Impassioned Enemies

Hazard dove under the water, sweeping downward with two powerful kicks. He saw Blaze immediately through the crystal-clear water, grasped her by one flailing arm, and hauled her up to the surface. He lifted her, dripping and shivering, so her head and shoulders were above water. Treading water in a slow pattern, he said, "I'm sorry. It never occurred to me you couldn't swim." His breathing was normal even though he was kicking slowly toward shore, the few minutes' exertion a trifle to a man in such superior physical condition.

With water streaming down her face and hair, her lips trembling, Blaze sputtered, "Damn you." But then Hazard's leather-clad leg grazed Blaze's thigh and the fervent fire in her eyes changed to something quite different.

Hazard, feeling the devastating shock, drew in a sharp breath. Instant need raced like flame along the sensual pathways of his mind and body.

Blaze felt the rush of pleasure, felt the flaring desire spread from the tingling point of contact like molten sunshine. Closing her eyes for a brief moment of dazed weakness, she shivered in his arms.

"You're cold," he whispered, feeling as though he must make love to her or die, his breath caught in his lungs. "Let me warm you." His mouth was suddenly close by, the words brushing against her cheek. . . .

*Don't Miss Any of
Susan Johnson's Tantalizing Novels*

The Kuzan Dynasty Trilogy
SEIZED BY LOVE
LOVE STORM
SWEET LOVE, SURVIVE

The Braddock-Black Series
BLAZE
SILVER FLAME
FORBIDDEN
BRAZEN

The St. John–Duras Series
SINFUL
WICKED
TABOO
A TOUCH OF SIN

and

BLONDE HEAT
SEDUCTION IN MIND
TEMPORARY MISTRESS
LEGENDARY LOVER
TO PLEASE A LADY
OUTLAW
PURE SIN

Available wherever Bantam Books are sold

Blaze

Susan Johnson

BANTAM

New York / Toronto / London / Sydney / Auckland

This edition contains the complete text
of the original edition.
NOT ONE WORD HAS BEEN OMITTED

BLAZE
A Bantam Book / published by arrangement with the author

PUBLISHING HISTORY
Bantam edition / September 1992

ISBN 0-553-29957-3

Published simultaneously in the United States and Canada

Bantam Books are published by Bantam Books, a division of Random House, Inc.
Its trademark, consisting of the words "Bantam Books" and the portrayal of
a rooster, is Registered in U.S. Patent and Trademark Office and in other
countries. Marca Registrada. Random House, Inc., New York, New York.

PRINTED IN THE UNITED STATES OF AMERICA

OPM 20   19   18   17   16   15   14   13   12   11   10

The following quotation is from an introduction by Henry Steele Commager to Ray Allen Billington's *The Far Western Frontier,* published in 1956.

"No other nation had ever expanded so rapidly or expanded so far without putting an intolerable strain upon the existing political and economic fabric—adding, that what is most impressive about the American expansion is the ease, the simplicity, the seeming inevitability of the whole process."

Jon Hazard Black wouldn't have agreed.

Blaze

Chapter 1

STRONG dark hands lazily stroking a warm spine . . .

A fragile woman smelling of summer roses . . .

Shadows and half-light in a deserted hallway . . .

The rubbed walnut paneling felt solid behind his back. Beneath his fingers, Lyon silk, delicate and heated, inundated his senses with pleasure. Slowly savoring the feel, his hands slid up the silken back of the woman pressed against him, glided over the ruched neckline of her gown to lightly close on naked scented shoulders. She smelled of violets too, and when he unobtrusively turned his head to glance down the darkened hallway, his jaw brushed across perfumed golden curls, soft as feathers.

"I hope you don't mind my coaxing you up here." A coyly whispered preamble.

1

"I don't mind," the deep masculine voice huskily replied.

"You're the most gorgeous man I've ever seen—north or south of the Mason-Dixon line," a honeyed southern accent purred, luscious as sable, while a voluptuous body moved provocatively against the man's obvious arousal.

A low, noncommittal murmur modestly acknowledged the sugared compliment while eyes dark as a moonless midnight gazed down at the pretty female held lightly in his hands.

The tall, sun-bronzed man with a faultless face like Attic sculpture, untamed raven hair, and arresting jet eyes, was dressed in full Plains Indian regalia: fringed elkskins decorated with ermine and quillwork; moccasins beaded in sinuous bands of gold, red, and black; an exquisite collar of bear claws and feathers spilling down his partially bared chest.

It was that heavily muscled chest which was currently the object of the lady's rapt attention; its contours were being caressed with long, lingering strokes. And the two figures, one powerful and tall, the other dainty and fragrant, pressed together in the dimly lit second floor corridor, were carrying on an abbreviated, softly murmured conversation between languid body movements and gently roving hands.

"Where are you from?" the extravagantly clothed woman, arrayed in lavish French court dress, whispered. Her hands moved down, slipping under the waistband of the leather leggings.

"Montana,"[1] the hawk-faced man replied on a sharply drawn breath.

"What tribe is all this from?" she asked in a soft, throaty tone, and while her question implied the costume, her fingers were touching his blatantly rigid manhood.

He swallowed once before answering, "Absarokee,"[2] and immediately felt the small hand suspend its exploration. Correctly interpreting the hesitation, he murmured in clarification, "Mountain Crow," giving the name the outside world knew.

The intimate fingers began moving again, drifting upward, luxuriating in the rock-hard sinew and muscle beneath her slowly gliding hands, and every nerve in her heated body melted into flame at the raw power underlying the dark skin. She could sense the years of physical exertion and training, could almost inhale the exotic smell of far-flung prairie and mountain. He was inches taller than most men, strong, quiet, the incarnation of majestic nature and freedom.

Why hadn't he kissed her yet? *Why?* she somewhat petulantly asked herself, when it was perfectly clear he wasn't immune to her charms. Lillebet Ravencour wasn't accustomed to such resolute control; men had been throwing themselves at her feet since she was sixteen. In a whisper of silk she stirred against his lean form, with a delicate balance acquired long ago—that perfect nuance, subtly ambiguous, between suggestion and demureness—moved into the male hardness and felt it swell against her although no sound came from the man holding her easily in his arms. Now he'd kiss her, she thought, and the lovely face framed in golden ringlets lifted expectantly.

But he didn't kiss her. Instead, his strong hands slid around her back and legs and, lifting in one smooth movement of shifting thigh and bicep muscles, put an end to their mating ceremonies. He carried her swiftly into the nearest bedroom, the lush folds of primrose silk billowing over his arm, trailing behind in pale, gleaming rivers in the corridor.

Later—only moments later—did he kiss her. He kissed her all over while he slowly undressed her. His mouth and lips and tongue caressed every curve, swell, hollow, every cresting peak and luscious plane. He kissed her in places she'd never been kissed before, intimate, dewy places, and she thought at first she'd die when his warm breath touched her there. . . . But she didn't die, of course, and when his tongue followed where his mouth and teeth so obligingly led, a tongue that licked and teased, she knew she'd never been so near paradise.

She regained her reason briefly when he rose to strip off his own clothes. Kicking off his moccasins, he pulled the leather shirt over his head in one swift masculine tug. "What if someone comes in?" she murmured, watching him toss the necklace on the bedside table with one hand and strip the leather leggings from his lean hips with the other. Stepping out of the fringed trousers, he left them where they lay, inches from a tumble of lace petticoats representing six months' hand labor of a dozen peasant women. Tall, broad-shouldered, lean near spareness through torso and hips, he walked the short distance to the bed, his erection beautifully formed. Lillebet's gaze dropped as if magnetized by the sight, and the fire between her thighs burned higher.

"Don't worry," he quietly assured her, his body already lowering over hers. Intent on the pulsing arousal even now sliding slowly into her womanly sweetness, his long-lashed eyes lifted and he glanced up at her face. Her eyes were tightly closed, her mouth slightly open, her breathing intermittently punctuated with little panting whimpers.

The lady seemed satisfied. He forgot about the question and bent to kiss the softly parted lips.

THREE blocks away, on a gently sloping street, elevated enough to offer a glittering view across the Charles River, a young girl with unruly flame-red hair stood at her bedroom window, looking out into the wet, dense darkness.

"Another night of fog," she lamented with a sigh, dropping the heavy lace curtain back over the small paned window. "I suppose it'll be too rainy to go riding again tomorrow."

The elderly woman readying the bed ignored the sigh and the dispirited comment. "Come sit down, Miss Venetia, and I'll braid your hair."

The nightgowned girl padded barefoot across the plush pink carpet and flopped dejectedly on the bed. "Dammit, Hannah, if I don't get out riding soon, I'm going to die of boredom!"

"Miss Venetia," her former nanny turned personal maid remonstrated, "watch your tongue. If your mama ever heard you, she'd have you put to bed without supper for a week."

Unmollified by the threat, the young woman with wide spaced eyes the color of clear mountain lakes wrinkled her face into a momentary pout. "Since I see her only at teatime on the rare days she's home and doesn't have a headache, it's not likely she'll ever hear, Hannah. Besides, Daddy doesn't care if I swear once in a while. *He* says one has to release one's frustrations somehow; and being a girl leaves out almost every other conceivable way of releasing frustration. Except shopping, of course," she finished scathingly. "as Mama spends her life doing."

"Come now, pet, it's not so bad." Hannah had been soothing these childish tantrums and gloom since Venetia first entered the world.

The slim young girl fell back on the bed in a lethargic sprawl, her tumbled red hair in jarring juxtaposition to the rose-colored bedspread. The eyelet bedcover had been selected, as had all the room's decor, by a mother stubbornly resistant to the imperfection of her daughter's coloring. Miss Venetia morosely threw her arms above her head and sighed again. "Oh, Hannah, it is. It's terrible. The only excitement in my life is riding and I haven't been riding in a week. Rain, rain, fog, rain, cold—every day. . . ." A third sigh—large and theatrical—drifted across the richly furnished room.

IT WAS, in fact, a typical chilly winter night in Boston, damp and misty, and the gas street lamps, enveloped in dense fog, glowed in a strangely eerie way.

Only a short distance away from the young girl complaining of the cold, in one of the opulent guest chambers of the Gothic revival mansion on Beacon Street, the night was far from chilled. Actually, it was extremely heated, and the sweat-sheened body of the lithe, dark-skinned man giving pleasure to the feverishly aroused woman beneath him attested to the fact.

His urgent hunger struck her as wildly barbaric, the magnificent body and willful hands did things to her which played havoc with her senses. A sense of being possessed—of capitulation—overwhelmed her, heating her passion deliriously. She was moaning, gentle whimpers of pleasure, breaking into breathy exhalations on each slow downthrust of the slim boned hips poised above her. With each withdrawal stroke, her white ringed fingers tightened on copper skin until the lower back of the tautly muscled man was bloodied and laced with scratches.

Immune to the clawed paths on his back, he was murmuring into the smooth curve of her slender throat: love words, sensual words, coaxing words, words in a strange, unknown language, and that strangeness further excited her . . . brought her to a cresting pleasure as intense as the expert rhythm moving deep inside her. A tiny bite of his strong white teeth on the soft flesh of her throat inundated her throbbing senses with a wave of passion. Her moist lips opened and she screamed as exquisite ecstasy peaked, tearing through her body, relentless as the rain pounding on the windowpane.

The man glanced at the door before swiftly covering her mouth with his, muffling the cry of illicit love. Only then, having silenced her orgasmic release from the guests below, did he allow himself his own gratifying climax.

Lying on his back afterward, his arm gently encircling the woman at his side, he wondered if she was the kind who asked about scalps. Since entering Boston society four years ago, a modest fortune in gold conferring instant acceptability, he'd discovered that society women responded to him in one of two ways—either with horror, as if a presumptuous servant had drifted in uninvited from the stables, or with undeniable lust. Females of the latter persuasion fell into two further categories—those sympathizing with tender condolence on the plight of the native American aborigine or those interested in the number of scalps he'd taken.

A pale hand floated up his chest, arresting his musing. The dainty belle murmured in her soft, musical drawl, slowly, as if questioning a simple-minded child, "Have you killed . . . many . . . *enemies?*" The last word was defined in long-drawn-out syllables.

For a moment, the man lay very still, from the glistening black hair lying tumbled on his shoulders to the ermine-decorated ankle bracelets he'd not had the time —or the patience—to remove. Then his mouth broke into a smile and, sliding his hands under her arms, he lifted her onto his chest. Gazing at the beautiful face a few inches from his he said, very, very quietly, "I've found so few enemies at Harvard this year, the killing business has been slow."

She squealed a little at the sound of the deep, cultured voice offering the prosaic answer and she quivered pleasantly against his body. An instant later, the lady's full lower lip pushed out in a coquettish pout. "Well . . . don't tell me before."

"You never asked . . . before," he softly replied, his grin widening.

"You led me on." The lush Charleston cadence was flirtatious.

"At the risk of contradicting a lady," he said, warm laughter in his eyes, "that point's debatable."

A slow, sensual smile greeted his remark. "What are you doing in Boston"—the delicate pause was scented with graceful suggestion—"otherwise?" Her small leg slid seductively between his.

"Besides this, you mean," he murmured, his easily aroused libido responding to the soft hips which had begun moving in a lazy motion atop him. "Going to school," he replied in a minimum way, positive the lady wasn't looking for a lengthy explanation, which would have had to begin with the California gold rush and the U.S. government's treaties with the Plains tribes in 1851. Hazard's father had understood the inevitable impact of those enormous migrations west, and when his only son was old enough, he'd sent him east to school. Considering the time, the place, and the woman's soft, undulating hips, Hazard condensed the complex reasons he was at Harvard and briefly added, "My father insisted I learn the white man's ways."

She lowered her head and lightly traced his upper lip with her tongue. "You," she breathed softly, "could give lessons."

His eyes were amused, his voice like velvet. "Thank you, ma'am."

He was being stroked and petted, her soft hands sliding over the muscles of his shoulders, down his chest, back up again. "Do you have a name?" she asked, her fingers slipping into the dark hair lying on his shoulders.

It checked him for a moment, the casual arrogance of her ignorance, but the intent was benign, so he answered laconically, "White or Indian?"

"Both." She brushed his shoulder free of his long dark hair.

"I'm known as Jon Hazard Black here. My Absarokee name is Is-bia-shibidam Dit-chilajash—Hazard the Black Cougar."

Pouting prettily again, a gesture Hazard thought particularly amiable to her redolent charm, she ran her lush tongue over her bottom lip and said, "You didn't ask me my name."

The thought hadn't occurred to him. "I'm sorry," Hazard politely dissembled; "you were so distracting. *Are* distracting," he amended, as the rhythm of her hips began to redirect the focus of his thoughts. "Tell me your name. . . ." His hands gently tracing the curve of her silky bottom paused momentarily when she whisperingly replied. But then she slid upward languidly and against his better judgment—since he knew tonight's hostess downstairs would very soon miss not only him, but his companion—his hands resumed their lazy massage. His rising maleness, at the moment, ardently contradicted good judgment. The velvet-skinned Lillebet, who, he'd just discovered, was his hostess's sister-in-law, gazed into his dark eyes and murmured softly, "So soon?"

"As you see," he replied with a charming smile acquired from similar conversations with highborn females eager to be seduced, "your attractions," he went on in a husky rasp while his slender bronze fingers slipped down the fullness of pink flesh and slid inside a hot, slick moistness, "fascinate me." He had not only learned to sip sherry and debate philosophy at Harvard, he'd learned every New England variation on the universal language of love. He then kissed her fingertips one by one and when he licked her thumb, she whispered, "Please, Hazard."

"Soon."

"Now, please, oh God, please." His lean fingers had continued stroking deep inside her with a controlled expertise any artist would envy.

"Hush." He kissed her lightly, then teasingly ran his free hand over and over the sensitive full undercurve of her breasts, stopping just short of the peaked hard nipples waiting for his touch. And when, after what seemed a breathless eternity, his thumb and forefinger closed over one pink crest and pulled lightly, the lady groaned, a low, quivering whimper. Sliding upward swiftly, he carried her with him. His hair caught and he felt an abrupt tug as the leather tie that held his hair pulled loose.

"Please!"

And his thoughts of the hair tie waned. Effortlessly, he lifted the golden-haired woman with pleading eyes and slid her ready sheath of love onto his hard length. He pressed down lightly on her slender hips. Her head fell back as she cried out softly, a trembling pleasure sound, and her tiny hands brushed a restless, feathery path across Hazard's chest. Lifting her lightly once or twice, he set the sensuous rhythm and then she took over, riding him, slowly, lingeringly. He lay back against the pillows, shut his eyes and, while his hands stroked her thighs, he luxuriated in the pleasure building by degrees.

His ears, attuned by practice and necessity to the slightest sound, heard doors softly opening and shutting down the hall, and the reasonable part of his brain suggested he discontinue this exercise in pleasure for prudence's sake . . . or at least turn out the light. The rash part of his mind knew there was neither man nor beast in Boston he feared, so he disregarded both alternatives. In addition, he was currently beyond reason and nearing an intensely felt orgasm.

He did look up when the door opened to gauge the extent of the danger, and his dark passion-hazed glance locked for a brief moment with that of his hostess. A flash of anger passed over her face before the door abruptly shut. An explanation and tactful apology would be required there, he thought, just before the woman above him collapsed in his arms and he allowed himself release, pulsing into her, drenching her warm honeyed interior with the liquid warmth of his lovemaking.

A HALF-HOUR later he was back downstairs, alone, his costume restored, his wide shoulders resting against one of the ballroom's decorative pilasters, a glass of brandy in hand, his dark eyes roaming the gilded, bejeweled, costumed members of Boston's refined society.

One of its number was absent upstairs, her coiffeur thoroughly ruined. He had every confidence the harried maid attending her mistress would rearrange all to order soon and Mrs. Theodore Ravencour would reappear in all her Pompadorian elegance.

Jon Hazard Black's exotic attire shone with its full magnificence, and only the most discerning would note that the braided leather thong formerly confining the thick black hair was missing, incongruously replaced by a pale blue ribbon hastily purloined from Lillebet's elaborately embellished gown. Somewhere in the rumpled disarray of silk sheets and comforters, a braided thong lay and, he hoped with an inner smile of pure mischief, it would be found by a servant straightening the bed rather than by the room's night occupants.

He'd been downstairs for no more than five minutes when his hostess, Cornelia Jennings, smiling and amiably chatting, gracefully crossed the crowded ballroom with no apparent destination in mind. Hazard knew better, knew he was her destination, and watched her slow progress with bemusement. She reached him after a time and when she was close enough to him not to be overheard, she said in a vehement whisper, "How could you, Jon! My God, she's my sister-in-law! Don't you care for me at all?" she hissed, her eyes suddenly bright with the glisten of frustration.

Looking down at the beautiful, troubled face, Hazard very soothingly said, "Of course I care. I adore you, Cornelia." As the tightness diminished slightly in her pretty face, he added in a low murmur, "You are, sweet, the loveliest . . . hostess . . . in Boston."

The fashionable young woman, swayed by the flowered compliment, became intent on more urgent matters at hand. Her pale grey eyes, gazing into his, lost their anger and flared hot with an emotion familiar to the tall man dressed in elkskins.

"Oh, Hazard," his hostess sighed as her hand, hidden by the folds of her voluminous skirt, stole into his. "It's been four days. I've missed you."

Hazard nodded, his dark eyes understanding. "I know. Exams, love—and a tutor who refuses to be agreeable."

Aware of his finely tuned responses, her dainty fingers tightened on his and in a stirring of silk gauze she tugged him away from the wall. "I've your favorite brandy upstairs." She met his teasing gaze with her own, ardent with inquiry, and moved slightly in the direction of the stairway.

He looked at her sideways, considering, then smiled into the hot, pleading eyes. When it had to be done, it could be done, Hazard reflected. He'd acquired that type of courage as a youth. And with the smitten ladies of Boston, he'd discovered this new application. Taking a deep breath, he tossed down his brandy and allowed himself to be led upstairs once again.

And for the second time in as many hours he found himself on silk sheets, doing his deft and imaginative best to assimilate the pleasant social civilities of upper-class Boston society.

Chapter 2

HAZARD'S school years in Boston blended a dual existence. He was, without complaint, sought after for his charm and sensual appeal. Attuned to flirtation and dalliance as due an Absarokee warrior, he easily accepted the multitude of female favors cast in his direction. But aside from the casual idleness of his amorous enterprises, he devoted the major portion of each day to a scholarly regimen. Obedient to his father's wishes, he utilized his time competently, faithful to his intended mission: to educate himself in order to aid his clan's transition into the future. He never forgot why he was sent away.

Encouraged by his uncle Ramsay Kent, relocated Yorkshire baronet, geologist, and adopted Absarokee married to his aunt, Hazard studied geology under the noted Swiss naturalist Agassiz, who had been invited to deliver a course of lectures at Harvard in 1847, subsequently had been offered a chair, and had stayed.

The Agassiz Museum at Harvard, founded two years before Hazard matriculated, became his second home. As a volunteer, helping catalogue the newly formed collection, Hazard soon found in Louis Agassiz a warm and gentle friend. Already in his fifties, Agassiz was a pleasant voluble man with a childlike devotion to science and an eager interest in the politics of the day. Some of Hazard's most genial times were those spent in the dusty museum work rooms talking with the professor. He learned from Agassiz, listened, and with the keenly bright idealism of youth, sometimes argued politics with him.

Through Agassiz, Hazard met Holmes, Emerson, Lowell, and Longfellow, first learned about the "women's rights" movement and was introduced to the antislavery and secessionist debates, a dynamic force in the society of the time. Social reform was in the air.

When a hiatus was needed from his studies, Hazard occasionally gave in to the coaxing of his less studious classmates.

"Come on, Hazard. Time to howl."

"Too much to do."

"Hell . . . stuff it until tomorrow." The young man in evening dress advanced another step into Hazard's neatly arranged room, dropped gracefully into an over-stuffed chair and importuned in a softly shaded Bostonian accent. "Come on. We're starting at Mama's 'Thursday evening.' She especially made me promise to bring 'that nice young man from the Yellowstone.' " A quick smile emphasized his words. "You charmed her to the tips of her egret plumes last time with all that talk about Longfellow and Hiawatha."

"Maybe next time, Parker," Hazard politely declined. "Really, I've lots of studying to do."

"My sister Amy'll be there."

"She's too young." Hazard remembered a young girl dressed all in white, looking very marriageable. Not his style.

"You're remembering Beth, Hazard. Amy's my sister married to Witherspoon. She particularly asked about you. Something about your dark brooding eyes, I think," Parker teased.

Hazard recalled the sister, even though he'd forgotten her name. She was ebony-haired, pale skinned, with a bosom that attracted attention and the kind of glance the term "bedroom eyes" had been coined for. She'd sat across the dinner table from him one night, but he and Parker hadn't stayed long enough that evening for him to discover whether Amy delivered more than amorous glances. "I don't know . . ." Hazard equivocated, his memory drawn to that unforgettable bosom.

"Tell him he has to come, Felton," Parker instructed the fair, slim man just crossing the threshold, equally resplendent in white tie.

"Have to, Hazard," Felton declared in the blunt delivery so characteristically his own. "Parker's Mama's At-Home Night is just for starters. Have a room rented at Shawdlings. It's Munroe's birthday today and we promised him Sarah and her friends tied up in a bow."

"Don't need me for that."

"Who the hell else can keep Munroe from breaking up the place if you don't? Have to come. He won't listen to anyone else."

"Besides, Hazard," Parker added, "Amy said her husband was out in Erie for a week. Don't know why she wanted to mention that," he said with a mocking raised brow.

"Erie . . ." Hazard slowly repeated, digesting the interesting possibilities.

"Two hundred miles away and no night train," Parker reminded him.

Felton and Parker exchanged entertained glances.

Hazard looked first at one, then the other. He too smiled. "Give me ten minutes to rig out," he said mildly.

Consequently, between classmates, bedmates, and bookish ways, the spring of Hazard's senior year at Harvard was extraordinarily busy. Schoolwork and papers required a certain amount of energy as did his simultaneous liaisons with the sisters-in-law on Bea-

con Street and an attentive Amy Witherspoon, all of
whom he managed to satisfy surprisingly often.

Outside forces intervened into this busy ménage
when the tensions brewing between North and South exploded at Fort Sumter in April. The battle lines had already been drawn at Christmas. After the holidays none
of the Harvard class from Dixie returned. South Carolina
had seceded, a Confederate Congress had assembled,
and Major Anderson was within the walls of Fort Sumter. South Carolina's legislature authorized the seizure of
all arsenals, arms, and forts within her limits. On January
3, Governor Brown of Georgia ordered the seizure of
forts Pulaski and Jackson at Savannah; on the 4th, the
authorities of Alabama seized Fort Morgan; on the 10th,
the authorities of Mississippi seized the forts and other
United States property within her limits; on the 12th, the
navy yard and property at Pensacola were taken; on the
28th, the rebels of Louisiana took the United States rev-
enue-cutter and the money in the mint at New Orleans;
and to complete the list, General Twiggs of Texas surren-
dered the United States forces and property in his hands
into the power of the rebels.

The War of Rebellion was just a matter of time in
coming and everyone knew it.

As early as January 16, Governor Andrew, only
eleven days after his inauguration, directed the Adjutant
General to issue General Order No. 4, which brought the
Massachusetts Militia into battle readiness. Concur-
rently, the legislature issued a statement that "it is the
universal sentiment of the people of Massachusetts, that
the President should enforce the execution of the laws of
the United States, defend the Union, protect national
property"; and, to this end, the State "cheerfully tenders
her entire means, civil and military, to enable him to do
so."

A few days later, on the 11th of February a great
meeting was held in Cambridge. The City Hall was
crowded. Hazard listened to John Palfrey speak briefly.
"South Carolina," he said, "has marshalled herself into
revolution; and six states have followed her, and aban-
doned our government."

Richard H. Dana, Jr., made the speech of the occasion. He said that the South was in a state of mutiny; he was against John Brown raids and uncompromisingly for the Union. He was opposed to the Crittenden compromise and held to the faith of Massachusetts. This meeting uttered the sentiments of the majority of the state.

When Sumter was fired on, Massachusetts was better prepared for war than most states. Her militia had spent the winter and spring nights drilling, recruiting, and organizing.

On the 15th of April 1861, Governor Andrew received a telegram from Washington to send forward at once 1,500 men.

Parker dashed into Hazard's room three days after Sumter, followed two steps later by Felton and Munroe. "We're joining up. You've got to 'list up' in Jennings' Company!"

"Jennings' Company?" Cornelia's husband? Not likely, Hazard thought. "No, thanks," he said. "Besides, this isn't my war."

"Don't you care about the slaves?" they all exclaimed, practically in unison.

He did, of course, and they knew it. Hazard had been quietly attending the antislavery meetings for some time, in sympathy with any human in bondage.

"Jennings has the best damn uniforms north of Richmond," Felton declared enthusiastically.

"Not a great reason to get shot at."

"The war won't be long."

"Over by fall, everyone says."

"Chance for glory, Hazard. It'll be a lark!"

Hazard had seen enough killing and death to disagree about the "lark" side of it, but he didn't argue with his bright-eyed friends. "Have a good time, then. I'm heading west as soon as classes are over. If you're ever in Montana, look me up."

"Hazard, we *need* you," they pleaded. "Who else can track like you and shoot like you and ride a horse like—hell, like it was part of you?" Munroe finished, the excitement high in his voice.

"Haven't ever seen a man jump on and off a galloping horse like you do, Hazard," Felton quietly remarked, "not even in the circus."

"Say you'll come," Parker demanded. "You're perfect for Jennings' Cavalry Company."

"Sorry, I can't," Hazard said.

But when Major Jennings came personally the following day to ask him to join the company and offered him captain's bars, Hazard had a harder time saying no.

Jennings wasn't deterred. "Let's have a brandy," he said, "and talk about it, Mr. Black."

And when Hazard said, "Call me Jon," Jennings knew he was talking to a reasonable man.

Neither mentioned Cornelia, masculine protocol concerning "discretionary affairs" functioning smoothly. Both understood women had their place in the society they frequented, but the coming war was strictly outside that sphere and its outcome depended on rational considerations, not emotion.

Over a good brandy, they got down to business.

"I need you," Jennings said, "Very badly. I wouldn't be here if I didn't. I'm putting a cavalry company together, and with you as scout I think we could operate damned effectively. Your reputation's formidable."

"Thank you, Major, but I've already told Parker and Felton how I feel. It's not my war."

"People in slavery are everyone's concern. Certainly you, more than most, must sympathize—" Hazard's cool look stopped him midsentence. "I'm sorry if I offended you," Jennings calmly went on, pleased to see he'd struck a sensitive nerve and determined to press that sensitivity to the limit, "but it might be instructional to you in other ways. An understanding of the Army's operation surely would be of use to you."

"I expect I could read that in a book somewhere and save myself being shot at by Johnny Reb," Hazard replied, equally calmly, although his dark eyes were not calm.

"Would money make a difference? I'm prepared to offer you whatever you want."

"I don't need money."

A heretical irreverence to one descended from eight

generations of Boston merchant princes, but Major Jennings smoothly said, "Forgive me. As you see, I'm willing to try anything."

"I'm sure you can find someone else."

"Not with your qualifications. I'll be blunt. You and I both know, under the circumstances (and that was the closest Jennings came to mentioning Hazard's liaison with his wife), if I had any other choice, I'd take it. But my men need you and that's why I'm here personally to speak to you. Wet-behind-the-ears pups like Parker and Felton and Munroe are going to be dead the first week unless men like you with experience can teach them some rudiments of survival. Our duties will be primarily raiding, picketing, and scouting, all unorthodox in tactics. It's not something you learn in Boston drawing rooms."

"Where did *you* learn?" Hazard inquired, curious for the first time about the man Cornelia lived with. Jennings was as suavely polished as two hundred years of wealth allowed, but under the gentlemanly exterior was solid toughness—and a natural directness Hazard couldn't help but admire.

"Fought with Scott in Mexico in '47. I was one of those green pups myself then. Just a damned lucky one, is all. I lived long enough to learn the ropes. And that's what I'm asking you to do. Help me teach these friends of yours what it's all about."

Hazard didn't reply. He looked out the window at the cherry tree blooming across the street from Young's Coffee House, thought of the wild plum trees in bloom in the low valleys back home, remembered Douglass' fiery speech last week and the far more poignant narrative of the woman who'd lost her husband and son on their escape north. It didn't seem right that a young child and his father should be hunted down with bloodhounds. Turning his gaze from the sunlit landscape outside, Hazard said, "I may go home from time to time."

Jennings face broke into a wide smile and his hand shot out to vigorously take Hazard's. "Anytime. Anytime at all," he agreed, gripping Hazard's hand like a sincerely pleased man. "I can't tell you how much I appreciate this. How much the company appreciates it. We're unofficially attached to the First Regiment, but we'll be moving out before them. When can you be ready?" he asked in the next breath.

Sliding his hand free, always slightly uneasy with the American practice of touching strangers in public, Hazard replied, "Two weeks. I've a last paper to prepare."

"Could I find you help with that?"

"I prefer doing it myself."

"Of course," the major quickly assented, having been warned of Hazard's peculiar notions about scholarship. "Two weeks it is. All your friends will be pleased. They were going to be the second assault wave if mine failed."

"You're persuasive, Major," Hazard politely answered, his smile gracious.

But Tyler Jennings hadn't tripled his father's fortune without a keen intelligence and he knew it hadn't been any of his arguments that had won the day. He had a strange feeling Hazard's mind had been made up prior to their discussion. "I'm damned lucky you're riding with us, Jon," he said, rising and holding out his hand once again. "Thank you."

"You're welcome," Hazard replied, courteously relinquishing his hand to the American ritual once again. "Do you think we'll really free the slaves, Major, or do you think it's simply another money war?"

So that was why he was doing it. A genuine idealism under that practical exterior. "We'll free 'em, all right. Damned if we won't. Starting in two weeks."

Hazard smiled at the ready assurance. "Good night, Major."

"Evening, Jon," Jennings said and started for the door. He turned back after three steps. "Send your measurements to my tailor—Walton."

"He has them."

"Ah . . . I thought that coat was his cut. Good. I'll have him start on your uniform tomorrow. Any preferences?"

Hazard shook his head, then reconsidered. "A patch on the left shoulder; a black cougar."

Jennings eyebrows lifted a fraction. "Your name?"

"Yes."

"Done."

FROM the 13th of April when Fort Sumter fell to the 20th of May, one hundred fifty-nine applications were granted to responsible parties for leave to raise companies in Massachusetts and they all left Boston with cheers and wishes of Godspeed from the enthusiastic multitudes.

After sending a note to his parents via Ramsay Kent, Hazard set off for what the politicians and northern papers considered a "brief summer war." The Sixth Cavalry Corps arrived at Annapolis on the morning of May third and landed in the afternoon. A week later they were camped in Virginia. The rout at Bull Run in July, where nearly 18,000 men in blue fled for their lives, put illusionary dreams of a three-month war to rest.

Jennings' was one of only seven companies of cavalry taking part in the Battle of Bull Run, but the firm front they displayed while covering the precipitate retreat probably saved a large proportion of the army from annihilation by Stuart's cavalry. The North had confidently expected to crush the Rebellion at once. Cavalry was an expensive arm and federal authorities had not encouraged volunteer cavalry. Owing to the broken and wooded character of the field of operations and the improvements in rifled firearm, veteran opinion had decided the role of the cavalry would be unimportant and secondary.

Bull Run changed that opinion. It also ignominiously altered northern assumptions of a speedy crushing of the Rebellion.

Jennings' Light was well suited to operate as a raiding expedition, depending on the country for sustenance, destroying railway lines, bridges, depots, provisions, and telegraph lines. Raiding was a way of life for Hazard, honed to perfection by years of training. Soon their company was unofficially known as the Cougars and their reputation preceded them.

As a moral factor and an engine of destruction, the cavalry raids were a great success. They destroyed millions of dollars' worth of Confederate supplies (increasingly difficult to replace as the war progressed) and cut communications, and often, due to their extreme mobility, the complete surprise of their attacks deep within enemy territory resulted in demoralizing and panic-stricken retreats.

Hazard met Custer early on when Custer rode into Abbottstown to take over his first command as brigadier general. The youngest general in the U.S. Army wore a black velvet uniform trimmed in gold lace and his blond mustache and mass of blond curling hair attracted instant attention. Hazard was one of the numerous field officers introduced to the new general.

The fantastic clothes didn't disturb Hazard. The Absarokee were far more resplendent in their dress. And unlike many of the other officers who resented Custer's promotion and romantic style, Hazard knew in the long run it was victories that made generals, not clothes. He had seen more than his share of fine dressers fired for poor fighting, and Custer's reputation for success was growing.

So when they met, they took note of each other, for Hazard's hybrid uniform of fringed buckskin and Walton-tailored tunic caught the interest of George Armstrong Custer. Their hair, too, shared a common length, and they had their youth in common.

"You're with Jennings' Cougars," Custer said, but there was curiosity in his glance and inquiry in his voice.

"Yes sir," Hazard laconically replied.

"But not a Boston native, I take it," Custer pressed.

"No sir."

Custer smiled at the cryptic answer. He'd heard tales of Hazard's escapades, of Jennings' Indian scout whose handling of explosives was magical. He could set a mine with unearthly precision and timing. He was also, it was said, the first man in and the last man out on forays to blow up railway bridges. And on the many occasions when escape seemed impossible, Hazard always found a way out. There was the time when pursuit wouldn't allow their raiding party the opportunity to blow up the locomotive, so they fired it up and headed home, tearing up track and blowing up the bridges behind them. They brought in eighty cars of rolling stock that raid and received personal recommendations from President Lincoln. Jennings made lieutenant colonel for that, and Hazard was awarded oak-leaf clusters for major.

It was also rumored Hazard was an important link in an underground railroad bringing out slaves from as far south as Georgia. And he and Parker had the dubious honor of being featured on a Confederate list of persons to be killed, for the brash arrogance of dining with J.E.B. Stuart on one of their spy missions into the South. So Custer smilingly remarked, "We're happy you're on our side, Major Black."

"Thank you, sir."

"Can we recruit any more where you came from, Major? You're invaluable."

"I'm all they can spare, sir."

"A pity."

"Yes sir," Hazard pleasantly agreed.

But their paths crossed frequently in the months ahead and they came to recognize in each other a reckless contempt for danger, a boundless confidence, and an inherent regard for destiny's calling.

Jennings' Cougars fought from Bull Run to Appomattox, taking part in grand charges at Chancellorsville and Gettysburg, at Gaines' Mill and Brandy Station. But they mostly fought as they were needed, mounted or dismounted, with saber, Spencer rifles, or Colt revolvers.

Dismounted, they held in check long lines of the enemy's infantry with Sheridan at Dinwiddie Court House; with Gamble's brigade at Upperville, crouched behind stone walls, they stopped a devastating charge. They helped rout Pickett's charge at Gettysburg and spearheaded the last advances after Petersburg.

Finally, it was nearly over. Lee's trains, heavily escorted, were found moving toward Burkeville in an attempt to escape south. A favorable opportunity for an attack of the long Confederate column occurred at Sailor's Creek, where Custer, with the Third Cavalry Division, including Jennings' Cougars, charged the force guarding the train and routed it, capturing three hundred wagons.

This success, supported by the position of Crook's cavalry division planted squarely across Lee's line of retreat, had the effect of cutting off three of the Confederate's infantry divisions. As the Sixth Corps moved up in the Army of Northern Virginia's rear, nearly the entire force was captured. This included General Ewell and six of his generals, fifteen guns, thirty-one battle flags, and ten thousand prisoners.

Sheridan at this time wrote to Grant. "If the thing is pressed, I think Lee will surrender."

And President Lincoln telegraphed Grant the brief message, "Let the thing be pressed."

It was pressed.

For two days the Federal Army pushed. Sharp fighting ensued, but by the night of April 1865, despair fell on the Army of Northern Virginia. Tired, desperate, and starving, Lee's army of brave, hardy men was finished.

The next day, a flag of truce called for suspension of hostilities, and the war was over.

ON THE day after the surrender at Appomattox, Hazard received news of his parents' death in a long-delayed letter that had been two months in coming. Ramsay had written as he lay sick. Sent along with a fur trader the first distance to Fort Benton, the letter had slowly descended the Missouri and then traveled cross-country from St. Joe. Printed in large, untutored script on the envelope when Hazard received it was an added message from the fur trader, succinctly blunt: *Kent dead Feb. 10.* The terrible tidings of his parents' and relatives' deaths enclosed within the letter shook Hazard to the depths of his soul.

A raiding party venturing too close to a wagon train sickened with small-pox had brought the disease back to the Yellowstone. Before the raiding party reached home, the pox had made its appearance, and when they arrived in camp, more than half the party were down with it. The scourge spread like wildfire through the susceptible Absarokee. The camp had broken into small bands, each taking different directions, scattering through the mountains in the hope of running away from the pestilence. All through the winter, the disease had continued its ravages, until it had run its course. Runners were sent through the country from camp to camp and the remnant of the nation assembled near the head of Big Horn River, the ranks of the proud nation terribly thinned.

Hazard had not only lost both his parents, but fully half his clan.

He cried when he received the news. Then he cut his hair . . . and immediately after, packed his saddle bags. The ritual slashing of his body must wait until he returned home. He'd need his strength for the long trail ahead. The war was over, and in many ways, in the mournful days to come, it seemed as though his life were over too.

His father had been his ideal. Brave, honest, gentle, everything a son could look up to. As head chief, he could have been a prideful man, but never was. He listened to everyone with kindness and as Hazard grew up, he tried to be like him. His mother had been a tall, handsome woman and his father's only wife. She could make the day bright with her smile, and her unconditional love had always nurtured and sustained Hazard.

It was a sad, bleak homecoming to the hundreds of graves and grieving clansmen when Hazard rode into his village three weeks later. After he'd seen to his parents' burial sites, he slashed his forearms and chest and legs, and with the blood slowly seeping from his wounds mingled a deep and terrible sense of loss.

THE young girl who once sighed at her bedroom windows on rainy nights in Boston had been transmuted into a slender, voluptuous woman, strikingly beautiful. The wide-set azure eyes, full of radiant curiosity, held within them a new maturity. She'd seen much of the ways of polite society and proper manners in those years. Her flame-red mane of hair was unchanged, the spoiled alluring mouth had only become more tempting, while the untamed temper and tendency to release frustration explosively were whispered by some to be a shade less than genteel. Many thought she addressed herself to life with a bit more independence than considered wholly respectable. These unfortunate attributes were laid at the door of her father's doting regard and enormous wealth.

Regardless of the gossip, Venetia "Blaze" Braddock, with her precocious, high-spirited beauty, was never without a score of ardent suitors. While she flirted, teased, intimidated, or spurned in her own scandalous fashion, she had not, in the parade of lovesick swains, found a man she cared to marry. Blaze was nineteen, and the more vindictive and uncharitable of society matrons remarked with snide satisfaction that she would soon be on the shelf. The untamed beauty had made her own bed, the slightly envious matrons whispered. She had snapped her fingers at every eligible party from Baltimore to Bar Harbor; it would serve her right if she turned into an old maid. Blaze would have laughed derisively had she known what was being said. Blaze Braddock had no intention of ever merely *settling* for someone to marry.

And her indulgent father agreed. "When you find him, honey, you'll know." he told her. He didn't confide that he'd discovered the truth of this adage outside his own marriage, empty now of everything but malice. He was hoping for better luck for his cherished daughter. "Until then," he generously admonished, "enjoy yourself, with my blessing."

"I'm trying, Papa, but most men are incredibly dull."

"They've been taught their manners, is all, darling."

"I'm not talking about manners. I mean their interests are so . . . so . . . worthless," she petulantly finished. "Do you know how shallow most of their brains are, Papa? A nail scratch would touch bottom. And when I bring up some topic of conversation that might be the teeniest bit interesting, they look at me blankly and then change the subject by telling me how beautiful I am."

"Well, you are, baby girl of mine; you turn their heads." Billy Braddock's look was that of every proud and doting father.

"I know I'm beautiful," Blaze calmly replied, impatience hurrying the last words, "but my God, Daddy, what the hell good is that going to do me if I die of boredom in the meantime with all these dull men I know?"

"Don't let your mother hear you swear, baby. You know how she feels about that."

Blaze shrugged lightly, that admonition so familiar it didn't require an answer. Then suddenly she giggled and, bringing her twinkling blue-eyed glance up to her father's, she said, "It would be fun, Daddy, just once to swear a blue streak in front of her and watch the smoke come out of her ears."

Billy Braddock tried not to smile. He'd always politely avoided overt discussions of his and his wife's differences.

"I'd say foot-high flames from her nostrils," Blaze cheerfully remarked and giggled again.

"Now, darling," the Colonel began, but a sudden image of Millicent's face after a "blue streak" struck his mind and a chuckle rumbled low in his throat. "It would be a sight," he laughingly agreed, "but promise me now—"

"I know, Papa," Blaze reluctantly acknowledged, her smile diminishing, "I never would. But the temptation's grand at those stupid teas of hers. Do you love me, Papa?" she suddenly asked, thoughts of her mother always causing unease and a sense of loss. Her eyes were large with childlike need.

The Colonel's arms opened wide and Blaze entered the familiar comfort of his loving embrace. "I love you, darling, more than anything," he quietly murmured.

Blaze's southern belle mother, never having taken an interest in family anyway, ignored the emancipated life of her only child. On the rare occasions when she spoke to her husband and their daughter was mentioned, Millicent Braddock would tersely remark, "She's very like you, William." It was not a compliment.

"Thank you," he'd always say, as though the underlying malice had escaped his notice. "Do you think Blaze needs new riding boots or a new fur coat?" he'd ask then in an effort to reach some common ground where civil conversation was possible. Millicent had excellent taste;

he couldn't fault her on that, and he relied on her judgment, at least in Blaze's younger years, in selecting a suitable wardrobe for his daughter. In later years, he and Blaze had gone alone on their shopping sprees, for by then Blaze had her own sure sense of style.

If he'd believed in divorce, the marriage could have been ended years ago, but it was a rarely elected choice in their social milieu. With wealth, separate lives were a civilized option.

So in the spring of 1865, the William Braddock family, in company with other wealthy investors from Boston and New York, rode west leisurely on a private train of elegantly appointed cars. The trip was an unhurried holiday and an opportunity to check their newly acquired land and mining camps. The weather cooperated with springtime splendor and while the men talked business and the ladies gossiped, Blaze daydreamed about the rugged, wild land of Montana. For a young woman who found life in society positively dull, and was uninterested in the antidotal outlets to female ennui—shopping and adultery—the summer in Montana offered a promise of challenge. A flare of unfamiliar excitement accompanied her on the journey west. She was swept by an unknown, inexplicable wind of freedom.

Hazard spent a month with his people, then moved up to Diamond City where the newest mining claims were being staked.

The eastern investors arrived overland from the railhead outside of Omaha, in twenty leisurely days aboard specially equipped carriages, and settled into Virginia City's finest hotel. The ladies kept to their elegant sitting rooms, rarely venturing among Virginia City's eight hotels, seventeen eating places, two churches, two theaters, eight billiard halls, five elegant gambling houses, three hurdy-gurdies, several bawdy houses, and seventy-three saloons, on its mile length of Main Street—the quagmires of mud from the spring rains made leisurely strolls impractical. The ladies had also been warned of the occasional violence, murder, and drunkenness abroad in this large and rough community.

The men rode upcountry to survey the new mines. Blaze accompanied her father.

The mining camps were strung out along the mountain streams required for sluicing or panning gold, rough and ready towns growing overnight when word traveled of a new strike. Although Blaze expected no special privileges as the only woman in the group, her father saw to it she had a private room at night when possible. When more humble conditions prevailed, a blanket was strung up to serve as a sketchy wall. On the nights spent under the stars, she and her father slept side by side in their rough bedrolls, often talking far into the wee hours. It was the first time her father had spoken of his childhood. The starlit heavens reminded him of summers sleeping out of doors as a youngster. A pleasant respite, he'd said, from the crowded hut that was home to his family.

"How did you ever decide to leave Ireland?" Blaze asked the first time he'd mentioned his youth.

"Everyone was dying or dead from the famine," he replied simply.

"Were you afraid to go alone?"

Her father was looking up into the star-studded sky when he answered, his voice as soft as his dying mother's had been when she'd said the words to him long years ago: "The streets are paved with gold." There was a short silence before he turned his head toward Blaze and in a normal tone added, "That's what everyone thought in our village." Then a faint smile appeared on his lined face. "Might be damned near true on this mountainside. We picked up some promising claims today," he briskly went on, shaking aside the melancholy memories of his adored mother.

"How many does your group have now?" Blaze inquired, responding to the casualness her father had inserted into the conversation.

"Fred says one hundred eighteen as of today and we've a long way to go."

After traveling for two weeks, the party of investors arrived in Diamond City. The possibility of an enormous strike was in the air. Good color had been showing up in numerous placer claims, indicating a very rich vein, and the investment group was buying up claims as fast as they could.

Blaze had decided to stay in town for the afternoon, but soon the heat in her little hotel room became oppressive. After a week of rain, the humidity pressed down like a fur mask. It was too stifling inside, she decided, after opening the windows in the rough-sawn structure serving as a hotel but getting no relief. Surely outside there would be a breath of a breeze. Somewhere.

Although there were few women in the mining camp, and those visible were of a certain profession, Blaze was unafraid; she was proficient with the two small custom Colts holstered on her hips. She was imbued as well with implicit confidence in her ability to take care of herself. The brown worsted trousers she wore tucked into high boots and the matching silk shirt had caused pursed lips of registered distaste when they had left her mother in Virginia City, but her father had found the upcountry clothes eminently practical.

"My God, Millie," he had said. Since Mrs. William Braddock hated being called Millie, her well-preserved face had flinched with further displeasure. "Don't tell me you want her gallivanting out in the bush in velvet and ruffles."

"I do not want her *gallivanting,* as you so colorfully put it, anywhere at all in this rude country. I wish, William, just once, you would remember that Venetia is a properly raised young lady. Or at least the attempt was made," she scathingly added.

"Godalmighty, woman," he'd exploded. She disliked that crudity even more, and if William Braddock had not been a millionaire many times over when he first uttered it to her at the Spring Cotillion in Richmond twenty years earlier, she would have suggested to his face that he go back to the potato fields of Ireland where he most certainly belonged. "Blaze is a person, not some sugar confection that's going to melt in the rain. This country's beautiful and she'll enjoy the trip."

"Very well, William, do as you like. I have made my opinions known and you have ignored them as usual. I hope you and Venetia have an edifying adventure in the *bush."* The last word was accompanied with a very lady-like shudder.

So, clothed in garments her mother considered scandalous, in a country her mother considered barbarous, with a supple, swinging walk that casually overlooked both opinions, Blaze ascended the hill from the gulch, away from the town, hoping the higher ground would catch an occasional breeze. The steady rain of the last few days had left the ground soggy at best, while the worst was apt to be more like quicksand. Before she'd traveled more than a quarter of a mile through the heavy haze of heat, Blaze's silk shirt was clinging uncomfortably to her skin. Rolling up the sleeves, she pushed open the neckline as far as respectability allowed, but the dark brown shirt had been a mistake, as it absorbed every searing ray of sun. She prayed for a waft of breeze, a touch of coolness, anything to alleviate the blistering heat.

Halfway up the hill, opposite the ominous "hanging tree" she'd heard talk of, where the local vigilantes had managed to hang 102 desperadoes in the last few months, the trail reached an impasse of unbroken mud. Blaze swore in a soft, articulate stream; the thought of returning to the hotel room was thoroughly uninviting, but at this rate she'd be baked to death by sundown. Reconnoitering several yards up the rocky landscape bordering the trail, she searched for some way around the long stretch of mud. The terrain turned to loose schist ten yards ahead, making the footing dangerous. As she contemplated the difficult ground with a sweeping gaze, her eyes fell on the half-concealed figure of an Indian sleeping in the shade of a rugged mountain juniper.

Crossing the short distance to where he lay, she stood at his feet and nudged him with the toe of her boot. In the course of the last weeks, Blaze had met several Indian scouts and none had seemed particularly terrifying. Furthermore, she'd been born with more than her share of audacity. "Get up. I need help."

The man didn't move. Unconsciously her sapphire eyes took in the tall, powerful form clothed only in leather leggings and beaded moccasins. He was magnificent. The lean-muscled upper body was clearly defined, his face was straight-nosed and finely modeled, and his hair, tied back with a strip of leather, was like black satin. For a silent moment under the scorching sky she was drawn almost hypnotically to this wild specimen. She noticed a fine lacing of scars on the honed, splendid body and wondered about their history. One diagonal slash slid under the skin-tight leather and her eyes followed its probable course until unaccustomed modesty reminded her such awareness could be dangerous.

Recalled to her surroundings, she quickly nudged the moccasined foot again, this time harder, in response perhaps to her awakened, agitated conscience.

He rolled over then, and his handsome fringed eyes slowly opened. With a glance of appraisal, Jon Hazard Black saw a slender, delicate woman of classical perfection; her hair gleamed on her shoulders, a tumbled, unruly, amber syrup; her eyes were large, her mouth soft and full, and when she spoke, her voice was commanding. "Didn't you hear me?"

Accustomed to servants and too familiar with being indulged in a world which had denied her nothing, Blaze's tone held a hint of irritation and imperiousness. Today was an aggravating day. It was unbearably hot, she was thwarted in her journey uphill and frustrated she hadn't gone with her father as usual. The sharpness instantly shattered the illusion of perfection.

"Carry me over that," she ordered, pointing at the stretch of mud. Then in an explanatory cadence, usually reserved for very young children, she added, "I . . . give . . . dollars." She pulled out a twenty-dollar gold piece from her pocket and held it out to the Indian.

Only the eyes responded in the unmoving man. Hazard, reared in the mighty Absarokee culture, son of a chief and a chief in his own right, reacted poorly to orders from women. That was when he was in a good mood. Otherwise he didn't react at all. Today was not one of his better days. He had had a furious argument with an agent for some mining group that wanted to buy his claim. When he'd said it wasn't for sale, the man refused to believe him. He eventually did, of course, at the point of a rifle, but Hazard never liked being threatened. And he'd been catching up on much-needed sleep when the woman walked up. Survival in these mining camps as well as in the mountains often depended on sleeping lightly, if at all.

"Forty dollars," Blaze stated curtly, thinking an increased bid would force a response, as she drew out another gold piece.

Not a ripple altered the unflustered rangy form. He was stronger than she was. It was no contest. Dark lashed eyes lowered once more in repose.

"Don't you understand?" Blaze exploded. *"Carry . . . me . . . over . . . mud."* Still receiving no response, Blaze paused in exasperation, stamped her small booted foot, and made the mistake of drawing her pistol. It was a stupid thing to do, and if less tested by the sun and less frustrated, she'd have known better.

In a blur of movement, swift and smooth as a striking panther, Hazard was on his feet and the gun was chopped from her with the hard edge of his hand. Blaze found herself hurtling to the ground with an abruptness that rattled her teeth. Pinned beneath a hard body, her heart began pounding wildly. Good Lord, she thought, he was angry, half-naked, an Indian. What had she done?

"Stupid bitch," he growled, his dark eyes smoldering with fury.

Thank God, he spoke some English at least. "I'm sorry," she cried in humiliation and acute fear. "Please forgive me . . ." Her breath was arrested halfway in her throat and her pulse pounded. Would he kill her, rape her, scalp her? What a fool she was.

Hazard's gaze moved from her face, falling on her throat just above her buttoned blouse, and he wondered if her skin underneath the modest neckline was as smooth and golden. The anger softened in the dark eyes and his expression changed, relaxing the grim line of his mouth. With his hands closed on her wrists beneath him, her breasts were crushed against his bare chest—nothing separated them but tissue-thin silk. She could count the beats of his heart, and felt them quickening against her.

Releasing one wrist, he took the brown silk of her

blouse between his finger and thumb and gently pulled the neckline to reveal the lace of her chemise and a curve of pure white breast. Her eyes opened wide under Hazard's gaze. He had never seen such vivid pools of aquamarine.

With increasing terror, Blaze felt his hardened maleness rising against her thigh and knew why his heartbeat had quickened. Should she scream? Would he kill her then? "Please . . ." she repeated, her blue eyes entreating.

His fingertips lightly traced the curve of her jaw, threading back through her tangled hair, and for a brief moment Hazard thought of various ways he could please her. He hadn't had a woman for a long time, since he refused to use the prostitutes in camp. He hesitated for a moment, his jet eyes masking his thoughts, but his better judgment prevailed; with a deep sigh, his hand dropped away. He lifted Blaze to her feet, and they stood face to face for a brief second. He towered over her by more than a foot. He picked up her gun and carefully returned it to its holster. She noticed his beautiful hands, with slender, hard fingers and very strong muscles. Without a word he lifted her into his arms, walked back to the trail, and waded into the mud.

Startled at first by the suddenness of his actions, Blaze soon felt a trembling sense of relief. But before the long walk was concluded, a new emotion agitated her mind. An unfamiliar, quivering feeling of intimate warmth, which had nothing to do with the sun, came over her. Held close to Hazard's bare chest, she felt the strong beat of his heart, the burning of his flesh against hers, his shoulder under her hands hard and reassuring. Glancing up at the chiseled profile only inches away sent an uneasy shiver rippling down her spine.

Hazard felt the tremulous flurry and, gazing down at the enchanting face framed in shining red curls and the tempting body, damned himself for having scruples. He was aroused and, if he hadn't seen so much fear in the wide azure eyes, he would have seriously considered indulging his desire.

Reaching high ground, Hazard set Blaze on her feet.

She offered him the two gold pieces with a timid smile and a second apology. He shook his head and, taking the coins, slipped them back into her pocket. A common enough gesture with uncommon results. When his strong fingers slid down the tight pocket of Blaze's trousers, releasing the coins, the unexpected intimacy seared them both. Hazard snatched back his hand in an almost violent motion and, turning abruptly, walked away. Blaze Braddock, shaken by a man's touch for the first time in her life, was left in a state of confusion.

Mingled astonishment and desire confounded her normally rational mind. The feeling was unprecedented, the probable cause—if seriously considered—against all she believed in. Not for her, bewitchment and charming sorcery. Her reality was clear-cut and reasonable. She had never believed in flighty romanticism.

With visible effort she shrugged away the unease, and with a toss of her head set her sights on the crest of the hill ahead of her. Continuing her journey, she consciously set aside any further thoughts of her encounter with the Indian as she strode off to join her father for the rest of the day. Finding him several claims down the valley, Blaze spent the remainder of the day absorbing the complexities of purchase agreements, partnership contracts, and claim staking.

Late that evening when the sun had set and coolness at last drifted down the mountain, Blaze retraced her journey from Diamond City, this time on horseback. When the group of riders passed through the mud that had upset her that morning, Blaze looked off the trail to the tree where the Indian man had been sleeping. The site was deserted, as she expected, but then her dark blue eyes swept up the valley wall. Was she hoping to see him again? Catch a glimpse of that magnificent face and form which had lingered in her thoughts despite ruthless efforts at suppression? Utterly ridiculous. He was an Indian, she reminded herself. A primitive aborigine, her mother would say. Unable to speak more than a few halting words of English, she remembered. But when her gaze fell on a glow of light high up the mountainside, and she realized it was a firelit cabin window, her heart tripped against her rib cage and a sudden warmth stole through her senses.

"Blaze," her father repeated, "didn't you hear me? We'll be back in Virginia City in time for the Territorial Ball at the end of the week. I thought you'd enjoy knowing that."

"Oh, thank you, Daddy," she quickly responded, wrenching her eyes from the dark mountainside and the solitary glimmer of light. "Did you say this week?"

"Saturday night, pet. And a penny for your thoughts. Care to tell your old dad what's absorbed you so these last few miles? You've been in a hell of a fog."

"Oh, nothing, Daddy. I think I was dozing a bit. It's been a long day."

"It'll be our last day out for a while. We're heading down to Virginia City tomorrow. You'll have a chance to rest in the comforts of the hotel the night after next. Damn, a hot bath in a real tub will feel good."

"Amen to that," Blaze said enthusiastically. She felt as though all the dirt of western Montana were stuck to her sweaty skin.

WITH the help of a lady friend, Hazard had recuperated from the ritual body slashing observed for mourning in his tribe and then had recommitted himself to his father's dream. His clan needed gold for their future; it wasn't as though there were choices. The placer deposits his uncle Ramsay Kent had been working didn't compare in potential with the newly discovered strikes. Since the first major deposits discovered at Grasshopper Creek in 1862, thirty million dollars of gold had been taken from the gulch. In 1863 and 1864, two more enormous lodes had been found at Alder Gulch and Last Chance Gulch. The pattern was repeated all through 1864 at Prickly Pear Valley, Confederate Gulch, Diamond City, Emigrant Gulch. The boom was on.

So Hazard was working two claims here, working very hard at what had appeared to be highly profitable claims, if his old mentor, Louis Agassiz knew his business.

But since the encounter with the red-haired woman,

in the lull of the ensuing evenings, Hazard found his mind distracted, drifting easily into fantasies about her. The soft cloud of russet hair, her sun-kissed skin and vivid blue eyes, particularly the luscious body, were recurring images. It annoyed him that she intruded into his musing so. She had annoyed him with her peremptory posture; she was a part probably of that moneyed crew out to buy up all the gold claims in the valley. Her offer of forty dollars for a two-minute task bespoke the careless negligence of the wealthy Hazard had known so well in Boston. That type of woman, both beautiful and spoiled, could always annoy him. He probably should have taken her that day, he selfishly considered. It would have quelled the annoyance and satisfied the lust. . . . If he had, all these unnerving images of her wouldn't be dancing before his eyes, Hazard reflected.

He needed a woman, that was all. It had been too long, and hell, he thought with cold-blooded hindsight, he could have protected himself even if she'd screamed rape. His claim was virtually impregnable to attack. It was one of the reasons he'd chosen the site; the position on the mountaintop would allow one man to hold off an army for a month or more. And whoever her husband or protector was, no man was going to put *that* kind of effort into avenging a woman's dishonor.

"Hell," he muttered aloud this time, and ignoring subconscious reasons to do with flaming hair and peach skin, Hazard abruptly decided to accept Lucy Attenborough's invitation to the Territorial Ball in Virginia City next weekend. He knew a dozen women in Virginia City who would be overjoyed to see him again, including, of course, the inviting Lucy, a perfect opportunity to end his overlong celibacy.

He didn't admit to the possibility that the woman he'd held in his arms—who haunted his thoughts—would be at the ball.

Chapter 3

THE night of the Territorial Ball was one of those pleasantly warm summer evenings depicted by painters and poets. The air smelled of new grass, fresh earth, and the sweet scent of tiny aspen leaves only beginning to emerge. The sun had sunk behind the surrounding foothills in a masterful display of flaming gold streaked across a shimmering sky. It was a sight which gave even the rough mining town a soft, inviting glow.

Blaze watched the liquid sunset from the window of her private parlor; her father was downstairs discussing business, while her mother, as usual, was taking an hour more than anyone else to dress. A servant delivered a glass of champagne with her father's compliments and, as she lounged before the window on a red plush armchair, Blaze sipped the wine and enjoyed the close of the day and the beginning of the night.

Yards of creamy lace and ivory silk hand-sewn with thousands of seed pearls spread luxuriously over her

crinoline and flowed to the floor in soft crushed folds.
The snug, revealing bodice of her gown was supported by
whalebone stays, so the filmy lace draped below her bare
shoulders was purely decorative. The pale fabric and lace
spectacularly set off her peach skin and golden apricot
hair. Long earrings of diamonds and pearls dropped
from her ears, shining against the delicate texture of her
skin. But reality defied the picture of perfection. Wayward tendrils were already altering her carefully arranged coiffeur. To the despair of her hairdresser, sent
away in a fit of pique, Blaze's curls had a rebellious bent
no amount of effort could control, and her stylishly
smooth hairdo was regaining its natural tendencies.

A pendant of matching diamonds and pearls suspended from a delicate chain hung tantalizingly in the
shadowed cleavage of her voluptuous breasts. Since a
state of studiously controlled half undress was formal
style for evening dress, Blaze failed to recognize how
provocative her dress was, her breasts pushed high over
the low décolletage of the gown brought west for just
such an evening. Shoulders were extremely bare this season, and the drape of lace between shoulder and elbow
served a multiple purpose. With the contours of the female form below the waist virtuously swathed in volumes
of petticoats and fabric, the area from the waist up was
left to remind men what a female was. The ruffle—so
stylishly new—set off the sheer nakedness of the female
shoulders while drawing equal attention to the soft
breasts swelling above corseted silk.

Slender, long-legged, arrayed in pale silk like a Re-
naissance bride, with the satiny skin of her shoulders and
half-revealed breasts lushly inviting, Blaze was guaranteed to turn heads at the territorial ball.

ONE male head denying any such intention was
lying back against the headrest of a large porcelain tub
drawn up to the west window of his second-floor room in
The Planter's House, Virginia City's newest hotel.
Stripped of the dirt and fatigue of several weeks of solitary mining, Hazard rested in the tub, leisurely enjoying
a large glass of brandy. Life had become more gratifying.

Disquieting images of autumn gold hair had been displaced by more palpable carnal realities in the shape of several Virginia City hostesses of various descriptions who had passed more or less time in room 202 in the past few days. Hazard's sense of pressing social duties had consisted largely of entertaining ladies in bed. In fact, he was expecting one of them to return in less than ten minutes. There'd be time *before* the ball, Lucy had insisted, and after the long, lonely weeks at Diamond City, Hazard wasn't about to say no.

All in all, he was enormously content. The rare yearning, for the unusual red-haired woman, was gone now, submerged by satisfying sexual abundance in the three days in Virginia City. Transient cravings based on prolonged abstinence were all the fantasies had been, Hazard rationalized; they had nothing to do in particular with the woman in tight trousers. And now that the abstinence was assuaged, she could be dismissed from his thoughts.

At the soft knock, he drained the brandy and called out, "Come in." As he turned his head toward the door, his dark eyes swept the elegant brunette dressed in pink mousseline de soie with ribbon flounces of Belgian embroidery precariously holding her full breasts from spilling out of the bodice. Hazard became suddenly attentive as Lucy Attenborough entered the room, shut the door, and leaned against it.

"Should I get out," he asked softly, his eyes meeting hers, "or do you want to get in?"

"I can't, Jon . . . my clothes . . . my hair. . . ."

"Take off your clothes, pet. I'll be careful with your hair." His glance held hers in predatory thrall. "Take everything off slowly," he said in a low, sensual rasp. "I'd like that."

She hadn't moved from the door, but her eyes glittered with hidden excitement as she surveyed her lover. Hazard was the most magnificent man she'd ever known, his scandalous eyes lured her with a dangerous attraction, his aquiline face was so beautiful he turned heads. Seated now in the bathtub—naked, bronzed, glistening with droplets of water across his broad-shouldered frame

—he was more of a man than ten of her husbands combined. Arching her back, she held his level dark gaze and felt the smoldering heat linger, then caress her body like licking flame. "How do you do it? How can you make me feel this way?" she asked, breathy, taut, flushing with pleasure.

"Charm of personality," said Hazard with a lazy smile, "together with lucid recall of the last four weeks without a woman," he teased. "Come, Lucy, you're too far away. . . ."

Any woman in town would tumble for him and he knew it. How many had already this trip, she didn't dare wonder. Taking a step closer, she shivered at her urgency. "I never know, Jon," she said with a trembling, ingenuous smile, "whether I want you to rape me or treat me like a virgin bride."

The seductive black eyes, slowly moving in speculative appraisal, stared at her. "Why not both?" Sliding deeper into the steaming water, he paused, almost completely submerged, his midnight hair drifting on the surface of the water and his heavy-lashed eyes slanting upward. "Decide," he said invitingly, "which you want first."

Short moments later, two dark friendly hands reached up, held and steadied the impatient slim, nude body, as the chief justice's wife, dipping first one dainty foot, then the other, joined Hazard in the warm silky water. And he was very careful. That's why women adored him, because he was slow and gentle and . . . careful. Much later, when every part of Lucy's body was taut with longing, when every inch of her smooth flesh had been bathed in warm sensation, she opened her heated interior to the slippery water and to something else as well. Peaking exquisitely, she whimpered for release.

"Patience, sweet," Hazard murmured. "I haven't started yet." And the soft intensity of the statement silenced her. The floor became alarmingly wet after that, as small charged waves crested over the tub's rim, but the lady's hair, as promised, remained untouched.

An hour later, they helped each other dress and before leaving, kissing him fiercely, Lucy unexpectedly pleaded, "Please, Jon, if you're really going back up mountain tomorrow . . . once more?"

He hesitated.

"Don't you want me?"

"I'm only thinking of preserving your clothes from" —his mouth smiled—"the rude savage."

Lucy's lashes came up to reveal heated desire. "Meaning you?" said the young matron in a hushed voice.

"Meaning me," Hazard echoed softly.

It was what she most adored in him, his wildness and unorthodoxy. Her eyes, holding his, were passionate, full of need. "Damn the dress," she whispered.

His smile, warm and rakish, was celebrated. "Your servant, ma'am."

So Hazard had the Chief Justice's wife despite petticoats, mousseline de soie, lace-trimmed drawers; and, he noticed later, her silk-slippered feet left only slight marks on his black evening jacket.

When Lucy left to join her husband at the ball, Hazard adjusted his clothes in a haze of contentment, and poured himself another brandy. He'd give Lucy time to make her excuses before he arrived. A half-hour later, he gently closed the door on the strewn, damp-carpeted room, stepped out onto Main Street, and set out for the Chief Justice's Territorial Ball.

AN OPEN carriage arrived for the Braddocks and they were driven the short distance to the large stone building serving as temporary quarters for the legislature. It was the only structure in Virginia City with a space suitable for a ballroom.

Their driver proudly pointed out the more resplendent dwellings and businesses. "That there is McBundy's Emporium; brought the stone three hundred mile on ox cars. Purty, ain't it? Past those willows is Forsyth's. See the one with the tower? And over yonder, on that rise, is Chessman's place. Took him a full two years to build."

While Millicent sniffed disdainfully at the Gothic

three-story jumble of gingerbread, Blaze politely said, "It's lovely, like a white palace."

"Ain't that jus' so. A palace, sure 'nuf."

And Chessman's mansion was very like a palace, gleaming pale in the sunset glow, an example of the curious juxtaposition of wealth and squalor so prevalent in the mining boomtowns. Side by side existed log cabins, shanties, tents, prosperous business blocks, and elegant homes. With the strike-it-rich possibilities of gold mining, an impoverished miner could find himself wealthy overnight. And when that happened, many spent their new riches in lavish extravagance.

Virginia City offered anything money could buy, from ice-packed oysters to couturier gowns. All merchandise was brought overland or up the Missouri, and though the freight charges forced prices high, there was always someone willing to pay. It wasn't like farming, where one worked and waited and finally eked out a modest living. Gold mining cast its lure out to people who craved instant fortunes. And it obliged many a gambling-minded man. Fortunes were made and lost and made again and money was spent on a princely scale. Virginia City may have been only three years old, but it offered opulence and luxurious living to anyone who could afford it.

"Really, how can anyone actually *live* out here? Everything is so . . . tasteless," Millicent complained. "And dusty, now that the *mud* has dried," she irritably went on.

"Can't expect a settled town right away. Takes time," the Colonel replied, smiling his apology at the driver, who'd turned his head around at Millicent's rude comments.

"There's no excuse, William, for *that* sort of thing, no matter how unsettled," and she lifted her silk fan a scant inch in the direction of a nearby tent with a roughly painted sign proclaiming Montana Belle its occupant. A line of men standing outside the gunny sack door flap were joking and passing a bottle of whiskey around while waiting their turn.

The Colonel cleared his throat gruffly. There's so

few white women, he wanted to say, but thought better of it in front of Blaze. "They're a long way from home," he replied instead.

"It's one of the main thoroughfares. You'd think at least," Millicent peevishly continued, "they'd find some-place—"

"Have you heard how large an orchestra will be playing tonight?" Blaze interjected, stepping in as she had so many times over the years when her parent's conversation turned discordant.

"They're from Chicago, I hear," her father quickly answered, relieved to change the subject. "Remember to save me a dance, sweetie. I know how fast your dance card fills up."

"Take care with your skirt, Venetia. They'll probably all wear their spurs," her mother cuttingly decreed.

"Yes, Mother," Blaze obligingly replied. The driver was stopping to let them down, and it was too fine an evening to argue about anything.

Colonel William Braddock, Mrs. Braddock, and Miss Braddock were graciously greeted by the territorial chief justice and his young wife who were acting as hosts for the evening at the governor's request. Lucy Attenborough was looking remarkably attractive tonight, as everyone who knew her would agree. Flushed, vivacious, she smiled warmly at everyone, including the elderly man at her side, her husband. It must be the summer air, several guests remarked; a night like this would bring a glow to anyone's cheek.

"Next thing you know," one elderly matron remarked to her companion of equal years, seated beside her on the perimeter of the dance floor, "we'll be hearing of a blessed event in the Attenborough family. That young bride of his was smiling up at George with something like adoration. Now when I was eighteen, mind, no one could have talked *me* into marrying a sixty-year-old man. I don't care how much gold he had."

Small towns being what they are, with everyone's business being everyone's business, her companion remarked with a smug, insinuating air, "One can only pray if she has a child, its skin won't be too dark."

Having gained the full and undivided attention—in addition to a wide-eyed look of astonishment—from the matron beside her, the smirking woman observed, "But the child would be gorgeous, undoubtedly gorgeous. Lucy visits the oddest places in the course of the day." But no amount of cajoling would wring another word from her.

Unsubstantial as these facts were, the perfume of sin was irresistible and before an hour passed, a current of intrigue had passed like wild fire throughout the room.

Leaving Millicent in a small parlor to sip sherry and gossip with the other wives traveling west with their husbands, Colonel Braddock escorted Blaze into the ballroom to claim her first dance. The music was a gay mazurka, lilting and merry, and those dancing threw themselves into the energetic steps with a high-spirited pleasure. Even in the midst of a room, crowded with guests, Blaze stood apart, her skin glowing warmly, her opulent pearl-studded gown a silken foil to her beauty. She was immediately besieged with suitors and dance partners, drawn to her startling loveliness with a certain predictability. The Colonel graciously gave way to his daughter's cavaliers, and she swung off in the arms of a tall, fair-haired gentleman who'd introduced himself with the soft drawl of a Texan. He danced well, told her she was more beautiful than the bluebells back home, and suggested they get married in the morning with a sincerity she found momentarily disconcerting. She smiled a polite refusal and was saved from further explanation by her next partner importuning for his turn.

She enjoyed herself, for dancing was always a pleasure, the people were open and engaging, and the talk, when she could turn it away from compliments, was often about the mining which so fascinated her. In the normal course of events, it might have been some time before she noticed the tall, dark-haired man in elegant evening dress among the hundreds of animated guests. Tonight, however, the moment he entered the room—cool, slender, expensive, with that swift, easy walk which bespoke ease and self-confidence—all conversation stopped, heads swiveled, and an uneasy silence settled over the large ballroom.

Not privy to the night's succulent item of gossip, Blaze had no idea why everyone was staring at the striking man, other than the fact he was beautiful. Perhaps he never walked into a room without the talk dying around him, she mused. He was distinctly a man of the outdoors, even in diamond studs and evening dress, and a closer look revealed he was undoubtedly an Indian. With a jolt Blaze recognized *her* Indian. Her heart raced. But palpitations aside, his beauty and heritage aside, why did every guest in the room continue staring at him? Watching from the dance floor, for her partner had abruptly stopped in his tracks, Blaze watched the conspicuously attractive man pause for a moment, taking in the silence, the expectancy, the rising hum of whispered comment.

His extraordinary black eyes swept the room casually, rested on Lucy, then moved with perfect equanimity along the haphazard grouping of officials making up the receiving line. Walking over in a wink of diamond studs, he calmly greeted some minor bureaucrats first. "Good evening. Pleasant weather. Yes, unusually warm for June," he remarked with consummate social ease. The dignitaries, by contrast, seemed edgy. Pretty, dark-haired Lucy Attenborough, next in line, looked up with a flash of a smile, and the elderly man standing beside her, his bald head glistening with sweat, followed her glance with a murderous scowl.

Hazard smiled back, ignoring the scowl, and extended his hand to the Chief Justice's wife, who unexpectedly blushed. With smoothly turned compliments he took her fingers briefly in his, then, passing along, put his hand out to the Chief Justice. "Good evening," said Hazard pleasantly. "I hear the legislative session finally ended. A relief to you, I expect."

"Yes, I'll have more time to spend at home now," the Chief Justice replied with cold-eyed resentment.

"I'm sure, sir, your wife will be grateful." Hazard's eyes were calmly open.

For the space of a heartbeat, the older man hesitated while Hazard absorbed the shock of his anger. But this was the man, everyone had heard, including Judge Attenborough, who'd killed three men last month. One did not carelessly annoy a man reputedly able to draw and fire five times in three seconds. Having made the decision, Attenborough's hand reached out and gripped Hazard's slender bronzed hand. "Enjoy yourself, Mr. Black."

Hazard's voice was steady. "Thank you. I will."

Collective breaths were exhaled throughout the room in sufficient volume to cause a gentle sigh to waft about the vaulted ceiling. The musicians who had been playing an indistinguishable tune in an indistinguishable tempo, so softly as to be scarcely audible, promptly resumed their rhythm and volume. The guests resumed dancing. Conversation erupted, deliciously agitated over the barely averted public scandal.

The tall Absarokee with glossy black hair just brushing his neck exchanged a few more polite phrases with the judge, who, with justice, treated him with suspicious reserve. His young wife foolishly regarded Hazard with doting eyes, which he studiously avoided while he bade husband and wife a good evening.

From the receiving line he went directly to the gaming room. Hazard Black didn't return to the ballroom until shortly before midnight, and when he did, his brow was creased with a frown. A note interrupting his card game was cause of the brooding look. As if rumor wasn't damned near tinder point already tonight (and he had smoothly brushed off enough pointed allusions during his gambling to know what was consuming everyone's thoughts) Lucy, apparently having lost all discretion, had sent a note in with one of her servants. She was one of the most sexually aggressive women he'd ever known. No doubt being married to a sixty-year-old man influenced that disposition; but Hazard Black never knowingly looked for trouble, and the only reason he was meeting her on the veranda per her written request was to avoid the more daunting prospect of having her march into the gaming room in pursuit.

The large veranda extended around the entire two-story building and fortuitously was ill-lit beyond the ballroom doors. Shrubbery screened the porch, and if a rendezvous was imperative, as Lucy's note implied, at least the location was private. Hazard purposefully strode to the small alcove near the back entrance; he and Lucy had swung on the swing on that veranda, hidden behind the tall bushes, the night they first met.

He found her near the back door, her forehead pressed against the jamb, a lacy handkerchief held up to her tear-stained cheeks. As he came up behind her, his flaring temper over the callous indiscretion of her note diminished. She looked so sad, so forlorn, and he knew her life with Attenborough wasn't all she wished. Gently gripping her soft shoulders, he buried his face in the curls at the back of her neck, murmuring comfortingly into the perfume of her skin, feeling the tension ease from her strained shoulders. Turning in his grasp, she threw her arms around his neck and cried, "Jon, I can't bear to see you and not touch you."

Looking into moist eyes, he said, "I'm sorry I avoided you, sweet." His voice was low, level, friendly. "But you must have heard the gossip tonight. It's bold as hell, and if Attenborough is pushed enough, he might feel obliged to call me out." Judge Attenborough was from an old Georgia family and still felt honor was defended with dueling pistols. "I don't want that and you don't want that. He could get hurt, maybe killed. Please, Lucy," he cajoled, "be sensible."

Whether Hazard would be defending his mistress, his courage, or merely his right to live his own life, the result would be the same. The Chief Justice would probably be dead and his wife the cause. Scandal could make her life unbearable.

While craving Hazard with a wanton desire bordering on obsession, Lucy was not prepared to relinquish her place with her husband and his three million dollars. After all, George couldn't live forever, and beautiful and ardent as Jon was, he was, by contrast, virtually penniless. Sighing heavily, she looked up through tear-splashed lashes and quietly said, "I know, Jon, you're right. I just want you so and you're going away tomorrow. Couldn't you stay another day?"

His mind quickly negotiated all the urgencies and obligations of his schedule against Lucy's tears, desires, her unnerving lack of discretion under stress. With an accepting smile he capitulated. "I can't stay another day, but I could postpone my departure until afternoon. How would that be?"

"Oh, Jon," she cried, her face alive with happiness. "Would you?"

He nodded once, saying in a gentle voice, "I'll be waiting for you tomorrow morning. Come whenever you can get away."

She laughed, triumphant as a captive let loose. "I'll be there at the break of dawn. That way I'll have you longer."

He smiled at her enthusiasm. "One thing, Lucy," he softly admonished, gently unlacing her hands from his neck and placing them in his own. "Take care, will you. A little prudence wouldn't be out of place. If I don't have to keep one eye on the door, I can devote more attention to you."

"I promise, sweetheart. I'll be caution itself. No one will even know I'm at the hotel."

"That would be nice, love, because today *everyone* sure as hell knew." He bent, softly kissed her lips, and then, opening the door, lightly pushed her through. "Get back to your guests. I'll see you in the morning."

Turning, she blew him a kiss and obediently returned to the ballroom.

Hazard leaned heavily against the door and slowly exhaled. A very touchy disaster had been averted. He'd rather not be forced to shoot the Chief Justice, judicial justice on the frontier being what it was and prejudice against the Indians escalating in direct proportion to the white man's greed for land and gold. Taking out a cigar, he struck a match, lit it, and lazily drew in the smoke. It was peaceful out here. The summer night was perfection and he needed a moment for the adrenaline levels to return to normal. He was thankful Lucy was so easily assuaged. The hysterical tone of her note had alarmed him; he had feared some public scene or impossible demand. While Lucy was an undeniable pleasure in bed, that was all she was, and for a disquieting moment he'd been afraid she was about to demand something foolish.

Recalling the swing in the corner, he decided to sit outside, smoke his cigar, and allow Lucy time to recirculate in the ballroom before reappearing himself. Summer moonlight rimmed and illuminated the tall man as he strolled toward the dimly lit corner of the veranda. Reaching the extremity of the alcove, he stopped dead, a sliver of moonlight illuminating his face. "Hell," said Jon Hazard under his breath, "bloody hell." Snatching the cigar from his mouth, he growled caustically, "Not only a stupid bitch, I see, but an eavesdropping one as well. I hope you were pleasantly diverted."

Sitting on the swing, shimmering white and pale in her silk gown, Blaze stiffened at his words and a thousand seed pearls glistened like fireflies in the moonlight. "I did *not* intentionally eavesdrop," she curtly replied. "If you could have kept your lecherous hands off the chief justice's wife for a few seconds," she witheringly continued, "I would have made myself known when you first arrived, made my excuses, and left. It's your own goddamned fault."

There was a hostile silence. The profanity checked his response momentarily. It might have been better phrased, he thought, but at least it reminded him of what she was. He had forgotten that beneath the simmering silk and shapely form was an imperious temperament. He had never been kicked by a woman before; had never been drawn on by a woman; had never been dismissively treated by a woman, he reflected in a rush. And until now, he had never been cursed by a woman. This willful female was single-handedly setting records of a kind that stoked his fiery temper. Swallowing alternative responses with supreme control, he merely said, "You have a vulgar tongue." But his face was dark with annoyance.

"And you have a vulgar mind," Blaze coldly replied.

Hazard's gaze was disconcertingly sharp. He smiled unpleasantly. "You find sex vulgar? Sinful too, no doubt. I pity your husband. The nights must be cold." His English was educated, his voice a derisive drawl, his accent softly western.

Her chin came up contentiously at his bad manners, and the moonlight caught for a dazzling moment on the lush curve of her neck and rising breasts. A man had never spoken to her so discourteously, and her voice, when she spoke, was icily correct. "Sex, as you so urbanely put it, is still a moot concept for me. Sin, I've discovered, is most often the obsession of small, wretched minds with nothing better to do. You needn't pity my husband. I don't have one. And when I do, I'm sure I'll be able to keep him warm in some adequately wifely fashion."

"Your blistering tongue's wifely enough," Hazard rudely said. "Unfortunately, men prefer other types of warmth."

Blaze shot to her feet in a flurry of shimmering pearls, fury sparkling in her eyes. "Mr.—"

"Black," Hazard supplied politely with a small bow.

"Mr. Black," she retorted, white-hot and hostile, "I find you contemptible!"

There was a pause. Hazard looked down at the glow of ash on his cigar and then his glance returned, enveloping Blaze in a shrewd, dark gaze. "And I find you"—his voice dropped to a whisper—"dangerous."

The word arrested her rising ire. "Dangerous?" she asked.

"Extremely," he replied drily. After a brief silence his face altered and she saw a polite charm he was in the habit of using effectively. "Will you give me your word you won't repeat anything you overheard tonight?"

The overture was coldly received, the request misread as a slap in the face. Blaze drew in a sharp breath of affront, which did alarming things to the high, soft rise of pale breasts pushing above the ivory silk and lace. Unconscious admiration shone in Hazard's dark eyes and he briefly forgot his heated anger.

"Would you like a signed statement?" she asked, the slightest malice in her tone. "Or *can* you read?" Her voice turned oversweet, "As I recall, at Diamond City, without evening rig and diamond studs,"—her small jeweled hand gestured vaguely—"you posed as a very different type of man. *Do* you read?" she insolently repeated, the provocation deliberate since neither his speech nor his dress suggested otherwise. "Or are you better at wrestling women to the ground?"

Hazard heard the caustic words with a rising sense of outraged disbelief. His lips parted and then closed in a straight, tight line. He had control of himself in a second and in another had matched her insolence. "I read a little," he murmured in a cool, constrained voice, fighting for equanimity before the female's unprecedented conduct, "and do all sorts of things to women, in addition to wrestling," he added in a husky rasp. She had finally goaded him past the point of acquired civilities. Sensitive of his Indian heritage, the relegation of unwritten Indian tradition and lore to some inferior position beside that of the white man's rapacious theme of progress was always guaranteed to provoke the worst in him. And that imperiousness was tiresomely excessive, he thought. For a woman. Within his own tribe he was a chief, well-born, a superlative warrior, trained to his fingertips, superior in standing to this spoiled white woman with all her wealth.

A glimmer of deadly derision appeared for an instant in Hazard's black eyes. "Why don't I show you," he said slowly, mockery tracing every syllable, "what I do to women? Show you those things that bring women like Lucy to heated indiscretion." His eyes scanned her slowly from head to toe, lingering leisurely on the stylish décolletage. "Why not sample firsthand some of the savage red man's beastly animal drives—*our alternatives to reading.*" The delicately derisive voice ended in a low, sensuous whisper, his eyes narrowing, becoming predatory. Tossing aside his cigar, he moved forward smoothly.

With a rustle of silk, Blaze retreated into the swing, staring defiantly back. "I'll scream," she managed, aware for the first time in her pampered life that she was facing a man she couldn't handle.

"Feel free. You wouldn't get the sound out of your throat before I silenced you." His voice was unhurried, his bronzed face under the thick black hair calm. "White men's schools may teach you to read, but the Indian ways teach you to move swiftly and silently. And up against danger, try using a book for defense." As he moved closer the smell of brandy was unmistakable.

"You're drunk!" Blaze cried half in affront, partly in dismay. "A damn dr—"

"Don't finish that," Hazard said sharply, his black eyes burning. If a man had so accused him, it would have cost him blood. "I never get drunk," he added in clear, explicit syllables. "Unlike other tribes, the Absarokee have never been ruled by the Masta-cheeda's liquor. It's a matter of pride," he finished simply.

He was still slowly advancing on her with a particular fluid grace, actually enjoying the fear in her eyes. The revelation that under the facade of imperiousness was only a trembling woman was unkind, but welcome, and it pleased him. That disclosure, or perhaps her stunning beauty and voluptuous opulence, more than the discovery, sent out familiar signals of desire. He felt the swelling against the fine wool of his trousers.

His hand slowly came up with a hushed delicacy, and as his slender fingers gripped her chin lightly the extravagant diamond pendants in her ears swung as prisms of light. "First," he said very quietly to the rigid woman, "I kiss them." And his head lowered to hers, half expecting her to pull away from his grasp. When she didn't, his other hand slid across the silk of her back and gradually pulled her close.

Blaze felt the gentle hands on her flesh, the fingers, work-hardened, not a gentleman's fingers, holding her chin lightly but ruthlessly, not inclined to let her get away. An extraordinary state of flurry overcame her senses, a confused rush of feelings, the same kind of thrilling longing and shivering fear she'd experienced when he carried her in Diamond City. And then she had no more time to think, for his warm lips touched hers, brushed back and forth against the soft fullness of her mouth, forced her lips apart in a breathless dissolving silence. The scent of him washed over her and the sense of a physical presence so much greater than her over-whelmed her mind.

She heard him groan softly, then with extreme and deliberate care he forced his tongue inside her mouth, tasting, licking, twining in a long, savage, sensuous pattern of withdrawal and penetration. And while his mouth and tongue ate at her, kissed and tantalized her warm, honeyed mouth, he gently accommodated her body to his, lifting her a little on tiptoe to fit more fluidly against his unmistakable arousal. "Then," he murmured in a particularly lush resonance against her mouth, "after I kiss them here, I kiss them . . ." His hand released her chin and slid down the warm, lilac-scented column of her throat, over the soft swell of breast where slim bronzed fingers, crushing a handful of silk and seed pearls, pushed down the décolletage and freed her of the confining fabric. The night air washed warm over her breasts in a languid pleasure before his dark head dipped. Just before his mouth covered one pink nipple already peaking in warm anticipation, he continued, ". . . here."

Blaze felt the soft brush of his breath just as his mouth closed wet and hungry on the cresting tip. The sensation streaking through her body was so excruciatingly violent her knees went weak, and if Hazard hadn't supported her, she would have fallen. Spontaneously relinquishing a multitude of genteel strictures drilled into her since childhood, flooded with thrilling new sensations ignited by Hazard's expert, coaxing touch, his relentless mouth and the unbelievable feel of him, Blaze's hands came up, slid into the overlong black hair, and pressed the tantalizing mouth closer. Hazard's mouth and nose and chin pressed into the ripe abundance of her breast, and fires burned in her blood; her pulse was racing into oblivion and she was tingling in hot waves of strange, exquisite longing deep inside.

With customary facility, Hazard was quickly past the point of prudence and, reading the signs expertly, lifted Blaze into his arms. He glanced around quickly, then down at her halfnaked body in his arms, and he knew he couldn't take her far. A rapid decision made, he walked down the steps and across the short stretch of lawn to the summer kitchen. The door was locked but he set his back to it, still holding her in his arms, and threw his weight against the molded pine. The flimsy lock gave way and they were inside. Heeling the door shut, he stood unmoving briefly until his eyes could distinguish shapes in the darkness. While he waited, his mouth toyed with hers, self-assured, confident, possessive. He sucked at her tongue until she whimpered a soft, breathy sound of capitulation, and finally, because he couldn't wait much longer, he cautiously moved toward the outline of a table.

He knocked over a chair getting to it, but kicked it out of the way and then moved the last few steps to the table. The fall of his splendid black hair brushed her cheek as he gently lowered Blaze onto the wooden surface and, bending low, brushed her lips with his. She clung to his face with warm hands when he tried to rise, so he kissed the graceful line of her mouth again, moving over a short moment later to trace the delicate border of her jaw and then languid his mouth slipped downward to the taut nipples achingly beckoning like extravagant wild rosebuds.

She cried softly when he touched her there, moaned little sounds of pleasure while his tongue caressed, held him fiercely to her as if she couldn't get enough of the soft savagery of his mouth and teeth teasing her nipples into begging peaks. Whenever he raised his head, she pushed it back. "Stay, please . . . stay," she whispered shakily, feeling the beat of her heart pulsing in strange new places, skittering in brushfire pathways from the tips of her breasts to the throbbing fire between her thighs.

But he couldn't wait forever; he wanted more than caresses. Unlocking the insistent hands, he held them aside and raised his head to taste her parted lips; with his tongue he plundered, ravaged, hungrily demanded. And left her trembling.

Swiftly his hand slid under the yards of silk and petticoats, glided up the velvet warmth of leg and thigh, and then—

Distinctly, a loud male voice shouted from quite near, "Blaze! Blaze! Where are you?"

She froze.

In the next heartbeat, she seemed to come to her senses. Sitting upright, covering her breasts with trembling hands, she whispered, "No!" in a small desperate voice.

"Yes," Hazard rebuffed, profoundly single-minded at the moment, reaching to recapture the soft silkiness of her bare shoulders, quite certain no one would invade the deserted summer kitchen. His mouth moved to regain hers. "Things you enjoy aren't bad for you, *bia*," he murmured against her lips, using the Absarokee endearment women found so reassuring. "You yellow eyes have it all wrong."

"No," she softly cried again, struggling to free herself, pushing him away with surprisingly strong hands. And before Hazard could decide whether she meant it or not, she had slipped from the table. Stunned and frustrated, he watched her run toward the door. In a few rapid adjustments she replaced the bodice of her gown, rearranged the lace drapery on her arms, opened the door, and disappeared into the summer night.

Jon Hazard Black swore into the grey shadows of the summer kitchen. He hadn't been left tormented with unconsummated desire since adolescence. Infuriated, he banged out of the building, exasperated with illogical women in general and one in particular. For a brief moment he listened to the lilting dance music coming from the glittering ballroom, and then, concluding he was past the point of civility that evening, walked back to his hotel and went to bed.

The following day, Lucy Attenborough received more attention than usual from Hazard. He had promised her the morning but he spent longer than that with her. Finally, very much later, when the heat of the afternoon had dwindled and the lethargy of a well-spent day enveloped the occupants of room 202, the only Absarokee prospecting for gold in Diamond City left the soft bed and warm woman and headed north out of Virginia City to his cabin on the mountaintop.

Chapter 4

THE next weeks were uninterrupted slogging hard work. Up with the dawn, Hazard built sluices, dug drainage, pickaxed and blasted deeper into the mine shaft he'd carved out of the hillside. He ate briefly each noon and then worked until sunset. His body, already powerfully muscled and bright-edged from years of training, took on a new toughness. The grueling regimen continued without break, day after day. At the end of the long workday, Hazard was normally too exhausted even to think—only sleep beckoned, not contemplative musing. But on the rare occasions it took him more than thirty seconds to fall asleep, a recurring image of red-hot hair, peach skin, and ivory silk slid uninvited into his mind.

Blaze, in contrast, had considerable leisure, and those unoccupied portions of her time were increasingly tenanted by vivid recollections of a boldly sensuous man. She disliked the arresting memories; no man's likeness had ever insinuated itself so into her senses. And with his image, of course, came remembrance of the unnerving, inexplicable response he'd drawn from her. Embarrassment flushed her skin each time she recalled her astonishing brazenness, her very near fall from grace. Only her father's voice breaking into the heated rapture had saved her. Without that reprieve, she would have readily and willingly succumbed to Lucy Attenborough's—and whoever else's?—very persuasive lover.

He was a womanizer of the worst kind, she decided after listening to the licentious rumor surrounding Hazard; everyone had a story about his way with women. He was the type of man who used women like frivolous playthings, with a casual male disregard she couldn't convince herself was cultural. After all, treating women as expendable receptacles for masculine passion was not without precedent in the white man's world. It was, she ruefully conceded, very obvious in the privileged world of wealth that she inhabited.

Yet within her own world, she refused to fit neatly into the niche reserved for affluent young ladies. The need to marry well, all the frivolous irrelevance so prevalent and cloying, the tedious boredom of fashionable society, were written in her future as surely as the days dawned. And that sort of stultifying, empty existence haunted her like a grotesque specter from hell. Consciously or not, she had fought against the final resolution of a proper marriage all her life. Over the years, occasional bursts of resentful tears rebuked the nasty quirk of fate which had sent her into this world as a susceptible female. Men weren't constantly boxed in and curtailed by hundreds of punctilious rules of etiquette. It was *grossly unfair*.

Owing, however, to her own fierce determination and a supportive father who gave rein to her capricious individuality, Blaze had circumvented many of the hindering strictures in her nineteen years. Unlike her female contemporaries, Blaze's striking thirst for knowledge had been fostered by her father's wealth. A succession of well-paid tutors in disciplines from the ordinary to the bizarre had entered the schoolroom of the house overlooking the Charles River. Blaze was educated in the conventional studies—classics, mathematics, geography, history—as well as the more uncommon disciplines of astronomy, Arabic, biology, metallurgy, and Chinese bronzes. She was—in the spring of 1865—beautiful, intelligent, a supreme egotist, a bit defiant, and intensely bored with the fatuous society in which she lived.

After a week more in Virginia City, subjected to the daily inconsequential chatter of her mother's friends, Blaze begged her father to set out with her again into the mining camps. At least on the trail she felt alive. If she had to spend one more day in the overfussy interior of Virginia City's grand hotel, sitting through another afternoon of tea and malicious gossip, she'd explode.

Very early on a Saturday morning Blaze left Virginia City with her father, a twelve-man group of business associates, and their three guides. The following week was spent following the route of the gold strikes, talking to prospectors, buying land whenever possible, discussing gold prices, interrogating claim owners on their findings.

The thirteen men in the group had combined to buy as many lode mines as possible. They had the resources to establish reduction works and processing plants, an expense most placer men couldn't afford. They also had the expertise in practical techniques of mining from parts of the United States and Europe that would make quartz mining, a long-term kind of gold mining, feasible.

Blaze listened while her father, his associates, and the miners discussed how to trace a vein, sink a shaft, break loose the ore, hoist it to the surface, crush it, and extract the gold from the resultant mass of ground-up material. She began to understand the problems involved in ventilation, hoisting, and timbering. She discovered that improved explosives and better drilling methods were allowing small operators an easier time of freeing gold-bearing rock from its matrix. She learned about stamp mills and the more primitive arrastra, used by the Mexicans and South Americans to crush gold-bearing rock. She began to appreciate the difficulty and intricacy of gold mining.

The weather cooperated with placid temperatures, in contrast to the hot spell of their earlier trip, and the activity was exhilarating. When feasible they slept in hotels (an optimistic euphemism for four walls and a roof), otherwise they camped in the open under the stars. The country was a combination of rugged, pine covered mountains and lovely green valleys, watered by clear, rushing streams. The party followed wagon trails where possible and, in less settled areas, traveled narrow deer trails. The scent of pines was pungent in the air, underbrush scarce beneath the towering virgin forests. A carpet of pine needles covered the coarse soil and wildflowers grew in a riot of color on the rust-hued bed of fallen needles. It was paradise to a young woman who'd spent most of her life chafing at the silken bonds of Boston society. Yet although she found the outdoors rustic and healthily fulfilling, Blaze was still very much a product of her upper-class environment. In the enchantment of the wild, rugged days on the mountain trails, she never once considered how the meals were prepared or the campsites settled so comfortably or even how her horse was saddled and ready each morning. An understandable oversight for woman reared in a household smoothly run by forty servants.

Two weeks later, the group stopped in Diamond City on the final leg of their return to Virginia City. For three days everyone was busy tying up and finalizing all the loose ends of their previous purchases.

Late the following morning, Yancy Strahan, Colonal Braddock's foreman, literally stamped into the parlor of the small house the party had rented and in a disgusted temper expressed his fury at "damn Injuns" in general and "one damn Injun" in particular. "That motherfucker!" he exploded in an incensed version of his soft Old Dominion drawl. "Threatened to shoot me if I didn't get off his claim in one minute! Don't they have reservations for them somewhere out here? Damn insolent savage. Who the hell's country does he thing this is anyway!" And even in the group of shrewd and avaricious businessmen who had developed "taking" into a fine art, no one had the audacity to answer him.

"Which claim is it?" one of the men seated around the large oak table asked.

"It's 1014 and 1015. This miners camp allows two claims per man, and they're smack in the middle of our lot," Yancy responded angrily.

"What's the fellow's name?"

"Hazard something-or-other," Yancy replied hotly. Blaze caught her breath sharply, more attentive as Yancy continued. "One of those idiotic Injun names. They just call him Hazard around here and make sure they stay out of his way."

"Dangerous?"

Yancy shrugged. "Killed three men in the last month. First one was cheating at cards they say and drew on the Injun when he called him on it. Guy didn't have a chance, the story goes. Blew him away before his gun was half out of the leather. Rumor has it he's quicker than anyone in the territory."

"Can we get to him?" someone asked, the voice as ambiguous as the words.

"That depends," Yancy said drily, "on the method. The other two he killed were trying to jump his claim. Came from different directions up the hill one night. He got 'em both."

There was a general clearing of throats, and then someone murmured, "At night?"

Yancy dropped into a chair and looked around the table. "They say he never sleeps." His voice dropped a tone and he more quietly said, "But hell, everyone has their price."

"Did you try—"

"Damn SOB wouldn't let me close enough to make an offer. Any suggestions should take that into consideration."

Seated next to her father, Blaze felt her pulse continue to race with each mention of Hazard. He was still there, then. The population of these mining camps was often transitory if a claim was unproductive. And she hadn't been altogether certain he *was* a prospector. After seeing him in evening dress in Virginia City, confusion had clouded her previous impression of him. Evidently, if Yancy's stories were true, the man had a multifaceted expertise: a killer too, not merely a womanizer and a prospector. Somehow it was hard to visualize—the murderous side—after having felt the gentle touch of his hands. Well schooled at murder, as well, it seemed, although, God knew, rough and immediate justice was prevalent in these lawless camps. Self-defense, Blaze knew, was the first law in the territory, maybe the only law, and no one thought less of you for holding on to what was yours.[3] "West of the Red River, no questions," ran the old rule.

So while the low murmur of male voices drifted around her, discussing how best to approach Hazard and make him change his mind, Blaze's thoughts were preoccupied with the remembered feel of his hard, masculine body. Almost as rapidly as these thoughts surfaced, she ruthlessly suppressed them and castigated herself for allowing such witless reflections. Hazard Black was no more than a primitive anachronism in evening clothes; under the facade was a barbarian, a killer, a brute of a man. And much as she loved the wild, untamed quality of the West, Blaze hardly considered those qualities acceptable in a man.

The conversation continued apace. Hazard's claims were the linchpin to the claims already purchased. If his land couldn't be acquired, its existence was going to cause untold problems in the future in terms of the Apex law.[4] From the looks of it, the men decided, Hazard's claims embraced the apex of a gold vein. According to the existing legal status of lode mining developed by miners' law in the early years of the California Gold Rush, if a claimant had the apex of a lode within the boundaries of his claim, he might follow the vein through the side limits of his claim as far as the vein extended. If Hazard's vein extended into the claims on either side of him, he could mine the gold under their claims legally. It could mean millions. Or it could be nothing. Gold veins were capricious, but none of the Buhl Mining men cared to gamble unnecessarily.

"Wasn't he at the Territorial Ball in Virginia City a few weeks ago?" Turledge Taylor, Vice President for Consolidated Mining, inquired. "Can't be a hundred percent Indian and invited there." He didn't know Lucy Attenborough had sent out the guest list.

Another voice offered, "I understand he's a chief's son. His parent's died last winter when smallpox took so many of those Mountain Crow. Gashed himself up like they do for mourning. It's a sign of their grief. Heard he was cut-up pretty bad. Strange people." At this, Blaze's mind raced back to the mud, and their first meeting, when she'd seen the scars crisscrossing Hazard's chest.

A dozen pair of eyes observed the speaker with interest. "Where'd you hear that?" two voices asked in unison.

The man looked discomfited for a moment, and he glanced apologetically at Blaze before he answered, "One of Rose's girls mentioned it." Everyone except Blaze knew which of Rose's girls that was. One of the young prostitutes at Confederate Gulch's fanciest brothel had taken Ed's fancy. She was only fourteen and he'd delegated much of his work to subordinates the last week or so in order to stay in Confederate Gulch. "His arms and chest are covered with scars, Fay said. Rose looked after him for a while."

"We're not dealing with the usual miner, it would seem," the man to Blaze's left interjected. "If money won't buy him, should we offer an alternate claim? Or maybe we could deal him in for a small percentage. He's probably a half-breed and a shade more civilized than the others. Or at least shrewder."

"I heard he's a Harvard man," Frank Goodwin said, "if you're talking about that fellow with long hair who sat in on our card game at the Territorial Ball." His heavy brows met in a frown. "Damn near cleaned me out."

"Damn near cleaned everyone out," his partner Henry Deville groused.

"Hard to believe," Frank went on.

"Harder to take," another man grumbled.

"No, I mean, it's hard to believe he went to Harvard. I know they let in those Siamese and Chinese princes and a Frog sometimes, even a Russian duke now and then, but not a half-breed. Hell, no, I don't believe it."

"Shit, I don't care if he's civilized enough to ball the Queen of England," Yancy brusquely said, ignoring Blaze altogether. "We need that parcel. Now, how're going to get it?"

"Why don't I go and talk to him?" Blaze very quietly said.

"Out of the question," her father curtly retorted. "You heard. He's killed three men lately."

"Really, Daddy, the man seemed quite—" Blaze paused, searching for the proper word since the one that came to mind—expert—would occasion licentious comment. "Pleasant with women," she finished in a level tone. "I heard him speak to the Chief Justice's wife and I briefly conversed with him myself. If it's the same man, I don't think he'll harm a woman. Let me try. At least I may be able to get close enough to talk to him."

Various opinions immediately broke out into a heated buzz of masculine voices. Blaze patiently waited. They knew, as she knew, that her suggestion was the only reasonable option short of massing an army. Yancy hadn't been able to get within speaking distance today, and both times he'd been driven off at rifle point. Without her attempt, they'd be returning to Virginia City one parcel short of an extremely profitable piece of mining property.

"I say we try it," Frank said.

"*I* say *no!*" Colonel Braddock snapped.

Bestowing on her father a calm, rational look that always seemed to convince him that what she wanted wasn't as rash as it sounded, Blaze countered, "Daddy, it's not as though I can't defend myself. You know I'm reasonably good with my Colts. You taught me yourself." She didn't mention that if this Hazard was the same Indian she'd drawn on in Diamond City in May, she'd have to rely on his good graces rather than her speed with pistols to protect herself. "Please, Daddy," she said, her smile ravishingly imploring.

Colonel Braddock vacillated, his eyes on his daughter's confident face, while his colleagues urged him to agree.

"Come on, Billy, it's broad daylight. What can happen?"

"We'll be standing right at the bottom of the hillside," another man added.

"He wouldn't hurt a woman. Likes women, rumor has it, . . . a lot."

Billy Braddock's scowl deepened with that remark and Turledge smoothly observed, "Attenborough invited him to the ball, remember; looked as much a gentleman as any of us, it seemed to me."

"Turledge's right, Daddy. He wouldn't have been invited to the ball if he wasn't acceptable." Of course Blaze knew exactly to whom he was acceptable. No need to mention that. She looked at him expectantly. She was his only child; he loved her and, dammit, never knew how to deny her anything.

Blaze was counting on that. One more quiet "please" and he helplessly acquiesced.

Chapter 5 ～⌒◎

JON Hazard stood under a clear sun at the crest of the rubble-strewn trail, hard, slender, hellishly curious, his rifle loosely disposed across his arms. Out of range of any firearm manufactured, squinting down the sun-baked landscape, he calmly watched the group of dark-coated men a thousand yards down mountain and inquisitively watched the slow ascent of the long-legged woman with hair like a cloud of shimmering sunsets. The trail was rough, uneven, littered with schist debris, all infinitely useful in gauging someone's approach.

She wore black twill trousers tucked into black highly polished English riding boots. Hazard transiently wondered which servant had been taken along to keep the boots so exquisitely shined. A white linen blouse, hand-tucked in scores of tiny pleats, enhanced the remembered golden glow of her skin, darkened to an almost unladylike hue since he'd seen her last. She must

have left her parasol behind in Virginia City, he satiri-
cally reflected.

He knew why she was climbing the hill. He recognized the group of richly dressed men at the base of the
mountain.

When she approached within ten yards, Hazard
shifted his position fractionally, his finger easing away
from the cocked trigger. Their eyes met; she flushed,
then paled so the delicate face was contoured with rosy
highlights. Admiration remotely stirred in his cool, dark
eyes. "You interrupted my noon meal. Leave your guns
outside." Without waiting for an answer, he turned and
walked back to his rough home, opened the door, and
went inside.

Leaving her guns, Blaze walked across the small
porch and stood at the entrance. Hazard was already
sitting and eating. His suavely muscled brown torso,
marked here and there with pale scars of healed wounds,
disconcerted her—both the inscribed mementos of battle
and the nakedness. He wore only antelope skin leggings[5]
and moccasins, his newly barbered hair, tangled and
damp from exertion under the midday sun, a thin sheen
of perspiration accenting the grace of his body. "May I
come in?"

He raised his eyebrows, studying the slim woman
before him. His memory of her had been accurate, although in daylight, she was younger than he remembered
—and more beautiful. "Of course," he said.

When Blaze entered the small room, he rose, moved
to the door, and shut it. Walking back, he paused, standing very close to her, and it seemed as though a warmth
emanated from him; his dark eyes turned their full attention on her. Her eyes drifted to his mouth of their own
volition and she remembered the burning fire of his
kisses.

His slender arching hand flicked toward the table.
"Would you care to join me?" he politely murmured as
though he'd never felt the fine silk of her skin or tasted
the sweet welcome of her desire. "Not up to your usual
standards, I'm sure," he serenely noted, his voice by con-

trast lambent heat, "but sufficient to keep body and soul together."

"Thank you, no," Blaze replied to the man known to most people diffidently as Hazard, her own memories of him suddenly too vivid. Unexpected qualms and unfamiliar feelings made her too nervous to eat. His food was simple: fried bread; a large steak, of elk or venison, she guessed; coffee; and a large tin container of raspberries.

"Try the berries anyway," he remarked, moving back to the table. "The boy from McTaggert's spent all morning picking them." He sat and began eating again.

"No, thank you," she repeated, determined to come straight to the point. She found him more disturbing than expected and the memories of the Territorial Ball too volatile to casually dismiss. Unconsciously squaring her shoulders, she said as calmly as possible, "I'm here to offer you a business proposition."

Glancing up, his gaze trapped hers and for a moment Blaze saw only luminous eyes and a dark, indulgent amusement. "A business proposition. I see."

Blaze relaxed. She'd known he'd be reasonable once one was close enough to talk to him. Yancy Strahan's business methods had never appealed to her either. Now it was simply a matter of agreeing on price.

Hazard wondered which businessman down at the bottom of the mountain owned her. She wasn't married, she'd said the night of the ball, yet was traveling with that group of men. Whoever it was must have brought her from the East; she was more refined than the available women out here. He understood what the business proposition entailed.

He could visualize her businessman protector now, telling her what to do . . . how to approach him . . . what to say; using her to try to get him another way— with a bribe and lure as old as man. So here she was, too nervous to sit down with him. Not sure exactly what to expect from a wild Indian who had threatened to shoot their last agent only this morning.

"You're aware your claim is contiguous to several promising properties," Blaze began, interrupting Hazard's reflections.

"Sit down. Do you have a name?" he asked, ignoring her opening gambit, and went back to his meal.

She hesitated briefly, for his presence was disconcertingly invasive, as though he'd touched her with his words and glance.

Lifting his eyes for a moment from his task of cutting his meat, Hazard said, "Do you?" and waited expectantly until she spoke:

"Miss Braddock." And sat down.

Ah, he thought, pretentions from a kept woman. Not Mary Braddock or Amy or Cora, but *Miss* Braddock. Would she be refined in bed as well? he facetiously mused. He ate then while Blaze in a small, dignified voice apologized for Yancy's discourtesy and began listing the claims around him Buhl had purchased. "So you see, Mr. Black," she continued, more assured without his dark gaze on her, "as an agent for Buhl Mining I'm prepared to offer you a very advantageous price for your claim."

She was really quite good, he thought. All the nuances of diction and substance were there. No doubt she'd been coached for the part. Hazard put down his knife and fork and pushed away his plate. "Fine. You're an agent of Buhl Mining Company," he mildly replied, but in the muted light, capricious with shadow, his face was civilly skeptical. "Just for the sake of argument," said Hazard encouragingly, "let's say I believe you." Sliding his chair back, he stood. Moving smoothly around the table, he pulled her to her feet. "Now then," he murmured, holding her straight shoulders, "what exactly are you willing to offer for my claim?"

His gaze, rested on Blaze's startled face, on the pale sunlight on her cheekbones, the slender bridge of her nose, on the ripe mouth. She seemed small, held close, and her soft lips, half open in surprise, were curiously beseeching. His hand moved to the buttons on her blouse and began opening one with unhurried fingers.

"I'm prepared—that is—Buhl's prepared to offer you—anything you want," Blaze softly stammered, mesmerized by his eyes, his touch, by the feelings that had sprung to life at his sudden nearness.

"Anything?" he quietly murmured. His dark fingers slipped under the linen and stroked the soft rise of one silken breast. "I like the sound of that." The feel of her skin was like rose petals, velvety and fine, and the thin chemise under the blouse was no obstacle at all to his sudden hunger. She opened her mouth to answer, but then his thumb and forefinger touched her nipple through the lacy fabric and the words lodged in her throat. Slowly, gently, he rubbed and teased each peaking crest into a rigid aching hardness. He hadn't kissed her yet, content to watch the lush sensuality infuse her face.

She stood very quietly beneath his hands. She was trained to be acquiescent though, he reminded himself. It was her job, the submissive pose. But he didn't mind. He was being offered a delectable break in his day and he'd be a fool to refuse it. He could take his time with her—that's why she'd been sent. So there'd be no interruptions. He might as well enjoy the bounties of corporate deviousness.

Her eyes were half closed, her breathing hushed, when he reached up to slip the cool linen from her shoulders, down her arms, over her small hands, freeing it from her body. His palms glided down the smoothness of her back; how fragile she felt under his callused hands. Tugging the blouse out of her trousers, he carefully laid it on the chair. The sheer white chemise, more lace than silk, scarcely concealed her upright breasts straining against the light material, nor the peaked nipples pressing like supplicants through the filmy undergarment.

Instinctively her arms came up to shield herself.

"Very nice gesture. Such a classic, but," Hazard said, pushing aside her protective arms, "I want to look at you before I fuck you." He deliberately used the coarse word, to remind her as well as himself that this scenario was bought and paid for by Buhl Mining Company—her owner, his adversary. She colored and appeared confused, but her sky-blue eyes were helpless when they gazed into his unflinching black depths.

He lowered his head with deliberate slowness to kiss her, excited despite himself by the stripping away of her habitual grace and poise. Whether artificial or not, the innocent confusion was erotically provocative and the throbbing in his groin swelled prominently against the leather leggings. She whimpered softly when their lips touched and this time her mouth opened of its own accord under his. He was being offered several heated degrees more than acquiescence in the gesture, and when he tasted the sweetness of her mouth, her tongue softly played with his, twined and teased, then winsomely danced away. He noted the difference immediately; she was responding like a young girl to a lesson previously learned. He marveled at the delicate sense of naïveté she was able to portray, gave her high points as an actress, and looked forward to a very pleasant afternoon.

"Mmmmm . . ." he murmured against the soft pressure of her mouth. "If you're the 'anything' "—he nibbled at her lush lower lip— "I'm buying." His hands played down the small of her back, pressing her closer, molding her lower body to his, until his pulsing manhood was like a living force between them.

"You don't understand," Blaze managed to whisper while the gentle swaying aggression of Hazard's need burned against her thighs, her stomach, pressed like a brand on her own aching want. And all the complexities of who she was and why she was here were reduced to trivia beside the raging tide of desire racing through her mind and body.

"I understand, *bia.*" The rough-soft voice breathed into her ear, his hardness brushing a languid pattern upward. "Perfectly." His mouth left a fiery trail down her throat, his teeth lightly nipping her satiny shoulder.

She shivered, trembled, died a little at the restrained hunger of the tiny bites, and her arms finally left her sides, drifting up in slow motion to grip his strong shoulders. Holding on against the mists of desire enveloping her, she dreamily murmured, "We should talk money. . . ." Still not completely lost to reason, she breathily added, ". . . Your claim—"

"Claims," he absently corrected, his hands already moving upward. He removed her arms from his neck and carefully placed them at her sides; then, grasping the thin

straps of her chemise, he slid them down, returning to
gently tug the fine embroidered silk over the fullness of
her breasts. The lacy bodice tightened, not designed to
be taken off that way. Single-minded now, Hazard improvised. Forcing her ripe breasts upward with one hand,
he gently eased the taut fabric over the swelling curves.
Blaze felt his hands like flame on her skin, the pressure
sure; she felt the filmy material slide over the cresting
tips of her nipples leaving her tingling with want. She
trembled, felt the silk of his hair brush her skin, warmth
rushing in an intoxicating turbulence downward from her
sensitive breasts to a new and irrepressible desire. Balancing tremulously on the heady fringes of the unknown,
in a soft rush of words, she whispered, "We really . . .
should talk . . . about—"

"Later," Hazard interrupted very softly, just before
he slowly drew the tip, the nipple, the entire aureole into
his mouth and teased gently with his teeth and tongue
until Blaze felt sure she would swoon from the pleasure.

In a remote corner of her brain, Blaze realized she
should break away, stop this irrational surrender to this
man who shocked and thrilled her simultaneously. It was
sheer insanity . . . but an insanity she was powerless to
resist.

Hazard only briefly considered how this luscious
woman sent up as a sweet bribe was corrupting his principles—only very briefly—and then his head lifted, his
hands moved downward and he began unbuckling the
narrow leather belt twined around her slender waist.

Blaze was pressed back against the wall near the
small table, crushed between it and the throbbing hardness of Hazard's lower body. His lean hips moved rhyth-
mically against her in slow dance of persuasion and lust
that caused a tremor in the fingers undoing the gold
buckle at her waist. She could feel the full length of him,
his roused masculinity like a battering ram testing the
way for entry. And when he finally opened the clasp and
slid the belt free, it was as if he'd opened her long-dor-
mant passion. Dropping the belt to the floor, he drew her
closer, slid a hand down her bottom, and, bringing her up

on her toes, forced her to meet the full urgency of his hunger.

Like magnets to the Earth's poles, Blaze's hands glided up Hazard's dark chest, lifted high on his shoulders, and, lacing her fingers around his powerful neck, she melted into his frame. "I shouldn't be doing this," she breathed in a sweet surrendering sigh.

It was the patently coy phrase and what sounded like a carefully orchestrated sigh that suddenly, like a cold drenching cloudburst, brought Hazard to his senses. He froze for the count of ten, looking down into the perfect face. Bloody hell, he thought, hot anger cresting in seconds, was he gong to fall into this strumpet's arms like so much docile meat? Not that he had any intention of selling his claim, but the whole easy acceptance of her brazenly offered body demeaned him.

Suddenly the crude and deliberate victimization by Buhl Mining mattered more than the lust licking through his veins. And, as suddenly, he knew he didn't want to be corrupted. Inhaling a ragged, brutal breath, using every ounce of will bred into him by the harsh, Absarokee tradition, Hazard crushed down the overwhelming emotions driving him to take this woman and very deliberately pulled her arms from around his neck and stepped away from her.

Turning, he walked the few steps to his chair and sat down, trying with all the strength of his considerable will to concentrate on something—anything but his hunger for this woman.

Feeling instantly cold and bereft when he walked away, Blaze, her eyes, pleasure-darkened from new, powerful yearnings beating at her sanity, didn't stop to think, only acted. "Come back," she softly pleaded. Her senses, her awakened body, were reaching toward some elusive enchantment, and not knowing why she felt as she did when Hazard touched her, Blaze only knew she wanted what he was about to give her.

Hazard didn't respond. His breath, a harsh, raspy rhythm, came from deep within his chest, now that the initial suffocating feeling had passed. With an irritated grimace, he shifted restlessly on the chair but he stayed where he was, braced hard against his body's searing drive.

Blaze knew, however innocent her knowledge of these things, that he hadn't wanted to stop. Something had forced him to walk away. And she also knew with an inherent femaleness that she could undermine that resistance.

And that was when the spoiled Miss Braddock came to the fore, the impetuous Miss Braddock who had been denied nothing in her life, the imperious Miss Braddock whose blood was on fire. "Come here," she repeated, out of pique this time, unfamiliar with being spurned, a sultry petulance permeating her voice. "I want to feel you . . ." The sentence was left incomplete.

Jon Hazard's treacherous mind finished the thought and his hand resting on the rough tabletop clenched convulsively. "You'd better go," he growled. "Just get the hell out of here," he added gruffly, all the ethical and unethical turmoil locked hard within him.

He heard her boot heels on the floor and tensed, his knuckles pale against his swarthy skin. The visual image of her backed against the wall, naked above the waist, her breasts softly swollen under his hands, her wide eyes warm and liquid with wanting him—the vivid portrayal added inches to his arousal. "I don't want to go yet," she whispered softly, like a young girl wanting something she shouldn't have. The tone was jeunesse dorée, willful, and transiently he wondered if she wasn't a hussy but some wealthy young lady fallen into disgrace.

His ambivalent musing was dramatically abridged in the following second, for her hand touched his hair.

She felt him steady himself after the initial, breath-catching shock, and as her small fingers, slender and pale, smoothed down the sleek blackness of his hair, Hazard sat unmoving, his breath almost in abeyance. Then her hand slipped down to his shoulder, her warm palm lying lightly on him, and an overwhelming sexual response poured over Hazard. He could no longer convince himself of the corruption. All he could think of her was her long legs wrapped around him.

Blaze focused on her pale fingers lying on his skin:

fragile femaleness on brown male strength; the erotic contrast of brute virility beneath her fingers like a tender rose on an anvil. Then she saw Hazard Black begin, automatically, to breathe again, felt the warmth of his skin move. Would it hurt, she wondered for the first time in her life? Could she take on all that driving power and ever be the same? Why was she drawn to this uncivilized man with the terribly civilized touch of a polished courtier?

Hazard had always prided himself on picking and choosing; with his charm and physical grace, he'd always been able to. He knew how to say no when he didn't want a woman. And he shouldn't touch her, *particularly* not this one. It was the reason she was sent up here. He would be falling into their unsubtle ploy with scarcely a struggle. He should say no and send her away.

For five full seconds all the reasons for refusing to respond to the provocative touch and coaxing words made sense, and then her hand slid down his spine, and his whole mechanism for feeling, thought, deed lay shuddering, hostage to that small hand. He became perfectly still, shaken by the agony of his mind until the devastating ache in his loins, disregarding every scruple, forced his reaction. Turning sharply, he looked up at her. Then, rising suddenly, he took two steps, forcing her back against the wall. One hand came up and planted itself beside her left shoulder. Lazily, his other hand rose, grazing her breast in its upward passage before it came to rest solidly by her right ear. He leaned close, the heat from his body bathing her heightened senses, and in a low, deliberate tone said, "You know what I'm going to do if you stay."

Her eyes were large and darkening, the unalloyed longing there to see. Even for all its severity, like a man suddenly annoyed, Hazard's voice had a heated, thrilling effect on her—like getting too near the flame. Fascinated, lured, against all her best judgment, she didn't move.

Then, abruptly, his face tightened. "Dammit . . . dammit to hell. Go. It won't work," he tersely declared. "Tell them it won't work," he harshly added one last time and his hands dropped. But despite the words, his need smothered her.

"I don't want to go," she said very simply, the offer in her eyes unmistakable.

Damn, he thought and touched her shoulders delicately with only his fingertips, a tentative touch as reluctant as his ambiguous feelings. "You don't want to go. I don't want you to go," he pronounced like a schoolmaster explaining an unpleasant assignment. "I suppose everyone in camp knows you're here. You're half naked already," he went on with the illusion of calmness. "We might as well," a shade of exasperation drifted into the rich voice, "get down to business." And the hands closing on Blaze's shoulders were like steel clamps, and this time the kiss was hard, brutal, possessive.

Hazard's urgent hands ran down the silky contours of her back, cupped her bottom, and hauled her fiercely close. There was no subtlety now. He had given her every chance to leave; he felt no compunction any longer. Twenty days' hunger, the arousal and frustration of the past half-hour crested like a rolling storm over the Rockies, while, astonishingly, the luscious woman reveled in the urgency and swiftly moving passion driving him. She answered his needs with melting flesh and soft cries of longing. If she was acting, he brutally thought moments later, carrying her over to the campaign bed in the corner, she should get an extra bonus for startling realism. Carefully placing her on her feet, he settled on the bed in a sprawl, his eyes never leaving the spectacular woman standing before him, and in a cool voice said, "All right. Undress. I haven't had dessert yet; it might as well be you."

Blaze, eyes downcast, blushed, inner conflict battling overwhelming desire.

Hazard's black eyes slid over her, observing the blush and hesitation with nerveless cynicism. "No need for coyness," he drawled. "But take your time. We've all afternoon." She was certainly aware of what was expected of her, of the reason she'd been sent up here, but if she chose to extend the amusement, he was amenable.

"By the way," Hazard murmured in silken accents, "your nipples are the most sensual I've ever seen."

It was as if his deep velvet voice had reached out to touch them and Blaze felt a fresh surge of desire coil deep inside her.

He saw the perceptible rise in the rosy peaks. "Don't make me wait too long," he said very low. "I'd like to touch you . . . everywhere."

Blaze stirred at the heated words, at the answering heat pulsing through her body. "I don't know . . . what to do," she murmured, her fingers curling against the twill of her trousers.

Hazard's black brows arched in surprise or ridicule or over some curious sense of respect. "Ah . . . very nice." Gentle derision underlay the approving tone. "Just the right amount of modesty. I like that."

"Help me," she whispered, standing before him in a half-dressed tumble of copper-bright hair and white flesh.

"Perfect," said Hazard encouragingly. "A rare talent —that simple innocence." His voice dropped a register, infused now with rich promise. "Later I'll help you. I'm very good at 'helping' women. But now, *bia,* amuse me. Finish undressing."

The words, the promise, the ardent anticipation licked at her desire. Her heart wildly pulsing, Blaze half raised her hands, paused for a moment, then determinedly grasped the chemise draped at her waist. Lifting, she tried to pull the wispy lace over her breasts.

It caught.

For a second, Hazard watched, then said helpfully, "Come here."

She moved across the few feet separating them and before the frightened response could reach her eyes, Hazard had cut away the garment with a slash of his knife. Returning it to the sheath strapped to his leg, he casually remarked, "I'm sure whoever bought that can afford another. Now the boots," he prompted, lying back down, lacing his hands behind his head.

In a trance, compelled by desire so powerful the world dematerialized, Blaze obeyed. Hazard observed the grace of her movements: the sensuous curve of spine, slender leg, extravagant breasts swaying slightly from side to side as she bent, then shifted her weight to remove her boots. Straightening, she stood, shivering a little, although it was a warm afternoon.

Hazard's eyes narrowed at the faint tremor and hesitancy. "Are you a tease, pet? Because if you are, I may be inclined to pay you back later." His arousal was aching now and, control or no, he didn't care to wait much longer. "The slacks," he ordered.

There was a capricious change in his tone and expression and in her innocence a moment of uncertainty numbed her. Impatiently, eyes smoldering with passion, Hazard sat up and, reaching out, pulled her close. "Temptress," Hazard murmured, his hands brushing up her hips and closing around her waist, "you're very, very good, but it's been so long for me. . . ." His fingers were moving to the buttons of her trousers. "The first time might have to be mine," he said in a low, husky tone, sliding the buttons free. An instant later, her slacks were stripped off. His heart began pounding in his ears at the sight of her long-legged beauty, covered now with only brief lace drawers. He untied the ribbon drawstring with visibly shaking fingers and they slid to the floor. He pulled her one step nearer and she was free of her clothing.

Drawing her between his legs, his fingers trailed over the curve of her hip, across her thigh, slipping up to the petal-smooth flesh he sought. She moaned softly, swaying under his hands. Steadying her, he softly breathed, "So nice of you to come and visit," in a parody of polite social exchange, while his fingertips stroked the pale velvet of her inner thighs, moving upward with a connoisseur's skill. Her nipples had risen like jeweled ornaments, and Hazard knew the meaning of those distinct erections. His fingers touched a dewy warmth, and the welcoming heat brought a sheen of perspiration to his body. Embracing her hips, he drew her closer, leaned forward, and kissed her silken curls.

"No!" Blaze gasped, jerking her hips back, shocked from her passion drenched madness.

"No?" Gripping her tightly, Hazard looked up and shook his head, shiny black hair brushing sensuously against the whiteness of her thighs. "Don't say no, *bia* . . . that's not in the contract," he murmured. "Remember, only yesses, only compliance, only everything I want to do to you." Against her faint resistance, Hazard firmly moved her back, hard hands shackling her hips, and very slowly thrust his tongue deep into her waiting honeyed warmth. She writhed helplessly against his steely grip, her frantic movement only furthering the progress of his softly caressing tongue. In moments, Hazard forced a shuddering moan from her and quivering she gasped in shallow rapturous sighs.

"That's better," he said gently against the damp, silken curls, but the woman didn't seem to hear. "I like a bitch in heat," he added in almost a silent whisper before his tongue touched her sweetness again. Mutually exquisite pleasure poured in torrents through their senses as if floodgates, locked too long, burst open by force. Blaze had never felt a man there, had never known the thrilling excitement Hazard so easily manipulated, was lost in an enchanted wonderland of ecstasy. After long moments, Hazard lifted his head and quietly said, "Look what you're doing to me."

Blaze's eyes remained shut and he wondered if she had heard him. "Look," he whispered again, and this time his palms ran sensuously over her taut nipples. Whether prompted by touch or tone, her eyes opened slowly and gazed downward, focusing on the telltale bulge in the soft leather pants. She trembled.

"I want you, Miss Braddock. You can see that, can't you?" His voice was liquid flame. "I want to touch you, Miss Braddock . . . all over. I want to feel your warm skin next to mine."

Her mesmerized glance hadn't shifted from the virile evidence of his need, nor had the stillness of her nude body altered except for a slight shiver. Was she finding it impossible to go on with this after all? Hazard speculated. Regardless of his orders, was bedding an Indian more than she could contemplate despite her easily aroused sensuality; did she have a core of prejudice, unknown even to her benefactor, impeding that final step? He knew her body was ready; the signs were obvious. The deductive conclusion brought his quick temper to crucible heat.

My God, here was a whore with more scruples than any white woman he'd known. If it wasn't so detestable, he would have found it amusing. Her fear annoyed him, galled him. He could rape her, of course. No one was going to stop him. And in her profession, surely, it was no novelty. But he'd never raped a woman and, even now in anger, didn't find the prospect appealing.

Damn, he didn't need a woman this badly. Let the slut go back. Drawing in a deep breath to suppress his aching desire, he said, cold temper grating suddenly in his soft voice, "Let's end this charade. Get dressed and get out. Tell them you tried. I've a lot of work to do."

Throwing himself back on the bed, he heard a quiet "No." Casting up elegant brows in surprise, his dark eyes took in the opulent woman with tumbled russet hair falling loose over her pale shoulders, noted the still taut pink peaks with a connoisseur's eye, saw the small hands clenched into fists at her side.

Was it some incontrovertible command? Could she *not* go back down unless she made love to him? Was she afraid of her protector as well as of him? Suddenly she appeared vulnerable and afraid.

"Oh, bloody hell," he muttered, then, reaching out, touched her hand. His slender fingers twined gently through hers; he tugged her close. "I'm sorry they're forcing you to do this. It's all unnecessary. Really, it is." The deep, quiet voice was polite, the tone kindly, the substance unimpeachably civilized.

Blaze Braddock, who prided herself on an undaunted self-control, whose reputation in Boston society precluded the usual commonplace feminine attributes, mortified, felt the tears begin to gather in her eyes.

Hazard noted the shiny glisten, saw her mouth begin to quiver, and, swinging his long legs over the side of the cot, pulled her on his lap. "It's over. Don't cry," he soothed, huskily. "They won't hurt you, don't worry. They couldn't have seriously thought this would work anyway." His hands were gently stroking, as a young boy would comfort a frightened puppy.

"It's not that," said Blaze failingly, under her breath, tears spilling down her cheeks. How could she explain all the tumultuous emotions in her mind or the unutterable sense of losing one's sanity. It wasn't any of the mining company officials causing the trembling and tears; she wasn't afraid of them. What frightened her was the edge of the unknown precipice she was balancing on, the threshold pleasures of love stretching her taut with powerful longings, her wanting this man in a way she'd never known before.

"What, then? Tell me." His voice was polite but wary, imbued with the same nuance of reticence which colored all his actions. He was holding her in the warm curve of his chest, his hands soothing absently.

"It's too complicated," Blaze replied with a capitulative sigh, her head dropping to his shoulder, flame hair cascading over his arm. With the gentle sigh, Blaze's last shred of moral indecision was cast away. She had never felt so wonderful, had never been bathed like this in warm pleasure, had never been consciously aware of each tingling nerve in her body.

Hazard, hearing the soft sigh, feeling the head touch his shoulder, momentarily tensed. That sigh and gesture were surrender and he knew it. What now? How important was it for him to quench his carnal urges and resist the enticement? Wouldn't it be simpler to put her clothes back on, push her out the door, and not disturb her essential intentions, which had nothing to do with this woman? But then her warm lips brushed against his throat, a light, tentative caress. For whatever esoteric reason, *she* had changed her mind. Uncertainty still curbed his reflexes, though, while the byzantine complexities of this situation disciplined his normal libido. This wasn't simple sex and pleasure. It was orchestrated, brutally bought and paid for. Damn . . . he didn't know what to do.

With a swishing toss of her scented hair, Blaze's head lifted from his shoulder. Her fingers played lightly over the broad planes of his chest, drifting slowly downward across his torso, hesitantly pausing at his waist where the leather leggings began.

The world was momentarily arrested.

Until suddenly her hand slid under the waistband of the leggings to the pulsing maleness straining against the leather, and Hazard drew in a sibilant breath.

"Kiss me," Blaze softly breathed, lifting the freshness of her face.

In an instant, gold, corruption, complexities, all the consequences were measured and dismissed, and he knew exactly what he was going to do. Laying her on the bed, he stood and took off his leggings and moccasins. Untying the sheathed knife, he left it within reach.

The bed was small and narrow and made for only one person. His strong knee crushed the sheet, and when his full weight was added, the springs protested. The bed shifted slightly on the wooden floor when he moved her beneath him and nudged wide her thighs. His mouth covered hers hungrily, greedily, and while he tasted her sweetness there, his excited manhood pressed against the soaked heat below. Past the point of preliminaries, whatever control he possessed, gone, with one hand he gave the slight guidance needed and was astonished, a moment later, to find his gliding progress into her abruptly curtailed. Impossible, he thought, feeling the gentle movement of her hips under him. He thrust forward again, suffocating in anticipation, and she moaned a little, but he penetrated no further than before. Impossible or not, incredibly, it seemed he had a virgin on his hands. He remained poised motionlessly for a fraction of a shocked second more before numbly collapsing beside her. What had he done to deserve such excruciating frustration, he thought, silently cursing every deity and spirit in the universe.

"Why did you stop?" Blaze desperately whispered, her hand hot on his arm. She could feel the breath lodged in her throat and, lost in sensation, only knew she must have him.

His head snapped around and incredulously he exploded, "You're a virgin!"

"Is that a sin in your culture?" Her blue eyes were

innocently wide, but under the cat's lashes, they were ardent and fierce with wanting.

"No," he quietly replied, thinking how freely Crow tradition dealt with making love.

She moved her hips, an exquisite motion as old as time, and murmured. "Well? . . ."

"Godalmighty," he said, lust surging through him. "Where in blazes did they find you?" With all the single men in Montana, he didn't think there was a virgin left.

"I'm from Boston," she softly replied. "Is that all right?" And she reached out for him, wanting to touch the man who ignited the fires smoldering deep inside her.

He arched away from her. "How the hell old are you?" he suspiciously asked, trying unsuccessfully to avoid looking at her, inviting and accessible, her red-gold hair spilling across his pillow. Although she had the body of a woman . . . good Lord, a virgin? She mustn't be very old.

"Old enough," Blaze whispered, her hand sliding down Hazard's arm, moving across to his hip. She desperately wanted him and she had never failed to get what she wanted.

His fingers gripped her wrist and stopped her. "Give me an answer, damn you."

"Nineteen." Old enough, his aching manhood said. Old enough, his hungry passion echoed. I thought you didn't like virgins, his dark spirit of reason insinuated, and furthermore—

Blaze stretched up to nibble at his lips, eradicating any practicalities after "furthermore." Her warm tongue languidly intruded into his mouth and his fingers uncurled from her wrist. He groaned, grasping her hard by the shoulders, knowing he should resist—and, in the next wild beat of his heart, knowing the time for resistance was past. With the feeling of being swept inexorably toward a whirlpool, he said in a soft whisper, leashed tight with restraint, "Are you sure?"

She nodded, her face only inches from his, her eyes so hot he could feel the heat spiral out.

"I hope I'm not going to regret this," he breathed,

rolling over her. Here, he decided, directly under his furiously aroused body, was someone's spoiled darling intent on tasting exotic forbidden fruit, and after having given her three chances to leave, damned if he wasn't willing to grant her her spoiled wish. Casting aside any responsibility or conscience due largely to a sexual appetite tantalized one step too far by the tantalizing Miss Braddock, Jon Hazard Black decided there were things in life that must run their course, and he set about to do what he did exceedingly well.

Her breathless young eagerness was his for the taking. He thrust forward, neither brutal nor gentle, but determined. She screamed, breathless and startled. And it was over. Hazard's lips soothed her cry with tender kisses; he murmured comfortingly in the soft cadence of his people's language, staying immobile while the love words washed over her. After the consoling pause, he began moving gently inside her, pampering, coddling, progressing slow inches at a time, withdrawing carefully, beginning again, until she welcomed him, genially. And no longer wanted to relinquish him. The virginal Miss Braddock was emitting soft moans and small sighs of pleasure now, encouraging his progress with intuitive understanding and tenacious hands. "It doesn't hurt now?" Hazard murmured near her ear.

"Is it always this good?" she replied in a sighing whisper, her lips brushing his in a lazy incitement.

His question answered, he withdrew enough to indulge her sense of "goodness" again, and then again, and . . . again, until very soon her appetite shifted voluptuously. There was no further timidity or shyness or uncertainty, she clung to him now, melted around him, undulated her slender hips to lure him more deeply. Obliging her, he drove in slowly, surely. Eagerly matching his rhythm, arching high in passion to meet him, predaceous suddenly in her wanting, within minutes she was shattering him into bits. In her startling desire, she was erotic, wild, unrestrained as a forest fire. Their mating was unladylike, ungentlemanly; it was breathless, fierce, tumbling, falling, hurtling, unlike anything he'd ever experienced before. When he touched her and she touched him, it was as if the world fell away and only reckless, insatiable desire remained. And at the last, when he sensed the intense abandon peaking, when he felt her first small convulsion begin, he poured in to meet her with tremendous, pulsing spasms.

Seconds later, resting his weight on his elbows, bathed in perspiration, panting, he regained enough breath to speak. *"B-icu bia* [a song of a woman]," he whispered, lightly kissing her flushed cheeks. Although he was empty, his arousal, burning fitfully, hadn't lost its need for her. Inactive, but rigid still, it rested inside her tight virginal passage. Blaze stirred a little and reached up a hand to touch his face. Without speaking, her eyes dreamy, she traced a delicate finger down his firm cheek and sighed contentedly. Then her hands slid down his back, pulling him deeper and the face she lifted to him wore a luxurious half-smile. "I want more," she impudently demanded, grown confident in her own powers.

"Don't you know," he replied with his own half-smile, "most men aren't as resilient as women?"

"I can feel you, though. You're not most men, are you?" The throaty contralto purred like a lioness. "I want you now."

"It doesn't always react to commands, Miss Braddock. You've got a lot to learn."

Limpid eyes calmly appraised him. "Teach me," she whispered, and lifted her mouth to his. It was a hungry, aggressive, intrusive kiss, and in the course of the next hour, they consummated their volatile passion like young animals, sometimes with insatiable fury, sometimes with sweet tenderness, always, for Hazard, with the piquant, critical attentions of the connoisseur. The glowing, spirited woman in his arms crested each time with great wildness and abandon until at last she was content.

HAZARD lay half on his side on the narrow bed, holding Blaze close. His mouth brushed against the tousled mass of flame-red curls. "You're a damned serious negotiator," he teased lightly. "If Buhl Mining is utilizing this bargaining method with any frequency, no wonder everyone's selling."

She dreamily murmured into the curve of his shoulder. "I was only going to talk to you."

"Your dialogue is utterly charming, Miss Braddock."

"Blaze," she offered, totally enchanted by the feel and taste and scent of him. "And you're to blame, Mr. Black. Has anyone ever mentioned how skilled you are at seduction?"

He modestly didn't reply.

Lifting her face, she looked from under sleepy cat-eye lashes into his amused dark eyes. "Well . . . have they?" she softly demanded.

"Yes," he said, smiling indulgently at her artless question.

"Oh," she responded in a small, startled voice, realizing suddenly, as she met Hazard's amused glance, that she'd been naive. Chagrined at her gaucherie, she quickly changed the subject. "Do you have another name or should I continue calling you Mr. Black?"

"I've quite a few other names, but most people call me Hazard. It's simple."

"And appropriate?" she said carefully.

"Not really," said Hazard at length, equally carefully, "since I go out of my way to avoid trouble." But he knew very well he was regarded by most as a kind of human ultimatum.

"You killed three men lately."

So she *had* heard. Brave of her to come up here in spite of the stories. "They all drew on me first," he said pleasantly.

"Would you have killed Yancy this morning if he'd threatened you?"

"Not unless he'd raised his rifle and sighted in on me."

"Some of the men were afraid you'd kill me."

He laughed. A warm, resonant sound. "Hell, no, not when more interesting options are available. Besides," he said charmingly, "you're no threat—only a distinct pleasure."

"You *will* consider selling though, won't you Hazard? They'll give you a good price. Whatever you want, I'm sure. You can take the money and live well for a long time." Blaze hadn't intended any of this to happen; the past hours were a fantastic, inexplicable deluge of passion and feeling which had simply overwhelmed her. Hazard seemed like a reasonable man; her offer was more than reasonable. Generous, in fact. She was sure he'd accept. At the moment, basking in some blissful paradise of contentment and well-being, she wasn't thinking beyond that.

Passion quenched, half reclining beside the beautiful woman who had so recently been his, the shadow of chill reality reminded Hazard what had brought her here. "My claim's not for sale," he said. His voice was completely without timbre, his face wiped clean of expression.

There was a moment of complete and cataclysmic surprise.

Then, as if stung, Blaze struggled up on her elbows, her eyes wide with astonishment. "Why not?"

There was a distinct pause while remote black eyes, heavy with cool sarcasm, scanned her from her creamy throat to her small bare feet. "Why should I?" His voice was deceptively mild.

Her dismay had brought her seated upright in the wreckage of the bed. "Well, for money, of course!" she retorted.

"I'm not interested in selling my mine, but I'd be interested in buying you. Do I have to negotiate with Buhl?" he asked, a slight edge to his voice, "or are you a free agent?"

"I'm very much a free agent," Blaze snapped, hot with resentment. "I'm also Colonel Billy's daughter." She said it with a deliberate arrogance, expecting it to make a difference, as it had all her life.

It did. Hazard was profoundly astonished. Everyone in the mining camps had heard of Colonel Billy B. He headed the group buying all the gold claims in Montana. He didn't think Buhl Mining was that desperate. Concealing his surprise, Hazard said in a voice dry as ash, "In that case, I don't think I can afford you."

"Are you in the habit of buying women, Mr. Black?" Blaze contemptuously inquired.

"No, you're the first. Bad luck your hot little body is out of my price range."

With a quick gasping breath, Blaze's arm flew out to strike, but his hand was there long before she reached his face, catching her wrist in a bone-threatening grip. As they breathed quiet anger, each resentful of the other's guile, a rifle shot rang out. Slamming Blaze down, Hazard ordered, "Stay there. Don't move," with soft, frightening venom, thinking what a fool he'd been to trust those bastards. Kicking his way out of the shambles of the bed, in seconds he was on his feet and standing at the side of the window, naked, his holster looped over his shoulder. His body was tense. No one. "Is it a signal?"

Blaze shook her head. "I don't know."

He turned to her, his suspicions palpable. "Don't move," he repeated, "or I may have to kill you." Pulling on his leggings, he picked up his rifle and walked to the door. Dark hair tumbled, eyes blazing brightly, his nostrils were flared in anger. With one hand on the latch, in a voice devoid of emotion, he said, "If you come out of this cabin, I *will* kill you. I mean it." It was a cold brutal tone he'd never used with a woman before. "Stay in bed and keep your head down." His eyes drilled into her. "If this is part of your performance—" He broke off. Turning abruptly in a movement of extreme violence, Hazard pulled the door open, slipped through it, slammed it shut, and was gone before the frightened look had fully crossed Blaze's face.

It didn't take long for Jon Hazard Black to make his plans known to the men at the bottom of the hill—the men with rifles, the greedy men, thirsty for his land or blood. His phrasing was precise and unequivocal, but spoken in a voice bell-like with anger. He stood there silhouetted against the shot summer sky, dark as the devil, capable, brutally rude, and no one in the group standing at the base of the mountainside was even fleetingly inclined to doubt what he said. "My claim is not for sale. I'm keeping Miss Braddock as a hostage just in case any of you seriously consider taking me on. I'll kill her at the first sign of treachery. Good day, gentlemen."

The words, stentorian and raised to pass down the

long distance, reached the cabin as well and each word was etched like flame in Blaze's horrified mind. He was keeping her here? He couldn't, she thought, but knew as instantly, he very well could. How *could* he, she heatedly considered next, and then, with a spark of annoyance, knew he would find it infinitely easy. She was out of the bed and halfway across the room when he came in. "No! Damn you, you can't!" she irrationally screamed. "You can't keep me here!"

Taking a cotton shirt of his, from a hook near the door, he tossed it at her. "I'm not *asking* your permission," he quietly said, "and if you could have repressed your female inclination to meddle," he added, cuttingly, "you wouldn't be here right now, ravished, naked, and my hostage. Whatever it is that drives you, Miss Braddock, to interfere in a man's world, to interfere, once too often, *in my life,*" said Hazard, his voice brittle with hard-controlled temper, "that fixation is what put you where you are right now. Don't blame me. Blame yourself." Willing his eyes away from her lush nakedness, so striking it made him uncomfortable, he ordered austerely, "Put that shirt on; you're distracting as hell."

Her flesh breathed sweetness and warmth and her magnificent breasts, round and still rosy from lovemaking, lay high and ripe for the taking. Naked, trembling with fury, he found her a heady, irresistible provocation. Lord, she looked good. Fiery, disdainful, haughty, and . . . too damned inviting. Restraining himself with effort, he cautioned himself against succumbing to her lure, as he had so easily before, when all his lofty principles had been burned away with a touch of her lips. He turned to slide his rifle back on the tack above the door.

"You bastard! You *can't* keep me hostage!" Blaze cried with white-hot rage, launching into a volley of obscenities, to which Hazard listened, his back uncompromisingly rigid. ". . . You *can't* do it," she finished in a breathless frenzy, standing stiff, pale, unyielding, clutching his shirt in one hand, refusing to believe what was happening.

Hazard turned sharply and stood, considering, across the small distance separating them, an ominous glint in his eyes. "Good God, you fool. Can't?" he said and laughed, a short unpleasant sound. "But I just have, Miss Braddock, and if you'd put a lid on your irreducible ego, you'd realize you're not out East now with your Papa and his friends and all their connections. There's no one here but me to enforce can or can't. So you can argue mountains into desert sand over how or what or why, but as long as I'm on the right end of my rifle," said Hazard with simple truth, "I can do anything I want."

There was a sickening silence. It was what unnerved her most—the unassailable self-esteem. "My father will kill you," she whispered finally, her hands shaking on the tightly held fabric.

"Not likely . . . if he fancies you alive. You've been promised a spectacularly close view of my rifle barrel should anyone get too near me." The ominous glint suddenly became hard as flint. "Now, put that shirt on, dammit, you conniving, avaricious little bitch, or I'll fuck you right where you're standing. Naked females have a predictable effect on me. Of course," said Hazard with a mockery of a smile, "that's what you came up here for, wasn't it? I wouldn't care to disoblige Buhl Mining's concept of business ethics. Just what were your orders— three times? four? How much was my claim supposed to be worth?"

Blaze hurriedly slipped the shirt on and fumblingly buttoned it under the dark, contemptuous eyes raking her. When she finished and was covered now to midthigh, Hazard said, suddenly impatient with trivial argument, "As long as you're staying we can haggle over the numbers later. Right now, we might as well lay down the rules. I spend most of my time outside . . ."

Blaze's face was unflinching. "I'll run away."

"Perhaps you didn't notice," Hazard remarked impassively, "there's a lock on the door. If you're going to be troublesome, I'll lock you in."

"You wouldn't," she curtly snapped, still dumbfounded at the idea of *captivity*.

He exhaled slowly and silently counted to ten. "I would and I will, if you insist on running away."

"I can't imagine how you can possibly make me

stay," Blaze disdainfully retorted, her whims having ordered the world to her perfection for nineteen years.

A cold, impersonal gaze assessed her briefly. "Then your imagination is uncommonly poor. I know a score of ways to make you stay, Miss Braddock, and several of them aren't pleasant. I won't go into detail. It would upset your digestion."

"You'd abuse a lady?" she breathed in astonishment.

"My apologies, of course," said Hazard with ironic politeness, "but I don't remember inviting you. Under the circumstances, it's up to you how you're treated. I expect my orders to be obeyed, that's all."

"You are a damned petty tyrant." Each word was lapidary and brittle with cold.

"No," he said, forbearingly, with a quiet sigh, "only a man trying to mind his own business. I think *petty* and *tyrant* more aptly apply to Buhl Mining, with their small nastinesses and autocratic iniquities. But we can argue economics some other time. All my evenings are free. Now," he went on in an uninflected, flat tone, "I'll expect you to make the meals, wash the clothes, and keep this cabin in some kind of minimum order."

"Are you *mad?* I'm no servant!" A lifetime of privileged wealth rang through her words.

"If you don't," and his voice sharpened for a moment beyond its level deliberate tone, "I'll make you infinitely sorry. If you're going to be here underfoot, you'll have to make yourself useful"—icy black eyes stared back at the pale, affronted beauty—"in all the usual ways. . . ."

Blaze stiffened, avoided the innuendo, and said mutinously, "I can't cook; I don't know how to wash or clean. All I know how to do is offer sherry or cognac and keep the conversation moving."

"Ah, well," Hazard said affably, "at least we'll be pleasantly drunk until you acquire the knack of domestic skills. I'm sure you'll manage eventually. In the meantime, it might be wise to have a case of cognac sent up."

She glared at the arrogant man. "Do you really intend to keep me here?"

Jon Hazard Black inclined his head.

"For how long?" she harshly asked.

"However long it takes to convince that bloody mining company I'm serious about not selling," said Hazard flatly.

Hard and fast as a richochet, she viciously shouted, "I hate you, you despicable savage. Everything they say about Indians is true. You have no honor, no decency." Frustrated already in her captivity, never weak or yielding, Blaze allowed her temper full rein. "You're cruel— barbaric. I wish they'd kill every—"

He listened, rage flaring into his eyes, for an acid five seconds before he was on top of her, his fingers biting into her shoulders like steel talons. "You can despise me all you please," he gritted out bitterly, "but I won't have you sullying my people with your ignorant epithets. There's more honor and decency in my small tribe than in the entire United States. And their values and beliefs are upheld daily at the risk of their lives. You yellow eyes only wreck and cheapen everything you touch." His breathing was harsh, his dark eyes brutally cold, soulless, his sickened understanding showing. "Now, you spoiled pampered bitch, listen to me and listen well," he went on curtly, quick-voiced and restless with repressed rage. "You'll do as you're told, when you're told. And if I hear another scornful word against my people," his voice suddenly cooled to its familiar irony, "I'll whip that luscious bottom of yours so you won't be able to sit for a week, or worse."

For a moment, she stood, her clear-eyed, angry gaze on Hazard's impervious stare. Furious as she was, Blaze, tight-lipped, decided not to test his ultimatum with its implication of violence more frightening than the threat. She was certain he meant it. The challenge died in her eyes.

"Very smart, pet," said Hazard, smoothly filling the pause. "You're learning fast."

"It's not as though I have any other goddamned choice," she acidly capitulated.

"A Mexican standoff."

"Meaning?"

"We both get off alive for the moment," he said mildly, reaching out to lightly pat her cheek. When she flinched, he only smiled. "Do you think," he blandly queried, "killing for personal principle ranks higher in virtue than killing for profit?" He shrugged fastidiously. "No doubt we'll find out soon enough. An edifying experience awaits us, Miss Braddock, don't you think?"

"You *are* a killer," she said softly. "They were right."

For a second, the line of anger between his heavy brows showed, then it was gone, control restored. He spoke quietly then, as he did in extreme anger. "At the moment," Hazard affirmed grimly, "I'm predominantly concerned with living rather than dying."

"You expect to die?" She was incredulous. "Over this claim?"

"I've learned to expect the worst when dealing with the white man's notion of civilized land development, and I've rarely been disappointed."

"Buhl's different," Blaze said in reproof, having, since childhood, participated in her father's business affairs and never, to her knowledge, known of a killing.

"As far as you're concerned, you may think so. I, however, do not," he replied with simplicity. Hazard was sensibly paranoid about the white man's treachery and put little stock in a virginal young woman's idealism. "In any event," he went on evenly, "I intend to prove more troublesome than anticipated. I don't want to sell."

"You're a fool, then," she retorted with some of her old defiance.

"Think what you will. I'm past the age where I have to prove myself to anyone. I have my own reasons," he said with the same weary courtesy, "for wanting to stay alive and keep my claim. So I'll fight for it, however necessary."

"Even if it means more killing?" Blaze pressed, never long in fear of anyone. And suddenly, he didn't seem so dangerous. Only tired.

Hazard took a long, soft breath and then expelled it. "Don't be naive, Miss Braddock," he said with cold, exhausted irony, "about Buhl's record on brutalization. They kill or I kill, and the loser gets a free pass to another life. The winner, of course, travels through this uncertain world a very rich man." His eyes were remote suddenly, and he moved away from her to the small window near the door, his profile rimmed against the brilliant sky. It was true. Only one winner was allowed, and on his worst days, he had terrible visions of defeat, convulsive and limitless, the land inundated by crushing tides of westward progress. Stretching lithely, he placed both long-shafted hands above the window and stared out at the scene below, empty now of the group of frock-coated men. His eyes were dark and lightless, his face strained with a private and difficult torment.

Hazard had no illusions about the ruthlessness of Buhl Mining Company and its officials. He'd seen them come in and take the land they wanted one way or another, without principle or pity. He'd seen them grappling for power, seen the desire in the men without ideals, to annihilate opponents rather than simply depose them. He knew, as well, they'd be aided by many of the territorial officials who were, more often than not, men of flexible conscience and limited concepts of social responsibility. But he knew how to fight as ruthlessly as they did and knew victory was as abruptly possible as defeat. He needed the claim which promised to be rich; he needed it for his people. As heir to his father's chieftainship, it was his responsibility to see to the clan; it had been ingrained in him in all the years of his training, his sacred duty to his clan, and he adhered to this trust now that his father was dead.

Since the Treaty of Laramie in 1851, unsigned by any ABSAROKEE,[6] but signed by forty chiefs of the Northern Plains, the beginning of the end of the old ways was signaled. His father had known it, understood that passively waiting for their territories to be taken piece by piece was as foolish as waging war against Washington. That was why Hazard had gone East to school, out of respect for his father's visionary dream for his people. He was to acquire the practical knowledge of the white man's world, so his clan could adapt to the inevitable changes in their way of life. And when his father died, he'd come home to take his place, to serve his people unto the essential finality of death if need be. Pride drove him in his special kind of commitment and necessity and an isolated dedication.

His tribe must have gold to buy guns, supplies, migrate if necessary to land still secure from the white man's greed. He was sending the gold back by messenger, keeping very little for himself, and if he was right, he had a very good chance on claims 1014–15 to mine the future security of his clan. He had great respect for the power of the spirits and the efficacy of great medicine and prayer, but when it came to winning against the encroachment of the white man, Hazard preferred relying on the power of persuasion in a million or so dollars of gold. He stood very still, staring self-critically into the afternoon sunlight, prosaically sure gold would win in the end, over yellow eye's promises.[7]

So. He meant to keep this claim, risking all for duty and compassion, while his own good sense of preservation suggested that Miss Braddock was perfect insurance for him to keep what Buhl so badly wanted. And, not to be forgotten, there was the lady's very responsive nature in bed. Very soon, they should get to know each other—better.

All in all, the next few months should be interesting, Hazard told himself, shaking off his fatigue. If they lived. *Bāc'dak' K'ō'mbāwiky* [While I live, I carry on], he fatalistically mused and turned back to his new and very beautiful companion.

Chapter 6

WHEN the evening star appeared in the sky, after a quiet if heated discussion, Hazard tied Blaze to him in two places, at waist and wrist, then lay down on the narrow bed and, exhausted, slept through the night for the first time in five days.

Lying very still, Blaze listened to Hazard's even breathing, until the slow, easy rhythm seemed part of her own respiration, until the warmth of the large man pressed close to her stole into her senses with an inexplicable rush of pleasure she could neither control nor deny. Cautiously she turned her head a millimeter in his direction, waited, then, observing no change in the deep, resonant breathing, slowly eased her glance around until he was fully within her gaze.

It came over her suddenly, as it always did—his unbearable beauty, the magnificence muted now in sleep to mere splendor. She watched him while the fading pastels of twilight disappeared into the void of night. Watched the play of light over the stark cheekbones, visually traced the perfect symmetry of finely chiseled nose. His sculptured mouth was prominently sensual—no austerity there, she noted. No, definitely not austere. And only with effort did she restrain herself from outlining that sensuous mouth with her fingertips. Even his brows were like delicate winged creatures, dark silky creatures that whispered to be touched. Blaze clenched her fingers tightly against the overpowering urge. And when his thick lashes fluttered suddenly, she caught her breath, fearful the sharp black eyes might open and find her own gaze transfixed. But he only sighed lightly, his fingers unconsciously tightening on the braided rawhide coiled around his hand.

As she observed him, taking in the sight and sound, the sage-sweet scent so much a part of these mountains it clung to everything, she suddenly saw, through unclouded vision, a different Hazard Black. Not the sensual, seductive man, as she had seen him, not the ruthless killer, as others saw him, not even an "Indian from an alien culture." She saw only a man, seeming as vulnerable as a child in his sleep. A man, beautiful beyond words but, transcending his physical perfection, beautiful in spirit, imbued with an indomitable courage, fearless against overwhelming odds. Odds any practical man would have refused. Jon Hazard Black had set himself against one of the most powerful mining cartels in the world. And he intended to stand his ground.

But later, in the roil and tumult of chaotic half sleep and black dreams, her logic and emotion at war, she felt the return of her initial outrage and resentment at his monumental arrogance at taking her hostage. How dare he, she thought with renewed vigor. *How the hell dare he!*

"You can't keep me here!" he heard her hiss as the first light of dawn appeared. Grunting softly, he rolled over, still half asleep, and the braided leather rope binding them tightened. The movement brought her hard against his back. He vaguely heard a quiet gasp and felt her stiffen. Then silence. Blessed silence, he thought, recalling her volatile temper.

She repeated the phrase in a scathing whisper. He

opened one eye briefly, casting a glance over his bare shoulder, and encountered snapping blue eyes. "Sorry," he murmured truthfully, for he knew already that his life had become endlessly complicated because of one Miss Venetia Braddock.

"Sorry? *You're* sorry?" she muttered incredulously. And then proceeded to read him the riot act until he exasperatedly answered in his own rush of temper, *"Enough!"*

But she wouldn't stop, the words tumbling out, furious and hot with defiance, like clubs beating and flailing at his head. He had to kiss her to arrest the torrent of abusive rage. A hand over her mouth might have worked as well, he admitted as his lips covered hers, but logic relinquished the field hastily to an unexplained desire to quiet her in a more pleasurable way.

She tasted sweet and welcoming, he thought, settling himself in an unconsciously fluid maneuver between her legs. How warm she was . . . and soft. Loosening the coiled rope from his hand, his fingers tangled in the silk of her hair, holding her like a precious gift, while his lips and tongue explored the luscious interior of her mouth.

He couldn't help himself. Didn't want to. She was here, his for the taking. And in a flashing second he realized how much he'd missed having a woman near. She felt like homecoming and rapture and soul-deep solace. When he raised his mouth the idyll was shattered.

"You . . . you . . . animal," she sputtered, her head turning fitfully in his grasp, her eyes glowering. "You odious, abominable—"

". . . savage," he finished softly and took her mouth again. This time in a hard, possessive invasion that put to use all the expertise acquired so pleasurably over the years. When he lifted his mouth a second time, long minutes later, his slow, sure skill had left her trembling and breathless. The sputter, modified, was now more like a sigh.

"This . . . will . . . never . . ."

". . . get any gold mined," Hazard whispered, a smile curling through the words. "You're right, sweet *bia*

. . . and I'll try to get you into the kitchen very soon"—
his smile widened—"so you can make me breakfast. Are
you ready to begin earning your keep?" He tugged her
closer with the rawhide still tied around her waist.

She didn't answer at first. Couldn't. Didn't want to.
Didn't know her own mind. But his fingers slipped between her thighs and slid upward like devil's sorcery, very
slowly at first, tantalizing, waiting for her to ask for more.
And when she arched her hips in response, his slim fingers eased into her sweetness. She cried out and reached
for him, her arms twining tightly around his neck.

He raised himself slightly against the pressure of her
hands and, looking down at her exquisite, flushed face,
asked again, "Are you ready to earn your keep?" His
fingers continued to stroke languidly and she moaned
softly with each delicate movement. Bending near, his
lips hovered in a whisper above hers. "Say yes, little rich
girl." His fingers drifted deeper and her nails dug into his
shoulders. "Say you'll cook for me."

His obliging movements stopped and she quickly
whispered, "Yes."

"And clean for me."

"Yes," she breathed.

"And do anything else."

"Oh—please, yes."

His fingers slid free and he moved over her gently.

"Now," she cried.

"Soon," he said and eased his body down.

The next half-formed plea died in a breathy moan as
he glided, hard and long, into her urging womanly
warmth. How could she, he thought with pleasure, feel so
excruciatingly fine?

How could he, she thought, with a shameful thrill,
arching against his spearing invasion, know I want him
so?

An hour later, when the rawhide shackle had long
since been untied by gentle fingers, and when Jon Hazard Black had given in to his hostage's demands as many
times as any able man would, he kissed her one last time,
rose from the shambles of the bed, and said, "I'm going

to bathe in the stream behind the cabin. Would you care to join me?"

"Is it cold?"

"Brisk."

"I know mountain streams. No, thank you."

He smiled. "Suit yourself. Breakfast in ten minutes?"

"Is that an invitation?"

"Not exactly. Call it . . . a diplomatic request." He could see the stubborn set of her jaw begin to form. "*Very* diplomatic," he cajoled, reaching down to touch her pretty mouth with a placating finger. "Relax, Boston, I'm no ogre. I'll help."

"Then let me go," Blaze said in a hurried rushing breath, fearful of staying with him for reasons that had nothing at all to do with mining claims.

Hazard's half-lowered eyelids covered eyes so dark they were unreadable. "I wish I could," he said quietly, "but the battle lines have been drawn. I'm afraid it's too late."

"You're serious."

Hazard paused a moment before answering. "You've led a sheltered life, Boston," he finally said. Tossing a towel around his neck, he continued in a moderate tone, as though discussing the merits of calling cards as a social gesture. "They're out to kill me. I consider that serious. That's why you're here. And that's why you're staying." A sudden flash of white teeth seemed to discount the undercurrent of danger. "I like my eggs soft-boiled."

He was gone in a noiseless tread, and she lay there stunned for several minutes. People didn't actually kill each other over a small section of mountain land, did they? Certainly not her father and his friends. Did they? For the first time a quiver of doubt intruded.

Wrapping the sheet around her, Blaze walked to the window and, looking out, glimpsed Hazard half screened by a clump of pines. He was swimming in a small pool contrived by damming up a portion of the rushing mountain stream. The sunlight shone off his sleek wet hair. Then he submerged, only to reappear moments later long yards away, shaking his head, droplets of water spraying like crystals from his streaming black hair.

When he started back to the cabin, all slender grace and hard rising muscle, Blaze went to the door, intending to meet him as a friendly gesture. After all, if she was truly a hostage—and it appeared the case; there was never equivocation when Hazard spoke, no matter how quiet the tone—she might as well be gracious about it. She pulled on the door latch. The door didn't respond. She tugged more determinedly. Nothing. She swore. Damn his untrusting soul. He'd locked her in!

HAZARD glanced at the empty table when he entered the cabin, then dressed with an economy of motion and clothing in buckskin leggings and moccasins. "Would you mind making breakfast?" he said to the stiff-backed woman silently staring out the window.

She didn't move.

"It needn't be anything elaborate," he added in the same quiet voice.

"You locked me in!" Blaze sputtered, spinning around, her cheeks flushed with anger, the sheet clutched defensively across her breasts.

"I can't take chances with this claim," he explained. Someday, maybe, he could explain to her just how much was at stake here. Depending on how their . . . friendship developed. "It's nothing personal. Rules of warfare, that's all."

"Now could I impose on you for breakfast?" The words were polite but firm.

"And if I say no?"

"I wish you wouldn't."

"I wish I weren't a hostage."

"Square one, again, ma'am," Hazard said prosaically. "Your move."

"I can't cook, I already told you!"

"And I said I'd help you," he patiently replied, his stance relaxed, his expression tolerant.

"I don't know what to make," she conceded.

"What do you usually have for breakfast?" he asked, all polite forbearance. "I'll have the same."

"Hot chocolate and strawberries," she replied, as if it should have been obvious.

"Every day?"

"Every day!"

"Even in the winter?" he asked, afraid of the answer.

"Daddy imports them. Do you mind?" she pugnaciously replied, a sensation of unreality flooding her mind. How had it happened that she, Blaze Braddock, was carrying on this incredible conversation at this ungodly hour of the morning with a virtual stranger who'd spent his entire life living *out-of-doors*. This dark Indian, however courteous his tone and accent, was badgering her to *cook* for him. She didn't even know how a stove worked, and last night's slight attempt at supper should have made that obvious.

Profoundly unexcited, he said, "No, not in the least. I expect your upkeep contributes a tidy sum to Boston's economy. Hot chocolate's fine with me," he added, as though the matter were settled to both their satisfactions. "As for strawberries, I'll see if Jimmy can find some this afternoon. In the meantime, use raspberries, if your sensitive palate doesn't object."

Blaze looked up, her eyes glistening with tears.

"Care to try?" Hazard coaxed, not surprised that a beautiful woman of her background wouldn't be a competent homemaker.

Blaze nodded, responding to the kindness in his voice.

"Good. You try the eggs. I'll fetch the milk from the stream, and we'll get this show on the road." He grinned.

She couldn't help but smile back. "Where's the chicken?"

He laughed. "That's McTaggert's problem. I don't even ask. The eggs are in the tin pail by the sink."

He had to teach her how to start a fire, show her where the water was kept, explain the finer points of his food storage system, and finally, distracted beyond bearing when the sheet she'd tucked around her fell open again when she forgot to clutch it tightly shut, he ordered in a voice tight with forced control, "Put some clothes on, Boston. I'll finish breakfast."

They filled up on bread and butter since the eggs turned out lamentably underdone.

"Oh, dear," Blaze murmured apologetically.

"Never mind," Hazard replied chivalrously, and reached for another slice of bread.

"It probably won't be for long," Blaze hurriedly interjected.

When Hazard's eyebrows rose inquisitively, she added, "I mean the cooking. Daddy will convince the others, I'm sure."

"Good," he said, but privately thought otherwise. There was an enormous amount of money involved—or the distinct possibility of an enormous amount of money. He'd seen men like Yancy's gang rate expediency over sentiment more often than not when a fortune was at stake.

Hazard rose from the table. "Thank you for breakfast. I'll be back at noon for lunch." Halfway to the door, he hesitated, turned back, and said, "Do you . . . that is . . ." He lapsed into Absarokee, the sibilant words softly exasperated. Returning to English, he went on, ". . . Would you care to, ah, ease yourself before I leave."

"So you can watch?" she demanded indignantly.

There was a momentary pause before Hazard flung back his damp head and laughed. "Is that," he asked when he'd regained control, "some Boston fetish I've overlooked, Miss Braddock? I could, of course, if you like," he said, a shadow of amusement lacing his voice.

Blaze's gaze was glacial. "Do I have a choice?"

"Not a comfortable one," Hazard said tenderly.

She flounced by him, convincing even without flounces, in black twill slacks.

He stayed discreetly inside, but cautiously began counting. If she wasn't back by two hundred, he'd have to go out and look for her. Now that the hostage idea was under way, it seemed a damnably simple solution.

He was on 193 and beginning to strap on his gun holster when he heard her step on the gravel north of the cabin. His swiftly moving fingers stopped, leaving the leg tie undone. And the adrenaline already anticipating a possible chase downhill was put on hold. But his voice when she entered the small room betrayed none of his mistrust. "Did you enjoy my outside facilities?"

Blaze looked at him sharply. Was he mocking her? The expression greeting her glance was warmly diffident, the trace of a smile, sincere. She relented in her ill-humor. When on his best behavior, Hazard was impossible to stay angry with. "The view's magnificent."

"I hoped you'd like it. We Absarokee call it *'Baré ráce ítsiram matsá-tsk,'* literally translated 'Our hearts are joyous.' It does that to you, the view from these mountains."

Hearing the softly muted inflection, melodic as a hymn, she tried the sounds on her tongue. "Bara ra-ice . . ."

Steeling himself against the warmth invoked by Blaze's childlike repetition of the words, mispronounced in a pretty confusion on the last three syllables, Hazard shakily reminded himself of his vow.

"Now if you can learn to say 'yes' as prettily," Hazard said with a trace of a drowl, "we'll get along famously."

Blaze's face clouded over. "Must you always be so damn provoking," she acidly inquired.

"For a woman," Hazard confronted her, his libido more comfortable with her adversarial posturing, "you're much too used to having your own way."

"For a woman—for a woman," Blaze sputtered, sparks beginning to ignite in her eyes. "What the hell does that have to do with anything?"

"Only that, like you, I've traveled quite a few miles across this continent and you may have noticed, Miss Braddock," Hazard blandly declared, taking down a buckskin shirt from a peg near the door, "it's a man's world."

He was out the door before the tin cup hit the pine door jamb. She had a remarkably good throwing arm, he noted in retreat. The thud of the striking cup was within inches of where his head had been short seconds before.

"Lunch at noon," he called back to her, fastening the latch into its locked position, his dinnerware crashing against the wall in rapid succession now.

Blaze stood in the debris of what had once constituted Jon Hazard Black's cozy cabin and called him every despicable name she could dredge up from her well-stocked inventory. It wasn't that Jon Hazard Black was, in fact, any of the multitude of names she called him. It was, rather, that Jon Hazard Black was the first individual in Blaze's self-indulgent life who had had the audacity—and the ability—to order her about.

"We'll see who does the ordering," she muttered into the silence of the pottery-strewn cabin. "We'll just see who the hell does what!"

Chapter 7

LUNCHTIME, as it turned out, was spare and silent, noteworthy only in the dramatically rearranged interior of the cabin. After carefully navigating the broken crockery with thinly shod moccasined feet, Hazard found himself some jerky in the cupboard, scraped pottery chips from the butter, and proceeded to make his second meal of the day on bread and butter. He ate in the heavily condemnatory glare of Blaze's sullen gaze and after finishing said, with a small exhalation of breath, "You know, Boston, you're going to have to clean this up."

"Now listen—"

Hazard's voice cut her short. "You listen first, then you get equal time." Blaze's lips pursed into a tightly drawn line, but she quieted. "Sit down." It looked for a moment as if she wouldn't. Hazard swept an inviting hand toward the chair and smiled his particularly winning smile that few could resist. "Please," he said, offering a conciliatory bow, and she sat.

"Since this is an . . . arrangement," he began, seating himself on the corner of the table, "neither of us anticipated, I suggest we keep it as civil as possible. Taking the obvious shortcomings of this small cabin into consideration, of course." He was neither nervous nor condescending, exuding instead a calm pragmatism, one moccasined foot swinging idly. "I won't live with tantrums in this small space, so you *must* clean this mess up. But enough of that. More important, I realize this will probably have ramifications on your future and I apologize for that, but I didn't start any of this—didn't ask for it, didn't want any part of it." He shrugged slightly. "But it happened, unfortunately, and since you now are my insurance against Buhl's machinations, I feel it would be best if we avoided the sort of . . . ah . . . intimacy that took place yesterday. And since this is at base," he said, all seriousness, "a business arrangement, I for one would prefer—"

"You needn't go on," Blaze interjected, her voice taking on the same cool detachment as Hazard's. At once both humiliated and relieved, his proposal, she understood as well as he, was the only reasonable alternative to an exceedingly uncomfortable situation.

Hazard received her acquiescence with contradictory emotions. He had been practical about the need for distance. What he'd prefer, in lieu of practicality, would be Miss Braddock's ready sensuality as a delightful and frequent respite to his hard gold mining.

"If we're agreed, then—" Hazard paused.

Blaze nodded and said, "I shall control my impulses without any trouble, Mr. Black, I assure you. I pray, however," she continued, rising from the chair with a petulant toss of her red-gold hair and a new caustic edge to the sweetness, "that Daddy comes to some arrangement with you very soon."

"Amen to that, Miss Braddock," Hazard agreed, noting his exquisite companion's sulk. "I'll add my prayers to yours."

Chapter 8

AT THAT moment, Colonel Braddock was following a Bannack Indian guide along a mountain trail on an urgent journey to find a go-between from Hazard's clan to save his daughter. Since Hazard wouldn't allow any of them to approach, it was imperative that the Colonel find an acceptable negotiator.

Hazard's ominous ultimatum had struck terror in Billy Braddock's soul. His daughter was the center of his life, his entire world, and he would willingly give up everything he owned to see her safe. His love for her had been unconditional from the first moment he'd laid eyes on her, all fragile pink innocence, on the day of her birth. And he'd vowed from that very first moment, his daughter would have all the love and luxury his own orphaned childhood had lacked. She would never know the grinding poverty and uncaring neglect of his harsh early years. And he had spared neither time nor money to fulfill his vow.

Father and daughter had become inseparable even before she could walk. A nursery had been installed on the top floor of the Braddock Block in downtown Boston, and with the relieved blessing of Millicent Braddock, who found motherhood a distasteful interruption to a busy social schedule, Venetia grew up under her father's doting regard. She'd become "Blaze" shortly after her fourth birthday, when the full glory of her vivid hair had grown to luxurious magnificence. And Blaze she'd remained, despite her mother's displeasure at the unladylike sobriquet. But long before Blaze was four, her mother had relinquished any interest in her daughter, embracing the upper-class dictum that children should be ignored until they became civilized enough to enter the adult world at eighteen. By that time, of course, there had been too many years of cool neglect for any rapport to exist between mother and daughter. Blaze was her father's pet by then, and that, too, blunted any hope of amity between mother and daughter.

Millicent Hatton had bartered her fragile beauty and old Virginia name for the richest fortune on the open market at the time, and under her terms of the sale, as she saw it, she had to neither like William Braddock nor indulge him—only marry him. Once wed, her duty was done. Before the honeymoon was a month old, Billy Braddock had known he'd made a disastrous mistake, but his young bride was already plagued by morning bouts of nausea. They returned to Boston immediately and, politely avoiding any discussion of their differences, took up their separate lives. They met occasionally at dinner, when by coincidence both were home for the evening, infrequently attended a social fete together, and because of Blaze they celebrated holidays as a family. It was a marriage devoid of all emotion, leaving Billy Braddock vast reserves of affection to lavish on his only child.

Yesterday, every inch the magisterial millionaire, he'd commanded his colleagues under no circumstances to make a single move toward Hazard Black's claim until he returned with a member of Hazard's clan to act as mediator for him. He knew from experience when a bluff is a bluff. And the Indian on the mountain yesterday had meant what he said. He intended to offer the Indian whatever he wanted to free Blaze, but a gnawing fear remained that perhaps this time money wouldn't be enough. Anxious, disquieted, Billy Braddock pressed on, restlessly vetoing a suggestion to make camp for the evening. "There's twenty more minutes of daylight," he declared, gently prodding his tired horse. They'd been riding upcountry steadily for sixteen hours, and for a man his age, the effort was draining. He'd been running on adrenaline the last two hours.

The guide finally had to warn him they'd lose their horses to broken legs if they didn't stop. The moon was behind heavy cloud cover that night, and their mounts had stumbled twice in the last few minutes. Reluctantly, Colonel Braddock agreed to stop, picked at his food, and lay awake all night waiting for enough light to start out again.

On the third day they found the first Absarokee summer encampment, but the Indians were Black Lodges, a related clan, but not Hazard's. The Many Lodges, they were told, had moved over the mountains a week ago looking for new pasture. Perhaps they could be found down by the Horses River.

Only taking time to trade for fresh mounts, Colonel Braddock and his Bannack guide traveled on, arriving at the upper reaches of Horses River two days later, where they found that the camp had moved once more. The summer migrations were on, each clan and its pony herds journeying from pasture to pasture in the foothills to escape the heat and insects of the sultry plains below.

The guide couldn't help noticing the white man's difficulty breathing in the thin upland air. But his recommendations that they stop and rest were always waved off. The yellow eyes weren't used to the high altitudes. Most of them, like this one, had spent too much time indoors and not enough time in physical activity. The man looked near collapse, his lips blue, his face pale and perspiring. The guide feigned a caught stone in his horse's hoof and was pleased to see color return to the white man's face after the short rest to examine the pony's "injury."

Chapter 9

HAZARD slept that night on the floor, buffalo robes serving as a mattress. Blaze told herself she was glad he was gentleman enough to honor their business-like agreement, but her dreams were of strong arms holding her and silky black hair brushing her cheeks moments before tender lips touched hers. The pleasure these thoughts sent coursing through her body warmed her flesh, and restlessly she tossed her covers aside. Hazard rolled over then, away from her alluring exposure, and faced the wall. Unable to sleep, his own desires more conscious and real, his dark eyes had strayed to the narrow bed a hundred times the last few hours. Blaze's voluptuous nude body—now fully exposed—was too tempting. If he trusted himself more, he would have gotten up and covered her again, but he was cognizant of his resolve's limitations, and he daren't go too close. Not the way he was feeling now, not with the urgency of his desire battering his sanity.

He finally dozed off long after midnight but woke, silently alert, just as the first slivered beams of morning sun slid over the mountains. Quiet, unhurried footsteps approached.

He was on his feet in one smooth motion and across the cabin, rifle in hand seconds later. The door slowly opened, a soft warbler trill announced the intruder, and Hazard relaxed against the wall, his mouth curving into a smile. A tall Absarokee stepped into the room and without turning, his eyes on Blaze's voluptuous sleeping body, addressed Hazard standing behind him. "*Show-da-gee ba-goo-ba* (Hello, brother). She's much too good for you, Dit-chilajash. Let me take her off your hands, Hazard . . . say eighty horses? She's going to cut into your work time like hell." Male drollery laced the soft Absarokee tongue.

"It's nice to have such a solicitous friend, but save your horses, Chadam Chelash; she's not for sale," Hazard said, slipping into his leggings. "She's my hostage, Rising Wolf."

Rising Wolf half turned toward Hazard, the long beaded fringe on his clothes catching the light, one dark brow raised. "Better yet. If she didn't cost anything, eighty horses will be pure profit." He was familiar with Hazard's pattern with women. They were all beautiful but transient. "I can wait awhile," he added with a smile. "Shouldn't take more than a few weeks, if I remember your style." They spoke in low tones, the sibilant sounds of their native tongue conducive to quiet dialogue.

"If I didn't value my life more than your pleasure," Hazard said, returning the smile, "I'd consider the eighty horses." Rising Wolf had the most discerning eye in the clan with horses, and his ponies were always superior. "Tempting as it is—this female has a temper like the hot springs up north—her presence here is guaranteeing my mine, and my life, at the moment."

"Really a hostage, then." Rising Wolf saw Hazard was serious.

"They tried to buy me out, run me off, and then"— Hazard's black eyes flickered in Blaze's direction— "bribe me."

"Who?" Rising Wolf was wondering if a small raiding party some night would handle the menace.

Hazard knew how his mind worked; it was, after all, the customary way of dealing with enemies. "Too many and too influential for that, Rising Wolf. It's the Eastern mining money that's been throwing their gold around for the last couple of months."

"Will it work? The hostage?"

Hazard shrugged. "The yellow eyes are crawling over this country like ants. Every week brings wagonloads more. It's my only choice."

"Too stubborn to sell?"

"Why should I, just because they've more money than I? This is a valuable vein I'm sitting on. Don't see any reason to hand it over to them. They've got lots of interests in this country—they can live without mine." He smiled faintly. "Not that their kind is likely to do that. But, hell, this whole thing could blow over in a few weeks, or even days, if some new strike with bigger potential comes through somewhere else."

"Need help?"

"With what?" Hazard teased, his mood lightened by Rising Wolf's familiar presence, the feel of home he always brought with him.

Rising Wolf chuckled. "When the pines turn yellow, as they say . . . No, I was thinking about some lookouts. We could set up out here."

"You haven't seen my new toy."

"You have another one besides her?"

Hazard laughed aloud at Rising Wolf's characteristic leer. The ringing resonance woke Blaze. She took one look at the strange Indian and screamed. Hazard moved toward her with a soothing gesture of his hand. Only then did her frightened eyes shift to Hazard's familiar lean form and the shock turn to recognition. "A friend," Hazard said, pulling up the light blanket over her shoulders possessively. "Don't be afraid." It was an unconscious action immediately reminding Rising Wolf of Raven Wing years before. Hazard had responded to her in the same solicitous way. And he'd never seen him behave that way since.

"Go back to sleep," Hazard softly said. "We're going out." And taking Rising Wolf by the arm, he steered him through the entry. After shutting the door and carefully placing the lock in place, he said, "Come," indicating a narrow trail between the pines. Following a brush-cut path a hundred yards up the mountain east of the cabin, Hazard moved onto a small ledge cut into the rock, pointed to an artillery piece and remarked: "The newest model, uses a copper fifty-eight-caliber rimfire cartridge, capable of being loaded while firing. It's accurate at five hundred yards and . . . can keep anyone away from the claim."

"What is it called?" Rising Wolf asked, admiring the multibarreled weapon mounted on a gun carriage.

"A Gatling gun."

"Where did you get it?"

"A friend of mine from school knows an ordnance officer at the Washington arsenal."

"And they just gave it to you?"

"It's pretty untried yet. In fact, most of the testing wasn't too successful. None of the veteran officers support it."

"Have you seen it in action? *Does* it work?"

"Rosecrans tried some of these in the Wilderness campaign. The time I saw it near Burgessville, it tore the hell out of a brigade of cavalry."

"So how did you talk them into sending it out here?"

"My friend had his ordnance officer from Washington rewrite the shipping orders. It was simple; they shipped it to the railhead outside Omaha and I had it freighted overland from there."

"You mean you didn't pay for it?" Rising Wolf smiled his appreciation of the U.S. government's unknowing largesse.

"Let's say I consider it a bonus for a field officer's meager pay."

"You should have gotten more," Rising Wolf mildly chastised, his tactical mind already visualizing the effects this gun would have.

"Don't think I didn't try," Hazard replied. "Even for this one, I think I owe favors beyond the grave."

"How much ammunition do you have?" Rising Wolf asked, well aware that it was always a problem for the Indian tribes, getting enough ammunition.

"Plenty."

"It would be superb against the Lakota."

"When the gold runs out, we'll take it to camp."

"How did you get it up here?"

"I had it winched up."

"What did you tell people was in the crate?"

"Mining equipment. Everyone's used to that. It comes by the ton either overland or up the Missouri."

"You look well set up."

"As I intended. Maybe a year from now most of the gold will be in our mountain cache, securing our people's future."

"And the woman?"

"She'll never last that long."

"Meaning?" Rising Wolf questioned softly.

"Nothing ominous," Hazard quickly responded to Rising Wolf's raised brows. "Only . . . I'm sure her father will reach some agreement with me much sooner than that. She tells me she's an only child." A smile flashed across his dark face. "My good fortune—worth at least fifty bargaining points more."

"Forget the bargaining points, I can think of better reasons to be grateful for having that woman in your bed."

"She sleeps alone."

"Tell that to someone more gullible—someone who didn't grow up with you." Hazard's discriminating instinct for beautiful women was as legendary on the plains as it had been in Boston.

"I mean it. I don't want the problems."

"Since when is making love a problem?" Rising Wolf's grin was widened.

"Generally I'd agree with you, but . . ." Hazard exhaled. "The circumstances are different."

"You really mean you haven't?"

"Not lately."

"So you have. I didn't think you'd let the *biahia*—that sweetheart—go untouched."

"I'm sorry now I did."

"Sorry?" Rising Wolf believed in pleasure with uninhibited enjoyment. "That's a strange attitude coming from you." And he searched Hazard's face piercingly, for the memory of Hazard attending the woman just minutes before was fresh and vivid. You didn't look at a woman that way and not want her, Rising Wolf thought.

"It's complicated."

"Women always are."

"More complicated than usual. I must fulfill my vision. There's no time for pleasure."

Rising Wolf understood. A vision must be followed.

And as a visionary, Hazard's revelations had been prophetic, giving them a potency and symbolic power. Years ago, as a boy on Wolf Mountain, fasting for four days in search of his *biricī' sam* (medicine-dream), he'd seen the white men coming for the gold already then, had seen the riders with the fire spears come down from the sky, had seen the sun darken with blood before the white men's disease had taken so many lives.

But he'd also seen a red eagle ride a black cougar over the men with fire spears. And he'd heard the animal apparitions tell him: The gold metal will bless your clan and bring it prosperity. Listen and learn and when the time comes, follow us. We give you these for your power. And when Hazard woke atop Wolf Mountain all those years ago, he'd found beside him a red eagle feather and a tuft of black cougar fur.

"Bala-ba-aht-chilash" (good luck), Rising Wolf offered.

Hazard accepted the wishes with a nod. "To the gold now. We'd better get it on the packhorses. The sun's rising over the horizon." Rising Wolf planned his trips so he arrived early, before Hazard left for the mine. It didn't take long to load the saddlebags since Hazard had rigged up a pulley to lift the heavy leather bags up the rugged cliff above the mine entrance.

"Are you coming home for the summer hunt?" Rising Wolf asked carefully, filling the painted leather bag with coarse gold dust.

"I was planning to, but . . ." Hazard paused. "Probably not now . . . with the woman."

"You could bring her along."

"I'd rather not."

Rising Wolf looked at Hazard closely. The women in Hazard's life since Raven Wing had all been for pleasure. Why *not* bring this one along? "We're all used to yellow eyes in camp," he noted. "No one would care." Rising Wolf smiled faintly. "Except the girlfriends waiting your return, of course."

"Everyone would assume she's a paramour," Hazard protested.

"And she's not," Rising Wolf quipped. "Or at least not all the time," he added facetiously.

"Not at *all* anymore," Hazard insisted, casting his smiling friend a quelling glance.

"Knowing you, Dit-chilajash, treading such a fine and virtuous line may prove difficult."

"I don't need anyone worrying about my love life, Rising Wolf," Hazard admonished. "Just keep your mind on the gold."

"The question is," Rising Wolf jocularly observed, "will *you* be able to?"

Hazard didn't deign to answer, but that in itself was an answer.

Ten minutes later the gold was all packed and they began hoisting it and loading the horses. It took considerable time before the string of ponies were all packed and Rising Wolf was making his way up the isolated mountain trail known only to the Absarokee. Along with the gold he took with him the fascinating impressions his acute eyes had gathered about Dit-chilajash and his beautiful hostage.

Chapter 10

"WHO was that?" Blaze asked when Hazard returned to the cabin.

"My *ba-goo-ba,* my brother," he translated.

"Do you come from a large family?"

"I was an only child. None of my brothers or sisters lived to walk."

"But if he's your brother . . ." she questioningly said.

"It's the custom in our tribe to address male relations of your wife as 'brother' and treat them as such."

"You're married?" Blaze asked, her voice not quite concealing the shock.

"Not now." Hazard said the two words very slowly as if unsure of the reality of his statement.

"What does *that* mean?" From her seated position on the bed where she had watched the sun rise, she stirred suddenly, all the lethargy of early morning precipitously banished by his short but uncertain reply. Long

bare legs flew out of the covers and in one swift shifting
impulse she was standing, face to face with Hazard, the
light wool blanket clutched around her like a royal cloak.
When he didn't answer, neither her question nor her
sharp look, Blaze murmured in a saccharine voice, "Not
now? How convenient. Maybe yesterday. Maybe tomorrow, but not *now.*" Her glance sharpened. "I should have
known. Another lecherous man of the world. I suppose
all that titillating gossip I heard about you in Virginia
City—the stories about Lucy Attenborough, Allison
Marsh, Elizabeth Krueger, and so on and so forth, failed
to mention your marital state because, after all, the
double standard operates in the Wild West just as surely
as it does in the East. For some reason I thought, out
here in the undisturbed majesty of nature, those deceits
hadn't corrupted. More the fool me," she exclaimed with
a short, unpleasant laugh.

"She's dead," Hazard quietly said, very much
against his will. Absarokee custom rigorously avoided
any mention of the deceased. They have gone to their
father, Ah-badt-dadt-deah, and like Him were sacred.
But Hazard knew Blaze would continue her diatribe until
he answered, so he reluctantly uttered the words.

Immediately Blaze was contrite, feeling guilty about
her false accusations. "I'm sorry," she apologized, her
blue eyes full of sympathy. "How did it happen?"

"I'd rather not talk about it," Hazard replied, his
body rigid with constraint.

"Of course. Forgive me."

An uncomfortable silence fell.

Wrenching his mind from the circumstances of
Raven Wing's death—a memory that even now, after
long years, still haunted him with remorse—Hazard tried
to restore the equilibrium of his emotions with mundane
talk. "Rising Wolf's gone and I came in to ask you if
you'd care to bathe today. I know you don't like mountain streams, but the water in the pool isn't so cool. The
sun warms it."

"Do you bathe every day?" Blaze asked somewhat
incredulously. She wasn't immune to the desire for nor-

mal hygiene but with the easy life of socializing in Boston, daily bathing was hardly necessary.

"It's a custom with my people."

"In the winter too?"

"In the winter too."

"It seems absurd," she said with a small shudder. "Imagine, in freezing weather."

"No more absurd than some of your customs. The crinoline, for instance: seductive as it can be in a wind or, at maximum, following a pretty lady upstairs, it is hardly the most practical of guises."

"Touché," Blaze acknowledged with mild distaste. "Let's not argue nonsensically."

"Agreed. Would you like to bathe first?" he asked with a pleasant courtesy.

"I don't care to at all," Blaze said, her voice identically pleasant but firm.

Hazard's lips came together in a straight line. "You'll have to eventually."

"I don't see why."

"Surely, Boston, even you can't be that obtuse."

"Are you calling me obtuse?" she retorted with an unmistakable flush of anger.

"I just have. Are you hard of hearing as well?"

"I don't care to be bullied."

He tamed his features, relaxed his voice. "And I don't care to stand here arguing with a spoiled child. To be blunt, Miss Braddock, if you don't bathe you will smell. And there's no room in this cabin for an—"

"Are you threatening me?" she broke in, her tone and pose haughty, spoiled, petulant. It was a novice's mistake in dealing with Hazard.

Muzzling all his preferred options, only dark brows came together in a scowl; his forbearance was extraordinary.

"Will you *kill* me if I don't bathe?" she provoked.

"Don't be stupid."

"Beat me then?"

"Tempting," he said with a saintly smile.

"How many people *have* you killed? Quite a few, I

suppose." It was like a catechism now. And a challenge. "How many?"

He stood very still, wondering if her foolishness or his control would break first.

"How many? Tell me—lots?"

"Enough." His answer was the model of noncommittal evasion.

"Put a number on it. I want to know how afraid of you I should be. How courageous you can be threatening a woman half your size."

Still he wouldn't rise to her bait.

"I won't bathe, you bastard," she asserted, tightening her hold on the blanket, and suddenly she looked like a plucky kitten, uncertainly fighting something much bigger and more daunting.

"It's not worth dying for, Boston," he said, smiling a real smile at last, and his strong arm stretched out and pulled her off balance. Falling toward him with a surprised look on her face, she was scooped up into his arms and held firmly against his chest.

"Put me down," she cried, struggling against his viselike grip. "Put me down this instant!" Her words were hissed into the sunny morning air, for Hazard's long stride had carried them out the door and onto the path to the pool. "If you don't put me down immediately, I'm going to hit you, dammit!" Her small hands curled into fists.

Amused dark eyes held her fiery ones briefly. "As someone trained in raiding and warfare and, I might add, only recently returned from four gory years of beating the South into a measure of submission, forgive me if your threat fails to strike terror in my soul." His mouth twitched with a repressed grin. "Very brave of you though," he added, the mockery at her expense incensing Blaze's already enormous sense of frustration. Hazard Black was the only man she'd ever met who refused to do her bidding. Not only did he refuse, but her insistence always seemed to fuel some private humor. Odious, contemptible man! How had she *ever* gotten herself into this incredible predicament?

As if reading her mind he said, "Just think, normally

at this hour of the day you'd still be sleeping between satin sheets, with the curtains drawn, while the servants only newly roused from bed wouldn't have even begun preparing your breakfast."

"Instead, I'm freezing to death on some mountain-top."

"It's warm," he said simply.

"Speak for yourself." In her present mood of fretful injustice, Blaze's sense of tact, never very conspicuous, had entirely disappeared.

"Would you like to get warmer?" he drawled, innuendo like fluttering butterflies after a rainshower. They'd reached the perimeter of the pool, the surface of the water at their feet silvery-smooth, as translucent as glass.

"I thought you had newfound scruples," she taunted him.

"Old Coyote teaches us to accept human frailty," Hazard blandly replied.

"That sort of flexible thinking must be easy on one's conscience."

"Realistic, I'd say. A quality you should develop. Daddy's not here. Daddy's money doesn't count at the moment. You're not insulated from the reality of the world any longer. And the sooner you accept it, the easier this will be for both of us."

"My, my," Blaze purred, looking up through thick lashes into Hazard's serious dark eyes, "aren't our lectures on life just too, *too* interesting."

"You're an unmitigated bitch," Hazard whispered ever so softly. "And," he went on, "if I hadn't been schooled against taking advantage of a woman's physical weakness, I'd very much like to beat some sense into you." He wished she'd slap him. He was ready for the excuse to slap her back.

But she didn't. She only replied in a coolly scathing voice, one usually reserved for a servant, "I might expect something like that from you."

"No, Boston, you're wrong," he defended, his sudden inclination curtailed by the chill in her voice. "Although the notion is tempting as hell."

"If I—I were a man," Blaze sputtered, incensed at

the overwhelming self-confidence Hazard exuded, "I'd kill you."

"You wouldn't get the chance. If you were a man, you'd be dead," he remarked impassively.

"Such certainty!" she angrily mocked.

"You're a pilgrim, a greenhorn, pet, and in this part of the country, greenhorns with big mouths don't live very long." Irritating as the angry woman was, the feel of her in his arms was doing disturbing things to his scruples. Only a steely determination kept him from bending down and tasting the hot fire of her full lush mouth. She tantalized him; even her unrestricted tongue intrigued him. She had a boldness about her which challenged him. Could it be that insolent daring, the inordinate tempestuous vitality that fascinated him? Or was it only the memories of her vitality translated into a sensual hunger that lured and charmed him, met his own with a burning glow?

"You haven't seen me shoot," Blaze retorted, unknowingly interrupting Hazard's heated memory just in time to save herself from his flexible human frailty.

"Someday, then, we'll have to test our skills and have a shoot-out. Would that appeal to your bloodthirsty nature, Miss Braddock?"

"I hardly think you, of all people, should accuse anyone of being bloodthirsty."

"Where did you learn this charming ability to turn every conversation into a verbal brawl? You'd do well to enter politics, where name-calling's evolved into a fine art. I'd bet my string of horses you'd hold your own with the best of them."

"I realize the favored feminine standard is the demure, the obedient, the shy. I suppose," she said bristling, "you're used to simpering, acquiescent women."

"The two need not be mutually inclusive," he evocatively replied, and she understood that he preferred acquiescence.

"I find that style of woman tepid as day-old tea."

"Delicately put, as usual," he mildly replied, "but in the interest of abbreviating this acrimonious dialogue, since I *do* work for a living—you have heard of work, I

presume, even in the rarefied altitudes of Beacon Hill—
would you prefer bathing with or without this blanket?"

"I choose not to bathe at all," she persisted.

"That, unfortunately, is not one of the options."

"I hope, Jon Hazard Black, that you burn in hell!"

"I hope, Miss Braddock, that you can swim." And so
saying, he threw her out into the center of the calm pool.

When she hit the water the scream could be heard
halfway to Diamond City. But a second later, she sank
from sight and Hazard plunged into the water in a flat,
racing dive, cursing himself for not taking the time to
find out if she *could* swim. Slicing through the water in a
few swift strokes, he reached the center of the pool
where the water dropped deep enough for drowning. He
dove under, sweeping downward with two powerful
kicks. He saw her immediately through the crystal-clear
water, grasped her by one flailing arm, and hauled her up
to the surface. He lifted her, dripping and shivering, so
her head and shoulders were above the water. Treading
water in a slow pattern, he apologized for frightening
her. "I'm sorry. It never occurred to me you couldn't
swim." His breathing was normal even though he was
kicking slowly toward shore, the few minutes' exertion a
trifle to a man in such superior physical condition.

With water streaming down her face and hair, her
lips trembling, Blaze sputtered. "Damn you—can swim—
bloody—blanket—holding—my—legs—arms." If looks
could kill, he would have ceased to exist then and there.
But then Hazard's leather-clad leg grazed Blaze's thigh
and the fervent fire in her eyes changed to something
quite different.

Hazard, feeling the devastating shock, drew in a
sharp breath. Instant need raced like flame along the
sensual pathways of his mind and body.

Blaze felt the rush of pleasure, felt the flaring desire
spread from the tingling point of contact like molten sunshine. Closing her eyes for a brief moment of dazed
weakness, she shivered in his arms.

"You're cold," he whispered, feeling as though he
must make love to her or die, his breath caught in his
lungs. "Let me warm you." His mouth was close sud-

denly, the words brushing against her cheek. Overcome by urgent desire, Hazard was no longer thinking, only feeling. His arms tightened, pulling her close, pressing her smooth, cool body against his.

She felt him like a hard heat, a large and wonderful arousal only moments old, brought to life because he wanted her. Wanted her despite his cool, reasonable words this morning, wanted her so badly a touch brought him the same scorching passion. Her pale fingers circled, then gently gripped, his wide shoulders. Feeling the small weight of her hands, he trembled, and it gave her pleasure—fierce, unfettered pleasure that Jon Hazard Black could be reached after all. From now on, she languidly thought with renewed confidence, she had a weapon against this jailer of hers. The sense of power unfurled, radiated through her mind, matching the enchantment she felt with Hazard's arousal moving against her thighs. Testing her newfound power, like a nubile child-woman would a new pleasure, Blaze stirred her lower body softly back and forth over the rigid length of Hazard's tense body.

A shudder shook the shoulders beneath her hands. It was her first faint taste of ownership. She turned her face imperceptibly, yet he felt it and waited, breath held, while she turned slightly more toward his warm mouth, turned the few final degrees until her soft lips melted obligingly and tempting into Hazard's. "I want you," she whispered, her small tongue tracing an enticing path over Hazard's bottom lip, "inside me."

Lust exploded in his brain—pure, unadulterated lust —and his mouth came down on hers, answering her request with an intense, driving fury, answering her in a hot, searing way that made her forget who had power over whom. She responded; all the nuances of her sensual longing and budding passion were delicious in their newness, a delicious, extravagant intensity she gloried in, for she was a spoiled young woman who believed that what she wanted she could have. And she had discovered in the just passed glorious, burning moment, that she could have Hazard Black anywhere, anytime, anyplace. It was victory—soaring, limitless victory. And sweet, redolently sweet, she decided with the tantalizing feel of Hazard beneath her hands. It was a sweetness one could become addicted to.

Speed, haste, now was all Hazard could think of. He held her tightly, as if the imprint of her body were salvation, as if the austerity he'd practiced that morning were only prelude, atonement for what was to come. A normal man is expected to gratify his passions, he recalled Old Coyote's words, the litany repeating itself insistently, his subconscious mimicking the fire racing through his blood. His hands released their hold and she found herself standing. Startled, she opened her eyes and blue surprise gazed into pitch-black eyes significant with unrestrained passion.

Her uncertainty dissipated, for there was no mistaking Hazard's look. She let the blanket drop into the water. "Promise me," Blaze murmured, her hand idly stroking the tense muscles of Hazard's chest, the silky feel of his wet skin acute to her heightened senses, velvety as quicksilver, "promise to love me . . . again . . . and again." He had only to touch her and she wanted him, wanted to experience all the enchantment of their loving, wanted to play in her newly discovered garden of delights, to frolic and lure with her newfound powers.

"I promise," Hazard exhaled softly, sweeping Blaze up into his arms again and moving to the shore. "Kiss me," he huskily said, his lashes close and spiky wet, "now."

With a wild shyness that suited her fledgling feelings, Blaze's arms circled his strong neck, her face lifted and she reached to touch his mouth.

Memory and need guided Hazard to the mossy softness beneath the alder bushes. Moments later as they lay together under the leafy green branches, their bodies damp and twined, their mouths warm and bruised, Blaze whispered, "Do you think I'm terrible?" The pink tip of her tongue teasingly licked at his mouth, the coquette playing at dalliance—bewitching and bewitched, feckless as an indulged child.

"Umm," he murmured, nibbling at her mouth in turn.

Her languorous eyes widened artlessly, the enchantress not yet surefooted in the game of love.

"Terribly eager," Hazard whispered, lightly brushing one wide-eyed brow with his lips. "It's unladylike," he mockingly reproved, a teasing smile curving his fine mouth. *"Terribly* unreserved," he softly continued, gently kissing her other silky brow. "And *terribly, terribly"*—the voice rich with anticipated pleasure caressed her cheek with its warmth as his body moved over hers—"desirable."

She smiled, a rare and beautiful smile as compelling as the candor in her eyes. "Love me," she ordered, her voice balmy with invitation. "Now."

"My pleasure, ma'am," Hazard murmured, easing away to shed his leggings.

When he moved he saw it—his sacred bundle—suspended from the tree near the shore. The small medicine amulet was the incarnation of his vision with all the sacred objects revealed to him in his dreams, invested with supernatural powers, giving him his power and blessings. The tied bundle was a protective talisman and the Spirit of his Life Force: a cougar skin wrapped around hallowed bits of earthly fragments. And those bits of stone and feathers and bone were what kept him safe, what he prayed to, what guided him, reminded him, even now, of his duty . . . searingly. Each hand-picked component was pregnant with meaning and *reminded* him, like surging tides of the past.

He came to his feet slowly, self-denial a stark affliction in this paradise of the senses. Putting a small distance between them, he stood still, hard pressed by desire. He didn't trust himself to touch her again. Finally, when her eyes opened in bewilderment, he said, "Forgive me. Would you go back to the cabin now?"

A cold drenching shower would have been less shocking to Blaze, with her body vividly awake, her longing no less urgent than Hazard's.

She lay in her mossy bower, as naturally as a wood

nymph, but the brilliant blue eyes were sharp and clear, the antithesis of the lyrical vision. And her pose was as greenly erotic as the wild flora on which she lay. "Don't do this," she said in her usual straightforward way. She was, he thought, the most beautiful woman he'd ever seen. Her eyes held his but he was silent. "Why?" she asked.

Discarding several answers, he finally said, "Someone has to be sensible."

"Why?" she repeated, innocent and simple.

He didn't have an answer she'd understand. Or even if she could understand all he felt about duty, the importance of his mission for his people, it wasn't the whole truth. And he wasn't about to explain to her that he found her so disturbingly desirable that he could contemplate endless weeks in bed with her. He didn't want her to know that. Or how he was infatuated with her like a giddy adolescent. How his need to touch her, the extravagant sensitivity he felt in her presence was like a magic spell. He had a job to do now and no time for infatuations. Maybe when this was all over, when his clan was safely provided for, he'd take a vacation back East. The place wouldn't matter to either of them. He was certain of her response, as certain as he'd been from the first steamy afternoon he'd looked up to see her standing above him. There was a startling affinity between them, and with his vaster experience, he recognized it as unique.

Blaze looked up at *him* this time, their positions reversed from the first encounter near Hangman's Tree a little over a month ago, and saw a man still as death, rigid in his withdrawal. There was no mistaking the tension. She felt it too, the burning need between them, like a smoldering fuse. But she didn't want to withdraw, didn't want to be sensible. Unconstrained by the motives that curbed Hazard, she openly acknowledged their attraction and wanted only to explore the hurtling beauty their identities provoked. Naive she might be in matters of sex, but she recognized desire in men's eyes—had known it since she'd left childhood braids behind. "Are you going to answer me?" she persisted, half rising on one elbow in a shamelessly provocative pose.

"No," Hazard responded, his voice brusque, the supple curve of her waist, hip, and thigh doing disastrous things to his control.

"I want you. I thought you wanted me. I don't understand what else matters."

It was a forthright proposition, and under any other circumstances, his answer would have been different. "Unfortunately," he said with regret, "almost everything else in the world matters."

"Can't it wait?"

"Or go away?" he suggested softly.

"That would be nice."

"It would be nicer if you'd get up and go back to the cabin."

She lazily surveyed his arresting hard male beauty. "Why don't you come back here?" She left an artful pause, then her small hand smoothed the soft moss hear her hip.

"There's a dozen or so reasons why . . . none," he said with a dry look of despair, "I could probably make you understand."

"Try me."

He laughed, the play on words enticing. "Well, to begin with—I work. Very hard."

"It didn't seem to bother you before." She was like a young child determined to have her own way.

"Discounting that," he went on, amusement rich in his voice, "we're adversaries."

"Oh, really?" she inquired, all coy disbelief.

"You change your mind in a hurry when you want something, don't you?" Hazard murmured, recalling the threats hurled at him yesterday—hell, minutes before, on the way down to the pool.

"It never pays to be rigid. Expediency," she purred, "is my watchword."

He felt the pulsing resume in his groin. "I think," he abruptly said, "we should continue this discussion when you have some clothes on."

She could sense his physical power and sharp need. "Does it bother you to look at me nude?" Her flirtatious tone couldn't have been improved on by Delilah herself.

"It bothers me that your father and his friends want to take my claim. After that bother, the rest pale by comparison."

"*I* don't want your claim."

"And *I* don't want your fine pussy," Hazard determinedly stated. "Don't look so shocked," he said, walking over and pulling her up. "Surely you know that's what we've been talking about."

The flirtatiousness was replaced by a quick flare of anger Hazard found infinitely safer to face. "You're rude," Blaze declared resentfully, pulling her hand from his grasp.

"And you're too hot a piece for me, Miss Braddock." For the first time Hazard's soft voice bit. "You might as well learn now that everyone isn't prepared to be enchanted by your"—he paused the exact fraction of a second for rudeness—"charms. So let's keep our distance. I'm interested in a platonic relationship," he continued, his glance temperate once again. "Cabin-mates, brother and sister, friends," he asserted. "Something that won't cause any trouble to either one of us."

"Platonic," Blaze said, as if she were examining a very mediocre piece of goods.

"Platonic," he repeated moderately. "It's *my* watchword." He kept his eyes safely trained on her left brow, logic, at the moment, struggling mightily to withstand his body's urgent demands.

A hot flash of pique illuminated the huge blue eyes at the parody, and then she said crisply, "Very well." Turning abruptly, she walked away.

Hazard watched her—the beautiful swaying walk, the slender, curvaceous body, the head held high—and damned himself for having scruples. Would there come a time when he could explain his vision to her, indulge their desire?

Spurned and now face to face with a challenge for the first time in her life, Blaze smiled contemplatively. She knew her father would rescue her, of that she was certain. In the meantime, Jon Hazard Black and his scruples, his fierce power and curious sensitivity, were about to be besieged by an assailant intent on winning.

Hazard didn't eat breakfast when he returned from the pool some minutes later. He only made himself two sandwiches and left for the mine. He didn't speak to Blaze, intent on keeping his distance, intent on avoiding any further discussion on the disconcerting, embroiling subject of making love.

COLONEL Braddock watched the Indian guide start a small fire, his own thoughts elsewhere: Was Blaze hurt, mistreated? Would the savage side of this Hazard man abuse his daughter? Under stress who knew how the man would react. Billy Braddock was also worried about Yancy. Unpredictable and short-tempered, Yancy was the last man he cared to leave behind in Confederate Gulch unattended, but Millicent had requested his support, so he'd consented. Yancy had come to him two years ago, well recommended by Alphonse DeSmet, so he'd hired him as a manager for his plant. He'd turned out to be first rate at organization; in fact, he'd handled the logistics of this entire trip superbly. But Yancy had a temper with underlings and like many of his southern counterparts was adamantly prejudiced against anyone with skin darker than his. It hadn't mattered before—the prejudice—because Yancy answered to him and he didn't tolerate discrimination. But Yancy might go off on his own after this Hazard and do something that could jeopardize Blaze. There was no way of knowing whether Blaze was with the Indian in the mine during the day or booby-trapped somehow in case of an attack, and heaven only knows what Hazard might do to her if they went up with guns. All the diabolical tortures attributed to the Indians raced through his mind. The Colonel shivered unconsciously. Whatever it took, he thought, to appease the fellow, he would do. Blaze was all he had in the world.

The smell of coffee reached his nostrils and his distracted thoughts returned to the fire, his guide, the sight of coffee bubbling in a tiny pot hung over the flames.

"Maybe it's my fault," he said, half aloud, his mind obsessed with the gravity of Blaze's captivity.

Hearing the murmured words, the Bannack guide looked up, his expression inquiring.

Colonel Braddock sighed, looked around like someone not quite sure where he was, and added, "I let her go. I shouldn't have. And now . . ." He sighed again, a deepening melancholy gripping him.

Whether the Colonel was explaining or talking to himself was uncertain, but Spotted Horse answered quietly, "Hostages. Do many in the old days. Keep peace. Won't hurt." He gave the coffee a stir with a peeled branch.

"Are you sure?" The Colonel's eyes were alive for the first time since their journey began. "Are you *sure?*" he agitatedly repeated.

Spotted Horse looked up. "Crow don't scalp," he declared. "Don't kill whites. Crow like Bannack," he continued more slowly. "Know white men like grass on the prairie."

Billy Braddock sat up straighter, felt suddenly invigorated. "How far did you say to Ash River? How long before we find Hazard's clan?"

"Maybe when sun sets again. River not far." He was pouring sugar into the pot from a leather pouch.

Blaze's father relaxed his rigid posture. It reassured, the fact that this guide seemed so certain of Hazard's motives. If hostages were used to keep peace, then Hazard would be willing to negotiate. But niggling doubts insinuated themselves again: How long would it take to reach the clan, return to the mine? In the meantime, how would Blaze respond to her captor? If he hadn't raised her like the son he never had, his mind would be easier. But he knew Blaze and knew how she reacted to constraint. He'd spoiled her, he realized, far too much, and it frightened him to contemplate what might occur if Blaze resisted Hazard Black's orders. Apparently Hazard wasn't a man to be crossed.

"Drink," the guide said, handing the Colonel a steaming cup of coffee. "Coffee help," he gravely asserted. "No tired."

The coffee was powerfully sweet, the way his guide liked it. But Spotted Horse was right. After drinking the coffee, he wasn't so tired, and when they remounted a short time later, the Colonel felt ready to ride over any mountain ahead.

Chapter 11

RECONCILING herself to hours of solitude, Blaze had settled into the armchair with a month-old newspaper from Virginia City when the door opened. Looking up, she saw a young boy standing in the rush of sunshine streaming in the opening. His shock of pale hair was disheveled, his eyes were grey and serious, and his sturdy arms were holding two string-tied parcels. "I brought some milk and meat," he gravely explained. "Ferguson butchered a steer yesterday."

Blaze had dropped the paper in her lap when she first saw him and, smoothing the pages lightly with her fingers, asked, "Are you the boy who picked the berries?"

"Yes, ma'am," he politely replied.

"Come in," Blaze invited, getting up. "Here, I'll take the packages." She carried them over to the counter by the dry sink. "Would you like something to eat?" she inquired, ignoring the measure of her culinary skills.

133

"No, thank you, ma'am," he courteously refused. Hazard had told him she couldn't cook when he'd stopped at the mine to get his orders for the day. He began stacking the plates from last night's supper.

"You don't have to do that. . . ." Blaze paused, uncertain how to address him.

"Jimmy, ma'am, Jimmy Pernell," he acknowledged, setting the salt and pepper neatly in the center of the table.

"It isn't necessary," Blaze began again, watching the young boy's swift, sure movements. He'd gathered all the used dishes on one end of the pine table.

"He told me to, ma'am," Jimmy answered, reaching for the dishpan hanging on a nail by the stove. "And he told me to help you with lunch too."

"Is he paying you?" Blaze was amazed at the assurance of his actions. He was stoking the stove now after testing the water in the reservoir.

"Oh, sure, ma'am," he replied, looking up from his task, "Hazard always pays real good. Mom washes and irons his shirts. He pays her five dollars apiece. And my sister Abby copies some of the new laws for him for a dime a word. And the baby can't earn no money yet, but Hazard says anyone that cute deserves an allowance just for smiling and cheering him up. He gives Joey money each week and Ma buys extra food with it. You don't have to worry none, ma'am. Hazard's the best."

Now there, thought Blaze, with an inner smile, is a very fine version of hero worship—and a sizable outlay for Hazard each month.

"What does he pay you, ma'am, for taking care of things?"

"Er—we haven't talked about it yet."

Glancing around at the unusual disarray, Jimmy kindly observed, "When you get the hang of things better, I'm sure he'll pay you fine, just like he does everyone else. He's fair as a prince, Ma says. That's a fact. And cleaner than any man she's ever knowed."

"I understand," Blaze said to the boy busily rolling up the sleeves of his homemade shirt, "his tribe has some custom about bathing."

"Don't know about that, ma'am, but Ma says God took away the mold after he made Hazard. He's one of a kind."

It sounded, Blaze decided with a twinge of resentment, as though Jimmy's mother might have a touch of hero worship herself. "How old is your mother?" she asked as casually as possible.

"Old," Jimmy declared in the way of children viewing anyone over twelve. Looking up from his arrangement of dishpan and rinse pan, he added, "She's probably got a couple years on you, ma'am. Do you want me to show you how to wash dishes? Hazard says you can't do nothin'. I can show you." The offer was sincerely made, without a trace of intolerance.

"Thank you," Blaze replied with a smile, "That would be very kind of you."

"No offense, ma'am," he said, surveying the littered cabin, "but what *can* you do?"

"I'm afraid my schooling overlooked . . . this sort of thing."

"Well, don't worry none," he reassured her again, "I'll help you out."

"Thank you, Jimmy, I'd like that." His childish frankness charmed her and she smiled at him again. "Now tell me, what do I do first?"

"Put hot water from the stove reservoir halfway up both these pans here. I'll get the cool water and then I'll show you how to wash dishes."

He washed and she dried—with beautifully embroidered towels stitched by Jimmy's mother and sister. For a rare moment, staring at the intricate flower designs, Blaze wished she'd learned how to embroider. She felt curiously out of place in the midst of what was obviously a warm group of friends.

After the dishes were finished, Jimmy swept up all the remaining bits of broken crockery with admirable restraint. He'd seen his ma throw a plate against the wall once and then burst into tears soon after his pa died a year ago. And he knew when grownups broke this many dishes, something wasn't right. So without a word, the piles were all picked up, put into an old box, and carried outside. "I think now," he said, returning and giving an approving smile to Blaze's effort at bedmaking, "we'd better start lunch cuz Hazard said he'd be in at twelve sharp."

He was a much better teacher than Hazard because he was a much better cook. "Learned from my ma," he said when Blaze complimented him. He was stirring up a batch of biscuits and making it look like an effortless exercise. "Put some flour on the table there, and I'll show you how to roll these out. Is the fire goin' good?"

He'd taught Blaze where to look now, and she reported back that it was indeed "goin' good." So in what seemed an incredibly short time, to someone who viewed bags of flour, sugar, and potatoes with as much familiarity as a foreign language, lunch was prepared. The biscuits had just been taken from the oven, while steaks simmered in butter-drenched onions in a large skillet and small new potatoes steamed in a milk sauce laced with wild chives.

"You're an absolute marvel," Blaze conceded, awed by the young boy's expertise. "How did you possibly manage to get everything done at the same time?"

"Just have to know how to count, ma'am. It ain't hard. The stuff that takes the longest, well, you start with that first."

"It seems so easy when you do it." Blaze sighed.

"You helped too, ma'am," he politely acceded, avoiding mention of all the near-disasters Blaze's attempts at helping had occasioned.

When Hazard walked in five minutes later, Jimmy gave directions and the food was arranged on the table. Hazard was lavish with his praise, and sincerely so. His own cooking was of the most rudimentary sort, so Jimmy's meal was deeply appreciated.

"He's really wonderful," Blaze agreed, and was warmed by a smiling glance from Hazard. "Although I'm afraid I was more trouble than help. Who'd ever think cutting an onion would be so difficult?"

"It weren't your fault it rolled on the floor, Miss." (Hazard had corrected his "ma'am.") "Should have told you to cut off one end flat first. And it won't take you long to catch on to rolling dough."

Blaze thought otherwise; the sticky dough had been as recalcitrant as Hazard of late, she reflected with a smile.

"You rolled dough?" Hazard asked, a pleasant smile curving his fine mouth.

"Mashed it ruinously, I'm afraid. First it stuck to the glass, then to the table, then to my hands." She brushed a distracted hand through her hair in a sweetly winsome way that made Hazard think suddenly she should have something to wear besides the black slacks and linen shirt. As if the men's clothes seemed out of place with the feminine gesture. If he'd thought much about it then, it was the very first provision he'd made to accommodate her. Making a mental note to see to her wardrobe, he gallantly said, "I'm sure Jimmy couldn't have done it without you."

Blaze's long-lashed eyes swept a flashing look at Hazard, the gallant remark reminding her of the exquisite man in evening dress at the Territorial Ball. It always disconcerted her—the civilized behavior, the cultured voice, the occasional lapses in chivalry. His image was so adamantly Indian here on the mountain, half clothed, dressed in beaded leather, all bronzed flesh and long black hair. But when she saw there was no mockery in the starkly handsome face, she responded in kind. "I'm sure he very well could, but thank you all the same. It never hurts to try some new accomplishment."

"Do you suppose, then, in a week or so, we can add biscuits to our hot chocolate and strawberry menu?" His grin was pure sunshine.

"Perhaps with much prayer and dedication," Blaze replied, her own mouth lifting in an answering smile.

Her blithe emotional openness charmed him. Their eyes met over Jimmy's towhead and a buoyant conviviality traversed the short distance.

"Would a prayer ceremony in the kitchen help?" he teased.

"Bite your tongue. My mother's forebears would roll

over in their Methodist graves." Her blue eyes were alight with laughter.

"I'd take my chances with distraught specters if my meals all tasted like this."

Jimmy didn't understand all that was going on over his head, but he understood the smiles and reckoned that dishes mightn't be smashed so much anymore. "I'll help whenever I can get away from McTaggert's and Ma," he offered.

He was rewarded with smiling thanks from both adults.

"See, you needn't waste any time with rites and rituals. Jimmy will see to my education."

"So amenable? What have I been doing wrong?"

"Just about everything," Blaze quipped, and added with decorum, "except for one thing, which you do very well."

The look passing between them this time could have scorched a prairie landscape in need of rain.

"Mind your manners," Hazard said very softly, after he'd recaptured the breath in his lungs.

"I've never minded manners much. So tedious," Blaze cheerfully replied, pleased by his reaction.

"And I don't suppose this is the time or place to change your mind."

"Oh, I don't know," she airily said, her smile lushly captivating. "I might be willing to change my mind about something if you wanted to change your mind about *some things.*" The last word was a low murmur.

Resolutely steeling himself to resist the rich sensuality, Hazard blandly observed, "Not likely, with what's at stake. Although," he went on, all gentlemanly courtesy, "I assure you, it's not from lack of wanting."

"How reassuring."

"My pleasure. And now," Hazard said, rising, "back to work. Thank you both." He bowed in a slow, relaxed motion, the muscles across his chest flexing with the movement. Pausing halfway to the door, he addressed Jimmy. "Stop at the mine before you leave. I'll send some gold back with you for supplies."

"Sure thing, Hazard. Soon as Miss and me does the dishes."

"Again?" Blaze blurted out, astonished that everything seemed to be beginning all over again.

"Maybe Papa will arrive soon," Hazard suggested, his eyes amused, "and save you from the drudgery."

Blaze grimaced slightly. "Either that, or may a full complement of staff appear while my hands are still lily-white."

She amazed him quite regularly. No timid woman here. She was sure of herself, devoid of fear. And splendid. A pity he couldn't enjoy her without all the restrictions. In different circumstances . . . But then, he reminded himself harshly, two more different people, and circumstances, and cultures couldn't possibly be imagined.

Blaze would have liked to walk over to him, standing there in the middle of the room, and kiss him lightly on the cheek. He could make her smile so easily, could warm her with his own smile; he made her feel curiously content for the first time in her life when he turned the full power of his dark glance on her. And the tall, lean, broad-shouldered body was beautiful, too. A pity, she thought, he felt so strongly about duty. Having been raised in an utterly selfish world, she found the virtue in duty intellectually valid, but emotionally unsatisfying.

"I'll see what I can do about it," Hazard said, interrupting her musing.

She looked startled.

"The lily-white hands," he explained.

"She can wipe," Jimmy interjected, at last finding something he understood in this adult conversation.

"Good. It's settled then." Hazard smiled and left.

WHEN Jimmy went down mountain an hour later, the list he carried in his head was extensive and his instructions were explicit: he was to say nothing to anyone about the woman in the cabin. As though the whole town weren't buzzing with the story already. But he knew even at his very young age how to be discreet, his loyalty to Hazard being second only to his family. So he was careful making his purchases; one of the young stockboys at Klein's General Store, happy for a twenty-dollar gold piece to sell him a large crated item after the store closed for the night. And if anyone asked, Jimmy knew he wouldn't mention who'd bought it.

The stockboy and Jimmy loaded Hazard's horses early the following morning—the horses Hazard kept in Pernell's pasture for a monthly boarding fee. And long before Diamond City was awake, Jimmy was halfway up the trail to Hazard's cabin, rechecking his list mentally to make sure he'd forgotten nothing.

Chapter 12

"I TELL you, Millicent"—Yancy had taken to addressing his employer's wife by her Christian name since the Colonel had disappeared into the mountains—with her tacit consent, he had noted—"there's no sense in waiting for the Colonel to return. One damn Injun. It's ridiculous to wait. Hell, we can blow him out of there in a minute."

Millicent Braddock reflected. Her husband had left precise orders—ones which left no doubt of what he wanted done in his absence—nothing. He knew Yancy had a reputation for violence not always in proportion to need.

"The Colonel won't allow any chances taken with his precious daughter," she reminded him. "It's all well and good to talk about blowing him up, but the Colonel would have both our heads if our actions endangered his darling."

Yancy and Millicent understood each other perfectly. Both had been obliged, due to the declining fortunes of their old Virginia families, to look afield for ways to mend their dynasties. But they'd never fully accepted this necessity. At least not with any graciousness. A burning resentment always smoldered under the surface, for neither of them had ever expected to have to work for a living. In Millicent's case, being married to the Braddock money certainly was work. For Yancy the humiliation was more overt. He'd actually had to find a job after the Civil War had dispossessed him of even the family's heavily mortgaged plantation.

"And you?" Yancy inquired with the barest suggestion of irony.

Millicent had spent a lifetime cultivating the nuances of a southern lady's conduct. "Why, Mr. Strahan," she admonished, just the proper degree of affront in her voice, "I *am* her mother. *Need* I remind you?"

"Begging your pardon, ma'am," Yancy replied, his eyes as devoid of feeling as hers, "I'm only concerned with the Colonel's property. It made me forget myself for a moment." His tone was as properly contrite as hers was properly affronted. They were like two actors playing excessively polite roles while their minds went over the evening's social engagements. It came as second nature to them both—the intricate set of insincere behavioral formulas. Each knew how the other felt about the Colonel, his daughter, and his money, but the game required certain politic rules.

Eventually they'd come to an agreement. It was simply a matter of the negotiations being couched in accepted propriety. The unacknowledged accomplices went in to dinner, something the Braddock servants were finding an increasing, if distasteful, occurrence.

Chapter 13 ❧

AFTER a second restless night, Hazard woke on his bed of buffalo robes and forced his tired body up. He stretched lazily, every muscle responding a millisecond late. Today, he thought, would not be a good day to face a crisis, with his brain and body sluggish from fatigue and Blaze's presence filling his thoughts with an exclusivity detrimental to concise thinking.

Quietly, he slipped from the cabin without waking Blaze and strolled down to the pool. The morning reminded him of so many from his youth: fresh, sunny, a whisper of a breeze rippling through the aspen. And he wished, in a fleeting moment, for that innocence again. A time of only his tribe on these lands, only the anticipation of some childhood pleasure—a horse race or a game of hoop and pole, nothing more pressing in the course of a day than the normal competition between boyish companions.

Standing on the mossy stream bank, he sighed and

the nostalgia dissipated. The sun still came up vivid and limitless over the same rugged crest of mountain landscape, but nothing else was the same. His people had moved north of these mountains, where white men hadn't come looking for gold yet or tried their plows in the mountain valleys. His innocence had vanished even before the yellow eyes had come into his life. And now he labored like the slave Blaze accused him of making her, labored inside the dim earth day after day, in hopes of saving his people from the fate of other tribes dispossessed by the white man's expansion. Gold was the answer. The ultimate answer for every problem. Well, almost every problem, he ironically noted. Gold wasn't going to solve this overpowering need he felt for his willful companion. He knew, of course, what would solve the problem. . . . Abruptly, he dove into the pool, hoping the chill water would briefly assuage the carnal direction of his thoughts.

WHEN Blaze woke an hour later, the cabin was still, trilling birdsong outside the only sound. Tossing aside the covers, she sat up, her glance sweeping the small room. He was gone already, his wet footprints, a reminder of his daily bath, still visible on the cool plank floor, the butter crock and remnants of sandwich-making left out on the table. It warmed her suddenly—the vestiges of his presence—and it unnerved her briefly that she should feel such tenderness for him. Until now, she'd considered her feelings for Jon Hazard Black blatantly and uncomplicatedly sensual. As one would enjoy a new bauble or toy or pleasurable taste—wholeheartedly and openly, but without the peripheral complexities that rushed in on her thoughts now. Brushing aside the unruly intricacies, she reminded herself that he was using her and she was using him, a fair exchange in her mind— hostage for teacher—until her father ransomed her. These days were an adventure she'd remember with a spiking rush of excitement all her life, for Hazard had given her her first exquisite sensual pleasure and she impatiently wanted more. Undaunted that her teacher had withdrawn his services, Blaze now contemplated some more amenable form of bribery, since her first forays had failed. Undeterred and motivated by an assumed prerogative, Miss Venetia Braddock of Beacon Hill set her mind on finding the key to overcoming Hazard's exceptional discipline.

JIMMY was there when Hazard came in for lunch, the food was prepared, the floor newly swept, and Blaze sported a spray of wild roses tucked becomingly in the top buttonhole of her blouse. It brought his mind instantly to the petal-soft feel of her breasts and, distracted by the memory, he didn't hear Jimmy's question until it was repeated.

"Didya start drifting south today?"

"Ah . . ." he said vaguely, as if waking from a nap. "Drifting. Yes. Made thirty feet this morning."

"Thirty feet!" Blaze remarked, amazed. She knew mining almost as well as her father did. "That must be some kind of a record."

He looked at her and thought roses suited her. "Black powder did most of it," he modestly replied.

"How do you haul it out?"

"A small dump car. I put in a few rails when I started working this claim."

"You *are* expecting the mine to produce."

"I wouldn't have invested so much time and effort if I didn't."

"Hazard went to Columbia School of Mines and he knows everything about mining," Jimmy interposed, pleased to illuminate yet another brilliant facet of his hero.

"Thanks, Jimmy, for the compliment," Hazard said with a smile at his small champion, "but I know far from everything. I took a couple of classes on gold mining, that's all. It wasn't so far from Boston."

Wide-eyed, Blaze accused, "You never said you'd lived in Boston."

"You never asked."

"What were you doing in Boston?" she asked, suspicion grievous in her tone.

"Going to Harvard." And then she recalled

Turledge Taylor's remark about talk he might have gone to Harvard.

"I never saw you."

"I don't think we frequented the same playrooms," he replied, an ingenuous smile playing across his face.

"I'm not *that* young."

"Young enough," he tranquilly observed.

"Meaning?" Her voice was verging on snappish and she was building herself into some kind of unwarranted temper.

"Nothing provocative, I assure you, Miss Braddock," Hazard temperately remarked, hoping to mollify whatever was goading her. "Only that, taking into account upper-class fixed notions of etiquette, my sojourn in Boston society preceded your debut, that's all."

Jimmy, watching the adults like a spectator at a tennis match, suddenly knew without a doubt who had broken the crockery. The lady living here with Hazard tempered up faster than a fox pouncing on a plump chicken. "Food's getting cold," he intervened, loath to be in the middle of a full-scale fight, although, he decided, casting a sidelong glance at Hazard, there was more of a smile on his face than anything else.

"Come, Miss Braddock, let's eat," Hazard invited. "It's a shame to waste all this effort." He seated himself at the small table. "Tell me," he went on, in a sincere, generous tone, as though the recent exchange hadn't occurred, "are these your muffins today?"

Blaze colored as pink as the roses at her neckline. How, she thought, could he infuse so much warmth in his voice? It was like being stroked with velvet. She decided then that Boston society must have been rather interesting the years Hazard practiced his charm on the ladies.

"She sure did," Jimmy answered, anxious to please Hazard, knowing he was supposed to be teaching the Miss to cook.

Smiling suddenly at the handsome face turned up to her, Blaze truthfully explained, "Jimmy allows me to stir. And I'm marvelous at throwing in the raisins. If Papa doesn't intervene, I may graduate to more intricate details . . . in the kitchen."

Hazard, waving Jimmy and Blaze to their seats, had already begun buttering a muffin. "Maybe we could hire you to live in, Jimmy. I've forgotten how good food tastes."

"I'd like to, but I can't," Jimmy replied quickly, his mouth full of muffin.

"Your mother needs you, I suppose," Hazard replied, savoring the flavor of new young carrots boiled with a touch of sugar.

Jimmy's eyes dropped evasively. "Yeah." He busily pushed his carrots into a pile.

"You'll be able to come up and help though, won't you?"

The fork stirred the carrot pile flat. Eyes downcast, Jimmy muttered, "Think so."

Noting the uncharacteristic nervousness in a normally ebullient young boy, Hazard put down his fork, swallowed the tender morsel of beef in his mouth, and softly inquired, "Think so?"

Jimmy's eyes came up fast, locked with Hazard's for one flashing moment, and then fell before the perplexed scrutiny. "Is something wrong, Jimmy?"

"No sir."

"Is the money all right?"

"Yes sir, it's not that."

"What is it, then?"

"Well, Ma saw—you know—what I brought up this morning, and—" His downcast eyes regained some of their usual sparkle. "It don't seem so odd to me, but Ma sort of pursed her lips, and, well . . ."

Amusement replaced perplexity in Hazard's dark eyes. "And?" he prompted, one finger lazily smoothing a nonexistent tablecloth.

"Ma says Mrs. Gordon was right all along."

"Right about what?" Hazard asked, a knowing smile beginning to curl the edges of his mouth.

"I don't rightly know, sir. Something about a thing called a tawdry hussy." Blaze choked on her food, but Jimmy didn't seem to notice. "Damned, oops, sorry, sir," he apologized, "if I know what that is. But Ma was right indignant and told me not to stay after sunset. How come, sir?" Jimmy innocently asked.

"I expect she's worried about you up in the mountains at night," Hazard calmly replied, his glance straying to Blaze's flushed face.

"But I stay here lots of times after dark."

"Maybe some grizzlies have been sighted lately." Hazard resumed eating.

"She didn't mention no grizzlies. What's a tawdryhussy?" Jimmy said the unfamiliar words in one unbroken breath.

It was Hazard's turn to choke. The small boy's face staring at him was plainly bewildered, while Blaze's heated blue eyes were burning into him. "Ah—actually— it's a matter of definition," he equivocated, "one of those things women take issue with. I wouldn't give it another thought. And do what your mother wants. Come up if you can."

"I sure will. It don't seem like she minds so much if'n it's daylight, so I'll come same as usual with your supplies, OK?" Jimmy had been afraid he'd lose Hazard's friendship when his mother had harangued him that morning about the large crate being loaded on the pack saddle. He wanted reassurance that all would remain the same between himself and the man who treated him with a gentleness he'd never known, even from his own father.[8]

"Fine, Jimmy, and tell your mother how much I appreciate your work. Now, would you run down to the stream and get a fresh bucket of water?" Hazard asked, knowing the woman across the table from him was about to explode.

"Right, sir. Right away," Jimmy exclaimed, jumping to his feet. "I'll be back in a jiffy."

He'd no more than crossed the threshold when Blaze blurted out, "The nerve of that woman! The unmitigated *nerve!* Who the hell does she think she is?"

"I wouldn't worry about it," Hazard said placatingly.

"I'm not *worried* about it. Why should I *worry* about what some *washerwoman* says about me?"

"Your snobbery is showing, Boston," Hazard observed wryly.

"My snobbery?" she sneered, the emphasis drawlingly apparent.

One dark brow raised fractionally. "Point taken," he said.

"I should hope so!" she snapped, rounding on him with a rush of movement. "You were about to take her side!"

He put both palms up in defense. "I wouldn't think of it. 'Hussy' isn't in my vocabulary at all."

"Knowing you, as long as they wear a skirt, right?"

"Or black slacks," he added, casting an admiring glance at her.

"Hazard, I'm not interested in compliments at the moment. Can you believe it?" she rushed on, hotly berating what she considered a gross injustice. "Of all the gall!"

Hazard's deep voice was tolerantly soothing. "Gossip is like that. Ignore it."

"I intend to! Damn her—*Hussy?*" she repeated incredulously, her fingernails drumming the tabletop.

"It's a small mining camp."

"Too damn small."

"Everyone knows everyone else's business."

"Why the hell would she call me that?" Blaze questioned, more bewildered now than resentful. "I'm a hostage, for God's sake." Immune to the world's opinion in general, Blaze took issue with the pettiness of the remark. The point wasn't what she did or didn't do with Hazard. That was her own business—she'd always done what she pleased with her life. It just astonished her that some laundress would comment on respectability in a rough, wild mining camp like Diamond City where vice itself was a business—a major business. "She probably wants you for herself," Blaze scathingly commented.

"Probably does," Hazard agreed.

Blaze's eyes snapped up. "Have you?"

"I don't see as it's any of your business," he replied, precise and fastidious, and went back to his eating.

The fork was halfway to his mouth when she

snatched it from his grasp. "Have you?" she repeated, not knowing herself why it suddenly mattered. Only knowing that it did.

Slowly lowering his hand to the table, Hazard stared at her quizzically for a moment. "Are you my mother?" he asked sarcastically.

"Do I look like your mother?" She returned his sarcasm, hers honey-sweet.

He stared at her for another silent moment, debating his answer, debating whether he cared to answer at all. It amused him finally, he decided, her hot-tempered inquisition. "No," he said.

"No, what?"

"No, you don't look like my mother."

"And?"

He smiled crookedly. "No, I haven't. Now may I have my fork back?"

The door banged open just then and Jimmy appeared, out of breath, with a pail of fresh water. Blaze tossed back the fork and Hazard resumed eating. Jimmy decided as the meal continued that it was twice as much fun being fussed over by two people as one.

Chapter 14

LATER that evening, in the lull after supper, imminent darkness having driven Jimmy home, Hazard finished cleaning his rifle, put it carefully away on its rack above the door, and walked outside.

Blaze, hearing the latch drop into place, thought with panic: Was he going into Diamond City? Would he be back tonight? Would he be back at all? Lord, would she be found by a search party in a month starved to death if he'd really left for good? Then the door reopened and Hazard came in struggling slightly under the awkward weight of a large wooden crate.

"You're back," she breathed spontaneously, relief evident in the soft exhalation.

"I was only gone two minutes," he replied, with the grin she was becoming familiar with. Setting the slatted wooden box down, he looked up with a lazy, half-lidded gaze. "Should I have checked in sooner?"

"You didn't say where you were going; you've never

gone out this late before. It's so dark when there's no moon. Oh, hell," she finished in a disgusted rush.

He found her artlessness charming. Always had. It was a curiously innocent quality in an ostensibly independent female. "Maybe I'll be forgiven such ruthless discourtesy," he said, straightening, "when you see what I've brought you." He gestured to the open crate in invitation.

"For me?" Blaze said, a throaty anticipation reminding him again how young she was. With the exception of her occasional hot-tempered reprisals, she really did view this all as some kind of adventure.

"For you," he agreed. And when she uncurled from the easy chair and stood, unrehearsed grace in motion, he caught himself staring. She was barefoot, her long legs accented by the tight black trousers, her slender body outlined by firelight. How long, he wondered, could he withstand his need for her?

A peal of delight interrupted his wandering thoughts and his glance focused on her face. "I thought you'd like it." His smile reappeared; her joy was contagious.

"How ever did you think of it? Wherever did you *find* it?" she exclaimed, touching the shiny rim of an elaborate copper bathtub.

"Since you seemed reluctant to endure my outdoor bathing facilities, I decided an alternative was—"

"Necessary?"

"I'd never presume to mention . . ." he deprecatingly murmured, a piquant sparkle in his eyes.

"Where did Jimmy find it?"

"After discreet inquiries—he knows all the young store clerks in town—he found one at Klein's. It seems Jimmy persuaded his friend to sell us this tub that one of the—er—working girls in town had ordered."

"It *is* a courtesan's model, isn't it?" Blaze said, smiling. Small porcelain inserts, inside, front and back had caught her eye. The scenes portrayed on the painted tiles, while mythological, were also provocatively salacious. "This is what Jimmy's mother saw."

"I'm afraid so . . . and that's not all."

"There's more?" She tried to keep from breaking into laughter.

"Only a couple of small items. Take a look under that linen sheet."

Lifting the fabric, Blaze took one look, turned to Hazard, and with a teasing smile said, "You *ordered* these or do they come with the tub?"

"An unfortunate series of events. What I told Jimmy to buy was two dresses for you. I thought you might appreciate a change of clothes." He sighed. "It didn't occur to me that 'respectable women,' the few we have here in Diamond City, sew their own clothes. The dresses Klein's and Bailey's and the hawker carry are for the . . . the other women."

"Jimmy's mother must have thought you were opening a brothel up here," Blaze cheerfully remarked, shaking out an outrageous creation in purple satin and feathers. "Do I have to cook if I wear this?" Her sidelong glance was replete with meaning.

Hazard caught himself just in time. The remark on the tip of his tongue matched the heat in her eyes. "You don't have to wear it at all," he said, his voice cool with hard-won control. "I meant for Jimmy to get something with those small flowers . . . calico, is it? Something comfortable."

"I've never worn calico," Blaze said, warmed by his gallant attempt to outfit her in "something comfortable."

"No, I suppose you haven't," he acknowledged, "but these I don't think are going to work. We'll reorder and have someone sew something for you. You specify the material if you think calico won't do, and send your measurements down next time Jimmy comes up."

"I don't know them." Her eyes lifted slowly to his, her face hauntingly beautiful in the firelight.

Hazard moved back a half-step, as if the withdrawal would ensure him safety from her inviting eyes. "I'll find some string around here. You could measure with that."

"Or rawhide?" she reminded him, challenged by his constant restraint.

"I'll find some string," he emphatically repeated. "After I haul some water up here for you." And he narrowly escaped outside. Resisting Blaze Braddock required a kind of courage he'd never cultivated. He was a novice at saying no to a beautiful woman.

Within fifteen minutes the boiler on top of the stove was filled and in another half-hour the water was steaming. Carefully lifting the heavy boiler off the stove, he poured the hot water into the tub. Cooling it with some water from the stream, he explained to Blaze, "Add as much cold water as you like from these buckets. You know where the soap is."

"This is all very kind of you. Thank you." No teasing now in her voice, no facetiousness glinting behind her long lashes. She was sincere, warm and appreciative. Harder, he discovered, to resist than her more blatantly sensual mockery.

His tone was brisk and, he hoped, pragmatic. "You might want to wear one of those garish satin things after your bath. At least they're clean. We'll get something more suitable in a day or two." Unconsciously, he'd said "we." He didn't notice, but Blaze did.

He was affecting her tonight in a way she'd never experienced before. The tub, the hot water, his solicitude for her taste in clothing, all were poignantly touching. He was a dazzling creature physically, but, more remarkably, a beautiful man with a core of gentle kindness she'd never seen before in the masculine world of her acquaintance. "You won't stay?" she asked very softly, for he was already moving toward the door.

He half turned back, and a hushed silence fell between them. He waited so long to answer she thought he might not have heard. She opened her mouth to say the words over again.

"No," he quickly said, his eyes telling her yes. Then, swinging around briskly, he walked out.

THE bath was heaven. The tub, made for a courtesan's trade, roomy enough for two; Blaze's leisurely bath, however, was solitary.

Hazard spent the time on the ledge overlooking the mountainside, his chin propped on the housing of the Gatling gun, his arms sprawled out before him along the smooth, cool barrel. The lights of Diamond City, at a short distance, were reflected as a pinkish glow on the underbelly of the cloud cover. The quarter moon, obscured tonight by heavy clouds, shone somewhere, but on Hazard's mountain it was black, the atmosphere heavy with activity, his own thoughts as turbulent as nature around him.

He thought of her a hundred times a day, he wanted to touch her no less often. Her smile and laughter—even her explosive temper—created a kind of warm companionship he hadn't experienced since Raven Wing died. Unfortunately, she was utterly untouchable—a woman linked irrevocably with a faction willing to kill him, more succinctly, linked with a world anathema to everything he held dear. His long-boned hands tightened around the multibarreled metal until, white-knuckled, the pain roused him from his musing. Enough, he resolved. His decision was firm. She wouldn't be here forever. He wanted no part of her, no reminder when she was gone, no complexities added to his already complex life. So he stayed there in the dark night, forcing his thoughts to the priorities that mattered—the mine, the gold, his people's welfare.

He wanted to be certain she was out of the bath and dressed before he returned.

WOULD he come to her? Blaze wondered, lying back in the warm water, resting her head against the richly embossed copper. Like a child wishing for an expensive toy, she wished he would. But also, unlike a child, she was fully aware of the difference between reality and wishing. He didn't come, of course, as she very well knew he wouldn't. But he'd been thinking of her when he bought the tub, when he'd ordered the dresses. He was, she knew, no more immune to her than she to him.

They would make love again, she knew. It was inevitable, as spring followed winter. She felt the excitement of attracting him, the excitement of her fledgling sexual power. She could feel the intensity between them like a scorching living force. And the anticipation of drawing him out from his reserved world of duty and moral obligation was irresistible.

WHEN he entered the cabin at last, the fire had died to glowing coals, casting burnt-gold shadows on his bare chest, his face reflecting muted saffron. Only his eyes and his silky hair shone black.

The moment Hazard saw Blaze, flushed, one slender leg curled under her, seated on the chair near the fire, he was shaken to the core of his conviction. He felt his heart miss a beat. She had chosen the black taffeta gown: an extremely low décolletage barely covered her pale, mounded breasts; white shoulders and arms glistened purity and innocence in contrast to the sinful black taffeta; jet bugles, lavishly sprinkled like midnight stars, caught the fire, accenting her provocatively upthrust breasts spilling out over the low-cut neckline. Then she moved slightly, her gleaming hair slipping over her shoulder like coiled copper and his adrenaline pumped wildly. With the same motion, the full, crisply pleated skirt fell open, crumpled silk shimmering with a life of its own. Suddenly her shapely legs were bared, as were portions of one hip and thigh, the revealing construction designed for a customer's ease.

She was a sorceress, half-naked before him, accessible as original sin, shimmering with heated invitation as cut velvet lures the eye to touch . . . an enchantress whose blue-eyed glance said, "You want me."

For the hundred-and-first time that day Hazard shut his mind to the tempting possibilities. "How was your bath?" he said very softly, his eyes focused on her supple, curving thigh.

She felt pretty and feminine in the sleek black silk, and alluring, the fragrance of the soap lingering on her warm skin. "Do you like the dress?" Blaze asked, ignoring his question, her voice low like his.

"Only a dead man wouldn't," he replied, his drawl velvety-smooth, his dark stare sliding upward in complimentary reassessment.

"It feels cool on the skin."

He didn't move. He felt his heart beating as if he'd run too many miles. "I can imagine."

"Did you notice the inventiveness of the design?" And she shook the skirt open another few inches.

"Of course," he said, his voice husky now. "My compliments to the designer. And," he added, "to the model. It may not be what you're accustomed to, but guaranteed, I assure you," he went on, his black eyes caressing, "to strike a ballroom speechless."

"Or a brothel reception room."

"Even that," he agreed quietly. "I wish," he gallantly continued in the mildest tone he possessed, "I could take advantage of the opportunity."

"I wish you would."

It always startled him momentarily—the candid impertinence. No artifice. No hypocrisy. White women generally practiced a fraudulent coyness, sanctimonious until the very last. "Not, I think," he said with a soft sigh, "as much as I do."

"Well, then?" She held out her hand with a delicacy that surprised and excited him.

All he had to do was reach out and touch the inviting hand, slide his fingers up her creamy arm, and slip the black taffeta off her smooth white shoulders. The dream was brief, however, and he came back to himself. "You don't understand, do you?"

Lowering her arm, she shook her head slowly and long shimmering hair, flame-red in the firelight, flowed over her bare shoulders.

"Your father will come for you."

"I know."

"And I don't want to be responsible for anything more than keeping my claim intact."

"Isn't it a little late for that?"

"Not," he said drily, "for me. In any case, there's no advantage to either of us." He stopped. "If you were an Absarokee woman"—he shrugged—"it would be different. But you're not. Our culture allows more freedom in these matters. Yours doesn't."

"I wish you'd stop intellectualizing this. My God,"

she exasperatedly declared, "you can't pretend you don't want me."

"I'm not that good an actor."

"Damn you, then," she said, rising suddenly. "I'm going to kiss you."

He laughed, but as the jet bugles brushed like glittering teardrops against her pale breasts when she walked, their shiny hardness intensifying the lush, trembling softness, a palpable heat enveloped him. She was very close, the stiff rustle of taffeta crackling like static in the fire-shadowed silence.

Reaching up, she touched the curve of his neck where it met his shoulder, softly brushed her finger over a wisp of black shiny hair caught in the supple arc of muscle and sinew. "I'm going to kiss you," she whispered this time.

He let her pull his face down so she could reach it, let her lips brush a threshold pulse of pleasure across his cheek, let her mouth almost reach his before he grasped the naked perfumed shoulders with fingers as pitiless as her seduction, bent his head down, and forced on her, with bruising and deliberate violence, an uncivilized savage kiss that changed at the end to a languid exercise in arousal.

She was shaken when he released her. Holding her at arm's length, for she was none too steady, his own face masked what hers revealed. It took him a moment to speak, but when he did his voice was near-normal. "You mustn't tease me, Boston," he observed, "or you'll get burned. I've been playing the game so much longer." Then, in spite of himself, Hazard grinned. "To think," he said with a chuckle, "I'm protecting *my* virtue. What idiocy. But sweet, spoiled darling," he murmured, his glance straight and true, "you can't have everything you want. I'm not available," he said, looking down into the beautiful pouting face, "for reasons that matter to me. And now," he went on, giving her a push in the direction of the bed, "I think I'll sleep outside tonight. Pleasant dreams." Picking up a buffalo robe, he walked away.

"Damn you, Jon Hazard Black," Blaze called after him, finding her voice at last as he strode through the door, the ebony taffeta only precariously containing breasts heaving high in resentful anger. "Damn you to hell!"

Get in line, he wryly thought, and set the latch in place.

Chapter 15

THE mosquitoes were fierce that night, hovering around him in small clouds, attacking in relentless hordes. He moved his bed twice before he found respite halfway up the mountain where a cool breeze kept the insects at bay.

Maybe he was being a fool about the woman, Hazard thought lying awake, the welcome breeze fresh on his skin. Old Man Coyote, the Almighty's irreverent helper, would have adjusted his sense of honor and duty in one capricious moment. But the Absarokee world view had been instilled in him as a child; the individual vision as a source of power represented a rationale uniquely Absarokee. Hazard's vision dreams had guided him always, a sharply defined cosmic and emotional stirring. And he felt an unease about the woman. He prayed that night for a sign. Maybe the woman was meant as a benevolent gift; maybe she didn't personify betrayal and greed. Maybe she was a gift from the mystical universe.

It was late when he woke, and unfortunately morning brought no clearer revelation to the turmoil in his mind. He hoped, with less emotional conviction than logic, that Colonel Braddock would appear soon.

Blaze was up and dressed in one of Hazard's cotton shirts when he came in for breakfast. "Did you sleep well?" she asked, cheerfully insincere.

"Not particularly." It was telling on him, the restless nights on the buffalo robes.

"Are you ready for breakfast?"

"Soon," he curtly replied, rummaging through his wardrobe for clean clothes. He abruptly turned around when her question finally registered. Had she actually made breakfast? She had, he saw. The table was set and something vaguely resembling biscuits reposed next to the charred bacon on the plate. He smiled, his sullen mood dissipating. She looked so damnably pleased with her efforts; she had even included a bottle of cognac in case he wanted a drink with his breakfast. Not a bad idea, given the condition of the food on his breakfast plate.

"Do you mind," she asked, seeing the smile on his previously somber face, "if I empty the tub outside?"

"No, of course not." And when he saw her struggle with the full pail of water she'd pulled from the tub, he added, "Let me help you." As it turned out, he emptied the tub himself while Blaze helped fill the buckets and thanked him prettily.

When he sat down for breakfast some minutes later, she said, "I'll be back posthaste," and before he'd tried the curiously shaped biscuits and black bacon, she reappeared. He was still contemplating whether his stomach was up to the punishment when she stepped over the threshold, an apology rushing before her. "I think I must have forgotten something in the biscuits. They're a bit hard and . . . well . . . I'm sorry about the bacon. I hope it didn't cost too much."

"I appreciate the effort, and don't worry about the money. If I didn't have a few thousand people to worry about, I'd be considered a relatively rich man, even by your standards."

"Oh," Blaze said, taken aback. Hazard's life hardly bespoke wealth, and she had never contemplated him in that light.

"Sit down," he suggested, waving her to a seat. "I wanted to apologize myself . . . about last night. It's nothing you . . . I have responsibilities."

Blaze sat down opposite him. "I know. Friends then?" she softly asked and put her small hand across the table.

"Friends," he replied, and prayed for restraint.

Blaze held his hand, warm and callused, and remembered where she'd felt it before. The memory brought a blush to her cheeks.

"Thanks for the breakfast," he politely said, looking for an excuse to drop her hand. The feel of her fingers curled under his brought his own reminiscing disastrously to the fore. "It was very nice of you." His voice was moderate, but his fingers when he unfolded them from her hand were trembling.

"Well, after the tub and dresses and everything," Blaze pleasantly said, determined to be as casual in her conversation as Hazard, "I thought I'd try." She glanced at the food on their plates. "It looks so easy when Jimmy does it," she ruefully conceded.

"I know," Hazard sympathized.

"You don't have to eat it." It was the first time he'd seen her contrite.

"And you don't have to wear the dresses," he gallantly rejoined.

She laughed and brightened, and he smiled that heart-stopping smile. A singing harmony, charitable and enchanting, passed between them.

Breakfast was revised to the usual boiled eggs, bread and butter, and milk, simple enough for them to manage.

"If Jimmy didn't come up we'd starve to death," Blaze admitted, her smile pure sunlight.

Hazard didn't tell her that, on raiding parties, they often subsisted on jerky and pemmican for weeks. He was familiar with rudimentary eating habits. "Perhaps a raise would be in order," he suggested with a grin, "to ensure our survival."

"By all means; I'll pay him too." When Hazard's brows rose in inquiry, she added, "If you'd accept my I.O.U. It might be a little touchy getting to my bank right now."

"Incredibly touchy, for me at least," he acceded, his eyes crinkling with laughter. "And you needn't pay."

"I've plenty of money."

"I'm sure you do."

"And think of the drudgery he's saving me."

"Speaking of drudgery," Hazard softly drawled. "And I hesitate to even bring up the subject. . . ."

What a change, Blaze pleasantly reflected, from a few days ago. "My jailer has mellowed," she couldn't resist teasing.

"Your demure acquiescence charmed me," Hazard mockingly replied.

She gave him a straight look under arched eyebrows. "You wouldn't like me if I was demure or acquiescent."

"I'd be willing to try," he offered.

"Fat chance," Blaze retorted, her eyes cloudless, her expression as cheerful as an admiral watching the last of the enemy ships sink from sight.

"How," he said with a theatrical sigh, "were you ever allowed to grow up so damnably willful?"

"How were you?" she countered.

"I don't suppose it would do any good to bring out the arguments relating to male and female roles in society?"

"Not a scrap." Another brilliant smile.

"I don't exactly know how to broach the subject then, but . . ." His tone was far too casual, and had she known him better she would have recognized the underlying irony.

"Yes?" She was feeling delightfully invincible, a not uncommon feeling for an extraordinarily beautiful daughter of a millionaire.

"My buckskins need washing." And inexplicably, he felt himself brace against her reply.

"Is that the drudgery you mentioned?" was all she said in a mild, unexcited way, having no idea whatsoever that washing buckskins entailed any more exertion than rinsing out a few soiled handkerchiefs.

He nodded and nominally relaxed.

"Can't you send them in to the servants or," she sweetly added, "to Mrs. Pernell?"

"They don't know how to handle them."

"Who usually does them then?"

"One of the women from my clan comes down occasionally."

Blaze could picture it: young, beautiful, acquiescent. The women probably drew straws or paid for the privilege of coming down and working for Hazard. Since she wasn't entirely naive about men nor naive about Hazard's reputation with women that preceded him lasciviously, nor, more important, naive about the man's incredible expertise at making love, her next question came to mind immediately. "How long do they stay?" she suspiciously inquired.

Her piqued curiosity gratified Hazard. "Overnight," he replied.

"Why did I bother asking?" Blaze's voice was arch with mock derision.

"I don't know," he interjected. "I've never professed to be monkish."

"Except with me."

"For numerous reasons—all logical."

"That," she said ironically, "is a matter of opinion."

"Would you care to learn how to wash buckskins?" he asked, trying to steer the conversation back to a topic which couldn't be argued into infinity.

"Do I have a choice?" she asked with sarcasm and a softly snide jeer.

"Certainly." He smiled and looked across the table at her with an open, guileless expression.

"But," she serenely murmured, feeling far from serene, "the choice entails an overnight guest—a female one."

"That's been the pattern." Hazard's smile widened.

Straightening, she placed her hands squarely on her hips, his oversized shirt riding up dangerously with the pose, drew in a large breath which did dangerous things to Hazard's libido, and said, "Ha!" The exclamation was accompanied by a glowering look.

"Does that mean you'd like to do it?" he replied, cheerfully ignoring the stern, unvarnished meaning of the exclamation, and striving as well to ignore the taut outline of her nipples temptingly visible through the worn fabric of his shirt.

"Only in contrast to listening to you make love to another woman five feet away from me, you mean?"

"Is that a yes?" Hazard wasn't about to respond to her last heated statement, not with his present thin line of control stretched to the limit.

"Damn you Hazard . . ."

He only waited, not daring to speak in the capricious, fitful mood enveloping him. Was he a fool to keep saying no? Would it really matter if he took what was so enticingly near and available? His eyes drifted over the precious jeweled beauty of a woman close enough to touch.

"Goddamn you . . . yes! Satisfied?"

"Very," he quickly said, relieved in ways he wouldn't care to admit.

"I won't have another woman in this cabin." It was the same imperious woman he'd seen so many times before. Whether in worsted trousers, pearled satin, or scavenged clothing, she was sure of herself.

"Fine," he said, the concession infinitely easy. The thought of another woman in the small cabin with Blaze was a disquieting notion. And for reasons he wasn't quite willing to face yet.

HAZARD showed Blaze what had to be done to the treated leather. Showed her how to soak the clothing in the clear water of the pool, how to scrub it with the mild yucca soap they traded from the Shoshones, then spread it on the grass, out of the sun. And within sight of the sluice box he worked all day, she scrubbed and washed and rinsed, seeing that Hazard's buckskins were clean, ensuring that Jon Hazard Black didn't have some other woman in his bed.

Jimmy didn't come up that day, and when Blaze remarked on it Hazard told her it wasn't unusual. He had other duties to attend to at home, and it wasn't out of the ordinary. Blaze thought otherwise but she was too tired to argue. Even too tired to bathe when Hazard offered to carry water up. And she told him so, half dozing in the chair by the fire. "Besides," she said, "I was in the water almost more than I was out, washing those damn clothes of yours."

"Thank you again. You did a beautiful job."

"I know, and I'll expect the usual payment," she sleepily replied, impertinent to the end. Hazard opened his mouth to reply and then closed it. She'd fallen asleep. He smiled at the sight of her curled up like a small child in the oversized chair. He realized she had worked very hard for him that day; he didn't realize, however, that it was the first time in her life that Blaze had worked for anyone at all.

Chapter 16

A HALF-HOUR later Hazard picked her up very gently, carried her to the bed, and tucked her in. He allowed himself a light kiss. "Thank you, *bia,*" he whispered, brushing her cheek with his lips. "You're a charming laundress."

In a dream Blaze heard the warm compliment and smiled.

Locking the cabin when he left, an hour later, Hazard was contemplating the shadowed back stairway of Confederate Gulch's most prosperous, elegant brothel. A silent perusal assured him the dark night held no secrets, and with soft footsteps he ascended the stairs to the second floor. Coming out into a red-carpeted hallway, the smell of waxed wood, cigar smoke and incense was distinguishably familiar. Without hesitation, he strode along the plush carpet, turned left down the corridor, and opened the second door on the right as if he were expected.

Although not exactly expected, Hazard had an open invitation and was welcomed, literally, with open arms. "Hazard, you sweetheart," the dark-haired beauty cried on seeing him. Rising from the plum velvet armchair, she glided over to him, arms outstretched, in a cloud of ruffled lace, expensive scent, and warm welcome. "It's been ages since I've seen you." She stood almost as tall as he in her satin slippers, and when they embraced, her splendid body fit meltingly into Hazard's as perfectly as matched bookends. She put her mouth up the scant difference in their height and waited for his kiss. It was warm, friendly, lingering, and inexplicably indifferent.

"You're looking marvelous," Hazard said, holding her half an arm's length away, his lazily appraising smile as perfect as she'd remembered.

Rose Condieu, gazing at the man she'd nursed back to health after his bloody mourning practices and reluctantly relinquished as bed partner when he'd staked his mining claim, dimpled engagingly and softly replied, "You look like hell," then added with barely concealed interest, "Is it that woman?"

"No," Hazard retorted, his smile widening. "You worry too much. I'm just working long hours."

"Getting any sleep?" Violet eyes the color of exotic orchids appraised him but could learn nothing except that he was more than a little drawn with fatigue.

"No problem," he lied smoothly.

"Everyone's talking about it, you know."

Hazard released his grip on her arms and, moving over to a chair near the heavily draped window, dropped into it. He leaned his head back and stretched out his legs before answering. "Didn't really think it would pass unnoticed," he observed, his low voice full of mockery.

"They say you're flaunting her as your trollop by keeping her."

He laughed derisively. "If I wished to flaunt her, I'd do it in a less private way. They knew what they were doing when they sent her up. It backfired and they're regrouping, that's all."

She clasped her ringed fingers and, walking over,

stood before him like an admonishing tutor. "You're up against some powerful people."

"But I've got the woman," he said, lifting his eyes to take in her face now that she was so close. "And I can bluff better." He appreciated her concern, but the warning was unnecessary. He knew, perhaps better than she, what he was up against.

"Did you know the Colonel's up mountain?"

Hazard shook his head slowly against the chair back, his thick black hair drifting over the rich mauve brocade, silk on silk.

"Looking for a spokesman in your tribe." She walked a step nearer, bringing the familiar rose perfume to his nostrils, and stood to one side of his chair, where the dark circles under his eyes were more pronounced in the shade of the table lamp.

"Good, he'll make an offer soon, then."

"You do look tired, Jon."

Hazard sighed, his fingers tightened, then relaxed and curled loosely over the rosewood chair arms. "I'm working like a coolie, Rose. Harder than I've ever worked in my life. And there's not a whole lot of time. How many *pioneers*"—the word was etched in sarcasm—"do you think have come into my country this month?" Bitter thought.

Rose lowered her eyes against the piercing cynicism. "Are you going to make it?" she quietly asked, for this new audacious act of his was more impetuously rash than she expected even of him.

"Rose, sweetheart," said Hazard, the thinnest edge to his lazy cadence, "I am proposing, if need be, to mortgage my soul down to its last iniquitous crumb in order to succeed . . . one way or another," he finished, his voice deceptively mild. Then suddenly he grinned like a young boy, and Rose caught a rare glimpse of the splendid youth before the disenchantment had come. "Godalmighty, Rose, let's not get morbid." He crossed his long legs leisurely, settling in, and said with relish, "Tell me the newest scandals in town. What prominent doctor, lawyer, or clergyman is frantically fucking whom? And what prominent doctor, lawyer, or clergyman's wife is piously fucking whom? I've missed the latest gossip the last weeks."

She stared at him, reminded afresh of his effrontery and his ability to amuse—nostalgically reminded. Rose smiled then and there was a new gentleness in her voice. "Feel like your usual? Then I'll give you a detailed account of who's rolling whom in the hay."

Hazard laughed easily. "Sounds wonderful."

When she left, he slid down on his spine in the cushioned chair, sooty lashes drifting downward to rest on swarthy cheekbones. Bone-weary, he could have slept a week.

Five minutes later she brought back her own private blend of black tea with sugar and fresh cream. Hearing her return, Hazard scrubbed a hand across his eyes, straightened in the chair, and accepted the delicately painted china cup. "Thanks, Rose," he said with a tiredness he couldn't conceal. "Do you know how long it's been since I've had fresh cream?"

Rose knew exactly how long it had been, but she remained silent. Although their liaison had been glorious, Hazard had always kept his feelings to himself.

"If I thought the woman could take care of a cow," he went on, "I'd buy one and bring it up there."

"Won't she work?" Rose asked. She would have gladly done any kind of work for Hazard, although she hadn't done any work for years now. But she held her tongue, having learned the hard way to guard herself against the profound error of naiveté. Hazard Black had never encouraged regular female company.

He drank some tea before he replied, "She's not used to doing much. Too many minions in her background," he observed, amused long-lashed eyes meeting Rose's over their teacups. "Unlike yours and mine." Hazard was being gracious. He had, in fact, been raised as a chief's son in a prosperous clan and never had to do anything for himself he didn't care to do. Putting his cup out for more tea, the china incongruously dainty in his large palm, he said, "I think I'm going to need better food up there. Miner's fare might keep me going but . . ." He shrugged a little.

"Getting soft on her, Hazard?" Rose quietly asked, pouring the amber liquid into his cup.

His calm face gave nothing away. It never did. Settling back, he slowly stirred sugar in. "I don't have time to get soft on a woman. She's insurance, nothing more."

Rose's eyebrows lifted provocatively and, without removing her fine eyes from Hazard, she murmured, "Nice insurance."

He ignored the unstated implication. "I wish she could cook. Jimmy's been coming up but his mother might put some restrictions on his visits, it seems."

"So Molly Pernell's jealous under all that sanctimonious religion," Rose acutely observed.

"With," Hazard murmured, "no good reason."

"You might be able to convince Molly of that, Hazard, if you talked real smooth, but don't waste the effort on me. I haven't a sanctimonious bone in my body."

Not inclined to get into any arguments about his sexual habits, Hazard instead asked Rose one of the favors he'd come down to ask. "With the cooking problem and need for better food, I was wondering if you'd do me a favor?"

Rose nodded her agreement.

"Could you shop for a few extra things for me here in Confederate Gulch and send them to Jimmy? He'll bring them up with the supplies from Diamond City. I'd like some fresh fruit and vegetables. Better bread. I saw peaches and grapes in Haroldson's window. Things like that. And strawberries, if you can find any."

"You're treating her well, Hazard."

He smiled enigmatically. "Only survival, Rose. I don't think she can burn peaches or grapes." He grimaced faintly, remembering breakfast. "But we'll see. So far she's got a perfect record. Oh, and another thing . . ."

"A better grade of champagne for the lady?" Rose inquired with a teasing grin.

His crooked smile was as casual as his voice. Elusive, he wasn't about to be baited tonight. "No, more practical," he blandly answered, setting his empty cup down.

"She needs clothes. I had Jimmy bring up two dresses, but they were a shade out of place in a miner's cabin."

"From Klein's?"

Hazard leaned his dark head back against the glossy silk and lifted his brows. "Unfortunately."

Rose stifled a gurgle at first and then threw her splendid chin up and laughed uproariously. Catching her breath a few seconds later, she inquired, "And Molly saw them?"

Another quick arch of his black winged brows. "So I'm told."

"That monumental gaffe may have taken you off her list of eligible men to marry," she teased, her grin still gloriously wide.

The pantherish black eyes widened for a moment and then settled into their slightly cynical slant. "Good. Since I have no intention of marrying anyone."

"That's what all men say until some sweet woman sweeps them off their feet. The Boston miss was untarnished goods, the story goes."

"Good God," said Hazard sharply, "are the details of her lingerie public knowledge as well?"

Rose's violet eyes slanted half shut, undiscouraged by Hazard's mild outburst. "Are you going to marry her?"

Two cool, friendly eyes met hers and glimmered for a moment with mocking levity. "Not me, Rose," Hazard pleasantly replied, "guaranteed." His voice continued lightly, as if she hadn't asked the burning question on everyone's mind in Confederate Gulch and Diamond City, "About the dresses now. Something sensible. I don't know fabrics, but whatever's practical. It's not the Taj Mahal up there. Or," he added, his mouth lifting into a small smile, "your reception room downstairs."

Rose could see there was no point in pursuing her inquiry. "How did the Colonel's fine daughter respond to the unorthodox dresses from Klein's? Was the Boston society darling affronted?"

Chivalry restrained Hazard from the truth. He noncommittally murmured, "She's not unduly refined," while he recalled all too vividly the image of Blaze in the firelight, all creamy flesh and provocation, the black taffeta gown revealing more than it concealed.

"Size?" She'd asked twice already and her eyes watching Hazard had taken on a searching quality.

"I'm not sure," he replied, finally realizing she was talking to him. "About Kate's size, I think. A shade taller, maybe. I'm sorry it's so vague, but, well . . ." His voice trailed off in an unusually indecisive manner for a nomally decisive man. Then his dark glance was suddenly direct and familiar again. "Can I count on you? Take out enough gold to cover your time, too, of course." Untying a heavy bag of gold dust from his belt, he placed it on the lace-covered table.

Rose gazed across the small tea table at the most beautiful man she'd ever known, resting calmly in her chair, one hand relaxed on his knee, dressed tonight in white man's clothes: black trousers, boots, long-sleeved shirt. Except for his hair, resting lightly on his shoulders, he bore no trace of his background. And even the long hair wasn't that remarkable on the frontier. Although he had a reputation as a killer and his earlier life as a youthful warrior had been one of continual raiding, his eyes, somehow, never seemed like the eyes of a man capable of killing. They didn't fit with the twin colts belted low on his hips. They were too gentle. Those heavy-browed eyes, their blackness containing a curious warmth, were trained on her attentively, waiting for her answer.

"Sure, you goddamn fool. You know I'd do anything for you."

The handsome face, all classic bone structure and perfect planes for which the Absarokee were justly famous, broke into a smile. "Thanks." Uncurling his lean form from its comfortable sprawl, he stood in one elegant motion. "Whatever you decide on those dresses will be fine. Four, five, six, something like that."

Did he plan on a long internment, Rose wondered, or did the Colonel's daughter change for dinner each evening?

"Oh, and chocolates, too."

Rose's eyebrows touched her hairline.

Hazard gave a brief shrug. "I like chocolates," he said, with a half-smile.

"Sure, Hazard, sure." Rose's large eyes looked him over slowly. "Couldn't talk you into staying awhile?"

Their eyes held for a moment and she saw it before he quickly repressed the emotion. "Mind if I beg off this time? I don't trust her alone up there very long. God only knows what trouble she can get into."

Rose smiled softly. "Whatever you say. I'm always here, though. Don't forget. And good luck with your insurance."

He nodded. "I'll probably need it." Moving to the door, he paused, one hand on the elaborate brass handle. "Some decent soap, too, would you, Rose?" he added. "Maybe Guerlain, if you can find it."

"Guerlain? Not for you, I presume."

He shifted slightly, his handmade boots catching the light of the oil lamps, and in the same low, quiet voice that offered only minimal explanation said, "No. She's not used to bathing in icy creeks like I am."

"Are you hauling water for her, Hazard? I never thought I'd see the day." The full extent of her shock was not betrayed by the lilting cadence of her cheerful tone.

"Self-defense, dear Rose. She wouldn't bathe every day otherwise."

"You damn Crows . . . cleanest Indians I've ever seen. Cleanest men I've ever seen, come to think of it."

"It's easy to be clean, Rose, when you're raised in country with clear running water. I'm trying to teach Miss Braddock that."

"Lots of luck, Hazard, with the millionaire's daughter."

"Thanks. I'll need it. She's harder to handle than a wild pony."

"I don't doubt," Rose murmured, "you'll manage."

"Ak-baba-dia-ba-ala-go-da-ja," he said. "God willing."

Rose leaned back against the velvet chaise after he left and pensively stroked her silken thigh. Hazard's conversation tonight had been a classic in the art of unclarity. With a shadow of envy, she perceptively concluded, Jon Hazard Black was in deeper than he realized.

HAZARD let himself into the cabin without a sound. Unhurriedly, he unbuckled his gun holster, and hung it carefully on its peg near the door. He was unbuttoning his shirt when Blaze, sweetly snide, purred, "Was she good?"

He turned at the sound of her voice, his eyes searching the shadows of the room. She wasn't in her bed. She was, he saw, after his glance moved laterally from her bed, in his; seated Indian fashion in the middle of the stacked buffalo robes. The shirt she was wearing was open enough to show a glimpse of one white breast, while her bare legs, crossed as they were, invited his eyes to the apex of her thighs. He placidly went back to unbuttoning his shirt, currently in a more benign mood than his hostile cabin-mate. Rose's company had calmed him, bringing the world into a manageable perspective. Although she wouldn't appreciate it if he told her, he often felt with her as he had with his mother—tranquil and renewed for the world's next onslaught.

"You smell like a whorehouse," Blaze resentfully remarked, the heavy floral fragrance of Rose's perfume pervading the small cabin.

"Actually," Hazard commented, undoing the cuff buttons of his shirt, "Rose's scent is too expensive for ordinary whores. It's quite popular with the society ladies out East, though." The allusion was deliberate.

Then the fragrance struck a memory cord in Blaze's mind. Many of her mother's friends had favored it. Blaze, considered too young for such heavy perfume, had never used it. "That answers one question at least. She must not be ordinary." Her lips were pursed, her expression sullen.

Hazard looked at her for a second. "Jealous?" He laid his shirt on a chair.

"Of course not," she snapped.

"Then it doesn't matter, does it?" He sat down to take off his boots.

"Isn't one woman at a time enough for you?" Her tone was feline and tantrumish.

He glanced up from tugging off one boot, his hand still grasping the smooth polished heel. "But I don't have one, do I?" he replied, amicable in an astringent way.

"Damn you, were you in bed with another woman?" Blaze wasn't interested in deductive reasoning at the moment. The attar of roses was so cloying, she knew he hadn't kept his distance from the woman, whoever she was, wherever she was.

"I don't answer to you," Hazard said, standing, his fingers moving to the buttons on the waistband of his trousers.

"I want to know!"

"So?"

"Jon Hazard Black!"

He ran an impatient hand through his hair and sighed. "Oh, hell, no, if you must know, and don't ask me why, damned if I know." It was, in fact, the first time in his life he'd turned Rose down. Sliding the black riding pants over his slim hips, he pulled them off and tossed them on top of his shirt. Raised in a culture where the male body was frequently unclothed, he walked over to the buffalo robes and stood above her, beautifully nude and perfectly at ease. "You're in my bed," he said quietly, willing his body not to betray him.

"And if I stay?" Blaze whispered.

His dark gaze, unwavering, surveyed her. "Can't."

"I want to."

"I'm too tired," he replied, his voice and manner formal, "to begin all that again. Leave or I'll move you."

She didn't.

When he picked her up, she slipped her arms around his neck, laying her head into the curve of his shoulder. She felt his arms tense. Seconds later she was dropped into her bed. "Sleep well," he said.

And she knew she would, because despite his long absence, despite the assault of pungent perfume, despite his not wanting to admit it, Hazard had *not* had a woman while he was gone.

Chapter 17

JIMMY didn't arrive the next day either, and Blaze only said "I told you so" two times. Both of which Hazard ignored. "Molly must be really angry with you," she mentioned, her voice dulcet with satisfaction. "Do you suppose I'm going to have to learn how to starch and iron shirts now?"

He was getting ready to leave for the mine and, looking up from pulling on his last boot, cast her what he hoped was a withering glance, but it fell on such cheerful confidence, it didn't stand a chance.

"I dare say," Blaze remarked to Hazard's stiff back as he reached for his rifle, "when I get back to Boston, I'll be able to oversee all the domestics with new efficiency."

If this was her idea of efficiency, Hazard thought ruefully, Boston was in for a surprise.

"I think I'll try muffins for lunch," she continued with the same aggravating sunniness.

Dark eyes widened skeptically. "Have mercy, Molly. Send up Jimmy," Hazard muttered, strapping on his holster.

"Pardon?"

He turned abruptly, inclined to bite her head off. Breakfast had been spare, lunch promised to be another experiment, and it was raining out. He was going to be wet all day, and the sight of her, hardly clothed in another of his oversized shirts, made him want to tumble her right where she stood. No preliminaries, no foreplay, no charming words. Only consummation. He'd never attempted the celibate life before, and he couldn't recommend it. He'd already cursed himself for a fool for turning Rose down. Maybe tonight he'd go back to town. It didn't take so long to get there. And a few hours in bed with Rose would mitigate this unnerving desire he had for the unbearably cheerful female facing him across his cabin. Damn, she was inviting. The sight of her, all tumbled hair and long bare legs, allayed the annoyance. You couldn't fault her for trying. So he said, instead, "Sounds good. Don't burn yourself." He *knew* the muffins would be burned.

"See you at noon, then."

"Right." He opened the door.

"My Lord, you're going to get wet today." It was said with the same boundless buoyancy.

He glared at her and left.

BLAZE tried, she really did, but for the life of her she couldn't remember if it was two spoons of baking powder or two of salt or one of salt and three of sugar. And the eggs . . . she had absolutely no idea how many eggs Jimmy had put in. Or were there eggs at all in the recipe? Helping someone cook was not precisely like doing it yourself. Hell and damnation, she softly swore. If only she had a cookbook.

It struck her so suddenly, she had to sit down. Seated at the rough table, the unplaned floor boards cool beneath her bare feet, her hands clasped very still on the smooth sanded top, she realized with a fluttering exhilaration that she actually wanted to learn to cook for him.

She *wanted* to please him, wanted to give to him, wanted his approval. All novel concerns in a life previously revolving around taking. She had over the past days neatly compartmentalized her feelings toward Hazard. They were sensual, she'd told herself, carnal, lustful. The normal reaction of a female to Jon Hazard Black. Nothing unusual. Really quite expected. He had, after all, a well-deserved reputation for pleasing women.

But then, she'd also been exposed to the complex qualities of Hazard apart from his legendary prowess. He was a mercurial man, wholly unpredictable, but warm and spaciously kind, impudent in his humor, infinitely clever, and imbued with a fidelity and courage she hadn't imagined possible in a single man.

And the need for a cookbook was the staggering instrument of her revelation—awesome in its unornamented simplicity. She cared about him, cared what he thought of her, cared that she couldn't cook or clean or do whatever women did for the men they loved. It took her some length of time, sitting there in the silent, small cabin, to fully realize how her life had changed. Without plan or arrangement and so removed from artifice and stratagem, any self-respecting novice debutante would deplore the ineptitude. But it had happened.

She didn't just want him in the physical sense, she wanted *him.* She loved him. An Indian chief from a strangely named mountain tribe. Was it possible? She hardly knew him. And with his curious reticence, would she ever know him? But the emotion sang through her senses—*I love him!* She said it aloud. "I love him." And then it occurred to her, the dark and ominous reverse side of that marvelous, wonderful declaration. Suppose —and with the events of the last few days vividly fresh in her mind, it was a distinct possibility—suppose he didn't want her.

As if by instinct, her back straightened, seated on the hard wooden chair in the isolated mountain cabin two thousand miles from Boston. Every nerve, every brain cell, every pulsing vein was put on alert. She hadn't acquired her undaunted spirit by accepting failure. She was her father's daughter, after all. "When it happens, Blaze honey, you'll know," her daddy'd said. And now that it had, miraculously, incredibly, with the same tenacity and determination with which she approached everything else, she intended to see her love returned.

Suddenly all the female gossip over the years, the secrets shared and confidences whispered, the undercurrent of feminine mystique—divulged over tea, murmured behind fluttering fans, archly pronounced by married friends, happy even *after* the honeymoon—was conscientiously recalled. And while the muffin dough lapsed into an irremediable amalgam, Blaze sifted and examined all the lessons learned about feminine wiles, scrutinizing all —however bizarre—with an empiricism that would have gratified the most pedagogical scholar. Then, discarding those she considered unsuitable, she began to set an inventive plan in motion, neatly artistic, subtly imaginative, sure, she felt, with her unerring confidence and Hazard's proven appetites, to produce results.

She was smiling when she took up the spoon to finish stirring the muffin batter. "Oh, dear," she breathed, her smile momentarily suspended. The dough was as solid as the wet earth outdoors. "Well, never mind," she murmured into the morning stillness, her smile reappearing. Muffins weren't his favorite anyway, she decided, placing the bowl in an out-of-the-way corner behind the wood box. He really liked those buttermilk biscuits. Now, was it one tablespoon vinegar to a cup of milk or one tablespoon milk to a cup of vinegar? From now on, true love dictated. She would certainly write the recipe down the next time Jimmy appeared, assuming Molly Pernell's moral ethics and jealousy allowed.

Anyway, she thought, settling on fried potatoes in lieu of recipeless buttermilk biscuits, one had to be magnanimous with one's rivals. Understanding and compassion were Christian virtues, after all, and if Molly Pernell found them elusive, she, the scent of victory already rich and strong, could be forgiving. With or without Jimmy, she'd learn to cook. Ah . . . and after tonight . . . Her mind drifted pleasurably astray.

HAZARD came back at noon, wet to the skin, greeted Blaze politely as he might a sister or an aunt, and sat down to his meal. Luckily, he thought, looking at his plate, he could eat raw meat—well, partially raw meat, the outside being meticulously charred. The fried potatoes were a venturesome attempt, and he complimented her on her effort. Unfortunately, they too were the same uniform black, without the saving grace raw meat possessed in flavor. He could not eat raw potatoes.

"The stove cooks everything so rapidly," Blaze explained, as if it had a life and spirit of its own.

"An unfortunate circumstance," Hazard agreed, unwilling to point out that the stove wasn't the cook.

"I'm truly sorry." She looked winsomely sincere.

"It's fine," he said, attacking his barely cooked meat. "Really."

"Are you sure?" she asked, all humility and innocence.

"I'm sure."

"You look so uncomfortably wet."

"The fire feels good." What the stove's roaring fire lacked in cooking qualities, it compensated for in heating potential. The heated cabin was a pleasant refuge from the steady, driving rain outside. Hazard's thoroughly soaked clothes were beginning to dry slightly against his skin.

"Do you think you should change?"

"Won't do any good. I'll be wet again in five minutes."

"Do you have to work when it's raining so hard?"

He looked at her for a moment, debating. He was driven—not by elusive Lady Fortune, like most of the miners, but by circumstances that didn't allow time off for adverse weather. How to explain all those ramifications to a society miss from the East. "Once you're wet, it doesn't matter," he answered, avoiding the more byzantine reasons for working seven days a week.

"If you wouldn't mind then—I mean—as long as

you're wet already—could you bring in some water for the tub when you come in for supper?" It was a simple request, guileless as her innocent expression.

"Of course," he agreed, unaware of the ulterior motives behind the prosaic request.

Chapter 18

HAZARD worked late that evening, striding in soaked and unusually reserved, carrying the first two pails of water. He filled the boiler, placed the extra pails by the tub, then quietly helped with supper, impelled by a gnawing hunger that required some edible food at least once every twenty-four hours. Although plain, the food was nourishing, and after supper he lay comfortably full and relaxed on his soft bed near the door.

Blaze refused his help with the dishes, and after the extra hours of work that day, he didn't raise any argument. She sang softly to herself while she worked, illuminated by the warm golden glow from the fireplace, and if Hazard hadn't been so dissociated from the concept by disuse, he would have recognized contentment.

After the dishes were washed, dried, and put away, Blaze pulled the copper tub in front of the fireplace and carefully began emptying the boiler on the stove, a pitcher at a time, into it. "You must have done some blasting today," she remarked, her tone chastely conversational. "Your clothes were dirtier than usual." Turning away from the stove, she smiled before carrying the large pitcher over to the tub.

Hazard made no move to help her. But as she walked by him, her slender bare legs close enough to touch, he drew in a long, deep breath and exhaled before replying, "Opened up a third drift." With his eyes following her long-legged stride, his tone was more casual than his thoughts.

Lamplight contoured her exquisite face, flushed from her exertions. "Will Rising Wolf be back soon? Or is it too early?"

"I'm not sure." Hazard's voice was suddenly gruff. She'd half turned to speak to him and firelight silhouetted the voluptuous roundness of her breasts through the coarse weave of his work shirt.

"I'm sorry. I didn't mean to pry," Blaze apologized, misreading the reason for his gruffness.

"It's all right." The words came out more curt than he intended, but he'd just seen her full breasts quiver gently when she twisted to face him.

"Have I offended you? I know it's none of my business about your gold and . . ." Her voice drifted away delicately, her apology offered with a fresh naiveté that reminded him suddenly that she'd been a virgin until four days ago. He could feel the rush of pleasure at the bewitching memory, could feel his arousal begin. Damn, he should get out of here, go outside while she bathed. Sleep outside. But the rain still drumming steadily on the roof was a deterrent. Damned if he was going to be wet all night as well as all day, he told himself.

"No need to apologize. Rising Wolf's schedule is unscheduled for the most part. I never know for certain when he's coming." Hazard was answering automatically, but the conversation wasn't holding his attention. He was staring at the shirt hem drifting about her thighs, only inches from a sweetness he recalled so graphically he felt his pulse rate accelerate.

"Oh," Blaze quietly responded, still facing him across a dozen feet of softly illuminated cabin, "I see."

And she tossed her head to displace an errant wave of hair that had fallen across her forehead.

It struck him then, the artful toss. And instantly, he was reminded of scores of willful females in his past. An inherent suspicion was born on that slow, sensuous sweep of auburn hair moving like silk in a breeze. Was he being manipulated by this young woman only recently introduced to lovemaking? Was the fresh innocence, the green-grass naiveté, as ingenuous as it appeared? Could she, with either a boundless arrogance or guileless ignorance, be seducing him?

Headstrong in his own way, as nervy as the impudent Miss Braddock, he waited, his mind quickening in anticipation, to see if she was brazen tonight or only innocuously determined to bathe.

She took her time filling the embossed tub, walking luxuriously back and forth across the golden light, apparently immune to the dark, mercurial eyes watching her with interest.

Her soft breasts moved under the light shirt when she walked, like ripe fruit in a summer breeze. The pale sheen of her legs, exposed to the shirttails falling to midthigh, were bronzed by the firelight, emphasizing the heated memory they evoked in Hazard's mind. Smooth, he remembered, and strong.

Blaze could feel his eyes on her, cool and assessing. But he hadn't gotten up and left. It could be the rain outside keeping him in. Or could it be need and passion? The longer he stayed, the longer he watched her, however controlled those penetrating black eyes, the surer she became.

And the surer he became, that no artlessness was displayed here. Rather the opposite. How far would she go? he wondered.

How far would she have to go, she wondered in turn, to move the apparently immovable man on his solitary bed? What would it take to readjust the principles he lived by—the arbitrary restrictions he'd placed on their relationship? "Forgive me for keeping you up," Blaze said, pouring in the last pitcher of cool water. Her azure eyes, when she lifted them slowly from her task, were not sorry at all.

"You're not keeping me up," Hazard said, his dissemblance as ready as hers.

She smiled then, invitation in the gentle curve of her mouth. "In that case, I shouldn't feel obliged to rush?"

"Don't on my account," he replied coolly, only the incandescent spark in his eyes belying the tranquil words.

"So kind," Blaze murmured, as if she were casually responding to a polite compliment at a garden party. As carefully as an artist adjusting his model to best catch the light, Blaze disposed herself to Hazard's gaze. She knew how the warm fire cast its glow, she knew how it gleamed, illuminated her form, glistened off her skin. She knew how long Hazard had been without a woman, and she knew from gossip in Virginia City that he was not inclined to celibacy.

Taking a hairpin from the table—one of three she'd worn in her hair the day she climbed the mountain to Hazard's claim—she swept up her bright hair lying on her shoulders, stood arms upraised, pinning the mass of hair atop her head. Her cool white neck was exposed in profile, her breasts, drawn up with the motion, stood upthrust, their nipples outlined through Hazard's shirt. And her pale legs were invitation with the elevation of her arms, up to the gentle curve of her bottom.

Hazard felt the terrible kindling of lust, felt his growing erection stretching the soft elkskin pants he wore, but he couldn't take his eyes off her. "A regular little Jezebel," he murmured drily. "Very lovely, but patently transparent."

"I don't know what you're talking about," Blaze replied to the man sprawled on the fur robes, his hands clasped behind his head. If she'd been able to see, she would have been gratified to observe his knuckles white with tension under the silky black hair.

"You know damned well what I'm talking about," he growled softly, and moved slightly to adjust the growing pressure against the pliant leather.

Blaze's clear blue eyes, innocent as spring skies, drifted over his supine form with angelic purity. "I simply hadn't time for my bath earlier in the day," she softly said, slowly unbuttoning the shirt, "with all the domestic details you insist on." She smiled a virtuous smile, unfastened the last button and dropped the cotton shirt to the floor. She wore nothing now, firelight rimming her. Her flesh breathed sweetness and wanting, and her high, rounded breasts trembled as if they felt his touch already. There was a smile on her lips, mysterious, proud, submissive, timid—but above all waiting. Infinitely soft and waiting.

Hazard unobtrusively sucked in his breath. "Very amusing," he said as casually as possible given the sudden quickening of his body. "Amusing, but useless."

"What a suspicious man." And so saying, Blaze partially turned and slowly bent over to test the temperature of the water in the large copper tub.

The alluring position, the satiny swell of her bottom, the languid curve of hip, thigh, slender leg, the deliberate exposure and teasing sight of all he so desperately desired, forced a deeply drawn breath from Hazard like that of a drowning man. I must not, he thought. I must not. But the sight of her recalled the last time he'd held that warm body beneath his and felt her close around him. For the space of five tautly silent seconds, he lay rigid, taking in the enticing female flesh, the provocative invitation so willingly offered and then, on a sudden expulsion of the suffocatingly held breath, he tossed aside the pillow under his head and came to his feet like a hawk rising, his lean, hard body borne on wings of fire.

He was across the small distance in two strides, pulled her upright, spun her round, and pinned her against the rough softness of the unplaned wooden wall with such force he felt her flinch. His body pressed with savage fierceness against the full length of her, forced itself against breast, hip, thigh, and Blaze, with a racing heart, felt the hardened arousal, strong and flagrant, burning to have her. "Damn you," he huskily whispered, his hands gripping her convulsively, his body straining into hers, "the pretty Bostonian bitch is in heat and the scent was irresistible, as you well knew. I hope your hot little body knows what it's taken on."

In mute answer, her small hands came up to cling to his firm muscled shoulders, her eyes reflecting the intensity in his. He silently cursed himself one last time before he capitulated and his hungry mouth took hers. It was a brutal kiss, impelled by his lust, frustration, betrayed sense of honor. He thrust at her with all the violence of detestable longing, of wanting things forbidden. She had won, and he despised himself for wanting her, for one brief second more before reason fled. He could not wait —only hot-blooded, ungovernable feeling mattered now.

He tore at his leggings, his mouth feverishly eating hers, hers opening under his, a sense of being swept away by a flood coursing wildly through him. With a frantic brutality, he savagely bruised her mouth, devoured her, struggling to free himself from the impeding elkskins. He pulled away, for two seconds, no more, and his erection was free. He took her quickly, standing, unable to wait the few moments it would have required to carry her to the bed or lower her to the floor. And she welcomed him with wildness and warmth, her arms flung around him as if she would bind him to her with a matching fierceness.

The top of his head felt as if it were lifting away. His surging need was released at once, flooding spasms deep inside her, and she met him with a violence that shocked them both. He covered her cheeks, her eyes with kisses. *"De awa-gee-shick, de awa-gee-shick,"* he whispered, his breath in fast, deep pants warm against her cheek, paradise flowing over him like corporeal enchantment. Her fingers slid into his hair and she lightly held the strong head as it moved over her face. And she felt on fire, glowing with a restless cataclysmic exaltation that only this dark-haired glorious man could quench.

In a few moments he was still, his face buried in her neck, their hearts thudding like jungle drums. Mere seconds had passed since he'd left the buffalo robes. Lifting his head, still breathing hard, he apologized in an abbreviated murmur, then carried her to the bed of buffalo robes, where he spent the next hour pleasing her leisurely in all the ways he knew so well.

He teased her after the second time, taking her to the brink and playfully stopping. Then one time she went on without him and after, she laughed, a warm, bubbling merriment. "I don't need you," she said, her grin wicked.

"That's the joy of it," he murmured, his hair brushing her cheeks, ". . . the discovery. It can be new each time." And with each woman, he reflected. And smiled in return at her beaming face.

"I want more."

"You"—Hazard kissed her—"always do."

"And more and more."

"Greedy child." He kissed her again. "Enjoying the banquet of life?"

"Ummmmmm." She sighed and reached up, pulling him closer.

Her arms were strong. It always amazed him. "Is that," Hazard asked, amusement rich in his voice, "a yes?"

She began kissing him, lightly, softly, trailing kisses down his face. She kissed his smiling mouth, his amused eyes, the curving line of his hard jaw. And he kissed her back, tasting the sweetness of her mouth and cheek and downy brows. Then she pushed him on his back in a quick, solid shove and began moving downward with her warm mouth and tongue. At waist level he touched her head. "You don't have to," he quietly said, uncertain of her motives.

Partially turning her face, her eyes came up and met his, eyes hot, steamy, and alive with passion. Her soft pink tongue trailed slowly over his taut stomach, then stopped. "But I want to," she murmured. And her head moved down.

He lifted his hand to pull her up but then her tongue delicately touched him there and his hand dropped away. With a swift intake of breath his belly contracted with the caressing upward stroke of her warm mouth and in seconds he was rigid with an intensity that almost hurt.

"Do you like that?" she asked some moments later, her tongue giving an affectionate lick. She looked up at him, past his swollen maleness rising proudly fierce, up past the horizontal plane of his stomach and chest.

His eyes opened at the sound of her voice and he forced himself back from the ragged edges of ecstasy. His dark lashes swept upward with infinite languor and he looked down at the soft-voiced woman lying between his legs. "Ummmm," he softly exhaled, several trembling horizons beyond conversation.

Her tongue came out again and touched his velvet smoothness, jarring his burning nerve endings. He gasped. "Is that," she said, a smile curving her full mouth, "a yes?" Her tongue lazily traveled up the pulsing veins to the massive crest. And drawing in a deep breath, he nodded.

She smiled again and slowly drew it into her mouth, and the focus of his body was under her warm lips. He tensed and his hands went to her shoulders, then slid up to cup her head.

Blaze was enjoying the sense of power her touching him revealed, enjoying the pleasure she gave him, enjoying his surrender to her. His fingers tightened in her hair and she sensed his tremble before it began.

Suddenly she was lifted up and found herself on her back, Hazard's need for her an instinctive driving force. He wanted to be inside her; he wanted to see her face when he climaxed; he wanted to see her face when she wrapped herself around him. It mattered suddenly that he touch her as well as she touch him, and he crushed her fiercely to him, sliding inside as if it were home. A primordial possessiveness overcame him, primitive yet complex. He'd never felt that way before, and if it were called to his attention, he wouldn't have welcomed the observation.

She responded to him with the same astonishing fire that struck him afresh each time, arching up hungrily to feel him deep inside, holding him with trembling fingers, low, at the base of his spine, so she could keep him a second longer with each downthrust. Bodies locked in melting delirium, the world was theirs, the universe within.

No wine or roses or gifts of precious jewels, no aphrodisiacs or passionate poetry, no coy preambles or elegant repartee. Only feeling. A naked, blind spark between two diametrically different people inciting a frightening longing as intense, as mutual as their joined bodies. It had happened to them both, without warning, a wild, rushing torrent sweeping everything aside in a spare, firelit cabin on a pine-covered mountain range three thousand feet above sea level.

The lovers were approaching the stratosphere and climbing. *"De awa-gee-shick,"* he whispered again into the tumbled curls behind her ear, *"de awa-gee-shick."*

"Now, Jon. Now." And she cried at the end, a soft, expiring whimper of loving release.

THEY lay very warm, very sated, on the buffalo robes, bright gilded by the fire. Sprawled on his back, Hazard held Blaze in a loose embrace as she lay half draped across his chest.

"De awa . . . de awa gee," she stumbled, mispronouncing the words, her breath little ripples across his skin. "What does it mean?"

His eyes widened in surprise. Although it was half formed, he recognized the phrase "I love you." He didn't remember saying it. He shrugged, a small casual shrug. "Love words, that's all. Endearments."

Blaze hadn't been able to see his eyes. She only saw and felt the shrug. "I know, but what kind of love words?" Her finger trailed over the ridges of his ribs.

"The kind women like to hear," he said, evasive to her persistence.

"Translate it for me." And this time she propped her chin on his chest and looked at him with that directness of hers that always reminded him of a curious ten-year-old child.

He touched her straight perfect nose with a fingertip. *"Bia-cara,"* he said, smiling, "it's one of those inverted colloquialisms that loses in the translating."

"Does *bia-cara* lose as well?" she asked, a tiny peppery spark appearing in her large blue eyes.

"No," he replied, feeling himself back on safe ground. "That, puss," and his fingertips slipped across the fullness of her lower lip, "means 'sweetheart.' And you are, *chad-gada-hish-ash*, my little red fox, the sweetest of sweethearts." He lifted his head from the pillow and kissed the curls near her forehead. "Do you think," he went on, shifting his position so he was resting back on both elbows, looking down at her, "we should make use of that tub?" It would be, he thought, an alternative to her questions, which he didn't care to answer. "I'm hot and sticky and you're hot and . . ." His foot came up and stroked the soft curve of her arch. "Should we?"

"Uh-uh, I'm too lazy," Blaze replied, her head still on his chest. "And besides"—she sighed, feeling the hard muscles of his torso under her cheek—"the water's probably cold by now."

Lifting her away as easily as if she were a kitten, he placed her beside him on the tumbled furs. "I'll warm the water, *bia-cara,* and carry you over to the tub." He was looking down at her now, his black eyes soft as velvet. "That shouldn't be too strenuous."

"In that case . . ." Blaze smiled a slow, lingering smile. She wasn't being refractory or imperious in her initial refusal. Far from it. She was only blissfully sated— a new and wonderful sensation she didn't want to lose. She was content. No, too mild a word, she decided. It should have shiny ornaments hung around it and golden garlands and fireworks for emphasis and then it would be the contentment she was feeling.

Kissing her lightly, Hazard left the bed, her eyes following him, absorbing his naked beauty, noting the fluid perfection of his lean, wide-shouldered body. Her gaze traveling slowly down his muscled back was startled to see the bloodied scratches her nails must have left. His voice refocused her glance as, facing her now, he said, "You make me very happy, *bia-cara,* even"—he paused, his smile turning into a wicked grin—"if you're the laziest woman I know."

She threw a pillow at him, which he deftly sidestepped, her smile as wicked as his. "I'm not either," she remonstrated. "I've just spent an hour entertaining you, and before that I cooked your supper—"

He groaned. "Don't remind me, I'd forgotten about supper. I don't suppose you'd want me to bring one of my clanswomen down to cook."

Her eyes narrowed. "You suppose right."

He laughed, charmed by her jealousy. "It may be," he said, still smiling, "a close thing, *bia-cara,* whether we starve to death first or you learn how to cook."

"Hazard Black!" She was a little indignant now, because she'd really been trying at supper. "I can too learn how. Get me a cookbook and I'll show you."

"You're on, puss."

Carrying the boiler over to the tub, he filled it again, placed it on the stove, and stoked the fire. If anyone in his clan had seen him then, he would have been teased unmercifully. Absarokee warriors didn't wait on women. At least not in public. In love, of course, they were like other men. Jon Hazard Black, while accommodating to women, had never waited on a woman before. This was a first. Yet he didn't even notice.

While Blaze lay abed, resting, warm, happy, utterly in love with the man she watched, Hazard rummaged through a leather pouch buried under some trade blankets on a shelf and, taking out a handful of dried grasses threw them in the boiler. "Lemon grass," he said, responding to Blaze's questioning look. "You'll like the fragrance in the water."

"How do you know all that?"

"I grew up here, *bia,*" he said, sitting at the table. "I know every inch of ground from here to the Wind River, every bird and tree and animal. Every blade of grass and sighing breeze. Every mountain peak and riverbank. This is my land." The last sentence was like poetry, softly muted.

Would she ever, she wondered, understand his sense of oneness with nature? She only knew *things*—acquisitions. He knew the earth, the planet they lived on, as though it were an extension of himself. "What did you do as a child?" she quietly asked, wanting to know the man she loved, wanting to understand this land of his, his culture and people.

Hazard glanced up, having drifted away in his own thoughts, and he looked at her for a moment as though she were a stranger. Her hair shouldn't be red-gold, but black and straight, he thought, her skin darker. Why was she lying on his buffalo robes? Then recognition came and with it a sinking sense of recall. Miss Blaze Braddock —his surety against dying. At least temporarily. The reason he still held his claim; the tenuous link between his tribe's survival and extinction. He should hate her. He did hate all she represented—the privileged wealth, the casual taking, the amusement in acquisition.

She lay on the fur robes with a natural abandonment, her right arm thrown over her head, bent gracefully, her back arched slightly, one slender leg raised, the other extended languidly. "What *did* you do as a child?" she repeated, not certain he'd heard her, his eyes so remote and distant.

"What most children do," he vaguely replied, his mood suddenly drenched with melancholy. There was something intensely familiar in the way she lay; it summoned up an old memory of another woman lying so in a young boy's lodge in a mountain pasture many summers ago. Staring at the woman, he moved to curb the memory, knowing he didn't want Blaze Braddock to become another indelible keepsake in his mind. She had, in her beauty and whimsy already engaged far too much of his present. Intuitively, he withdrew, regaining his sense of what was proper, reestablishing his mental redoubts against emotion. Putting Blaze Braddock back in her place: a hostage; his guaranty he'd see tomorrow; and after tonight, having relinquished his honorable attempt at celibacy, she would take the position she'd wanted from the first, the one he'd perfunctorily disputed—that of mistress. Now that his mental wrestling was resolved, he intended to make use of her—often. "Come here," he said, holding out his hand. "Sit on my lap and tell me about your childhood instead. Mine was uneventful."

He held her while she talked, only half listening, the sound of her voice soothing the morbid creatures that threatened his future. He heard every few sentences, smiled occasionally, kissed her lightly on the cheek, the ear, ran his hands lazily down her back, her warm flesh the immediacy in his life at the moment—the scented talisman keeping the evil spirits at bay.

She glanced at him while she talked, casting sated, adoring blue eyes over the strong face so close to hers.

His eyes were half wild and restless and so beautiful beneath his fine arched brows, she found herself staring at them often as one might admire a flawless rose over and over for the pleasure it gave. And his high-bridged nose was a perfect sweeping line drawn with a sure hand. She reached out and slid a fingertip down its smooth length, as if by touching the pure, true straightness, she might feel a sensation akin to its perfection.

Absently, his hand came up and brought her errant finger to his lips. It was the casual courtier who languidly dropped a kiss on it.

"I love you, you know."

The simple words shattered Hazard's inattentive, transient peace. His hand abruptly dropped away. Her eyes, he noted at first startled glance, were as serene as her expression. *No*, was his first wrenching reaction. No, it's all wrong!—a silent rebuttal ringing through his mind.

"Can you handle it?" she calmly asked, his reaction much as she'd expected. He was silent for a few moments more, one hand still light on her back, and warm. "You don't know what you're saying," he slowly replied, picking his way carefully between responsibility and conscience.

She only nodded her affirmation, her blue eyes placid and contained.

"Young girls always think they love the first man who—"

"Takes their virginity?"

"I was going to say makes love to them."

"Oh, really?" she said, her expression skeptical and manifestly suspicious.

"So I've heard," he quickly amended.

The skepticism vanished and the smile, the one like sunbeams over a field of golden poppies, appeared. "I don't care about anyone else. I love you. You needn't worry," she went on, her tranquillity unflustered, "I don't expect you to love me." While a novice at love, she was no novice at handling men; it would never do, she realized, to press for an answer so soon.

"Once your father comes back for you, we won't

ever see each other again. You'll marry some young scion of equal wealth and class and raise wealthy young children."

"I may stay here," she refuted.

"What for?" It was blunt and almost discourteous.

"To oversee Daddy's mines," she said, unruffled by his sharpness. It was feeling at least, and she found it eminently more satisfying than cool detachment.

"And take over my country."

"Just the mines."

"It's the same thing. Someone says the word *gold* and the landscape's overrun."

"I could help you."

He smiled abruptly, a boyish smile, vivid with mirth. "I know. And you *are,* sweet *bia,*" he said, his tone one of deepest admiration; "you really are." His mouth dipped and captured hers. He didn't want to talk about the mines and the white men and what they might be doing in a year, a month, a week . . . all the obstacles and impediments. He didn't want to remember any of it right now. He wanted to forget, if only for a night.

He pulled her close, his right arm around her shoulders, his slender fingers reaching up her neck, resting on her jaw, keeping her head immobile so he could taste her mouth, slide his tongue inside, and feel her respond— hold her like his own pet prize for as long as he wanted her. His other hand found the heavy undercurve of her breast, his palm drifting slowly upward over her cresting nipple, then back again, the tip hardening into his palm —the languid back-and-forth motion triggering the floodgates of desire for both of them.

"I love you," she whispered when his mouth left hers briefly to nibble at her lower lip.

"I know," he huskily replied, the nibble, sharpening suddenly. "And I need you, *bia-cara* . . . to put out the fire."

He placed her very carefully in the Morris chair, kissing her gently on her warm, soft lips, his hands like a jeweler's, brushing her curls away from her shoulders. Then, easing her legs apart, so slowly she felt a thrilling anticipation in the lingering movement, he knelt between her legs and bending forward kissed her breast. He sucked one pink tip very lightly at first, so lightly her senses were attuned to his merest brushing touch. She arched up in quivering expectation, but his tongue only languidly circled the stiff, tingling peak, then moved to fondle her other rosebud crest. The gentle feeling of his mouth, warm and teasing, was tantalizing promise, and each small nibble or grazing lick sent spirals of pleasure racing downward until she felt she must have him or die.

Reaching out, she tried to touch him; his arousal, she saw through a haze of desire, was as ready as hers.

"No," he softly said, pushing her hands away.

"I won't wait." It was the imperious tone even in her breathy demand, wanting what she wanted. She reached out again, but he stopped her easily, his fingers closing loosely around her wrists.

"You have to."

"I don't want to—" She struggled against his grip, but effortlessly, he held her away.

"You're going to be a handful for your husband, Boston," he playfully teased. "I hope he's got plenty of stamina, with your pressing need to give orders. What if you don't always get your way?"

"But I always do."

"Did," he corrected, his dark eyes impaling hers.

"You're tiresome." She pouted, her lush lips pursed invitingly. "Why does everything have to be some kind of challenge with you?"

"You haven't learned to be malleable, puss," he murmured. "That's why. You want to run the show, but I don't follow orders—especially from a woman."

"I don't mean it that way," she whispered, sliding a few inches down in the chair until she was enticingly close to Hazard's rigid maleness. "Would you like it better if I waited for you to ask me?" The poignantly innocent eyes she raised to him would have melted stone.

He laughed, amusement spilling out of his eyes. Laughed at her theatrics, at his misplaced scruples, at the beautiful adventuress with flamboyant hair and an extravagant temper he curiously felt he must master. "Oh, hell," he capitulated, his smile pure magic, "what's the damn difference . . ."

And when he carefully placed her legs around his waist, adjusted her comfortably in the chair, and entered her, they both felt the world tremble.

LONG moments later, stroking the dark head lying in her lap, Blaze softly declared, "The water's hot."

"Now *I'm* too tired." The words were muffled against her thigh. Hazard had collapsed on the floor beside the chair and buried his head in her lap, his damp hair like black ruffled satin on her legs.

"I'll get it ready." She attempted to rise, but his body was immobile.

"Give me five minutes," she heard in the same muted tone.

"Be my guest." She felt the chuckle rather than heard it. Five minutes passed, while both in their divergent ways were very much at peace. "I thought Absarokees were the cleanest people on earth."

"Why do women always use guilt?" he groaned, but he didn't move.

"Don't go to sleep." Blaze shook his shoulder.

So he roused himself for her, and moments after lifting his head from her lap, hauled himself to his feet. He was exhausted. "What I really need more than a bath is some sleep," he said, his glance caressing Blaze in an affectionate way.

"Just a quick bath," Blaze pleaded.

"If I get into that tub with you, nothing's going to be very quick."

"How nice."

"You're damned exhausting, you know."

"But lovable," she retorted.

He smiled, fondness apparent in his dark eyes. "But lovable," he graciously agreed.

"I'll fill it," she offered.

He sighed. "I'll fill it." He had taken two steps when he stopped. "If you promise one thing."

"Anything," she happily affirmed.

"Don't say 'more'—at least," he added, "until after midnight."

"Promise." She grinned.

He grinned back and walked over to the stove.

The bath was pleasant and refreshing. Hazard leaned back against the headrest and sighed contentedly, his arms holding Blaze snugly tight. She was seated between his legs, her back resting against his chest. "Have you ever taken a bath with a woman before?"

"No," he lied.

"Why not? It's very nice."

"No time," he lied again.

"I think a tub for two is a glorious invention."

"Thought of at least four thousand years ago, sweet. Sex is not an original idea."

"Really?" she teased. "You mean we're not the first?"

"The first on this side of the Big Belt Mountains in Montana Territory, in a cabin on claim 1014—maybe—but I wouldn't bet on anything more than that."

"Such a cold, callous realist."

"The world does that to you, *bia*—takes away the illusion. Often at the point of a rifle. I can't speak for Boston society misses, of course; the disillusion for them might be articulated more in terms of an emerald ring smaller than a pigeon egg."

"You needn't be so sardonic."

"Sorry, you're right. Tonight there is illusion along with some other extremely enchanting . . . sensations." His fingers gently stroked the curve of her hip.

"And society misses don't just count their jewels. We do all sorts of things," she said with just a hint of lofty condescension.

"Anything useful, though, *bia-cara*, is the moot question . . . besides that," he added, smiling into her upturned eyes. "Tell me, pet—seriously now, my hunger pangs are coming a very close second to my carnal appetites at the moment—do you think you could do one of your 'all sorts of things' and make a chocolate cake once I get you a cookbook? I have this overwhelming desire for chocolate cake."

"More overwhelming than your desire for me?"

"Never, *bia*," Hazard responded, the perfect gentleman, his smile alight with mischief. "You are the chocolate cake of my existence, and I much prefer eating you to anything in the world."

"Libertine," she said, laughing and twisting in his arms and splashing him with a handful of water.

"It's all your fault," he reproved, hauling her up on his lap. "Damned if there's a thing I can do about it."

"Is anyone asking you to?" she sweetly asked.

Chuckling, he touched his lips to her nose. "You're the most forward female I've ever met, chocolate cake of my life." She was more forward than he'd ever allowed for—more than he'd ever encountered.

"More forward than Lucy Attenborough?"

He seemingly calculated for a moment. "Yup."

"Good," Blaze said, a very satisfied look on her lovely face. "I was wondering then . . . if I word this properly . . ."

His smile began slowly.

There was a minute tilt at the corner of her eyelids, and a corresponding one at the corner of her lips, that denied subtly but unmistakably the literal obeisance of the words that followed. "I mean in order not to offer any unseemly challenge . . ."

The amusement reached Hazard's eyes.

"That is . . . considering how well you seem to be . . . refreshed . . ." Blue eyes met his with unwavering need and she could feel his refreshed vigor rising smoothly against her thigh. "Only one more time," she whispered.

"Heaven forbid," he quietly remonstrated, his smile warming the softness of her cheek.

"I didn't mean it literally," she murmured, purely, naturally, without artifice, the last syllable gasped midway between a sigh and small cry, for Hazard, his large hands holding her easily, obeyed her with a smile and slowly eased her down his militant arousal. Can one die, she thought, of joy?

Much later, Hazard carried a very sleepy, very content young woman over to the soft bed of buffalo robes and tucked her in. She was sleeping before he finished arranging the supple blanket over her. He looked at her and smiled; sweet as cottonwood candy in the spring, he decided, viewing the fragile, flushed face and tumble of silky hair. Sweet everywhere, he reflected, blissful weariness seeping into every pore of his body. She needed him, she'd said over and over that night, but damn, he needed her too, and until tonight, he hadn't realized how much he'd missed having a woman.

Turning back to the tub with a small shrug of dismissal, as if such thoughts were best not considered and, at worst, dangerous, he contemplated the puddles of water on the uneven plank flooring. He could leave the mess until morning; Blaze could take care of it. Or could she? He grinned to himself. Or would she? Hazard had been raised to view all household duties as woman's work, and in this preconception he differed very little from any nineteenth-century male regardless of race. "Oh, hell," he muttered and reached for a towel. In ten minutes, the floor was wiped dry, the tub emptied outside, all the damp towels draped over the porch railing. Then he lay down next to Blaze and slept better than he had for days.

Chapter 19

HAZARD woke early in the morning, in accordance with the Absarokee maxim "Do not follow sleep to the end, but waken when it requires determination." Leaving Blaze asleep, he took his clothes and walked outside into the sunlight. He left the door unlatched.

When Blaze woke sometime later, her first reaction was disappointment. Hazard was gone. She'd wanted to find him still beside her, wanted to whisper good morning and be warmed by his smile. He smiled like no other man she knew—a slow, lingering smile that started in his eyes and then curved his mouth upward with a tentative reticence like his quiet speech. And then suddenly the smile touched you intimately, as if no one else existed in the entire universe, as if he had reached out and embraced you.

He was too charming, Blaze warned herself, too perfect, too experienced. A man with a sensual reputation; a man from a tribe with a sensual reputation. He called it natural. The righteous moralists among the whites had always called it scandalous. The Absarokee simply offered both men and women freedom, he'd said. Theirs was an egalitarian society where women owned property, where descent was matrilineal—at least in theory, he'd amended with a smile—where women as well as men could choose their lovers, could choose to divorce, could choose to remarry. This in an age when women were chattel everywhere in the world. Even his words were persuasively charming.

I want him, though—a pulsing rhythm of thought signaled along every singular pathway of her brain—I want him. Too charming, too perfect, too experienced, too seductive, not only to her, Blaze ruefully reminded herself, but to any woman. She knew all that; she understood. But it didn't matter a scrap. She intended to have Jon Hazard Black for herself. And she hadn't acquired the sobriquet Blaze for the color of her hair alone. Her eyes shone now with a purposeful intensity that had never yet been thwarted.

Throwing off the fur robe, she sat up and glanced around the room. Would he be back for breakfast or had he taken food already? She couldn't tell, but she noticed that the tub and towels and water puddles were gone. He was unbelievably endearing, this man who'd insisted not too many days ago that he'd have her hide if she didn't learn to do the work.

Was it possible he cared for her in the same way she did him? Or was it only that he was gallant as well as charming, chivalrous in the true meaning of the word? None of the men in her world back East would have cleaned up after a woman; they would have been both disdainful and ultimately inept. Neither of which Hazard was. In a way, he was the most gentle man she knew. And he was never disdainful of another human being or inept. Not Hazard.

Finding a shirt to wear, she surveyed the kitchen, wondering if she should start breakfast, when she noticed that the door was ajar. A thin sliver of sunlight cut across the rough floor and she moved toward it uncertainly, as a prisoner would contemplate a green grassy field. She pushed the door open another two inches and waited. Then a moment later, suddenly brave, she threw the door open and stepped out onto the low roofed porch.

It was quite lovely, she decided, this new, shiny sun-lit world of hers—the mountain range in the distance, the green pine and paler aspen, the fresh perfume of clean morning air. Uncertain of her future, uncertain of her lover's susceptibility, acutely aware that Hazard had tangible duties that superseded both his wishes and hers, she nevertheless, with buoyant youthfulness, felt a thrilling sense of happiness. For right now, at this precise moment, she was where she most wanted to be. And of one thing at least, she was certain. She did love him.

Moving off the porch, Blaze slowly walked around the cabin, the sensation of freedom exhilarating. Barefoot, she walked carefully over the rough gravel, paused for a moment in the cool, damp grass under the wild cherry tree near the creek, and then wandered down the pathway that led to the rim where Hazard had stood short days ago watching her approach.

She stood on the very crest, looking down the schist-strewn trail she'd climbed that day, and marveled at how a person's life could be altered irrevocably in so brief a time. The slate was warm under her feet, warm and soothing, like the morning breeze lightly ruffling her long hair and swirling Hazard's shirttails against her bare legs. She took a small step and curled her toes over the ledge.

"I wouldn't go any further if I were you." The voice was familiar and cool and charged with enough volume to reach her, each syllable clearly enunciated.

She turned casually, annoyed by the implied cynicism. She hadn't realized she'd been onstage the last few minutes. Her gaze slowly scanned the mountainside in the direction of Hazard's voice. It took perhaps thirty seconds before she found him, high up above the mine entrance, some three hundred yards away. She began walking toward him.

He didn't move, only watched, taking in the beautifully formed body scarcely concealed beneath the shirt, the face exquisite in both its beauty and character, her flame hair that made him want to bury his face in it. And he wondered, as he watched, if his stubborn, thorny, independent hostage would have taken a second step forward if he hadn't called out.

"What is it?" Blaze asked when she was close enough, indicating the artillery piece with a small nod of her head.

"A Gatling gun."

"It looks lethal." Her glance took in its size, the numerous barrels, the strung cartridge belt leading into the firing mechanism.

"It is."

"Would you have used it on me?" she softly asked.

"I have to be careful," he said, after an age, ignoring the question he wasn't sure he could answer. "Until I learn to know you better."

Her downy, irregular eyebrows rose, a dark silky incongruity in a perfect face.

He smiled and added, "In other ways, I mean. And I must say," he annotated, "I look forward to the discovery with profound . . ." He paused, looking at her as if seeing her for the first time.

Blaze smiled now, reassured, and finished for him, "Delight?"

"Ko-dak."

"What does that mean?"

"Amen."

Hazard began work late that morning; he'd never made love before in the shadow of a Gatling gun. The morning sun and air bathed their senses; the rush of enchantment roused their passion; the wonder of discovery piqued their inventiveness, and the world disappeared, or rather, the world became them.

"HOW long are we supposed to sit and wait for the Colonel to come back?" Yancy grumbled. He was on his second bourbon after dinner and the ascendant issue in his mind came to the fore.

Millicent sat across from him, composed and relaxed. They had convinced the other members of the mining group to start back for Boston ahead of them and she had just bidden goodbye to her oldest friend, Elizabeth Talmadge. It had taken some convincing, but as the days stretched on, Millicent's arguments had gained ground. William had instructed them to "sit tight and do nothing," after all, she reminded them, so their presence was hardly a necessity. And they all knew Billy Braddock as a man who took charge of his own affairs, a man who wouldn't appreciate any interference. She was feeling supremely content at the moment and increasingly confident. "Now that all William's friends are gone, we may not have to wait at all," she calmly replied.

Yancy's glance was suddenly predatory and alert. "You mean one dead Injun won't matter now?" He smiled faintly.

Millicent helped herself to an inch more sherry, took a dainty sip, and, setting the glass down, said, "I think an unfortunate accident to William and *then* one dead Indian would be a more suitable sequence." She looked over to where he sat opposite her on a brocaded settee and lifted one brow inquiringly. "Does that make sense to you?"

"Love it," he replied, his smile widening.

"Highway men, I thought, would be appropriate. Another slaying after the dozens in the neighborhood lately will hardly cause comment, I'm sure. Gold robbery and its attendant violence seems a primary occupation out here."

"It might take a while to find him up in those mountains."

"Why not wait until he returns? Can you trust some of your men?"

Yancy nodded. "We could set up a small camp on that north trail into Crow country. Catch them before they get too close to town. I could send some trackers out too. Might speed things up."

"How long would that take?" Millicent casually remarked. She could have been inquiring about the stage schedule, for all the emotion in her voice.

Yancy was wondering himself how long it would take before he could marry the Colonel's millions, but he answered Millicent's more immediate question with a shrug and a quick narrowing of his eyes. "Considering he's been out for so long," he went on to explain, "it can't be many more days before he starts back with or without the tribesman he's looking for. A few days, a week at the most, I'd say."

"Wonderful," she replied with a complacent smile. "Now then, I think we should settle on the exact number of men and arms you're going to need to storm that mine. If you give me a money figure, I'll have that overly friendly banker next door measure out the gold tomorrow. Do you need anything else?"

"All you need is money, Millicent. You and I know that. Everything else arrives on schedule after that."

"My daddy used to say something along those lines. You seem very much like him at times, Yancy. I like that. Come here and sit beside me. You haven't touched me since this morning."

Chapter 20

A WEEK later, in the grey hour before dawn, Rising Wolf looked in the window, pursed his lips, and exhaled softly. His gut feeling about Hazard and the woman had been right after all; but with Hazard one could never be sure. By the time he entered the cabin his initial surprise was controlled.

Hazard, hearing the moccasined footfall, had relaxed the hand reaching for the pistol he kept near, checked quickly to see that Blaze was covered, and was pulling on his pants when Rising Wolf entered. The softly spoken Absarokee woke Blaze, but she lay drowsily quiescent, letting the sibilant cadence wash over her.

"Tell me what day, so I'll know who won the wager," Rising Wolf said. His smile was so outrageously benign Hazard couldn't miss his meaning.

"I'd forgotten what a bunch of gossips you and your friends are," Hazard replied, casting Rising Wolf an appraising glance. "I don't suppose it would do any good to feign ignorance."

"You must have known it was an opportunity for a lottery no one in their right mind could pass up. Knowing you," Rising Wolf continued, glancing meaningfully toward Blaze, "as well as we all do."

Knowing the issue wouldn't be put to rest without an answer, Hazard gave in with good grace. "Eight days ago." Diverting his gaze briefly to Blaze, he found her awake. With a smile to her, he murmured so his voice didn't carry past Rising Wolf, "Now let's drop the subject in front of the child. She may not understand the language, but your confounded leer is universal."

Unchastised, Rising Wolf continued to smile. "Red Bear won, then. Personally, I didn't think you'd hold out that long. I'd picked the day after I left last time."

"Thanks for the pledge of confidence."

"Hell, Hazard, what do high principles have to do with making love? That never corrupts. It's the fear of it that corrupts. Making love only brings you nearer to heaven."

Hazard laughed. Rising Wolf never took life too seriously.

"I like your heaven, by the way. When you get tired of her . . ."

"Don't hold your breath. She's not the kind you get tired of."

"Inventive?"

"Spontaneous." Pleasure showed in his eyes, lifted his mouth into a smile.

"The spontaneity may be bartered away any moment, and then what will you do?" Rising Wolf reminded him.

Hazard found himself forgetting that often these days. Found himself forgetting Blaze had a family and another life outside his world.

Rising Wolf saw Hazard's smile disappear, saw the instant sobering.

"Has anyone seen her father?" Hazard asked abruptly, a score of possibilities racing through his mind.

"No."

"Rose says he's out looking for the summer camp."

"Rumor has it he's dead."

It's over, was Hazard's first startled thought. If Colonel Braddock was dead, all the rules of the game were obsolete. "Whose rumor?" he quickly asked.

"The Lumpwood band. One Heart heard it from his wife's brother."

"How sure are you?"

"One Heart's brother-in-law saw the body."

"Could it have been some other white man?"

Rising Wolf shrugged. "Possibly. I'm not sure." He smiled. "They all look alike."

"Damn."

"Is it a problem?"

"Could be. The Colonel's more apt to be amenable than some third party."

"Why don't we just bring a guard down. Twenty or thirty wolves, say. . . ."

"I don't want that. All the third-rate politicians running the territory would love to call in the army. And since the end of the War Between the States, every ambitious officer looking for a promotion is galloping over the Northern Plains hoping like hell to start an Indian war. I'd just as soon not be some glory boy's excuse for a colonel's bars."

"We could kill quite a few with your new artillery piece." As a tactician, Rising Wolf was superb, and his eyes gleamed with all the pregnant possibilities of the site Hazard had chosen at the top of the mountain.

"And lose the mine," Hazard reminded him.

"Are you so sure it's important? We've always been a prosperous clan. Why do we need more than we have now?"

"The yellow eyes aren't going to stop coming. Not with the gold. And the buffalo won't last forever." It wasn't the first time the two men had gone over this ground.

"There's people who'll disagree with you about that," Rising Wolf said pleasantly.

"They can disagree," Hazard said just as pleasantly. "In the meantime, I'll stockpile gold."

"Jon," Blaze said, softly interrupting, "do you want me to try to make some breakfast?"

"So she's learned how to cook?" Rising Wolf inquired in Absarokee. He understood English as well as Hazard. They'd been raised as brothers and shared the squaw man Alonzo Kent as a kindly uncle. Their English was upper-class, learned mainly from Alonzo Kent, Baronet, the younger son of a younger son who had been sent abroad for his health. He'd reached Montana Territory before it had been named in the train of a German prince collecting New World fauna and flora and was near death with consumption when he first saw the Yellowstone. Hazard's clan was camping nearby, and his aunt took Alonzo in and cured him. They fell in love and he never returned to England.

"Thank you, Miss Braddock," Rising Wolf politely said, offering Blaze a casual, elegant bow, "I'd like breakfast very much."

"You know English," she exclaimed. "How very nice. Hazard, why didn't you tell me?"

"You probably haven't had much time to talk," Rising Wolf murmured in their native tongue, innuendo flagrant in his husky tone.

"Cute," Hazard retorted brusquely, then turned back to answer Blaze. He thought of the hundreds of thousands of fragments and people and anecdotes of his life she knew nothing about and was nonplussed for a moment. "A white man married our aunt—he was a fur trader," Hazard diffidently said, "and we both learned English as children." She looked very desirable lying abed and it annoyed him momentarily that Rising Wolf was attentively surveying her in languorous semidress. "I'll bathe while you attend to breakfast," he abruptly remarked. "After you." He indicated the door with a gesture of his head, and Rising Wolf preceded him outside. "Put on your slacks this morning," Hazard ordered sotto voce as he prepared to follow Rising Wolf. He wasn't in the mood to share her, even visually, with Rising Wolf.

"They shrank when I washed them," Blaze whispered back.

"Put on a pair of mine."

"They're too big. I *could* wear one of the dresses you—"

"No. Put on the pants," he said, each word quietly emphasized.

"Yes sir," she murmured, recognizing his jealousy.

"And we're getting some clothes for you, immediately. Now no games, Blaze. I want you wearing pants when I get back."

"Yes, master," she sweetly purred.

Her meek compliance raised a trace of distrust in Hazard's mind. She was rarely submissive; he corrected himself—she was never submissive. He jabbed a peremptory finger at her. "And a shirt," he added for safety.

When they returned some time later, Blaze was monitoring the bacon sizzling in a pan on the stove, and a swift glance told Hazard it wasn't intolerably burned for a change, only pleasingly crisp. He was also grateful to see she had actually followed instructions for once. She wore one of his shirts tucked into a pair of his slacks, rolled up several times at the bottom and belted into gathers at her narrow waist. Relieved she was fully clothed, he overlooked the fact that she looked like a waif from an orphanage. "Are there eggs left?" he asked, the familiar routine of helping Blaze with the meals so commonplace he fell into it naturally.

"You used them yesterday," Blaze replied without turning from the stove. "I don't remember."

Seating himself at the table, Rising Wolf looked up at Hazard and said with a mocking grin, "Learning to cook too?"

"Hazard's a marvelous help," Blaze exclaimed before Hazard could reply. "If it wasn't for him, we'd starve."

"You'll have to show me your cooking skills sometime when you come back home," Rising Wolf declared, amusement in the rich timbre of his voice, although his face was blank as a statue.

"Not likely," Hazard muttered, knowing he'd hear endless jokes about cooking the next time he visited camp.

"And he washes dishes and cleaned up the floor and everything after the . . . well . . . the other evening," Blaze went on more delicately when she heard Hazard clear his throat in warning. She was proud of his gallantry. Turning, she saw he was mildly embarrassed. "I'm sorry," she quickly apologized, wiping her hands on the oversized pants. "I forgot about all your masculine prejudices."

"It's all right," Hazard acknowledged.

"Yes, he can astound everyone at the summer hunt," Rising Wolf asserted, a teasing light in his eyes.

Glimpsing the sharp look Hazard cast at Rising Wolf, Blaze inquired, "What's a summer hunt?" And to herself, she wondered why he did not want it mentioned.

"Tell her," Rising Wolf prompted, entertained by Hazard's awkward and precarious situation.

Reluctantly he complied. "The clans gather to hunt and socialize," he tersely said.

"How lovely! Like a grand picnic. Will you have many relatives there to visit?" Her voice had risen in excitement like a young child's.

"I won't be there to find out," Hazard said, quietly but emphatically, and, turning back to Rising Wolf, glared at him for bringing the subject up.

Lapsing into Absarokee, Rising Wolf suggested, "You could look for the father, if you came."

"If he's alive, he'll find me," Hazard replied in the same melodic tongue.

Rising Wolf shrugged and spoke in English once again. "Everyone will miss you this summer."

"It can't be helped," Hazard retorted in cool, clipped accents.

Blaze glanced cautiously from one man to the other; she realized she shouldn't interfere in Hazard's life any more than she already had, and there must be some private matter they were discussing in their own language. It was Hazard's decision, after all, she acknowledged, but . . . she hesitated for only a fraction of a second more before her impetuosity overcame her finer motives of sensitivity. "Could we go? Could we? Please, Hazard, it would be such fun."

"No."

"Why not?" she cheerfully charged, as immune to his refusal as any others in her life. "I've never seen an Indian village, or a summer hunt or even an Indian except you and Rising Wolf and our scouts."

Hazard's back stiffened. "It's not a sideshow arranged for your amusement."

"Don't be so touchy, dammit. I didn't mean it that way and you know it."

Rising Wolf's mouth dropped a bit before he caught himself. He'd never seen Hazard talked to like that before—not by anyone and certainly not by a woman. But then he'd never known Hazard to cook for a woman before, or clean up for a woman. In the half-second that elapsed before Hazard replied, given the Hazard he knew, Rising Wolf fully expected him to lash out in some way.

"I'm sorry," Hazard apologized, and Rising Wolf's mouth gaped open further. How often in Hazard's life had he apologized to a woman? "But we can't go," Hazard went on gently. "It's impossible."

"Because of the mine?" Blaze asked, her tone more understanding. Hazard looked mildly uncomfortable and she had misgivings suddenly about her insistence.

"Yes," Hazard affirmed, glad of a ready excuse Blaze would accept. He had no intention of exposing his need for this woman to every person in his clan. And if he took her to the summer hunt, she might see it as a charming adventure into an unknown culture, but he, personally, would find it harrowing.

They would both be under constant scrutiny and everyone would know his wanting Blaze transcended casual need. Wanting a white woman that much could diminish his power as chief. And the public flirting and courtship normal and prevalent at the summer camp could cause untold problems. He knew how Blaze responded to the mention of other women in his life, and while he understood, in theory, jealousy was beneath a man's dignity, in regard to Blaze, dignity be damned.

Furthermore, much of his time would be required for council meetings, and his friends would expect him to join them hunting, gaming, racing, all usual activities enjoyed at the summer encampment. All male activities. It wouldn't work.

"Perhaps some other time, then."

"Perhaps," he noncommittally replied.

Rising Wolf left very soon after breakfast, with a well-laden string of pack ponies.

Blaze only inquired about the summer hunt once more during supper that evening, inquired in very general conversational terms.

Hazard's reply was curt and negative.

She wouldn't bring it up again.

Chapter 21

ONLY minutes after eating, Hazard began buckling on his gun belt.

"Town again?" Blaze asked softly, loath to see him go. Town at night meant Rose, and her jealousy boiled up despite his abstinence last time. And the danger would be constant and very real if Yancy was as worked up as he'd been the day she came up the mountain.

Hazard nodded.

"Rose?" She couldn't keep herself from asking.

His head came up, his fingers still tying on the leg strap. "Only for your clothes," he said, his dark glance level. "Jimmy should have been here by now." He finished securing the holster to his thigh and straightened. "I want you to have clothes to wear."

"Because of Rising Wolf?"

"Yes," he said simply.

"It's not worth a suicidal trip into town."

"It is to me," he quietly replied, then smiled a quick,

easy grin. "And it's not suicidal. No one saw me last time and no one will this time either." He was dressed all in black except for his moccasins, expecting he might have to move faster than boots would permit. Despite his facile explanation to Blaze, he knew small-town rumor may have heard of his last visit, and the possibility of a reception committee was a consideration.

"Wait until Jimmy brings them. Rising Wolf won't be back again for days."

"That's the point. Jimmy hasn't come. Evidently there's some problem. Rose knows everything in the county. I'll find out."

"I don't suppose it would do any good to beg and plead?" Blaze winsomely asked, the firelight warm on her fine-boned face.

"I won't be gone long," Hazard said, forcibly restraining himself from responding to her delicate beauty and entreaty. "Two or three hours at the most," he added. Reaching for his rifle, he slung it over one shoulder and then shrugged a leather pack over the other. "Do you want me to bring some books back for you? I know how tedious the days can—"

"Damn you, Hazard. Do I look like I want you to risk your life for some damn books for me to ease the damn tedium?" She'd risen to her feet in her fear, and tears of anxiety and frustration had welled into her eyes. "Do I, damn you, look like I want you to die?" she said in a trembling voice.

Hazard set his rifle down and with his habitual fluid grace strode soundlessly across the narrow room. He looked down at her apprehensive face for a silent moment and then pulled her close. He'd never realized how susceptible he was to her moods. "Don't cry *bia-cara*," he whispered, kissing away her tears. "Don't cry. I'd be a fool to take any chances when I've you to come back to." He nibbled on her lip, a light teasing gesture. "You know how I need you," he murmured.

Blaze's wet, shiny eyes lifted and met his. "Really?"

"Word of honor," he said and then smiled that heart-stopping smile.

Blaze's mouth quivered into an answering smile, a

sweet rush of joy inundating her senses. "Hurry back," she whispered to the man who touched her soul.

"I'll run all the way," Hazard softly replied.

And he did, setting out in a loping stride that he'd been taught could be sustained from sun to sun.

WHEN he neared the outskirts of Confederate Gulch, where scrub pine and alder bushes marked the perimeters of civilization, he stood motionless for several minutes, his eyes scanning the disreputable hodgepodge of buildings in the shallow basin below. The town was a jumble of houses, stores, streets, timber mine frames, tents, log cabins built to the needs of the miners without regard to plan. But Hazard knew each building, knew where each street meandered, knew most of the inhabitants by sight. Like a scout, his eyes scoured the scene, quartering the area, reassessing it, moving to the next section with a methodical thoroughness that he'd learned, on raiding parties into enemy territory, could mean the difference between living and dying.

Satisfied at last that no one was waiting for him in the immediate vicinity, he carefully moved into the deepest shadows and stealthily made his way to Rose's.

He saw them first. As he'd expected. Lookouts posted front and back at both entrances to Confederate Gulch's finest brothel and gambling hall. He didn't recognize them; they weren't locals. These had the look of eastern pilgrims. Backtracking, he approached Rose's from the far side of the block and, assessing the distance to the roof of Malmstrom's Leather Shop, decided he could just reach the chimney in back with his lariat. The supple rope made from braided buffalo hair was a requisite item on any Absarokee raiding party; since horses were wealth and raiding a means of obtaining them, every Absarokee warrior was an expert with a lariat by ten years of age.

The loop fell perfectly over Malmstrom's back chimney and, after two strong tugs to determine whether the masonry was sound, Hazard climbed hand over hand up the taut rope to the wood shingled roof. Leaning against the chimney, he recoiled the lariat, then tied it with a slip knot to his belt. He sat quietly for several moments judging the variety of roofs he'd have to traverse, reconnoitering, now that he was above street level, for lookouts posted on any adjacent buildings. Satisfied he was alone, Hazard gripped the shingles through his soft-soled moccasins and carefully moved eastward toward Rose's establishment six buildings away. The imposing limestone and wrought-iron elegance dominated the far side of the block.

Morality hadn't arrived yet in Confederate Gulch. That always came later, if the gold lasted long enough for more stable settlement. In the boom months of a new strike, even the first few years, there was no law except miners' laws, no principles except the concept of "get rich quick," no formalities for judging right or wrong except the fastest gun or knife; and territorial justice, although in theory prevailing throughout the territory, was a hundred miles away in Virginia City. The leading industries were saloons, gambling houses, dance halls, and places like Rose's. Later on, the socializing available at Rose's would be relegated to areas off the main street. But in these frantic new growing times, hers was the biggest structure in Confederate Gulch, splendidly constructed of pink-hued limestone carted overland from Fort Benton.

Rose had always insisted on the very best, ever since she'd been old enough in New Orleans to know what the best was. Although she had been born on the wrong side of the blanket, her mother's protector had been generous to his beloved mistress and natural daughter. Until her parents' death in the typhoid epidemic of '59, Rose had had all the advantages money could buy. But when they died, her father's family chose not to recognize her, although she had the Longville looks there was no denying: violet eyes, skin as white as magnolias, hair black as night and silky smooth. Unfortunately she was, through her mother's side, one thirty-second black. To avoid the taint to the Longville name, she'd been abducted one night by a Longville employee, shipped upriver, and sold at Natchez. Her owner died the same night he purchased her and deflowered her—from a slit throat, the papers said. Served him right, Rose had thought, if he didn't have brains enough not to fall asleep in a drunken stupor after he'd abused his newest slave. She was, of course, wanted for murder, the papers reported, but by that time she was halfway to St. Louis with the contents of her short-lived owner's money box hidden in her baggage.

She'd set herself up in business, or rather, set up business at St. Louis the summer of '59; Rose Condieu had never actually worked at her business. She'd had enough money not to have to. Her choice of career was a decision based on the rather limited areas open to women without family who chose not to eke out a living on a subsistence level. And more important, it would offer her the protection of the local law enforcement officials who patronized her establishment as her guests. Southern justice was adamantly malevolent toward slaves who killed their masters, and Rose planned to be careful.

Within a year, her undertaking was the most successful of its kind in St. Louis. But when news of the gold strikes came four years later, the adventure appealed to her. She was still young, only twenty-three years old— and St. Louis was becoming boring.

The wrought-iron second-floor balconies made access from the roof simplicity itself. Hazard dropped down to the railing and then to the balcony floor in one light swinging motion, silent as the dim shadows between Rose's and Shandling's Hardware. Easing the balcony's French doors open, he pulled aside the gold brocade drape a narrow half-inch and looked into the bedchamber. Roxy, lying on her back, was entertaining a customer, but her gaze was wandering, mild boredom evident in her expression. When Hazard stepped into the room, he raised his hand in salute and smiled. The aging businessman, for his wife's benefit supposedly at a meeting of the Masons that evening, had his back to Hazard and was seriously involved in his own enjoyment. Quietly crossing the room, Hazard reached the door, Roxy watching him with a small smile on her face. Carefully, he opened the door, glanced up and down the hallway, and, seeing no one, blew Roxy a kiss and slipped out of the room. Roxy's mischievous wink in return had been both suggestive and humorous, and Hazard was still smiling when he entered Rose's suite three doors down.

Rose's startled glance gave way to recognition. "You're a fool, Hazard," she said, her admonishing tone bordering on vexation, "and smiling about it. This place has been under surveillance twenty-four hours a day since your last visit."

"I'm smiling at Roxy's particular style," Hazard replied, bright, imperviously cheerful, ignoring Rose's nettled admonition. "Although," he went on with a quirked grin, "Reggie Weaver looked like he might not make it through another 'Masonic meeting' without an apoplexy."

"Is that how you got in?" Rose was checking the bow windows facing the street to see that the heavy silk drapes were tightly shut.

"The entrances looked slightly busy," Hazard conceded drily.

"You shouldn't have come."

"Thanks for the friendly welcome," Hazard said, dropping his rifle and leather pack and settling into a velvet armchair.

Satisfied the curtains were securely closed, Rose turned back to Hazard. "He's got every scoundrel in town hired to kill you," she warned, "not to mention the bodyguards he brought with him from the East. And posters went up yesterday. He's offering one hell of a nice price for your head."

"He? Not the Colonel."

"No. Yancy Strahan. The kind of no-account *gentleman* who gives the South a bad name," Rose disgustedly added.

Hazard grinned. "I thought you despised the South."

"Not the South, Hazard, just some of the asses who thought they owned it and anyone with skin a little darker than theirs. And don't try to change the subject. You know damn well who is out to see you dead. Which brings me back to the beginning of this conversation. Why don't you leave right now and go back the way you came before someone notices something?" Her voice was firmly persuasive, her large violet eyes filled with concern.

"Nothing to notice," Hazard soothed. "Relax. No one saw me except Roxy, and she's not likely to kill me."

"Only with kindness, if you'd let her," Rose drily agreed.

"Now, Rose, you know you're the only woman for me." Hazard's smile was easy and winning.

Until his last visit, Rose was quite confident she had more than her share of Hazard's attention. But confidence had been dislodged by the evidence that Hazard's hostage had replaced her. Knowing Hazard's sexual appetites, it didn't surprise her; after all, Miss Braddock was near him twenty-four hours a day and Hazard had never struck her as either celibate or ascetic. "No one's going to have you, Hazard, if you stick around here too long. Except the undertaker."

"Why has this Strahan fellow taken over suddenly?"

Rose walked away from the window and in a whisper of silk and fragrance perched on the arm of a loveseat. "Rumor has it he and the Colonel's wife are mighty friendly."

Hazard's eyebrows rose in mild astonishment. Millicent Braddock had struck him the few times he'd seen her as a thoroughly asexual female. Too thin, too controlled, too perfectly put together, such that a sudden jolt would shatter the fragile confection. "You don't say," he murmured, alive to the changes this could make in his life. While the Colonel might be overly cautious about his daughter's safety, Yancy Strahan, on the two occasions he'd spoken with him, appeared immune to any humane motives.

"Sleeping together, Hazard. I have it on good authority," Rose explained, as if Hazard were too dense to understand all the resulting ramifications.

"Do you think they've heard the Colonel's dead?" He'd already dismissed the sleeping relationship as minor compared to the cryptic significance of the Colonel's apparent disappearance.

"Good Lord! Is he?"

"He might be."

"Jesus, Hazard, if he is . . ."

"It's just a possibility," he assured her. "Some third-hand gossip from Rising Wolf. I'm not certain."

Swiftly coming to her feet, she took two nervous steps toward Hazard, the hem of her lilac gown fluttering silkily over the intricate flowered carpet. "Hazard, get your sweet body out of here. My God, if he's dead, your life's not worth much. Strahan's dangerous, I'm telling you. He hurt a couple of my girls when he first came into town. I told him after that he wasn't welcome here. Luckily, I had Buck and Tom to back me up because he wasn't going to be reasonable about his ouster. Yancy Strahan doesn't care who he hurts. It's a fact, Hazard. So will you get the hell out of here?"

"Don't panic, Rose. I can handle Yancy Strahan."

"Maybe you can, and maybe you can't; his type doesn't fight fair. They never even fight their own fights, Hazard, if they can avoid it. He's a bully through and through. And he's got half an army of hired thugs with him." Just then a knock on the door echoed sharply through the sumptuous room. Rose stifled a cry of alarm.

Without speaking, Hazard signaled her to answer the door. Picking up his rifle and pack, he quietly moved through the archway into Rose's dressing room.

Rose's cheeks were flushed when she opened the door but her voice was deliberately calm. "What is it, Edward?" Her recently hired monte dealer stood diffidently in the hallway.

"Keene wants credit, Miss Condieu. Over the five thousand limit you set for him. He's raising a damnable fuss." The monte dealer's eyes scanned the room over her head with the ingrained appraisal of a thief while he waited for her instructions.

Harvey Keene was apt to be the new judge from their district and, keeping that possibility in mind, Rose said, "Give him another five thousand. But after that, he's got to talk to me. His law practice isn't *that* good."

"Very well, Miss Condieu." His voice was smooth and unctuous, and his dark eyes, had Rose noticed, suddenly flashed fiercely. A two-inch strip of mirror, barely visible through the decorative carved archway leading into Miss Condieu's sleeping quarters, reflected a slim portion of silky black hair and black-clad shoulder.

The new monte dealer, sent into Rose's by Yancy Strahan, had just earned Yancy's promised reward. "Sorry to disturb you," he apologized deferentially. And he turned away, his heart tripping against his ribs. The damn Indian was there! *Inside Rose's suite as big as life.* Despite the patrols, prowling the town since they'd discovered he'd been down to see Rose. Despite the guards front and back. Despite the reward posters nailed up, offering a small fortune for him, dead or alive. How the hell had he done it? Not that it really mattered. He wouldn't be around long enough to answer the question.

The newest of Rose's monte dealers walked down the stairs and right past his table and Harvey Keene. The temperate night air cooled the flush of excitement warming his skin. Yancy had said he could be reached day or night at The California Hotel. The promised fifty thousand dollars was all Edward Doyle could think about as his long-legged stride carried him down the street to the hotel.

"NOW," Rose insisted, looking at Hazard lounging against the carved arch, her pale forehead marred by a scowl, "get the hell out of here."

"No tea this time?" Hazard teased.

"Not a chance," she snapped, totally unnerved by her dealer's visit. Rose had never trusted Edward Doyle, only hired him because he was good with cards. Some sixth sense told her now it had been a mistake. "I don't trust him," she said levelly and, lifting her hands in a small helpless gesture, softly pleaded, "Please don't stay."

"You're really worried." The anxious flutter of her hands was so uncharacteristic, Hazard's voice lost its teasing mockery.

"That man and the mother of your . . ."—she hesitated a moment, searching for the right word—"hostage are as ruthless a team as I've ever seen. Two sledgehammers under their soft southern drawls. And yes, I'm worried as hell."

"Sorry, Rose, I didn't mean to upset you. I came for the dresses and other things if you have them," he quietly explained, "and then I'll go."

"You came for the *dresses?*" She couldn't keep the shock under control.

"The dresses," he repeated. "You wouldn't have a couple of books you can spare," he inquired mildly. "And a cookbook," he added. "I promised I'd bring one back," he finished with a small smile that lit up his eyes.

Exasperation caused Rose to explode. "Do I look like I own a cookbook? Do I look the least bit domestic? Hazard, have you lost your senses?"

He gazed at her, dazzling tonight in lilac georgette, beruffled and ribboned, and softly replied, "Pardon me, Rose. My mistake." He smiled then and enigmatically said, "It must have chocolate cake in it. Would your cook have one?" he helpfully inquired.

"My chef, Hazard, would run you through if you called him a cook. His talent is spontaneous, anyway, learned but not written down. It's all in his head."

"In that case," Hazard thoughtfully murmured, "would you order one? I promised her—"

"Dresses, Guerlain, chocolates, cookbooks—what else did you promise her, Hazard?"

His smile turned faintly wolfish. "She's persuasive," he said.

"I'll bet." Violet eyes narrowed slightly, and Rose looked at him with a lenient tolerance that had always endeared her to him. "Just so long as she doesn't persuade you to buy a wedding ring along with everything else."

"Her hair's the wrong color, and her skin," he tranquilly answered, unruffled by his own intrinsic prejudice. "We're not talking permanence, only books, if you have some you don't mine lending. I know you have them sent out from Ming's in Virginia City."

"Lend?" It was a small breathless gasp. "I think you've gone mad, Hazard. Watch my lips, darling. There are men out there *itching to kill you.* Do not, under any circumstances, consider bringing these back," she said, snatching an armful of books from a nearby table. "Keep them! *Do not return them! Do not return at all!* I mean it, Hazard. Not until Yancy Strahan is gone or dead. Nothing stands in that man's way. He's the kind who'd bring out murderous instincts in a nun, he's that rotten. Understand?"

"Thanks for the books," Hazard nodded, sliding them into his fringed pack, "and for the warning. I'll be careful." His instinct for survival came from necessity and the rigors of tribal training. It was his strength. He stood and then waited, quiet, relaxed, his composure serene.

Rose wanted to holler. She was a hot-blooded, volatile woman and Hazard's impassive calm in the face of this—this—horrendous danger grated on her nerves like a high-pitched scream. "What are you waiting for?" she demanded.

"The dresses." His voice was temperate, his smile forebearing. "If they're ready."

"Do you have a goddamn death wish?"

"On the contrary," he said, smiling a little more, thinking of one very lush reason for living, all rosy flesh and heated beauty, waiting for him in the cabin.

"I hope you live, dammit," Rose exploded, stalking over to an armoire, "to let her see that charming smile again." Jerking out a dress at a time, she flung them at him. "Personally, I don't think she's worth the risk!" Spinning around she threw the last dress into his arms.

"You're a sweetheart," Hazard blandly responded, familiar with Rose's hot temper and its equally rapid abatement. "I don't suppose you found any Guerlain."

If it was possible for a human to steam, Rose began to steam. "Good Lord, *how* could I have forgotten?" she replied, sarcasm dripping syrupy-thick. Turning back to the armoire, she reached up to the top shelf, snatched a package down, and hurled it at Hazard like a lethal weapon. "We wouldn't want Miss Braddock to wash with ordinary soap, would we. Hell no!"

Putting his hand out with an ease that belied the required speed, Hazard plucked the hurtling box from its trajectory and tranquilly placed it atop the six dresses packed swiftly into his leather bag. "I owe you, Rose," was all he said.

"I'd appreciate it if you'd get yourself out of here so I'll be able to collect someday!"

"I'm on my way . . . except . . ."

"Except what?"

"Well," he paused and grinned. "The chocolates."

"All I can say," Rose sighed exasperatedly, "is I hope you live to enjoy them."

"I'll do my damndest." A minute later the box of chocolates was being laced into the bag with the books, dresses, and soap.

"Anything else?" Rose sweetly inquired, watching Hazard tie the rawhide strings tight. "A maribou fan, perhaps, for my lady, or emerald ear clips for when she dresses for dinner?"

Hazard's head snapped up. "That reminds me. Jimmy hasn't come up. Do you know why? Is it Molly?"

"No, he broke his arm."

"How?"

"Apparently a barrel rolled off a freight wagon the wrong way when he was helping unload. Ron Davis, a clerk at Klein's, knows Jimmy so I sent him up to get some information when he didn't come for the food you wanted."

"Who's Ron Davis? A customer?" Hazard asked.

"A friend." Rose smiled, adding, "who'd like to be a customer, but I've never worked, as you well know."

"Can you trust him?"

"He'd do anything for me."

Hazard raised a brow in understanding. "In that case, would you send him up to Jimmy's with a message for me?" He slung the pack over his shoulder.

"If you hurry and get out of here, I'll do anything, including murder. You're not safe here, I'm telling you." The odd glow in Edward Doyle's eyes suddenly struck her ominously, a delayed reaction swimming up from her subconscious.

"If I don't come back for a while—"

"Don't! Good God, don't!" Rose interrupted.

"I just wanted to say," Hazard went on, reaching out

to take her hand, soothing her wrist with gentle strokes, "I might go back for the summer hunt. Let Yancy cool his heels for a few weeks."

"And her?" Rose asked, her orchid eyes watching Hazard's face intently.

"She'll go too. My insurance," he said, omitting the fact she'd become much more to him.

Rose knew Hazard's answer was evasive. No one risked his life over dresses and chocolates for a woman who was *just* insurance, but he'd admit it in his own good time, she knew. "Can he take the claim in your absence?" she asked, concerned not only for Hazard's physical well-being but for his future as well.

"Not legally. It's all filed right and proper. Besides, he won't know we're gone."

"When will you be back?" The touch of his fingers was exquisitely tender. And comforting even now when her nerves were skittish.

"Two weeks, three, a month maybe. When Jimmy's better, you could have him go up every few days as usual. That way no suspicions will be raised. We'd still be there as far as Diamond City's concerned. And thanks again, Rose, for everything." Hazard's fingers lingered another moment then he dropped her hand. He was reaching for his rifle when the door crashed open.

The man standing in the doorway, blocking the light from the hall, held a custom-made sawed-off double-barreled shotgun trained on Hazard, his finger curved precariously over the hair trigger. "Don't move, you mother-fuckin' redskin," snarled Yancy Strahan.

Hazard thought he was beyond umbrage at gratuitous slander directed at his race; he'd lived in the white man's world enough years to have heard it all. Heard it and discounted it as so much ignorant rhetoric by a race the Indian viewed as ill-bred, noisy, childishly impatient, and devoid of good manners. But he felt a virulent hatred, like venom from a snake bite, spreading through his senses at Yancy's coarse command—potent, out-of-control hatred. And for the first time in his life he was prompted to kill a man on impulse alone.

Rose screamed.

"Shut up, you slut," Yancy said, stepping quickly into the room and kicking the door shut, "or I'll shoot you too. I'm just itching to shoot you, mother-fucker," he growled, looking at Hazard. "And I will too, just as soon as you sign your claims over to me."

Hazard slowly eased himself straight, the rhythm of his breathing returning to normal. He had time to think. Yancy needed him alive for his signature. "It won't be legal unless it's recorded," Hazard ventured.

"Then we'll fuckin' well record it."

"Just you and me?" Hazard quietly asked, his eyes trained on Yancy's flushed face. Whoever had fetched Yancy must have found him drinking somewhere. The smell of bourbon pervaded the room. And the recording office was six blocks away, Hazard pleasantly thought.

"You and me," Yancy bluntly replied, "and the five men out in the hallway and the ten men downstairs and the dozen men front and back." Like so many bullies, Yancy relished center stage only when reinforcements were close behind.

For Hazard's purposes, Yancy's need for importance made the odds considerably more advantageous He glanced at him standing solidly in front of the door like a bull, exhibiting none of the refinement southern tradition extolled, devoid of the elegance or civilized veneer so assiduously cultivated by aspiring white gentlemen. Yancy was brutishly strong, over average height and heavily muscled, with the fair skin and sandy hair of his Scots forebears. The kind of skin that only reddened under the sun, or like tonight, with too much bourbon. Hazard could see that the pale eyes were dilated and a slight tremor affected the workmanlike hands holding the shotgun. Too much whiskey. Good. Another advantage, provided he didn't accidentally pull the trigger. "How does the Colonel feel about this?" Hazard calmly asked. "I might have Miss Braddock set to detonate if I don't return."

"Piss on the Colonel," Yancy declared in a blustery tone.

He was feeling pretty secure, Hazard thought. Had they received definitive news on the Colonel's death or was Yancy simply foolish enough in his sodden state to ignore Billy Braddock's wishes?

"And I'd cry at the redhead bitch's funeral," Yancy gloated, and laughed. A smug, pleased laugh, the laugh of a man already counting his money, if Millicent Braddock was sole heir.

"You might change your tune when the Colonel comes back and cuts off your balls," Hazard softly replied, watching the flush rise up Yancy's neck at the rebuff.

"Shut up, mother-fucker!"

"You might keep it in mind," Hazard provoked, his gaze intent on the shotgun's trigger, gauging the distance between himself and Yancy.

"I can take care of the Colonel." The liquor was talking now—Yancy's tone was bourbon-charged bravado. "Along with the Colonel's lady," he boldly added, his future fortune within grasp. After all, if the Colonel was still alive, that could be remedied without much trouble, and with the Colonel and this Indian out of the way, Yancy's intoxicated brain contemplated, the ladies would be easy enough to handle. When he married Millicent Braddock, whether the daughter liked it or not, he'd have the Colonel's fortune. "Get a pen," he ordered Rose. "And paper."

Rose looked at Hazard, her expression remarkably collected.

Hazard, raising his brows, glanced down at his long hands. Then his dark eyes came up and he nodded his head in assent.

"You won't get away with this," Rose declared, her eyes cold and dismissive. "Some miners don't like your strong-arm tactics."

"Shut up, bitch, or I'll cut your throat."

No man had talked to Rose like that since she'd fled Natchez. Pride stiffened her back, and only Hazard's soft murmur broke through the noxious loathing surging through her brain. "Steady, love. Get the pen and paper."

She looked at Hazard for a moment before she focused on him, before the quiet words registered through the violent repugnance. And only Rose, who knew him so well, heard the controlled rage behind the flat tone. He smiled reassuringly and winked, the knife blade sheathed on his calf warm against his skin. His fingers flexed lightly, an unconscious gesture.

She nodded, a charged current passing between them, then pulled the desk drawer open and reached for the perfumed lavender paper.

When Hazard sat down at the table in the center of the room, he chose a chair facing the door and Yancy. Pen poised over the paper, he waited.

"Put down the date," Yancy commanded.

Hazard wrote the date, his dark, heavy script like a sword slash across the pastel, scented paper. Then waited again.

"I agree to sell claims . . ." Yancy hesitated. "Put in the right numbers," he added.

Hazard wrote.

A voice shouted through the door. "Are you all right, boss?"

Hazard willed Yancy's answer with every nerve in his body. Against several men he didn't stand a chance.

"Everything's fine," Yancy drawled, his voice full of success.

Hazard was silently thankful and began breathing again.

". . . to Yancy Strahan, *S-t-r-a-h-a-n,*" he spelled. "Then sign your name." Yancy's southern voice held a mellow hint of elation.

Damn greedy sucker, Hazard thought, knowing it was Buhl Mining who'd bought all the other claims. Evidently Yancy was going to do some privateering against his employers. Some people don't have sense enough to know when they're ahead, he decided, and dropped the pen on the floor in an apparently awkward stroke.

"Clumsy bastard," Yancy declared, only mildly perturbed. Everything was falling into place with the perfection of clockwork and he was feeling pleased with the night's work. This Hazard everyone was so frightened of was just another dumb Indian. Adjusting his stance, he waited for Hazard to pick up the pen.

Hazard leaned over slowly, feeling for the pen with his hand before he lowered his head sufficiently to see under the table, in a balanced pattern of motion detached somehow from his thoughts. The embossed gold pen had left a path of black liquid splotched on Rose's carpet, Hazard's mind idly reflected, his adrenaline already surging. Where to strike, he fleetingly debated, the assessment of Rose's carpet already replaced by matters of logistics. Yancy's belly, groin, barrel chest. Each was considered, then rejected, in an exercise involved yet uninvolved, motionless for a suspended moment of time. If Yancy wasn't killed instantly, no easy task with a knife, he must at least be silenced. The neck, Hazard decided. Possibly lethal if the jugular was hit; incapacitating in terms of a scream in any event. He felt his breath go out, released from the tension of decision.

Ostensibly reaching for the dropped pen, Hazard's lean dark fingers touched the slender horn knife handle, its texture comforting like a friend's voice. Sliding the honed blade from its sheath into his palm, he came up from his bending posture in a powerful, smooth arc; the stiletto point of steel cupped in his fingers was aimed directly at Yancy's throat. The flashing blade caught the light for a glittering spasm before it buried itself into Yancy's fleshy neck. Wide-eyed terror convulsed the flushed face and a terrible gurgling sound came from his gaping mouth as he clawed at his neck.

From dropped pen to hideous choking sound, mere seconds had elapsed. A moment later, Yancy Strahan fell to the floor.

Both Rose and Hazard glanced briefly at the body. Rose spoke first. "Go, and hurry." She kept her voice down.

Hazard didn't move. "Will you be all right? Any problems with the body?"

"Are you kidding? We have fights here every night. Besides, Judge Faraday is a loyal ally since I donated twenty-five thousand dollars to his election fund last year."

"He might be dead." Hazard indicated the bleeding body.

"I hope like hell he is. Now go," Rose hissed, giving Hazard a shove.

"If you're sure you're OK."

"Hazard!"

"*Bala-ba-aht-chilash* [good luck], then," he said, smiling, and shouldered the leather pack. Picking up his rifle, he carefully eased his body through the brocade draperies. He stood in the shadows between drape and balcony door for a moment, surveying the street below. A cluster of men milled outside the main entrance but there was no one on the balcony, he noted with relief. Opening the door only enough to slip through, he stepped out. The drapes billowed briefly with the small rush of air, then Rose heard the door quietly click shut.

She glanced at the gold clock on her desk, then at Yancy bleeding on her carpet. If the guards didn't come in, she'd scream in five minutes. By then, Hazard would be out of town, provided he eluded all the hired guns.

His back pressed against the glass-paned door, Hazard paused for the briefest moment, giving his eyes a second to begin adjusting to the dark. He scanned the roof next door. Empty. Relief pulsed through his sharpened senses. Sliding his rifle across his back, he checked to see that the leather pack was secure, then soundlessly swung up onto the balcony railing. From this point until he reached Malmstrom's chimney, if anyone looked up, they'd see him. Taking a deep steadying breath, he reached up to the roof, found a fingerhold on the scant inch of protruding millwork, and pushed away from the balcony railing. He swung free for an instant before one foot caught the roof edge and he hung in the reflection of the saloon lights for a fragment of a breath, gathering the second surge of power he'd need to pull himself completely onto the roof. The pack didn't help any; it was heavy and awkward. Calling on his reserves, he gripped his precarious hold tighter, contracted his muscular shoulders, and slowly drew himself up over the narrow eaves. Flattened on the shingles, he lay still and listening . . . waiting to hear if he'd been spotted. Nothing. Only the normal night sounds of a mining camp in the evening: the saloon pianos, the low roar of raised voices, the sounds of fiddles and banjos in frightful discord, ribaldry, profanity, and an occasional fight. Raising himself to his knees, he carefully looked north and south where the patrols might be. He saw several of the hired guns, huddled in small groups, smoking and talking, but no one was looking up. Good. He tensed his legs to jump the six feet to the lower roof next door, centered the pack on his shoulders, settled the rifle in place. And jumped.

He was in midair when he heard Rose scream.

He was scrambling up the roof of Shandling's Hardware when he heard the balcony door splinter open.

He was hurtling over the ridgepole of the roof when the first bullet whined over his head.

Twisting slightly at the apex of his flying tumble down the far side of Shandling's roof, Hazard caught a split-second vignette of a man sighting down a rifle barrel, his form outlined by the golden glow of lamplight from Rose's suite.

Tearing over the remaining five rooftops, he caught snatches of shouted orders from the street below. But the voices were always one or two buildings behind him. If he didn't break a leg, he thought, landing hard after a flying leap over a darkened alley, he could stay ahead of them.

He didn't pause at the chimney to uncoil his lariat. He only had time to swing his legs over the side, hang by his fingertips to his full length, and then drop the last twelve feet to the ground. The fall jarred his spine, spiraling pain upward like stabbing knife blades. He rested on his knees briefly absorbing the worst of the clawing spasm, but the nearing shouts brought him to his feet. He sprinted toward the darkest shadows, in the direction of the creek.

He knew where he was going. They didn't. He should be able to outrun them. All the races of childhood came back now in a rush of memory—all the images of young boys dashing across windblown prairies, their long hair streaming out behind them, their bodies wet with sweat, moccasined feet flying over verdant greenness. And the tallest youth always outstripped the others, fleet as an antelope. Hazard smiled at the vivid imagery, warmed by the poignant memories of his growing up time, when this land was Absarokee land. And now white men called it theirs—wanted his blood. He laughed in a flurry of high spirits and accelerated in a burst of speed.

Not tonight, he thought, his soft-soled moccasins skimming across the last street of Confederate Gulch. They wouldn't be having his blood tonight.

Chapter 22

HE STOPPED to collect two of his horses at Pernell's mountain pasture. The ponies quietly whinnied when they caught his scent. He tapped them lightly on the nose to silence them, and after looping his lariat into a makeshift bridle he led them away. When he was sufficiently away from the ranch, he vaulted onto Peta's back for the trek up the mountain. He led the buckskin on a short lead and quietly talked to them on the journey to the mountain cabin, telling them they'd be back in the high mountain valleys for the summer hunt. They seemed to understand the exhilaration in his tone; their heads lifted, their ears came up and their nostrils quivered in soft answering snorts. Hazard walked the ponies the last rough mile up the twisting trail, but Peta kept nudging him in the back with her nose as if impatient to be home. "So the summer hunt appeals to you, too, Peta," Hazard murmured, and laughed when she nudged him again in apparent response. "We both want

to go home," he buoyantly retorted. "Home," he murmured with quiet joy and swung up the last steep stretch
of path as if it were a paved roadway.

It was grand pleasure to think of going home. He
hadn't been back in three months, and with the exception
of the few days in Virginia City, he hadn't had a break
from the arduous drudgery of mining in as long. Home.
It conjured contentment, solace, good sport, genial
friends.

BLAZE glanced at the clock for the thousandth
time. Two, three hours, he'd said. It was nearing on five.

I suppose he's having too good a time at Rose's to
notice. I might have known, she thought. Here I am worrying and fretting and he's probably finishing his fourth
brandy. Or worse, her unsure brain whispered. "Or
worse," she said aloud and rose heatedly to her feet one
more time to stamp over to the window commanding a
view down the mountain. She'd nearly worn a path there
already in the last two hours.

At half past nine, she'd gone out on the porch thinking she'd heard a sound. The moon was sliding through a
break in the clouds, and for the short minute it lit up the
landscape, she'd strained her eyes. Nothing. And no
more sounds.

He didn't care that it worried her sick, his going into
town. Her abduction was public knowledge. He had to be
a marked man. Her father couldn't control everyone in
town. She wondered sometimes how much control he
had even over bullies like Yancy. Hazard didn't care that
she was sick with fear, all for some dresses. Damn male
possessiveness. As if a few inches of her leg showing were
worth a suicide trip into Confederate Gulch. Blaze supposed he'd only be satisfied when she was properly covered in front of his friends. She had a mind right now to
tear those damn dresses into shreds when he got back. It
would serve him right for all the grief he was causing her.

She'd stayed out on the porch listening for a long
time, thinking a dozen times she'd heard his footfall. But
he didn't come and the chill night air finally drove her in.

She glanced at the small brass clock on the mantle.

10:20. Good Lord, where was he? Damn you, oh, damn you, Jon Hazard Black, if you've gone and gotten yourself killed over some trifling dresses, I'll never forgive you. "Never," she breathed, her hands clenched tightly in her lap. She sat for the next hour in the armchair, stiff and nervous.

11:30. I should just go to sleep. That would be best. All this worry and he's probably rolling in the hay with Rose. Don't be stupid, Blaze Braddock. Here you're half in tears with fear and he's probably whispering sweet nothings in some whore's ear while they're all tucked in, cosy as two turtledoves in her fine warm bed.

I'll just go to sleep.

If I could.

Well, I'll pretend to sleep.

What was that? Loose gravel was tumbling down hill. That couldn't be Hazard. It sounded like horses. Was that a horse nickering? He'd walked into town. He wouldn't be traveling with horses.

She flew to the window.

Hazard!

Oh, sweet, good, dear, kind God, it was Hazard!

HE HAD a wide smile on his face when he walked into the cabin, and Blaze was running to him before he'd taken two steps inside the door. Throwing herself into his open arms, she clung shamelessly to him, her fear in his absence terrifying in its conjecture, the sweet joy of his safe return, instant delirium. She covered his face with kisses and he smilingly kissed her back, tasting the innocence of her delight. After long, blissful moments, Hazard gently pried her arms away and, holding her so he could see her face and read her reaction, asked, "Would you like to go to the summer hunt at Arrow Creek?"[9] His smile was infectious, his dark eyes warm with lazy affection.

"Yes," Blaze replied instantly. "Yes, yes, *yes.* When?" Now that Hazard was back, perfection had returned to her life—perfection and contentment and a happiness she had stopped trying to understand.

"No patience?" he teased.

She cast him a sparkling glance from under heavy lashes. "Remember to whom you speak," she reminded him with a vivacious smile, "when you mention patience. The woman who seduced you twice in this very cabin."

He laughed.

And she said "When?" again, a little more emphatically.

He took her face gently between the palms of his hands, bent his head down so he was at her eye level, kissed her mouth very softly, and said, "Now."

She squealed with delight. His hands fell away when she danced two small steps of elation, and she saw the blood for the first time. "You're hurt," she cried, reaching for his hands.

"It's nothing." He sidestepped to elude her. The palms of his hands were ripped from the rough shingles and his need for haste.

"There's blood!"

"Scratches, that's all," he explained, then added, "We should leave."

"If we don't leave here very soon"—it dawned on Blaze, looking at him squarely, at the bloody torn hands so plain to see, although Hazard denied the severity of the wounds—"might it make a difference in the state of our health? And damn you, Jon Hazard, don't lie to me."

Her deep blue eyes were watching him intently, and he discarded the notion of dissembling. "It might."

"Who's after you, as if I didn't know?"

"I may have killed him."

"Where?"

"At Rose's."

"May?"

"I left in a hurry."

"Can they find their way up here in the dark?"

"No, and at base, I don't think they'll risk your life to come up here at all. But—"

"What?"

"Suddenly I want to go home. No terribly rational reasons. Maybe I'm tired of people shooting at me. I need a rest cure. And you wanted to go anyway. You don't mind, do you?"

Mind? she thought. I wouldn't mind living on the Earth's most blighted square of space if you were with me. Mind? Going to see your home, your relatives, the way of life that made you the splendid man you are? All she wanted, now that he had safely returned, was never to have him leave her again. "No," she calmly said, instead, sure he'd be terrified at the real intensity of her need, "I don't mind at all."

Hazard packed two more sacks with clothes, food, and fur robes, carried them out, and arranged them comfortably on the horses. Coming back in, he asked Blaze what he probably should have asked sooner: "Can you ride?" And then looked at her in the context of a rider for the first time. Attired in one of his shirts, she wouldn't last an hour on the trail. The light cotton dresses he'd just brought back from Rose's were, ironically, no longer useful.

"Yes," Blaze replied simply. She'd spent most of her youth on horseback. It was the only pastime allowed women of her class that had any element of excitement.

"Traveling at night can be dangerous. The horses occasionally stumble."

"I'll manage." She smiled at his concern.

His dark gaze taking in the unsuitable shirt, he hesitated another moment, then walking over to the storage shelves, took down a doeskin envelope, large, flat, and tied with elaborate beaded bands in stark patterns of black and white. He placed it on the table. "Wear one of these," he said. "For riding," he gruffly added. And, turning abruptly, he walked back outside.

Blaze untied the braided leather that held the beaded bands in place and folded back the supple doeskin. Inside, carefully wrapped in ermine, were three women's dresses. One of pale yellow doeskin, one of elk-skin and one in a fine white leather she didn't recognize. All were elaborately fringed and beaded. The white one was covered with hundreds of elk teeth, each suspended from delicate beaded ornaments of unusual pastel shades. Months of handiwork had been lavished on each garment; in some areas, the beadwork literally covered the leather.

It was obvious, what with the almost ritual packing, whose dresses these were. He'd saved them after his wife's death. How long had she been dead? How did she die? What was her name? And then an uncharitable surge of jealousy flooded her mind. Did he, she apprehensively wondered, both curious and dismayed, have children by his wife? It had never occurred to her, that he might have children; even the thought of Hazard's having been married seemed inconceivable. Yet he had been and he must have cared for his wife very much, she sadly reflected, to have kept the dresses with such ceremony.

I don't want to wear them, she morosely thought. Every time he looks at them he'll think of her. And being back with his people would only serve to revive old memories. Why should she wear them and renew those sorts of remembrances? I won't wear them, she petulantly decided, I simply won't. It was insensitive of him to even suggest it. Her ready temper flared. Imagine, wanting her to wear his dead wife's clothes, she reflected with smoldering sullenness. The nerve! Storming out of the cabin, she stood on the top step of the small porch and shouted at Hazard, who was a mere four feet distance, adjusting the half-hitch rawhide bridle on the buckskin's lower jaw. "I won't wear them!"

Startled, Hazard looked up. "What's wrong with you?"

"With *me*? What's wrong with *me*? *Nothing's* wrong with *me!* I just don't want to wear your dead wife's clothes!" she screamed. Jealousy, envy, fear of losing him, fear of never having had him, apprehension over the differences in their cultures, the differences in their experience and feelings, the suddenly real threat of Buhl Mining versus claims 1014–15, all contrived to generate the hysterical scream.

"You can't ride in that shirt," was all Hazard said, ignoring the hysteria, not wanting to discuss it at all. "You'll need them," he finished matter-of-factly.

"Go to hell," Blaze retorted, not in a practical frame of mind.

It had taken a small piece from Hazard's soul to

take down that doeskin envelope. It represented not only a wife he'd once loved, but a youth so far removed from the present that the memories had begun to lose their fine edges. Years were merging, faces blurring, words spoken only half remembered. It hadn't been easy to offer the dresses; they were the last traces he had of Raven Wing, a reliquary to both her and his carefree youth, a time neither he nor his clan would ever see again.

Lord, he hated it when she screamed. He wasn't familiar with screaming women. A muscle high over his cheekbone twitched. "I wouldn't have offered them to you," he said, his voice cool, "if there'd been any other choice, believe me. And I dislike you screaming."

"I dislike being offered some damned holy, treasured keepsake of your wife's," Blaze shouted, an undefinable sadness underlying her anger. How could she ever expect to become a part of his life? She was alien to everything in his world.

"What do you want me to say?" he asked gravely, his hands still now on the bridle leather. Necessity had driven him; she couldn't ride for two days in that shirt.

His feelings were too new for him to consciously recognize that his gesture had represented something more than necessity. It was a final relinquishing of Raven Wing's memory, of all she'd been to him, of all she personified of his youth. No woman had ever replaced her completely in the secret recesses of his soul, despite all the playing at love since her death. Until now.

But logic had ruled his life too many years and duty, as well, so he was no more aware of what the giving up of Raven Wing's dresses meant than Blaze did. They were objects, that's all, useful at the moment, he rationally noted, ignorant of the tenuous texture of emotions that prompted his decision.

"If you don't want to wear them, don't. I just want to go home," Hazard said. "Now." And suddenly he felt as though he'd been tired for a year. "Ride your bottom bloody for all I care," he added, jerking the last knot in the bridle. The abrupt wrench caused the buckskin to fling her head up in fear. Hazard's slender fingers soothed her, brushing down her nose, his voice a rich undercurrent of resonant endearments.

"I'll wear a pair of your trousers," Blaze insisted.

"Fine." He looked up, his eyes meeting her coolly over the buckskin's nose. "Whenever you're ready."

Turning in a huff, her back stiff in anger, Blaze reentered the cabin. She didn't look around when Hazard came in a moment later, but kept her back to him, intent on her struggle with the oversized waist on Hazard's blue cavalry trousers. When the door slammed again, she only muttered about odious men, odious men still in love with their dead wives.

She had to roll the pants legs up several times in order to walk, and she was still softly cursing Hazard's damnably cool indifference when she left the cabin not even looking around the room as she departed. "Fast enough for you?" Blaze acidly inquired, emerging onto the porch.

"You're the fastest woman I've ever known," Hazard replied, equally acidly.

"And you've known plenty." The remark was intended to be denigrating.

"Unfortunately, one too many," Hazard drily said, vaulting bareback onto Peta.

"In that case, why not leave me behind?" Blaze offered resentfully, standing motionless near the buckskin. "It'll save Daddy a lot of trouble."

"And lose my claim? Not on your life. Let's go."

"How am I supposed to get on this horse?" She eyed the light padding intended as a saddle, the stirrups buckled short.

Peta was prancing impatiently. "I thought you said you could ride."

"I can once I'm up on the damn animal."

With a disgruntled sigh, Hazard slid off Peta and walked over to her. "I forgot to hire a groom to help you up. Sorry, my lady, we're so primitive here in the wilderness," he mockingly commented, and taking her around the waist, he lifted her neatly onto the slight saddle from the off-side. Unlike the white men, the Absarokee always mounted from the right.

"There's no bit," Blaze noted, looking down at him.

"Observant," Hazard remarked coolly.

"How do I control him, Mr. Black?"

"Use your knees, princess, or do you want me to lead him?" he sarcastically suggested.

"No!"

Shrugging, he swung up on Peta and gathered his reins. He expected he'd have to lead her before the night was over. White people rode, but no one handled horses like the Absarokee. When Absarokee children could first sit up, they were tied into a high-backed pack saddle and from then on became an integral part of the migrations of the tribe, riding their own ponies. By the time they were four, they could ride by themselves, and by seven they were accomplished horsemen. They also had callouses on their backsides from years on horseback. Hazard didn't recall Miss Blaze Braddock's being similarly endowed. And that rough twill would be hell compared to the soft leather of his fringed leggings. Not his problem, though, he noted, and kicked Peta into a canter.

Blaze struggled a little at first, but with Peta in the lead, the buckskin was more inclined to follow than choose its own route. She experimented with the light bridle, with knee pressure, and before too many miles discovered the horse she was riding responded to the merest touch. Hazard could have told her that. He'd trained it.

Hazard stopped once just before sunrise to water the horses at a small creek lined with quaking aspen. He'd started to lift Blaze down but she'd shaken his hand off her arm and slid down herself. They ate pemmican and bread in austere silence and resumed their journey soon after.

He didn't stop again until midafternoon. And he wouldn't have then except he'd noticed the clenched line of Blaze's jaw a half-mile back. She was in pain, he could tell, and he silently admired her stubborn courage. Only waiting to find a suitable campsite, he pulled up soon after on the bank of another bubbling stream bordered with flowering cottonwood and lacy pine. This time when he offered to help her down, she allowed him to, and he set Blaze very gently on her feet. Although he hadn't intended resting overnight, he said, "This clearing looks comfortable. We'll stay here tonight."

Hazard started the fire, cooked and served their supper, cut enough pine boughs to make an *acta 'tsé*, an Absarokee-style lean-to, and laid out a soft mattress of ground cedar and sweet sage thick as a feather bed. He hadn't teased or scolded or bullied or said "I told you so," and for his kindness Blaze was close to tears. Damn, how could he be so patient and kind? And damn, why did she love him? And damn and bloody blast, why did he still love his wife? It wasn't fair! It was a great miscarriage of justice, for after nineteen years, when she at last found the man she loved, he was still in love with his dead wife.

She desperately wanted to know why he still felt that way, but it wasn't something you could just blurt out and ask. Even Blaze realized that some things were sacred; a person was entitled to his privacy. And if Hazard didn't care for her, certainly she couldn't make him care. What a waste, she thought, all those years cultivating all the graces one was told would charm a man. Not that she had exactly cultivated them. But she had listened anyway; she'd heard about them and, in her own uninhibited way, accepted some as practical means to an end. And now, when she'd found a man she could love so much that nothing else mattered in the world, she'd come up against a stone wall. A beloved dead wife of a stone wall. Why had no one written a chapter on that exigency in the finishing-school texts?

Well, she had some pride, anyway, some respect for another person's feelings. Even if she wanted to know, *very desperately*, why he still loved his wife, she certainly wouldn't ask. "Why do you still love your wife?" she heard herself ask, looking straight at him across the small fire left after the supper had been cooked.

Hazard's eyes flared, then his lashes dropped.

He won't answer, Blaze thought. It's too painful. He still loves her too much.

My God, he thought, is she hallucinating? What

prompted that question? And he said, "Are you all right?
I know your bottom must be sore. Are you in pain?"

"Don't try to change the subject. I want to know."

He didn't answer for a moment, realizing she was
driven by some demon. Finally, he said, "She's dead."

"That doesn't answer my question."

"Is it important? Because my people feel it's disre-
spectful to talk of the dead."

Her eyes, the color of stormy seas, were very large
and strikingly intense. She nodded her head.

Persistence was her strong suit, he ruefully thought.
Exhaling softly, he began to speak. "When someone's
dead," he said very slowly, "you can't love them anymore. You can love their memory, or the pleasure they
gave you or the joy in living they may have intensified.
But you see, once they've joined the spirit world, the
person you loved is gone. The grass still grows, the flowers still smell as sweet, the buffalo travel the land. Memories aren't the same as living, though. Do you think it's
possible to love someone who's no longer alive?" He
asked the question with a quiet curiosity.

It was Blaze's turn to pause for an answer. "I don't
know," she said at last. "Why did you save the dresses,
then?"

Hazard was seated on the ground very near the dying fire. Pulling up a handful of grass, he tossed it on the
low flames and watched the smoke spiral up before he
responded. "The dresses were part of the memories, part
of my youth." And he drew from recollection, the raw
enthusiasm of his adolescence, when ideals were a substitute for judgment, life was play, and the future entailed
nothing more lively than horse raids and begetting children. It seemed a millennium ago.

"How old were you when you married?"

Absorbed in recall, Hazard didn't reply until the
question was repeated. "Seventeen years"—he smiled
faintly—"as you yellow eyes say. We say seventeen snows
or winters."

In the glow of the fire his heritage was purely traced
on his face and form. His dark hair fell forward with his
head bent slightly down, and his black eyes stared into

the flames as if the answer to her probing questions were centered in their red-hot iridescence. The smooth texture of his skin was darker in the shadows of the evening, his leather-clad body at home here in his country.

"Were you happy?" Blaze braced herself for the answer, wanting to know and not wanting to know.

"Yes."

The quiet reply hurt more than she'd imagined. "What happened?"

"She died."

"How?"

"By her own hand." His voice held a curtness that hadn't been there before. Rising Wolf had finally pried his fingers from Raven Wing's cold wrist and led him away. No one else had dared. "And now," he went on, shaking away the unwelcome image, "the inquisition is over."

Even Blaze, nervy and impetuous, didn't have the audacity to continue.

"I'll sleep on the outside," Hazard mildly remarked, as if he hadn't divulged anything unusual, when, he had, in fact, made the mysterious dead wife even more mysterious.

How had she died, Blaze wondered, her eyes unconsciously arrested in widened surprise.

"We leave at sunrise; we've another long day ahead of us." The words were moderate, explanatory, calm, and he was waiting for her to precede him into the pine-bough shelter.

The mystery would have to wait for another time, Blaze thought, and made to move. She gasped in pain and fell back down. She'd been sitting quietly since Hazard had lifted her down from the buckskin and had half forgotten the extent of her soreness. The rough fabric of Hazard's trousers had rubbed her skin raw in the course of their day on horseback. Hazard was at her side in an instant, lifting her into his arms, his touch gentle. A moment later he had carefully placed her on the sweet-smelling bed. "We're both too stubborn," he murmured, gazing into her cerulean eyes gleaming wetly from the shock of the pain. "I'm sorry, *bia*. I should have noticed sooner that you were hurting."

"It's my own fault," Blaze conceded, warmed by his apology. "I could have said something."

"Not the indomitable Miss Braddock," he teased, his smile flashing against his bronzed skin.

"You're looking at the least indomitable woman in the world right now. I'm not going to be able to walk for a week."

"I can take care of that."

"This is one time your self-assured arrogance sounds sweet as a heavenly chorus."

"I brought some salve along." His grin was benign, ". . . just in case."

"Very smug men," Blaze sweetly replied, "have always annoyed me." But her smile was the kind that could charm tarantulas away from a four-star meal.

"And obstinate women, me." Hazard's slender hand brushed the corner of her smile. "With one notable exception," he softly added.

"I suppose I should have worn one of the dresses."

"There's nothing like leather between you and a horse," he agreed. "I brought the dresses along in case you changed your mind. But," he went on hurriedly, aware of Blaze's sparking glance, "we'll get you your own just as soon as we reach the village. I didn't intend the dresses to be hurtful. They were simply all I had handy."

"Really, no deep ulterior meaning attached?" The hope in Blaze's voice was naively poignant.

"None, I swear. Maybe you'd rather wear trousers." He recalled the few times he'd seen her before she became his hostage, and she'd had trousers on two times out of the three. "We could have some made for you. Although"—Hazard paused, then determinedly continued—"you decide . . . dress or trousers. But they should be leather. At least for the long rides. Otherwise—" He grimaced. "Oh, hell, we'll just have to put together a wardrobe for you. *You* decide what you want."

"Do Absarokee women wear trousers?" Blaze asked, recognizing his resolute effort to be tactful and mediatory.

"No."

"Would it bother you if I wore trousers at the summer camp?"

It took him a moment to consider. "You're entitled to wear what you wish." He was being excessively accommodating for, in fact, he would be the brunt of much joking if Blaze wore trousers. "I won't presume to—"

"But no women in your clan wear trousers."

He shook his head.

"If I can move tomorrow, I'll try on one of those dresses," she said, smiling, "and save you from embarrassment."

He grinned suddenly like a small boy. "I can take care of myself, Miss Braddock. You needn't sacrifice for me."

"It's no sacrifice. They're gorgeous dresses, but . . ."

He waited and softly repeated the conjunction when she didn't go on.

"Do you mind?" she whispered low. "I do want my own dresses when we reach camp."

"You'll have them," he quietly declared. "As many as you want." The Absarokee were the most resplendent of the Plains tribes, priding themselves on their appearance and dress. "And what we can't buy, we'll have made," Hazard promised, intent on having his woman lavishly clothed. It didn't strike him until much later that night, cradling Blaze as she breathed trustfully in his arms, that he'd thought of her as *his woman* and meant it.

THE salve proved as miraculous as Hazard knew it was. Blaze woke feeling wonderful, and it wasn't exclusively due to the salve. Several other factors contributed to her extraordinary sense of well-being. The morning was fresh, warm, sundrenched. And most important, she awoke in Hazard's embrace. He'd held her gently all night, afraid to move lest he wake her, conscious that she was exhausted after the long hours on the trail. He was used to not sleeping; when out on raiding parties, there'd often be many days without rest when pursuit was intense. In those circumstances, one simply swung over to a fresh mount in the herd just captured and continued riding.

He'd dozed a little during the night so he hadn't gone completely sleepless. But he'd spent a lot of time staring into the smoldering fire and analyzing the concept of *his woman* that had finally forced its way into his conscious thoughts. Problems arose; the obvious ones concerned the mine, less blatant ones involved the success of any future they might have. Not new problems, old ones. With an additional reflection to confuse an already muddled predicament. Was Blaze Braddock's unique sense of adventure, he wondered, simply spilling over and encompassing a sensual caprice as well, or was she capable of more? Were her feelings committed past a frivolous lark?

Hazard had been entertaining himself too many years with willing and amorous ladies to be certain himself where frolic stopped and love began. But while he came up with no answers, of one thing he was certain: he did want her as *his woman.* To relinquish her, to send her away, even to ignore her sexually for some moral concept of honor, as he'd first attempted, were no longer viable options. Selfishly, he wanted her. She pleased him in countless ways, brought joy to his life. And pleasure— more profound and intemperate than any he'd known before.

"I feel much better," Blaze purred, startling him from his musing. "What in the world is in that stuff?"

"Mostly buffalo fat," Hazard replied, adjusting his arm, stiff from its immobility, "with some yucca plant, nettle, camomile, and I forget what else. A few incantations and smoke from sacred tobacco," he added with a smile.

"Are you teasing me?" Blaze asked, nestling against him, her eyes the way he liked them best—enormous with cheerful curiosity.

"I forgot the hummingbird feathers."

"Now you're teasing."

"Nope. True as E-sahca-wata's laugh."

"One of your folktales?"

"This one about Old Man Coyote reminds us of our humanity, and frailty."

"Tell me."

"Sometime. Say tomorrow, when we're indulging our laziness in my lodge at the Arrow." His dark brows rose. "And now, *bia*, it's time to leave if we want to reach home before dark. Now, Boston princess," he whispered, brushing her hair aside from her cheek, "you have to get ready." And bending, he kissed her tenderly on the eyes, then dressed her, fed her, lifted her onto Peta, and swung up behind, arranging her in his lap. He wouldn't hear of her riding today, although Blaze insisted she was perfectly fine.

Hazard held her that day as they rode higher into the mountains, and only a man with muscles strengthened by years of physical training could have so effortlessly endured. They stopped at a creek just outside the range of the scouts—which he called wolves—set round the encampment and washed. Hazard dressed in full regalia with all the accoutrements of his position as chief: wolf tails at the heels of each beaded moccasin, indicative of striking coups; falcon tail feathers with eagle breath feathers tied behind one ear, his medicine and spiritual guide; iridescent blue and green sea shells from beyond the mountains by the Pacific where the Salish lived, hung from both his earlobes, pierced with a heated awl by his mother on the second day of his life;[10] fringed leggings adorned with ermine tails that marked him a leader of an expedition returning with booty. A beaded shirt,[11] half open over his strong chest, revealed a necklace of bear teeth.

Peta was decked out too, in a rich bridle and breastplate traded in the annual spring meeting with the Shoshone—they'd obtained the Spanish riding gear from the Southwest tribes. The polished medallion glowed, ornamented with flowing feathers and strings of beadwork. A knotted rope hanging from Peta's neck told of the cutting of an enemy's picketed mount. And the number of horses captured could be read from the stripes of white clay painted under her eyes and on her flanks. Hazard modestly used the symbolic number three, his lucky number, knowing each stripe represented many more.

When he had finished dressing he added a heavy silver necklace to Blaze's costume, matching the pale saffron doeskin dress elaborately beaded in shades of silver and azure. Then he held her still and carefully combed her hair with the porcupine-tail comb common to the Northwest Plains tribes. His strokes were gentle and skilled, and under the late afternoon sun her red-gold hair soon shone like satin. When he was satisfied, he lifted her onto Peta and vaulted up behind. Carefully holding her across his lap, he nudged Peta with his knees. The breath feathers behind his left ear stirred in the light wind.

Chapter 23

THE wolves spotted them first and sent out their wailing cries. Hazard smiled, the sound a familiar childhood memory.

Two scouts, eager in their youth, came galloping out of a draw and thundered across the open grassland toward them, hauling their ponies to a rearing halt a few short feet from Hazard and Blaze. "Welcome, Dit-chi-lajash," they cried, wide smiles of greeting on their handsome young faces. "We were afraid you weren't coming!" Blaze recognized Hazard's name in the flow of Absarokee words.

"I missed you young cubs too much to stay away," Hazard smilingly replied to the eager youths on their prancing ponies. Noting their surreptitious glances at Blaze, he gestured gracefully at her and said, *"Buah,* Blaze Braddock." And Blaze smiled at them, understanding it was an introduction.

Still young enough to lack some of the necessary

social graces, they sat open-mouthed for a moment when Hazard said, *"búa."* Speaking rapidly, Hazard prompted them and they both stammered an English "El-lo."

"That, I'm afraid, is about the extent of their English," Hazard said to Blaze. "They're sons of my mother's sister and," he finished with a smile, "a great nuisance at times." Hazard murmured a few brisk phrases in Absarokee to them and, with a gesture much like a salute, they wheeled their ponies and galloped away. "They're going to ride ahead. Something they're eminently suited for. At this age, they only know how to gallop."

So when Hazard and Blaze entered the village sometime later, the whispering had already preceded them as Hazard knew it would. *Uah* (his wife) drifted from mouth to mouth. "Hazard the Black Cougar has taken a wife" went from lodge to lodge. "A yellow eyes," they murmured, and the young women who had been recipients of Hazard's attention in the past whispered less charitable phrases. "He won't keep her long," they said. "A yellow eyes can't please him as a wife." Hazard the Black Cougar had long been famed for his beauty and attentiveness, and his former lovers disliked hearing they'd been displaced.

The tepees from the mountain and river divisions of the Absarokee spread across the whole grassy river valley. They were divided into clans, circles of lodges arranged in a familiar pattern with all doorways facing east. As with all Plains Indians, horses meant wealth. And this camp was rich. For miles around the hills were covered with ponies of all sizes and colors.

Hazard rode slowly through the crowds of people pressing around them. He smiled and acknowledged their greetings, answered dozens of inquiries with quips which made everyone laugh. They all noted how carefully he carried the yellow eyes woman. And none of them had forgotten the origin of the elaborately beaded dress the yellow eyes wore. They all remembered how many horses Hazard had paid for it. For his first wife. His Absarokee wife. How much power, they wondered, did the beautiful flame-haired woman hold over their chief?

Hazard stopped before a pure white lodge, taller than the others and beautifully painted, unlike most of the tepees. With Blaze still in his arms, he slid off Peta. Standing in the center of the admiring crowd, he spoke to those gathered round, listened to them, paused sometimes before answering—other times answered with no more than a smile. Small boys pushed to see him and those who dared touched him. He was the legendary Ditchilajash, the chief who had more coups than anyone in memory. After a polite amount of time Hazard nodded, turning back to the lodge, then spoke rapidly and concisely as if issuing orders.

A pathway was cleared for him to the doorway of his lodge. He was, Blaze thought, like some conquering hero, and impossibly complicated feelings assailed her. It was as if he had a light side and a dark side—two different people—and she hardly knew either. Striding toward the entrance, he spoke twice more to a young man who bore a remarkable resemblance to him, although still in his youth and some inches shorter than Hazard. The boy laughed. Hazard smiled and murmured a few more words before bending slightly and passing into the interior of his lodge with Blaze.

Careful as he lowered her, he placed Blaze on a bed of fur robes, one of two on either side of the entrance. The dwelling was as elaborately decorated inside as out. Painted skins hung from above eye level, lining the entire inner surface. Light streamed down from the smoke hole high overhead, and a soft diffused illumination from the afternoon sun shimmered through the pale leather.

"Are you tired?" Hazard asked, pulling up a woven willow backrest and sprawling comfortably beside Blaze's bed, leaning against his own *icërekō' tsi 'te.*

"No. You wouldn't let me do *anything* today," she replied, her smile mischievous.

"Later—tomorrow—you should be completely healed and you can have the run of the camp."

"And of you?" Blaze winsomely asked. "Since you turned me down this morning." She had wanted him so badly in their soft bed of ground cedar, but he'd gently refused, afraid of hurting her bruised body.

"For your own good, minx. Not for lack of wanting. And yes, tomorrow, I'm available. Remind me," he said grinning.

"With all those people who seem to know you and want your time, will it be possible?" she inquired, half in jest and half seriously. "You're extremely well known." It was a prodigious understatement of the chief's position she'd just viewed.

"They're all from my clan, *bia*. I'm one of their chiefs, as was my father before me. I know everyone and everyone knows me," he casually answered, seemingly oblivious of his fame.

"How many are there?"

"My clan[12] is one of thirteen and we've forty lodges.[13] In terms of people, around four hundred. We're part of the Mountain Absarokee, sometimes called Many Lodges. In the summer, we meet with the River Absarokee, the Black Lodges, and socialize. Everyone's related in convoluted ways. It's like a large family gathering, with all branches present. Probably five hundred lodges altogether are here now."

"And you know them all?"

"Most, although I've lost track of some of the newer youngsters."

And they all know you, she uneasily thought; know you and want some part of you. She'd seen the women's glances. One would have had to be blind not to. She thought of the women's covetous eyes and said, "Do you have any?" ignoring the hesitancy of politesse.

"Any what?" he said in apparent ignorance. But it could be evasion; Hazard had never struck her as particularly slow.

She wasn't to be put off. "Children," she explained.

It was silent in the cool interior. Hazard's sprawl went suddenly rigid. Lord, he knew her so little, knew less what she was thinking. Knew only slightly more about his own thoughts concerning her. Why was she so damnably inquisitive? The answer to her question probably required an entire restructuring of her cultural ideas on family—of which there was no time, at present, he brusquely decided. "None by my wife," said Hazard shortly.

For once in her life, Blaze was shocked into silence. She tried to speak twice, but the words wouldn't separate neatly from the jumbled confusion in her mind.

"It's not the same in our clan," he said mildly after a very long time, after the silence had lengthened and the first suffused shock had subsided on Blaze's cheeks—and after his own painful memories had been locked away once again. "Men and women have lovers, wifes are abducted at times. There are different choices with us."[14]

"Who has the choices?" Blaze asked, finally finding her voice, wanting to know how Hazard's children were born, wondering if the choices were masculine prerogatives as they were in her world.

"Men and women both. Since women own property as men do, they have more freedom. That's not to say most marriages aren't stable and long-lasting. Most are . . . but—"

"There are choices," Blaze softly finished.

Hazard sighed. "Right," he said, knowing his truncated version of a very complicated cultural phenomenon was not going to satisfy Blaze's inquiry about his children.

"Was that last boy you spoke to outside yours?" She was trying to stay calm against the tidal wave of emotion washing over her.

Hazard's expression softened and the graveness left his eyes. "You noticed the resemblance?"

"It was very striking," Blaze answered as tranquilly as possible. She was numb with jealousy.

"No, he's not literally mine, although he's designated *barä'ke,* my child, in terms of clan relationship. You'd call him a cousin, I think. Our relationships are quite different from yours. Red Plume is my father's sister's son." Feeling uncomfortable, Hazard attempted to end the conversation. "Let's drop the subject," he suggested. "It's endlessly complicated and not based on any of the white man's cultural traditions."

"After you tell me what I want to know," Blaze murmured, insistent.

"Why?" Hazard bluntly asked, preferring to avoid controversy.

"Because I'm jealous," she said very softly, "of any woman you've ever been with."

He looked away restlessly and uneasily slid down an inch or so on the willow backrest. She unnerved him with her candid honesty. After years of dealing with women in terms of honeyed love words and superficial endearments, he was forced to respond to this remarkably frank and independent woman in ways very new to him. He had to think for a moment to avoid the familiar pacifying phrases from his past. "You don't have to," he replied simply, at last. "You don't have to be jealous of any of them. And if you weren't still recuperating, I'd prove it to you."

"I get so angry with you," Blaze responded unexpectedly.

"You may have noticed," he drily retorted, "you have the same affect on me occasionally."

"About all the women in your past, I mean."

"Would you want me to protest about the men in your past?"

"There weren't any," she reminded him.

"Well, if there were."

"They wouldn't have mattered."

"And neither do mine," he quietly insisted.

"But the children . . ."

"They're with their mothers. Descent is through the female line. When they're older, the boys may want to live with me, in our way. When that time comes, a decision will be made. They're still young."

"Are there many?"

"No. Three. And the circumstances are . . ." He ran lean fingers through his hair in exasperation. "I'll explain sometime when—"

At that moment the lovely young boy who looked as Hazard must have at his age called out *"Dee-ko-lah,"* the polite announcement of a visitor. "Are you there?"[15]

Hazard readily replied, welcoming the termination of a discussion which would only cause problems.

Behind the boy trailed six women, all carrying food.

Within minutes, a substantial meal was set before them. One women burned sweet grass so the lodge smelled fragrant and fresh. And then visitors paraded in.

Hazard was seated at the rear of the lodge, facing the door, *acō*—in the place of honor—with Blaze on his left in the most respected position for a guest. One older chief brought up what all the others were thinking when they saw Blaze seated on Hazard's left. "She stays," was all Hazard said. Since it was a social occasion other women were present, but not seated in such exalted positions. There was some low-voiced grumbling, but no one opposed him.

After a formal greeting of welcome, the visitors were asked to sit in a certain place, then invited to smoke. The pipe was passed around the crowded circle and all the men smoked. And since this was a social occasion and not a council, the young males were also allowed to participate in the pipe ceremony.

Following the offering of the pipe to the four directions of the compass, a great variety of food was served, beginning with the most succulent delicacy, roasted buffalo tongue. A stew was served of buffalo meat, squash, and wild celery in dishes made from the bleached shoulder blades of the buffalo. Pumpkin cooked with box elder syrup, wild turnip baked in hot ashes, and camas roots cooked in a pit over hot stones followed. Boiled artichokes, lushly green and seasoned with sage, contributed a colorful foil to bowls of ripe grapes and blackberries. The special sweet saved for important occasions such as this was brought forth to a murmur of delight. Cottonwood ice cream, a jellylike froth scraped from the peeled surface of the tree and tasting exactly like ice cream, was piled in milky clouds on a large wooden platter. The meal was an extravagance in preparation and display, suitable for a chief of Hazard's rank, and at the first taste, Hazard realized how much he'd missed meat cooked in the Indian way. And nothing in the world, he thought contentedly, compared to the delicate flavor of cottonwood ice cream.

A busy hum of conversation drifted around the sea of guests dining with Hazard and Blaze. Rising Wolf sat next to Blaze and interpreted for her, at least the portions that he felt were suitable. She was more than once the topic of conversation, and to the variety of questions, Hazard replied calmly. He explained she'd come to the mine as a bribe, he'd kept her as a hostage, and she'd now become his woman. There was some discussion over her exact position. *Bia*, they asked, or *bwa-le-jah*—sweetheart or friend? *Buah*, my wife, Hazard said firmly, seeing shock invade more than one set of dark eyes. Somehow, with clarification, many had felt she would be less than he had announced this afternoon. Fervently, many had *wished* she would be less. Eyebrows raised at his firm pronouncement, and for a moment there was an uneasy silence.

"Are there any objections?" Hazard asked, attentively regarding the circle of startled guests. "Good," he declared into the ensuing silence.

It wasn't as though white people hadn't married into the tribe before. Since the early days of the nineteenth century, many white men had married within various Absarokee bands, and all had been accepted eventually as full members of the tribe. The only difference here was that one of their *chiefs* should choose a yellow eyes woman. That had never happened before.

"Tell me," Hazard ventured into the stillness, "are the buffalo near enough for the hunt?"

From that point, Rising Wolf's interpreting resumed. No further discussions arose over Hazard's new wife. Plans were made to hunt in two days' time, animated anecdotes were exchanged about previous hunts, and, after being served a sweet concoction of wild raspberries, hazelnuts, plums, and honey, the guests departed.

"Does everyone always listen to you so obligingly?" Blaze inquired as Hazard dropped the door robe behind the last guest. She had noticed the few abrupt silences, heard Hazard's curt replies, recognized her name and the occasional shocked reactions.

He walked across the width of the large lodge and dropped into a sprawl beside her on the bed of buffalo robes. "Everything's open to discussion in our tribe. No single person makes all the decisions."

"It seemed that a few of the older men took offense at some of the things you said."

Hazard shrugged and stretched out on his back. "Can't please everyone all the time," he philosophically replied. "Some of the older men are less open to compromise."

"That's pretty true everywhere."

He nodded abstractedly, his eyes on the starry night visible through the slowly spiraling smoke wafting up through the smoke hole. "The world's changing so fast," he softly said, thinking how small they all were under the canopy of endless sky. "If we don't adapt, we won't survive." He didn't speak for a moment, and when his eyes turned to Blaze his tone was less pensive. "There're only six thousand Absarokee Indians; twice that many people live in Virginia City alone."

"Do you ever despair . . . with those odds?" He had never talked about his people before, and the melancholy was pungent in his voice.

He smiled. A small gentle smile. "At least a hundred times a day—or a thousand," he softly added.

She wanted to offer him comfort, help in some way, ease the sadness behind the smile. "Hazard, I have money; I know people, I can—"

His dark fingers curved around her wrist. "Hush, Boston princess. *Hú'kawe*," he murmured, pulling her onto his chest. "No more serious talk, *bia*. None. We're here for fun," he whispered, "fun and play. So kiss me, darling Boston."

He held her close all night and they slept like exhausted children, safe now after weeks of uncertainty, at home in the chief's lodge in the center of the encampment. Protected and guarded.

Chapter 24

THE camp's morning activities woke them. The dogs barked first, followed by the high-pitched sounds of children at play, and soon the full bustle of bathing, fire building, food preparation—all the early day occupations—buzzed around them as they continued dozing.

"Ummmm," Hazard murmured later, stretching leisurely. "I haven't slept like that in months." Rolling on his side, he bent to kiss Blaze—a soft good-morning kiss. "And how is the loveliest redhead in camp?"

"The only redhead, you mean," she lazily responded.

"That too," he said, smiling. "Ready for bathing?"

Blaze only slid further under the fur robes.

"That excited? At least we'll have the river to ourselves. Everyone else bathes at sunrise."

Blaze groaned.

"Fortunately no one expects you to act normal," he teased.

"Good," came a muffled reply from under the mounded furs.

"Not normal. But . . . civilized. Come, *bia*, you have to bathe. Do you want me to lose face?" His tone was mocking.

The body beneath the robes gave no indication of moving.

"I guess I'll have to carry you down to the river."

Blaze sat bolt upright and furs slithered away in gleaming folds. "You're being a bully again, Hazard," she blurted out, prickly in an instant, but looking much more like a soft, tousled kitten with enormous doting blue eyes.

"Perhaps we could negotiate this, *bia-cara,*" Hazard murmured placatingly. "Item one: Permissive as our culture is, certain requisite precepts remain, namely, cleanliness. Item two: I could find a warm, sunny spot where the water isn't too deep and will be hot enough even for you. Item three: I cannot, sweet pet, haul water for you here. Even I have my moments of consequence. And item four: If you come down to the river and bathe with me like the dutiful wife everyone here assumes you are, I promise to—"

"Stop a minute," Blaze demanded, scrambling onto her knees, her heart beginning to accelerate in irregular pitta-pats. "Back up a bit."

"I promise to—" His eyes were lit suddenly with a flame she'd never seen before.

She cleared her throat. "Farther back."

His voice was level. "Everyone here assumes—"

"Farther."

It had surprised him too, how easily the words flowed from his tongue, and he knew what she was asking. Looking at her directly, he repeated without sarcasm, as if the words had a compelling life of their own, "the dutiful wife?"

Blaze's gaze was also direct. "Now why," she very softly said, "would people assume that?"

"Because," Hazard replied gravely, "that's what I told them."

"Are we married?" Her voice shook like the quaking aspens outside.

"In the eyes of my people, we are."

"You didn't have to tell them that, did you?"

"No."

"I could have been your . . ."

"Paramour," he finished. Reaching over, he brushed a coppery curl behind her ear. "But I didn't want you to be."

"Because you love me," she said, awareness vivid in her eyes.

"I . . . It's been so long," said Hazard slowly. "There're so many problems . . . too many . . ."

"Why, then?"

"I didn't want any shame attached to you, because you're with me." It wasn't only a matter of conscience, but he wasn't prepared to confront the fullness of what it was. "And you have to be with me," he went on, "at least until your father arrives."

"And then what?" she softly asked.

"Let's not think about it for the time we're here," he said quietly. "Can't we just enjoy ourselves? Can't we forget your world and what it's doing to mine? Can't we forget next month, next year?" The image of the future had never seemed more vulnerable. "Please," he said, scarcely above a whisper. Nothing more tangible than a sense of personal honor drove him and at times his spiritual reserves were at a low point. He didn't want to face any questions that had no answers. He only wanted pleasure and ease, pure in its simplicity.

Listening to Hazard's whispered plea, Blaze realized, unlike her own pampered life, this young man she loved had taken on an enormous responsibility for his people. He'd gone East, understanding that the Absarokee way of life was in peril, and understanding as well that his duty lay in minimizing that peril. If he could learn the white man's ways, he might have the tools and weapons to stay the corruption, mitigate the losses. He knew what he must do, why and where it led; knew all the sacrifices honor must make to expediency; understood the shabby compromises the future held in store.

He was under pressures she'd never contemplated in her own self-centered life. And when he softly pleaded, "Can't we forget?" she understood he wanted to close the doors, at least temporarily, on every world but their own.

"What does a dutiful wife wear on the promenade to the bathing facilities?" she asked with a smile.

Hazard's dark eyes warmed instantly, dissipating the momentary bleakness. "A robe, a dress, anything. Hell, wrap that fur around you and I'll carry you down."

She looked up saucily from under lacy lashes. "And what of your consequence?"

Pulling her to him, he covered her face with kisses, light, dancing butterfly kisses, joyful buoyant kisses. "To hell," he murmured, "with my consequence." And lifting her into his arms, he carried her through the sunlit camp, past smiling glances, ribald comments, speculative murmurs, knowing eyes, down the path lined by drooping willows.

And the private bend of the mossy-banked river he carried Blaze to, shaded by willow shrubs and tall cotton-woods, was warm and sunny as he'd promised, and unveiled for Blaze a new and joyful glimpse into the boyish spirits of the mercurial man she loved.

It was a warm and golden day that fed the senses an overwhelming banquet of pleasure. They splashed in the azure water, played tag in the slow-moving current, washed each other with the sweet yucca soap, and, when their heated young bodies demanded, made love under the willows while warblers sang overhead.

In all their loving, she'd never seen anything as beautiful as his body that day, broad-shouldered and sculptured, glistening with pure mountain water, dusted golden with sunshine, lean and lithe as his namesake mountain cougar.

He made love to her and she to him as if it were the first time, kissing, undressing, tasting each other's lush flavors, the sun burning above, a pale second to the brightness of their love. He was the best thing that had ever happened to her in a life lived amid the luxuries of the world. He was the absolute best.

He told her in his own lyrical tongue that her beauty was the beauty of the sun as it slips down behind the mountains, her voice like the soft music of wind in the pine trees, her eyes the limitless blue of his own country's skies. Her expression was tender and solemn when he murmured the Indian words, and when he was finished, she told him, very very softly, "I am yours. And you are mine. Absarokee doesn't matter. Boston doesn't matter. Where you go, I go also."

He didn't answer. Only smiled and wrapped her arms around her neck. "Hang on tight," he whispered and rolled onto his back. After settling comfortably, she lay on him drowsy and replete, her breath wafting softly across his throat. "How do you like the summer hunt so far?" he murmured, his fingers lazily stroking her spine.

"Has anyone told you that you're the world's best host?" she languidly inquired, unmoving, like a kitten being stroked.

"Do you want the truth," Hazard amiably replied with a faint smile, part wolfish, very boyish, all beauty, "or something more diplomatic?" He grunted when she punched him and found himself looking into peppery, narrowed blue eyes. "In that case," he said after he caught his breath, his tone mockingly serious, his dark eyes alight with amusement, "the answer is no."

It took soothing after that, playful soothing, to placate his feisty companion, but they both reveled in the game, Blaze's teasing as provocative as his. And of course, the game had a predictable and delicious ending.

Much later, when the noon sky filtered apricot sunshine through the soft green leaves, Hazard asked, "Are you getting hungry?"

Blaze was lying on the crushed pungent grass beside him and turning her head slightly, raised one mischievous brow. "Is that a serious question?"

Schooling his mouth from its impulse to smile, Hazard said with a modicum of gravity. "Swear to God."

"A little," she replied, throwing her arms above her head like a coltish child.

"I'll send for food."

"Here?" Blaze looked around nervously, but all she

saw was varying shades of green and gold. "What will people say?"

"They'll probably say, 'He must love to make love to her; I thought he'd get hungry sooner.'"

"How embarrassing." Her cheeks had flushed rosy. "Why, because I'm hungry?"

"You know damn well what I'm talking about," she retorted, her voice low and heated.

"Weren't you the one," he patiently, inexcitably asked, "who wanted me to keep my schedule open for you today?"

"Well, yes, but—I mean—"

"I did, that's all, and I knew we'd have to eat eventually. I'm not allowed to cook here." His brows rose and fell quickly. "My consequence, you know. And I knew we couldn't rely on your cooking, if you'll pardon my mentioning it, ma'am," he teasingly finished.

"Did you actually tell someone you'd be busy all day making love to me and that you'd need food later?" Her arms were crossed under her head now and her glance was piercing.

"Not *someone,* precisely," he mildly answered, "and we don't say 'making love.' We call this pleasure *ah-x-abaw.*"

"Don't quibble, Hazard. Whom exactly did you tell?"

"The ladies," he said in a conversational tone as one might use discussing the weather, "who cooked for us last night, and the men who wanted me to ride out and scout the buffalo herd today."

"Oh, my God," Blaze gasped. "Everyone knows."

"Look, sweet," he calmly explained, watching the blush creep up her slender throat, "there's nothing to be embarrassed about. You're my wife. This is all the usual married stuff. And with one look at you, anyone could see I didn't marry you because you could cook and sew." He ran the tip of a blade of grass down her sun-dappled body. "You are the joy of my life, *bia,* and I don't care who knows it."

The simple words were a balm. Blaze looked up at Hazard, his hair—uncut since June—a silky black fall, his classic face warm with affection, his lean body luminous in the light. "You *are* my life," she whispered, and she knew her heart wasn't wrong. Despite Hazard's reluctance about tomorrows, undeterred by his evasive reaction to the word *love,* she was militantly sure that she and Hazard could overcome whatever odds were stacked against them . . . she knew their love was right.

"Terrifying prospect," he whispered back. "But I'll try to live up to your modest expectations." He had the look of a man not quite sure the natives were friendly, but cautiously hopeful.

They returned to the lodge to eat, Blaze not comfortable about eating by the riverbank. Hazard indulged her uncharacteristic prudery with only a minimum of teasing, reminding her that anyone who outclassed Lucy Attenborough in audacity should hardly be concerned about such mundane irregularities. He received a kicked shin in reply and orders to return her to his lodge.

Hazard smiled often on the walk back to the lodge; his replies to the cheerful comments addressed to him were equally lighthearted. Blaze hid her face in the solidity of his shoulder and counted his steps across the grassy plain.

The women who brought the food giggled when they left, except one tall, slim woman who looked at Blaze coolly and then spoke briefly to Hazard. His reply was terse.

"Friend of yours?" Blaze remarked after she left, capable of recognizing a former girlfriend when she saw one.

"Apparently not," Hazard replied, a trifle distractedly. He was digesting Little Moon's provocative comments. One of the young braves, it seems, was bragging about abducting Blaze. That sort of bravado was to be expected in a coterie of rash young bloods, but Little Moon's promise worried him more. She'd said she'd come and visit him some night.

It wasn't uncommon for lovers to slip under the tepee covers at night, especially in the summer, especially in the easy atmosphere of the summer hunt when dalliance was at its peak. He'd refused her, but he couldn't be sure she'd honor his wishes. If only Blaze understood all the idiosyncrasies of Absarokee culture. It was like a dance—complex, subtle, formalized by convention, an arrangement of humans moving in intensely convoluted ways. Oh, hell, he'd face the problems as they rose. Perhaps they wouldn't surface at all. In any event, he couldn't possibly educate her in a thousand-year-old culture in a few days. So, cavalierly disregarding the possibility of problems, he surveyed the variety of food arrayed before them and smilingly said, "Maybe we should have a food taster if Little Moon helped prepare this."

"Ah . . . a jealous girlfriend."

"*Former* girlfriend," Hazard corrected and tentatively tasted some stew.

"If you're still alive in ten minutes, I'll try some of that."

"Right. Hell hath no fury . . ."

"So you turned her down."

"Absolutely. I'm taking this marriage business seriously." He had by now tasted three other dishes in addition to the stew.

Blaze assessingly watched him dip a spoon into a fruit concoction. "You believe in living dangerously. I wouldn't trust that woman an inch." Her smile was guileless.

Hazard looked straight at her for a moment, his mouth twitching uncontrollably, and then he fell back against the robe-draped willow backrest and laughed out loud. He laughed until tears came to his eyes, and Blaze cautiously wondered if he was convulsing from a fast-acting poison. He quieted at last, wiped his eyes with the backs of his hands, clasped his fingers behind his head, and lay motionless against the shiny furs.

"What was so funny?" Blaze asked, relieved to see him still hale and healthy.

"The irony, pet, of your remark about living dangerously. As if some small bite of food can matter when I've lived my whole life on a knife edge. Do you realize we Absarokee are surrounded by powerful enemies? The Lakota outnumber us ten to one; the Blackfeet almost the same; the Shosone and Striped Arrows together are eight or ten times stronger than we are. They all want our hunting ground because it's the best in the world. And I should worry about food? Sweet puss, you're a darling," he said, his dark eyes expressive in the afternoon light, "but you don't know a scrap about the world or survival."

"I've a trust fund available when I'm twenty-one and it's my own money to do with what I wish. I could help the Absarokee survive." It was a rich young woman talking, assured and confident.

"This may sound cynical, puss, but I doubt very much whether the trust fund would be made available to me. In any case, I don't want or need it. My claims are rich—the best north of Virginia City. There's enough gold there to serve my needs. How," he said, sitting upright and reaching for a cup of cool water, "do we continually get into this subject when all I want is to hold you, make love to you, and forget everything for now? Look," he casually remarked lifting the cup and spreading his arms wide, "I haven't died. Come and eat, princess. You're going to need your strength. I've given strict orders not to be disturbed until tomorrow morning." He had, in fact, changed not only his schedule, but everyone else's as well, to conform to Blaze's wish for his time. Taking a drink, he smiled at her over the rim of the cup.

Blaze smiled back at him. "Is this like a honeymoon, then?"

He carefully set down the cup. "Would you like it to be a honeymoon?" His voice was low, modulated with inquiry.

She nodded, never sure of his baffling moods, only sure of her own feelings.

"A honeymoon it is, then." The expression in his eyes was unreadable but his smile was enchanting. "Let me feed you," he murmured, picking up a piece of roasted meat in his slender fingers and carefully placing it in her mouth. "And let me comb your hair for you," he whispered lightly. "And take care of you."

"If you do everything, what am I supposed to do?" Blaze very softly asked.

"You can take care of me, Boston, in your very special way." His lean hand caressed the line of her jaw.

"Is that all? Don't I have to work?" She stopped his hand with hers and nibbled on his fingertips.

"I'd rather," he murmured, her licking tongue on his fingertips sending heated messages to his brain, "you devote your energy to me in other ways."

"How nice," Blaze softly replied, then, taking his hand in hers, slid it downward and placed it over her breast, "since I'm very good at that."

"Yes, you are," Hazard agreed, his glance beginning to heat. "Very good, indeed. But eat first, princess, because I intend to take advantage of your natural proficiencies for the rest of the day and you're going to need sustenance."

The afternoon drifted by in a sequence of pleasure which enhanced all their affinities, never once invaded by the demons of discord. She was insatiable, and he'd never enjoyed himself so much.

It was late afternoon when Hazard said, "Clothes," in a startled abrupt murmur, followed by a soft expletive. With a brushing kiss across Blaze's hair, he set her aside and rolled off the bed of buffalo robes. Walking over to the lodge door, he lifted the flap a fraction and spoke briefly in Absarokee.

"Who's there?" Blaze quietly asked, sitting up.

Looking over his shoulder, he said, "I forgot," then turned back to the slight opening and went on in a soft flurry of Absarokee. He was answered by several women's voices and many giggles.

"Your harem?" Blaze inquired in oversweet accents when he dropped the flap ear and came back to her.

"With you, love, I don't have time for a harem," he smilingly replied.

"Or the inclination?" Blaze retorted, warmed by the smile but still green-eyed and needing assurance.

"Absolutely," Hazard quickly agreed. "Or the inclination. Those ladies outside aren't for me; they've brought your wardrobe and I forgot. I think they've been waiting quite a while, so I apologized like mad. You'd better try the clothes on now."

"*Whose* clothes are these?" Blaze uncertainly asked, wondering how a new wardrobe could be assembled so rapidly.

"They're all new. The women make dresses, shirts, moccasins, robes, whatever, for trading. I mentioned yesterday I wanted to buy clothes for you this afternoon. Unfortunately, it slipped my mind until a minute ago." Reaching for his leggings, Hazard said, "I'll invite them in."

"No!"

He was stepping into one pant leg and at Blaze's exclamation looked up. "No? I thought you wanted your own dresses."

"I do. Tell them to leave everything and I'll try them on later."

"Sweetheart, the dresses are going to need fitting," he replied, pulling up the leggings and lacing the belt through the loops.

"I'll do it."

He finished tying the belt before he quietly asked, "You sew?"

"Well . . . when I was young . . ." Blaze began to stammer. "I mean . . . I think I—"

He looked down at her and perceptively observed, "You *don't* sew."

Blaze sighed and bit her bottom lip. "No," she admitted.

"We probably should have someone who *can* sew," he pleasantly remarked, "fit them then, don't you think?"

Blaze stared at him for a long moment before she grudgingly agreed, "I suppose. But someone I don't know," she warned, recalling Little Moon's earlier visit.

"You don't know *anyone* sweetheart."

"Someone *you* don't know."

"I know everyone."

"That isn't what I mean," she said darkly.

"Fine," he said understanding at last.

"Someone old," Blaze added.

He laughed. "I'll see what I can do."

When he stepped outside, Hazard explained his wife

was shy and then proceeded to buy all the dresses in order not to offend anyone. Afterward, he politely sent the ladies away, save one old woman.

Blaze had slipped on one of Hazard's buckskin shirts and was standing near the bed when they entered the lodge. She reminded him of a youngster in an over-sized shirt, her feet bare, but she stood regally. Only her eyes reflected her uncertainty. He introduced Willow, explaining to Blaze that Willow was known across the northern plains for her exquisite quill designs. Then he carried in a large stack of fringed and decorated dresses while the women tentatively smiled at each other. "Start with these."

"Do you think you have enough here?" Blaze asked teasingly, her hands lightly brushing over the multitude of luxurious leathers he held out to her.

"Would you like more, Boston?" he inquired, answering amusement in his glance. "I'll send out the crier."

"You're too extravagant."

"I have an extravagant woman to please," he said very low.

"You want to please me?" she happily purred.

"In infinite ways, *bia-cara*," Hazard murmured, "after you try on the dresses."

"Try them on in front of Willow?" Blaze hesitantly returned.

"Do you dress yourself at home?"

"Sometimes," she hedged.

"Pretend this isn't sometimes," Hazard coaxed, well aware Blaze had a lady's maid or two in her background. "Humor me."

Blaze faintly grimaced. "If you insist."

He smiled. "I do."

Willow, standing to one side, had taken in the scene and understood despite the English, that Dit-chilajash was pressing and his woman resisting. Willow's eyes twinkled knowingly when Hazard smiled at his last firm word, and she stepped forward to help. "The star design is made for a chief's woman," she said to him, "and the beaded one from Fawn. Tell your woman to try those on first."

Hazard translated for Blaze, placed the dresses on the bed, and pulled out Willow's special dress decorated front and back with an intricate spiked star of multicolored quills. "The star design brings luck to its wearer," he added, holding it out. "Come, *bia,* put it on."

Blaze hung back. "You're embarrassing me."

"There's nothing to be embarrassed about. Willow's seen a nude body or so in her day, and I"—he paused and smiled—"prefer you nude. I did what you asked; all the other women were sent away. Now you keep your part of the bargain."

Blaze gave in gracefully and after putting on the first dress, which Willow adjusted at the shoulder, waist, and hip, felt less uncomfortable.

"Your wife is very beautiful," Willow said, marking a shoulder seam with a chalky bit of limestone.

"Thank you," Hazard replied, repeating the compliment to Blaze in English.

Blaze had received such compliments all her life, but somehow it meant a great deal more coming from this old woman who was a member of Hazard's clan. She so wanted to be a part of Hazard's life. "How do you say thank you in Absarokee?" Blaze asked, and when Hazard told her, she carefully repeated the phrase. *"Aho-aho,"* Blaze slowly repeated, with a large smile and a small curtsy.

Willow curtsied back and they both laughed. She's like Hannah, Blaze thought. She's just like Hannah. Joy warmed her heart.

Leaning comfortably against his willow backrest, Hazard enjoyed the fitting session. He'd never had the opportunity before to look at Blaze for this length of time. Something or someone would usually intervene: work, conversation; more often than not, in the quiet of their evenings, it was his lust. Alone, he'd never have simply looked this long. So he quietly relished the beauty and perfection of Blaze's face and form. Her skin was peach-gold beneath the translucent lodge walls, her hair a drifting sheen of copper. She moved gracefully at Willow's elementary commands, lifting her arms to pull off a dress, ducking her head into a held garment, shimmying her hips gently to let the soft leather slide down her body. She was timid, tentative, beneath Willow's ministrations, a revelation to Hazard, who had seen determination and commanding presence more. She *was* different here at the summer camp, less decretory, more —dare he used the word?—obedient. And then he smiled at the absurd notion and, lifting his heavy lashes, caught her glance over Willow's grey head.

He winked.

She smiled.

And a delicious sweetness passed between them.

Several dresses later, they argued briefly over a neckline cut too low for Hazard's taste. Fascinated, Willow watched the dispute, only understanding an occasional word but clearly aware of the issue.

"That one won't do," Hazard had said, motioning for Willow to remove it.

"Wait a minute." Blaze gestured Willow away. "I like this dress. The beading is almost liquid, it's so dense. And I like the colors." It was lush cream leather, supple as velvet, blue and green beading in wave patterns radiating outward from the deeply cut neckline.

"No."

"I happen to want it."

"No."

"Don't take that tone with me."

Hazard controlled himself, retrenched, altered the autocratic command. "Sorry, *bia,* keep it if you wish." But when he spoke to Willow after the dress was fitted, he added in a quiet Absarokee aside, "Don't bring that one back."

Willow nodded. Dit-chilajash had won. But she gave the woman her due. The yellow eyes woman stood up to Dit-chilajash as bravely as a man. He wouldn't always win, she knew. Not with this flame-haired woman. Willow had known Hazard's first wife from babyhood, had made her wedding dress; she'd watched the young couple grow up together, helped nurse Raven Wing as she lay dying. This relationship she'd seen today was different, as if the Black Cougar had met his equal, not just his mate. She wondered what the infant would be like born of two such parents. The yellow eyes was pregnant; it was plain if you knew what to look for. Did Is-bia shibidam Ditchilajash (Hazard the Black Cougar) know?

LATER that evening, after slipping down to the river to bathe, Hazard and Blaze lay under the willows and listened to the young men serenading their sweethearts with their flutes. The delicate music floated through the warm summer night, melody overlaying melody, notes intertwined, romance personified in the pure night air.

"Are you happy?" Blaze asked very late that night when even the love songs had finally quieted and only the wind in the trees broke the stillness.

"Is this a test?" She couldn't see him in the darkness of the lodge, but she could hear him smile. He only yelped quietly when she pinched him, and then conceded into the blackness, "Yes, I am. And what of you *biacara?*" he questioned in turn. "Do you like our summer camp?" By force of habit, he found himself avoiding soul-searching inquiries.

"I like everything. It's perfect. You're perfect." On his best behavior, joy and contentment a natural inspiration. Hazard had enchanted his new "wife" through the lazy, languid day. A day set aside for them alone, a day in which the world was kept at bay.

He laughed softly at her immoderate response. "And if this perfection had to let the world in tomorrow, what then, puss? Would you still like it?"

"Of course. As long as you're with me," she answered with the open, limitless emotion he found both bewitching and disconcerting.

"Does that mean you'll go on the buffalo hunt tomorrow?"

"Will other women go?"

"Some will."

"Isn't that lucky. Now I can say I'd love to. I would have gone anyway, but now it sounds polite rather than disagreeably pushy."

"It sounds as though I'm going to have a shadow." He was holding her in his arms and thinking how different his life had become since he'd met her.

"That's the general idea," Blaze cheerfully replied, then abruptly asked, "Am I allowed to kiss you in public?"

"Would it do any good if I said no?"

"No."

He groaned theatrically. "I foresee my consequence in tatters."

"Just as well. Consequence," she pronounced mischievously, "is much overrated."

"Might I recommend discretion, at least?" he asked with amusement.

"You can recommend all you want," Blaze sweetly replied.

"An Absarokee chief has a chief of his own, it seems," he said with a chuckle.

"You might say that," Blaze agreed, her smile part mischief, wholly female.

He ran his palms leisurely down her back and pulled her closer. In matters of love she could rule him with his blessing. And he told her so.

"I wasn't envisioning so circumspect a role."

"I thought perhaps you weren't," he responded, all courtesy and tact. "Maybe we should get back to the discussion of the buffalo hunt."

Blaze giggled. "Coward."

"Diplomat," he disagreed, warmth curling through his voice. "I'd never dream of ruining this delicious rapport. . . ." And he changed the subject in a way he'd perfected years ago.

Chapter 25 ～≫

SUITABLE clothes were found for Blaze in the morning, and she, along with other sweethearts and special wives—all vividly dressed—rode their lovers' prized buffalo ponies out to the site of the hunt. The men never rode the buffalo ponies until the actual hunt in order to keep them fresh; the women, light on their backs, wouldn't tire the strong mounts.

They rode along Arrow Creek in the shadow of the cottonwoods. It was cool in the shade of the towering trees, the sun only beginning its journey across the sky. The herd was grazing just south of The-cliff-that-has-no-pass, a fast hour's ride. It would take them twice that long at this leisurely pace. Rising Wolf and his current sweetheart rode just ahead of Blaze and Hazard in a line of riders stretched out a mile or more.

While the hunters and their companions slowly followed the meandering creek, the young braves, stripped down and on display, raced alongside the procession, showing off their riding skills for their sweethearts and lovers. It was the most dramatic equestrian prowess Blaze had ever seen. In a split-second movement, they nimbly sprang off, then back on, their ponies while at an all-out gallop; agile as acrobats, they lightly balanced standing atop their speeding mounts, hung effortlessly beneath the bellies of their racing ponies, a hairbreadth from the flying hooves.

One lithe, muscled warrior turned a cartwheel on his horse's back, slid gracefully astride once again, and a scant five feet from a collision from Peta, careened his thundering pony aside.

"Be-se-che-waak, Dit-chilajash"* (I like her, Hazard), he tossed over his shoulder as he galloped away.

Rising Wolf's girlfriend giggled. Blaze was still awe-struck at the daring display.

Twisting half around, one hand resting on his horse's rump, Rising Wolf said in Absarokee, his smile wry, "Spirit Eagle's in his usual form, I see."

"Someone's going to have to teach him a lesson someday," Hazard replied in his own language, his tone carefully modulated.

Someday may be here sooner than you think," Rising Wolf replied, a grin supplanting the faint smile. Dainty Shield giggled again and whispered something to Rising Wolf. He turned back to Hazard. "Little Moon says—"

"I already heard," Hazard said.

"A new position for you," Rising Wolf said, chuckling. "How does it feel?"

"What is all this about?" Blaze interjected into the Absarokee passing back and forth, saving Hazard from having to probe his feelings on this new experience. He had always wooed women as Spirit Eagle had done today, openly in the way of their clan. Now his woman was the pursued for the first time and he was on the defensive.

"Boys' games. They like to show off," Hazard casually replied, but his territorial defenses were warned.

"Like you used to do?" Rising Wolf teased, the Absarokee a gentle drawl.

"You talk too much," Hazard growled, but he was smiling, so Blaze knew he didn't mean whatever he'd said.

Further along the way Hazard issued a list of instructions for Blaze's safety. "Once the herd starts moving, there's no stopping it. It may look magnificent and dramatic when you haven't seen one before, but anything remotely in its path is dead. Stay well back of the other women. Peta will mind you. Don't be foolish and don't take any risks."

"Do I look like someone who'd ride into a herd of buffalo?" Blaze asked somewhat indignantly, having patiently listened to Hazard's monologue of directions for the better part of five miles.

Hazard, riding beside her, turned his head and gave her a look of cordial assessment. "In my experience, princess," he said amiably, "you seem to do anything you set your mind to."

"That may be," Blaze as amiably conceded, "but I'm not inclined to race a herd of buffalo."

"I'm relieved to hear it."

"And I don't skin buffalo either."

He laughed. "That could make you the toast of Boston, darling. Maybe you should try." The dark look she cast him prompted him to add quickly, "Don't worry, love. Unlike other tribes, skinning buffalo isn't a woman's job. The men kill, skin, and butcher the buffalo and bring it back to camp. When I dump it in front of the doorway, it becomes your problem."

"Where do I find a frying pan that large?"

"And then again," he swiftly amended, recalling her cooking and not at all certain her remark was meant facetiously, "I'm sure we can make other plans."

"Now *I'm* relieved," Blaze laughingly responded and they both rested a little easier.

AS THE riders came within a mile of the buffalo, there was no talking except by signing. Buffalo, like most four-footed animals, were wind-readers, but there was nothing wrong with their hearing, so the barefoot ponies on well-grassed sod and the silent riders were noiseless as they approached. When they'd traveled another half-mile, the scout loomed up on a butte signing with his robe. It meant the herd was in sight and close. The signal caused everyone to spread out. Sliding from his pony, Hazard stripped off his skin shirt and leggings. Silently, he and Blaze traded horses, and kissing her lightly, he mounted his buffalo pony. The scout on the butte swung his robe twice around his head and dropped it. Before it hit the ground every buffalo pony was running, leaving little curls of dust in the grass behind them. Hazard's roan pony, decked out in feathers at tail and foretop, went wild at the scent and, without urging, sped like the wind toward the herd. At the top of the ridge, the buffalo —two thousand or so—were in sight, all spread out grazing. Before the clouds of dust starting rolling, Blaze caught a glimpse of Hazard shooting his first buffalo. He was leaning forward close to the roan's neck, his toes hooked under the pony's foreleg for balance, and firing with one hand. After that the galloping herd pushed him out of view.

An hour later the dust had settled over the grassy plain and hundreds of dead buffalo littered the landscape. The women rode down then with the young boys and old men, leading the pack ponies. Blaze found Hazard a mile away butchering a fat cow. He was sweating under the hot sun, cutting with precision in strong slashing strokes, his hands drawing Blaze's attention, as so often in the past, to their grace and strength. Several large portions of meat were already stacked on the hide he'd skinned.

"This could take a while," he grunted, heaving another large cut of meat onto the robe. "You might rather go back to camp."

"How many do you have to butcher?"

"I shot five, but my uncles are taking care of three of them." Hazard looked at the sun. "It'll take me at least another two hours." The sun was almost torrid as it reached its zenith. The buffalo horse was lathered and panting; Hazard's bare body clothed only in a breech cloth glistened with sweat. "Why don't you get out of the sun?" he suggested, blowing a strand of hair out of his eyes.

"I don't mind the sun," Blaze replied, jumping off Peta.

Looking at her, bare-headed, bare-armed, bare-legged, he said, "Boston society won't approve of your brown skin."

"I'm not going back, so I can get as brown as I like."

Hazard didn't respond, but continued, his knife cutting and carving with a sureness honed by scores of buffalo hunts. All he could think of was the pleasure in her staying.

"Did you hear me?" Blaze asked, dropping down on the trampled grass in a flurry of beaded fringe.

Hazard's knife stopped then. Half turning his head, he gazed at her from under dark lashes. "And if your father has different ideas, or your mother maybe, or Yancy Strahan?"

"Do you *want* me to go back to Boston?" She waited for his answer without breathing.

His gaze didn't flinch. "You know I can't think about what *I* want. I have to worry about my claim and my people."

It wasn't the answer she wanted, but it wasn't negative either. She resumed breathing. "Discounting those problems," she impulsively pressed, her voice suddenly timid, never in her coddled life having wanted anything so fiercely.

"If we discount those problems, we discount the world, *bia,*" he quietly said, jabbing abstractly at the ground with his knife point.

"Just say we could."

"A dream world." He smiled indulgently. "Is that it?"

"Yes. Then what? Say it is, Hazard, then what?" she demanded.

"Then, sweet puss," he softly said, "I'd want you with me. I'd never consider living in my dream world without you."

"It's going to work out," Blaze happily replied, with irrepressible spirit. "Just wait and see."

"As it always has for the pampered Miss Brad-dock?" Hazard mildly inquired.

"Just so," Blaze impetuously agreed, and in a whirl of happiness and flying fringe she launched herself at Hazard. She knocked him backward, falling atop his sprawled form, and kissed him capriciously, heedless of others, only knowing he was her whole world.

His own reactions as rashly ungovernable with Blaze's soft body pressed into his, Hazard returned her kisses. Smiling and laughing and kissing, they rolled like puppies at play, the clean fragrance of crushed grass like heady perfume in their nostrils. "You're a tempting distraction," Hazard whispered long moments later, half out of breath, their positions reversed with his glistening body atop hers, "but—"

"But what?" Blaze lightly panted, the playful wrestling having winded her as well.

"But the ants are going to eat the two buffalo I'm supposed to be butchering."

"Really?" Blaze playfully murmured.

"Word of honor. Perhaps a raincheck for—"

"An hour from now?"

Hazard quickly glanced at the two carcasses he'd yet to complete butchering. "Make it two and I'll show you a quiet mossy pool not too far from here."

"Deal," she said with a wide grin. "Let me help."

Pushing himself away, Hazard drily said, "If you help, it'll take three hours."

"I shan't raise a finger," Blaze quickly acceded.

Hazard set a new record skinning the second buffalo.

Chapter 26

THEY rode to an abrupt break in the terrain a few miles distant, where a deep chasm cut through the undulating grassy highlands and a strange bluff loomed like a tower at its entrance. Dismounting, they were immediately cooled by the shaded slope thick with foliage and undergrowth and cascading trees that had partially fallen down the bluff and chasm walls. "Wait," Hazard said, leading the horses through the dark, wild underbrush before returning for Blaze.

The ground sloped steeply down and after twenty paces into the lush vegetation the silence was rich and fragrantly verdant. Sunlight, gold and pale yellow, found its way in serene shafts of light through the overhead canopy of green. They passed silently through the hushed wildness of growth and burgeoning fertility, the scents of blooming wildflowers and green-tipped elders pungent in their nostrils. Holding Blaze's hand to guide her through the strange undercliff, Hazard looked at her with a smile.

And then suddenly he was holding back a ladened plum bough and inviting her forward.

Blaze stepped into a little green meadow studded with clumps of buttercups and drifts of wild roses. It was a tiny south-facing dell surrounded by enormous soaring ash trees and cottonwoods—a kind of opulent paradise. Two cherry trees framed the inlet of a large, clear pool that trickled away to the east over a rustic outcropping of moss-covered rock. Warblers and thrushes sang overhead. It was rare and beautiful like a jewel.

"Would you like a swim?" Hazard asked. "I would. Unless, of course," he teasingly said, "the sight of blood excites you." His glistening bronzed body, stripped to a breechcloth, was smeared with buffalo blood.

"We Boston debs were always taught," Blaze mockingly replied, her eyes a twinkle, "to ask a man to wash off the butcher's blood from his body before making love. It's rule number two."

"What is rule number one," he sardonically drawled, "in this hierarchy of etiquette?"

"Take off your own gown first in case your escort didn't follow rule number two," she sweetly replied, her smile merry.

"And do you adhere to this fascinating protocol?" he silkily murmured, advancing toward her.

"Of course," Blaze demurely retorted, pulling her dress over her head and dropping it at her feet.

Hazard's dark eyes heated. Blaze stood slimly erect, her delicious breasts upthrust like offerings waiting to be touched. "Come here," he murmured.

"Unthinkable to break the rules, sir," she drolly replied with a wicked grin. "I'm going to swim." She turned and ran through the cool grass toward the pool. It pleased her to tease Hazard; he played the game of love effortlessly, sportively, like a man who enjoyed giving pleasure to women.

She was already in the water when she called out to him, "I'll race you to the other side. The winner wins . . ."

Hazard was swiftly untying the rawhide strings of his

breechcloth when she dove under. "What does the winner win?" he shouted as she surfaced long yards away.

"You!" she shouted back, languidly treading water,
reminding him of a woodland sprite surprised at her
bath.

"What if *I* win?" he countered, kicking off his moccasins.

Her smile was obvious even from that distance.
"You won't!" she cried, flipping under water with graceful precision and disappearing from sight. When she
broke the surface, breathless, seconds later, she had a
half-pool advantage over Hazard, who was slicing
through the water behind her with the power stroke of a
natural athlete. She was, Hazard saw, a first-class swim-
mer and, though he gained steadily on her, they were not
grossly mismatched. She cut through the water like a
whipcord, and it wasn't until they were nearing the opposite shore that Hazard managed to pull level with her.

"You're going to lose," he said, swinging his hair out
of his face.

She didn't answer, only smiled, then dove under in a
flash and forged toward shore with a dynamic kick that
left a trail of frothy bubbles in her wake. He followed her
with a smooth jackknife dive and, easing his own strong
kick a few yards from shore, arrived gallant seconds behind and flopped beside her on the mossy shore.

"You lost," she sunnily declared between gasping
breaths. Lying prone on the ground, her face turned toward his, he thought her soft cheek pressed against the
emerald moss was like silk on velvet.

"You're damned good, Boston," he smilingly com-
mended, his own respiration ragged, *"for a woman."*
Waggish amusement slid lacily through the smiling
words.

Blaze sat up abruptly, the sunlight gilding her wet
body like liquid gold, her breasts trembling slightly with
the sudden movement. Hazard felt his arousal begin to
swell against the cool ground. "For a *woman?*" she repeated. "That's going to cost you, darling."

"What," he asked, rolling over, nude and splendid,
his face innocently bland, "does it cost?" Tucking his

hands beneath his wet head, he looked at her with a roguish smile.

"Our wager was the winner wins you. I won. Now *you* are mine."

"Was that ever in doubt?" he pleasantly said.

"You have to do everything I want you to do," she serenely explained.

"My pleasure, ma'am," he murmured, his gaze slowly roaming her body, his desire stiffening.

"To begin with, come here and kiss me," she ordered.

Curling upward, he leaned across on one elbow and did.

"Not bad," she thoughtfully noted a moment later, as if there were some internal guide to excellence. Her mouth broke into a small grin and she demanded, "Do it again."

His kiss was languidly thorough this time but almost chaste. He hadn't touched her with his hands.

"Will it improve with practice?" she inquired nonchalantly.

"We can only hope, ma'am," Hazard wolfishly replied. "With madame's cooperation, of course."

"Even if I don't choose to cooperate," she softly enunciated, "you must do as I say. Everything." Her teasing smile lit golden sparkles in her eyes.

"How nice," Hazard said. "I've never done this before."

"You're my chattel, Hazard."

His eyes widened appreciatively. "Do I get a turn in this charming game?" he asked.

"No, darling, only one winner allowed. Now stand up."

He stood.

"Walk over to that tree."

A moment later, leaning against the trunk, he raised inquiring eyes to hers.

"Touch yourself," she said.

"Must I?"

"You must," she emphatically asserted. "You're my chattel."

With a light shrug and a faint smile he did. His thumb and fingers closed around himself and with a light sliding motion of his slender hand, a swollen dimension was added to his arousal. Blaze watched his lovely rampant length and felt a trembling heat shiver down her spine. He stretched then, sliding his fingers through his damp black hair and flexing his back, like a pet gladiator on display or a splendid palace guard who had come to notice and found favor because of their beauty and size. "Do you like it?" he asked, gracefully dropping his hands to his sides.

"I think *I'd* like to touch you, now," Blaze said in a low, breathy voice. "Come here." He walked over like a great dark cougar, his lithe body fine-muscled, his erection beautiful, and offering to her. Standing near, he quietly waited, playing her game with his familiar seductive charm. But when her lips touched him and her half-open mouth closed around him, her warm tongue delicately roving, his self-control broke and he trembled slightly.

Looking up after a moment, she softly asked, "Should I kiss you again? Does my vassal like that?"

Hazard's dark eyes were heavy-lidded when he looked down at her. "Like I enjoy breathing, ma'am," he murmured and, sliding his fingers through her hair, pulled her back. Before long, Blaze's own desires matched the stark evidence of Hazard's need, and she felt the heat curl, flame-hot, to the very center of her pulsing core.

Moving away, her heavy-lashed eyes came up. "I think I'd like to feel you inside me," she slowly said, her face rosy with the fire beating through her senses.

"I thought you might," Hazard softly replied, his own heart thudding in his ribs. "Would you like it standing, ma'am, or there . . . where you are?"

"Here," she murmured, her eyes half closed, and leaned back on her hands.

Dropping down on his knees before her, Hazard gently pushed her legs apart. "You're very kind, ma'am, to the hired help," he whispered, sliding his warm palms up her slender legs, his hands dark on her pale flesh.

"I've changed my mind," she asserted when his

heated fingers touched her thighs, although her breathing had quickened. "I don't want to anymore."

"Boston princess," Hazard said very slowly, savoring the separate words, "you're going to have a slave revolt on your hands unless you reconsider."

Blaze lifted one shoulder in a small shrug. "Well, perhaps a little, then," she magnanimously agreed, as if granting a favor.

Hazard's eyes narrowed the tiniest fraction. "A little . . . like this, ma'am?" he gently inquired, moving up to touch the hot center of her desire.

"Ummm."

"And this?" He slid inside her a teasing inch. Her eyes closed as Hazard's hard body pressed her back onto the moss and followed her down. She could feel him begin to fill her and pleasure like opium dreams flooded her mind.

"And now, ma'am," he lazily drawled, withdrawing slightly, "that's enough."

Blaze's eyes snapped open. "No!" she protested, reaching up for him. Obligingly he sank back in, penetrating deeply, feeling her close tightly around him, hearing her smothered cry.

And then he withheld himself again. "Do you want more, ma'am?" he huskily inquired, watching her face.

"Yes . . ." She moved her hips to feel him so beautifully inside her. "Oh, yes!"

"Now, then, *bia-cara*," he whispered, touching his lips to hers, "the slave becomes the master. I don't think I want to anymore," he murmured. "Maybe later." And he moved back a fraction.

"Hazard! I'll have you shot, you impudent wretch!"

"Not right now, you won't," he softly replied, gliding back in.

"After, I will," she whispered on a caught breath.

"Then what will Your Highness do tomorrow," he teased, "when your hot little body starts tuning up . . . when you remember how I felt inside you . . . and remember what I did to you? What will you do then?"

"I'll find someone else," Blaze pettishly exhaled.

"But would he know how to touch you here?" he

softly thrust upward. "And here?" He moved against the quivering heart of her need and she whimpered. "Would he know that your breasts tingle when I bite them just this hard? Not too hard . . ." he said a moment later, sliding his mouth over to her other taut nipple, "but just enough." And his teeth gently tightened on one pink peak.

"Please, Jon. Don't tease. I want to feel you."

"Like this?" he asked.

"Yes," she sighed.

"And this?"

"Oh, God, yes . . ." The world began slipping away.

"And this?" His hands slid under her lush bottom and lifted her to meet him. Ecstasy washed over her.

"In that case, Boston, *you* must do what *you're* told, or I won't give you what you want." His rich, luxurious voice curled around her.

"Hazard," she softly implored. "Do you want me to beg?"

"Lord, no," he genially retorted. "Just hold your breasts up for me to kiss. They're not close enough for me."

She didn't move.

"I think I'll go for a swim." Pulling away, he sat up.

Blaze's hands came up and pushed her round opulent breasts upward so they stood in high peaked presentation, the nipples displayed prominently.

"That's better, princess," Hazard murmured approvingly. "See, you can follow orders after all. Which one should I kiss first?"

Her eyes wouldn't meet his gaze.

"Look at me, pet. This one?" Hazard softly inquired, leaning over and touching one turgid tip with a light flick of his finger. Her breast stirred and Blaze moaned, shifting her hips to meet the spiraling urgent heat tumbling downward. "Or this one?" And Hazard's mouth closed over her other swollen nipple and gently sucked. He slid one hand between her thighs and slowly explored while with the other he excited the nipple of her other breast. Playing and probing, he caressed her until, her mouth half open, she cried a small strangled sound deep in her throat and reached up to clutch his shoulders, her nails digging into his skin. "Are you ready for me, love?" he murmured, gently easing her hands from his shoulders and placing them at her sides.

She looked up at him with smoldering eyes.

"Are you open for me? Slide your finger over your lush pink flesh and tell me."

She hesitated.

"You must, darling, or I won't know," he said in a rough-soft voice.

Closing her eyes, Blaze brushed her finger over the dewy sweetness and moaned at the shattering surge of desire it provoked.

"Once more," Hazard whispered, watching the creamy fluid drip languidly over her slender fingers. And when she did, she shuddered. "I think," he said very softly, lifting her hand and sliding her drenched finger into his mouth, ". . . you're ready." She tasted like wild, pungent fruit, and he could no longer wait.

He kissed her and she kissed him wildly, blind to everything but the feeling beyond bearing. Her tiny explosions began as he drove gently into her and he lay quiet and patient inside her until her last exquisite pleasure had drifted away. Then he kissed her gently as the spring sun kisses the new tender green shoots, and his strong heart, echoing his love and need, took them to paradise together.

After, when all the games were over and all the delicious pleasures had hushed into sated calm, Hazard rolled away and sat up. Blaze lay beside him on her back in dreamy abandonment. Her hair had dried in loose and tumbled disarray. Her eyes were closed. He sat perfectly still and watched her, entranced by her, his feelings strangely imprecise—part sexual; part friendly affection; some oddly paternal as if in this simple setting her innocence struck him more strongly, and some still undefinable.

Reaching out, he cupped a butterfly gently in his hands, remembering the endless youthful hours spent in practice until at last one could accomplish the quiet task of capturing a butterfly. He carried it over in his closed hands and delicately placed it on Blaze's smooth white stomach. Her eyes opened at the feathery sensation and she saw the precious creature poised like a shimmer of gold. It was yellow and saffron and black with great fragile wings.

"I'll give you the treasures of the world, *bia-cara,* wife of mine," Hazard whispered, stroking one flaring golden-striped gossamer wing so lightly the frail thing showed no fright. Those were the same hands that had hacked away at the buffalo short hours ago, with such power and strength, Blaze thought. The same hands that killed, the same hands that gave her indescribable pleasure.

"I only want you," she softly replied.

Their eyes met. The butterfly flew away.

"I'm yours," he said quietly, his handsome face tender, "always."

Chapter 27

BY THE time Hazard and Blaze returned to the village, the drums had begun beating, sunset colors streaked across the sky like flame on the distant grey mountains, and the smell of cooking buffalo from the fires made even the birds in the trees hungry.

They dressed hurriedly since they were late, Hazard in feathered leather and Blaze in one of her new dresses ornamented with sea shells and beads. Hazard spent extra care on her hair, combing it into shiny waves. "You don't have to do everything," Blaze protested when he kneeled, lifted one of her feet, and slipped on a new beaded moccasin. Hazard looked up at her, remembering the silky pleasure of her at the pool that afternoon and, with the barest hint of all he wished to say and do for her, serenely noted, "You can tell how much a man loves his woman by how he cares for her; it's the way of our nation. Look at any woman's hair and you'll know the extent of her husband's love."

"It's a very lovely custom, and astonishing in a nation of warriors. I can't imagine a white man caring for his wife's hair."

"A life of warfare doesn't preclude sensitivity. And I can't imagine a white man being other than the barbarian he is. You see," he said with a faint smile, "we have our intolerant prejudices as well." He slipped on her second moccasin, rose, and took her hand in his. "Come, we're late. Half the village has preceded us by now, and as one of the chiefs, I should have been there early."

"Do I have to dance?" This was her first mass social occasion, and she felt strangely insecure.

"It's easy," Hazard casually replied. "You know how to dance. I saw you in Virginia City."

"That's different."

"I'll show you how," he replied, pulling her out the door.

SO UNDER the full moon suspended like a golden ornament in the blackness of the summer sky, Blaze Braddock, lately of Boston, put her hands on her lovers' strong shoulders, felt his hands circle her waist, and, falteringly at first, followed the slow gliding movements of the *pō'pate disú a* (owl dance).

Over Blaze's head, Hazard occasionally caught a glimpse of Spirit Eagle, the brave of whom Little Moon had spoken. He wasn't dancing but standing apart in the shadows, a few yards from the circle of dancers, his eyes trained on Blaze. Hazard understood youth was like fire, reckless and dangerous. He also understood Spirit Eagle was in competition for a chieftainship. He'd have to keep an eye on him—and on Blaze—in case Spirit Eagle *was* contemplating abduction.

Then the drummers intensified their rhythm, deepened the base and heightened the natural trill of their smallest drums, signaling the introduction to a new dance only recently brought in from the Hidatsa. A ripple of excitement swept through the press of dancers. The River Absarokee had first witnessed the dance when visiting the Hidatsa, and the dance had been introduced to the Main Body only a few years ago. The Main Body had been surprised when they first saw it, for in it the men and women participants kissed each other publicly. But the dance was eagerly assimilated by the young women at the summer encampment, because there were many good-looking men among the Main Body. The *bī ra i gyé disú a* procession, led by two chaste girls and made up of all the good-looking women—married and single— began forming when the drum beat accelerated.

"What's happening?" Blaze asked, seeing the procession begin to form, aware of the charged current sweeping the crowd.

"It's another dance, but stay here."

"All the women—"

"You don't know the steps," he ambiguously replied and his hand slipped possessively around her waist. Turning his head briefly, he said to Rising Wolf beside him, "Watch Spirit Eagle; I want him waylaid if he starts in this direction." The brisk order was murmured in Absarokee. Rising Wolf merely nodded in understanding.

By this time, the women had forced a circle around a group of men and were dancing in a swaying clockwise movement around them. A herald walked into the center of the circle, crying, "Young men, give presents to the young women you like and kiss them. If your heart is greater, so that you want to marry them, give them a horse and none will run away."

A young warrior arrayed in a fine breechcloth having inspected the women, was the first to put his arm around a beautiful young girl. He gave her a beaded blanket and a kiss. Soon everyone was participating. Some men offered painted sticks, representing horses, and if the girl accepted they were married. Some women refused the offers of gifts, waiting for the men they wanted. Some of the old women went around whipping the young men and women who hadn't risen to dance while a ring of spectators watched. Soon almost every young and comely person was dancing and kissing and all were enjoying themselves immensely.

Hazard had been the object of much intent inspection—he was famed for his beauty, and wasn't dancing. Blaze, too, was thoughtfully regarded by more than one bold-eyed young buck, but Hazard's arm firmly around her waist served as deterrent to further boldness. But before long, two old medicine women came up to Hazard and would not be gainsaid, although Hazard attempted to refuse. Blaze didn't understand the words, but she understood the old women's threatening gestures and Hazard's polite opposition.

Rising Wolf spoke rapidly to Hazard. Hazard shook his head and murmured a short reply but Blaze heard her name mentioned. "Go," she said to him. "It's your duty." And she smiled at the two old women, who were still jabbering agitatedly before them. She was in a benevolent frame of mind, attuned to Hazard's responsibilities as one of his clan's leaders and still basking in the perfection of their afternoon in the secluded leafy dell. It all looked fairly innocuous anyway, she thought.

"You don't mind?" Hazard softly inquired, gazing down at Blaze with darkly serious eyes. Familiar with her reckless temper, he'd attempted prudence.

"No. Really, I don't. Go. It's expected of you."

A third old woman had joined the others, and they were all inciting Hazard now, with fierce gesticulation and high-pitched admonitions.

"Sure?" Hazard repeated, aware of the obligations required of him but determined to avert any controversy with Blaze.

"Go."

Rising Wolf spoke briefly and Hazard replied in a rush of soft Absarokee before allowing himself to be led away.

"What was that about?" Blaze asked Rising Wolf.

"I told him to avoid, well, er, old friends, and he said he was going to insist on kissing a virgin, to keep everything perfectly innocent." Rising Wolf shrugged, like a nervous young boy explaining away some transgression. "He didn't want to offend you, but, as you can see, he's always been much in demand."

"I'm not offended, really. No more explanations are necessary." Blaze felt a charitable glow of congenial tolerance. "Everyone wants to please him, don't they?" she continued.

"He's the best," Rising Wolf calmly replied. "Always has been."

And then her altruistic glance followed Hazard as he lifted an elaborate bear-claw necklace over his head and carefully placed it around the delicate neck of a spectacularly beautiful young girl. A small, slender girl who looked up at Hazard with radiant adoration and yearning. It was that hungry look that created the first fissure in Blaze's liberal and benign tolerance. And she felt the first tiny stirring of temper growing like ripples in a pond.

Hazard's dark head bent low to kiss the girl, his hand gliding by habit around her waist while he held her head lightly in his palm. This second observation crumbled a larger portion of Blaze's benevolent facade. And when the fragile girl threw her arm around Hazard's neck and melted into his tall body, the smooth marble of Christian charity crashed to the ground. It was a long kiss, intolerably long, measured in Blaze's hot flashes of resentment and the breath-holding gaze of hundreds of pairs of eyes. "Who's that girl?" Blaze demanded, her eyes swinging around and impaling Rising Wolf's nervous glance.

"We don't speak of the dead," he equivocated.

"Make an exception," Blaze snapped, her tone unflinchingly imperious.

Rising Wolf sighed. "That's Raven Wing's younger sister."

"*Who's* Raven Wing?" she huffily inquired. "One of his old girlfriends?"

"Hazard's first wife."

Hot tears filled Blaze's eyes, tears of frustration, rage and humiliation, and she could feel her throat closing with the pressure of the sobs she was trying to smother. Before she betrayed herself in front of all the curious eyes, Blaze spun away into the darkness surrounding the dance area. Rising Wolf snatched at her, but she slipped between two women and melted into the blackness. He couldn't shout her name; he didn't want to cause a scene. Shouldering the women aside, he raced into the darkness between two lodges, Hazard's words echoing in his ears: "Watch Spirit Eagle." Just before pushing the ladies aside, he'd searched the space where Spirit Eagle had stood all evening.

It was empty.

HAZARD managed to extricate himself from Blue Flower. He had only intended a platonic kiss, enough to satisfy the old ladies. Nothing more. Blue Flower, unfortunately, had other ideas. She was as ready as a woman could be, he observed, easing away with a polite smile and moving into the crowd. Relieved, he exhaled softly, his gaze automatically searching for Blaze. When he saw Rising Wolf pushing through the press of dancers, his pulse rate accelerated.

"I lost her." The words were curt and blunt and troubled.

"How?" Hazard asked, already knowing why.

"She ran off so fast I couldn't stop her. That long kiss . . ." he obliquely noted, his eyebrows rising.

"Damn hussy wouldn't let go. Your style, not mine. Where's Spirit Eagle?" he sharply inquired in almost the same breath, the girl dismissed, the kiss forgotten.

"Gone."

"Damn, I could feel it coming."

"He's been challenging you for a long time."

"I know."

"You've been gone so much in the past few years."

"Umm." Hazard was only half listening, fully aware of Spirit Eagle's preoccupation with a leadership position. The challenge had never worried him. Until now. Hazard didn't want Blaze used as a pawn in a power struggle, although he acknowledged that she alone could be the motivation for the abduction. Any man would want her.

"Do you think she can find her way back to your lodge?" Rising Wolf asked.

"Not at night. There's too much sameness. I'd say we check Spirit Eagle's lodge first."

"That sure?"

"He's gone, isn't he?"

"Maybe he joined the dancers," Rising Wolf hopefully suggested.

"My roan against your sorrel says he didn't." Hazard's terse voice was as sure as Rising Wolf's was uncertain. He was already twenty yards away and sprinting when Rising Wolf shouted, "Only if you give me odds," and charged after him.

BLAZE knew she was lost almost immediately. She'd run into the darkness with no destination in mind, only a driving need to escape the lurid spectacle of Hazard and that woman. After racing blindly between rows of lodges, she stopped, panting, and glanced around. Nothing looked familiar. Only row upon row of deserted tepees, all their inhabitants participating in the dances and merrymaking down by the river.

How would she ever find her way back to Hazard's lodge? Not that it mattered anyway, she testily decided. He'd probably be too busy for the next few hours with the little beauty he was eating up in front of hundreds of interested spectators. It would serve him right if she didn't go back there tonight. And she wondered for a moment, turning slowly around in an attempt to get her bearings, whether she'd be able to find the willow bower near the river. That would make a comfortable bed.

The valley basin was mainly flat, so it was hard to know which direction to take, but the blaze of fires at the dance area at least indicated the general direction of the river. Turning toward the lighted glow in the sky, she intended to skirt the dancers and hopefully find the willows. With Hazard as guide, she'd never paid much attention to directions, and he'd always carried her. Those memories only rekindled the flames of her temper. Damn his libertine soul; all the stories in Virginia City were true. He'd never turned down a woman in his life. And she, it seemed, had as little sense as the rest, no more immune to his soft endearments and sensual expertise than any of the others.

Anger at herself, at him, at the hussy kissing him, along with nascent urges for vengeance, all tumbled around in her mind in confusion. Inhaling a deep breath of clear night air to steady the tumble and dull the rancor, Blaze determined to first find the bower. A night alone would give her the opportunity to decide what she wanted to do regarding Jon Hazard Black and his abominable predisposition for females of every persuasion.

She'd taken no more than five steps in the direction of the bonfires when a young warrior, richly dressed, his long hair gleaming in the moonlight, walked toward her. He smiled and held out his hand, making the sign for friendship. Blaze didn't recognize the word in hand sign, but she understood the message. She smiled back, and Spirit Eagle thought Hazard a foolish man for letting her out of his sight. He spoke softly in Absarokee, telling her she was beautiful.

Blaze shook her head, indicating she didn't understand, but when he held his hand out again, an idea was born on her rankling resentment. Why not dance with this beautiful young warrior? If Hazard, however reluctant he pretended to be, could dance and kiss the pretty young women, why couldn't she kiss the handsome young men? After all, that's what the dance taking place down by the river was all about. Everyone was having a good time. Why let futile rage and envy ruin a pleasant evening? She'd simply follow his example and participate in the crush of sweethearts enjoying themselves under the mountain stars.

Blaze placed her fingers in the hand extended to her and returned his smile. "Dance," she said, swaying in pantomime. Spirit Eagle's arousal ignited and he pulled her closer. "No," Blaze softly retorted, tugging back a little. "Dance . . . down by the river. Dance." And she made a small gliding motion.

"Ah," Spirit Eagle responded, smiling. *"Disék,"* and he moved gracefully in a repetition of Blaze's step.

"Yes, yes . . . dance," Blaze agreed, anger at Hazard urging her on. "Let's go down to the river and dance." She pointed in the direction of the fires.

"Hú kawe," he said, and Blaze recognized the word for "come." His fingers laced more comfortably in hers, and when he gently drew her, she followed. As they walked through the camp, she cast small sidelong glances

at him. He was younger than Hazard, but he carried his lithe body with the sureness of a proven warrior. His hair was long, much longer than Hazard's, and when he turned and smiled at her, she decided the Absarokee men deserved their reputation for physical perfection. He was starkly handsome.

They walked in silence down several empty avenues, only an occasional dog lazily noting their progress. Spirit Eagle turned to smile at her frequently, and Blaze smiled back in a friendly exchange without words. She was relishing the opportunity to pay Hazard back with a flirtation of her own, and this splendid young man was pleasant, friendly, and very accommodating.

It wasn't until they'd walked some distance that Blaze noticed they seemed to be moving away from the luminous radiance of the bonfires in the night sky. She stopped abruptly and Spirit Eagle's grasp tightened on hers. "The dance is back there," she said, turning a half-step and gesturing with her free hand.

He didn't seem to understand. *"Hú kawe, bia,"* he quietly replied and began walking again, tugging Blaze along.

Her stomach pitched nervously, for she'd recognized the entirety of that short phrase—"Come, sweetheart." Why was he calling her sweetheart? Was it an innocuous form of address or something more personal? Suddenly she felt very much alone in the deserted camp. And unsure. Maybe this friendly walk and polite smiles were less innocent than they appeared.

Damnation, she thought pettishly, I'm not going to docilely allow myself to be led away in the wrong direction. "Stop!" she unceremoniously demanded and suited her actions to her words. She might as well have tried to stop a force of nature. Spirit Eagle didn't even break stride; his grip only hardened and he pulled her along effortlessly.

"Just a damn minute!" she shouted and struck at him with a clenched fist. It was like hitting a solid wall.

He paused then for a moment and looking down at her said, *"De-yea-x-wah-saw-weeh-ma* [I won't hurt you]. *Be-le-she-chila-lema* [You'll like me]." He was so sure of himself, and any number of women he'd pleasured would uphold his assertion. Reaching out, he trailed his fingertips down the slender grace of her throat. When she sharply thrust his hand away, he laughed and murmured something so low the words were only a husky murmur, but the message in his eyes was unmistakable. "Come," he repeated, and resumed walking.

No longer cooperative, Blaze dug in her heels, but it hardly slowed him, save for the tiny furrows left by her moccasin heels in the grass. They traversed another fifty yards in this fashion, with Blaze verbally threatening and denouncing and Spirit Eagle appearing not to notice. He stopped at last in front of a lodge and leaned forward slightly to lift the entrance flap aside.

Taking the small opportunity of his distraction, Blaze twisted sharply, slid her fingers free, and with adrenaline-induced speed, ran. Although fleet, she soon heard him behind her; first his footfalls and, as he gained on her, his unhurried breathing. Her own respiration was forced after two hundred yards of all-out flight, and as she drew in a labored breath, she found herself swung off her feet from behind and lifted into strong arms.

She began struggling, pushing at his solid chest, pounding on his shoulders, kicking the air with her feet, but he only chuckled, tightening his grip, and whispered some of the words she'd heard Hazard whisper to her when they were making love. He murmured them softly, soothingly, as one might to a recalcitrant child, and at the last, the words held a question.

He was bending his head to kiss her. Had he asked her to kiss him? Held high in his arms, her eyes large with shock and fear, she could see his mouth only inches away.

Suddenly into her field of vision Blaze sighted Hazard turning a corner of the avenue in a flat-out run. Automatically fear vanished, but jealousy reminded her that Hazard deserved some payment for that long, long kiss with the girl in the dance. Spirit Eagle's back was to Hazard and he was still unaware of his approach when Blaze glimpsed Rising Wolf clear the same corner in a sprint. She was smiling faintly when she lifted her lips to accept Spirit Eagle's kiss.

Sweet revenge, now that rescue was near.

Hazard hadn't seen Blaze's resistance.

He hadn't heard any of the verbal defiance.

He hadn't seen her run away or kick and struggle.

He only saw her held in Spirit Eagle's embrace, only saw her kissing him. And jealous rage exploded in his mind.

"Enjoying yourself?" he drawled in English, walking the last few yards, controlling his urge to strike out.

Spirit Eagle spun around.

"Let her go," Hazard coldly ordered, the Absarokee unnaturally harsh.

"Maybe she wants to stay." Spirit Eagle's challenge was flagrant.

"Do you want to stay?" Hazard coolly asked, reverting to English, and even in her own anger Blaze didn't dare respond in the affirmative to that tone. Hazard's eyes were too remote.

She shook her head.

"There," Hazard said, impassively. "Now let her go."

Spirit Eagle loosened his grasp and Blaze slid to the ground.

"Take her back to the lodge," Hazard instructed Rising Wolf, who'd arrived directly behind Hazard.

"Just a minute," Blaze objected. "I won't be sent off like—like—"

Hazard looked at her disdainfully. "Like some misbehaving trollop?" he finished, his smile unpleasant.

"Don't talk to me about misbehaving," Blaze hotly retorted, taking a threatening step toward him. "Did you tire of the games of the dance?"

Hazard grimaced. "We can talk about that later," he said, not inclined to conduct any grand-scale verbal battle in front of Rising Wolf and Spirit Eagle.

"Oh . . . later. I see, *Your Highness,* I'm to be dismissed then?"

"That's the general idea," Hazard softly replied.

"And what if I don't care to be dismissed by every

woman's *dream lover,"* she archly retorted, her tone acidly sweet. "That young girl down at the dance's lover, Little Moon's lover, Lucy Attenborough's lover," her voice was rising as the list grew. "Elizabeth Motley's lover, Fanny—"

"Shut her up and take her away," Hazard snapped.

And in the next instant, midway through the next woman's name in the lengthy list, Blaze was swept off the ground. "Sorry," Rising Wolf apologized, placing his hand over her mouth, leaving her speechless for most of the distance back to Hazard's lodge.

SPIRIT Eagle was smirking. "Maybe you'd like me to take her off your hands."

"Maybe I wouldn't."

"Does the great chief Dit-chilajash allow himself to be ruled by a yellow eyes woman?" His tone was insulting.

Hazard ignored the insult. "I'm warning you off, Spirit Eagle. Don't touch her again. Don't talk to her. Don't go near her."

"We could fight for the yellow eyes," Spirit Eagle challenged, anxious for an opportunity to publicly triumph over Hazard.

"You know better than that. I don't fight over women." Hazard's tone was final in its clarity. Was it necessary to explain age-old tradition?

"Coward?"

It was startlingly rude, but Hazard remembered the impertinence of youth and only served verbal warning. "You'd die finding out."

"Pussy-whipped, then!"

Hazard shrugged to indicate the unimportance of Spirit Eagle's remark. "Just stay away from my woman. This is a one-time warning. You won't get a second chance."

"It discredits a man to show such favor for a woman. You're becoming like a yellow eyes. You shame yourself with such weakness. To crave a woman is to fall short as a warrior."

The young pup was frank enough, Hazard thought

ruefully, but he was past the age himself when youthful dogmatism narrowed his understanding of men. He carefully explained, "I understand your challenge, Spirit Eagle. All those in the past and now this one. It's the path of a warrior to seek glory and leadership. I understand all that impels you." Hazard's voice was patient. "I even understand," he went on thoughtfully, "you wanting her. And I was raised in the same ways you were," he said as a father would to a rebellious son, "so you needn't talk to me of shame and dishonor. You needn't remind me of the different motives that rule men's and women's lives. But this is different, and that's why I'm warning you. I'll do as I please about her." Hazard's tone was sharp now and cutting in its plainness. "Don't cross me on this or I'll—" He closed his eyes briefly, unsure himself how far he'd go in his need for her. When he reopened them, they were bleak and cold. "Just don't," he finished.

"I could abduct her. You couldn't do anything then."

"It's not the season."[16]

"It will be again."

Hazard smiled faintly. "Not for me."[17]

"So it's true, then. I hear you carry water for her and cook for her like a woman." Spirit Eagle's young face held disdain.

"I do what I please," Hazard replied quietly, fathomless reserves of self-confidence lending assurance to every syllable. "You're young and have much ahead of you. I suggest you find another woman. But if some misplaced sense of honor or pride presses you, I just want you to know," he continued, cool-eyed and exact, "if you try to come for her, you'll have to get by me first."

"She's going to make you weak."

"You're welcome to try and find out. Anytime," he offered, waited calmly, then receiving no answer walked away.

RISING Wolf, standing guard outside Hazard's lodge, felt a hand on his shoulder as Hazard's voice, low, level, and friendly, said, "Thank you. I'll talk to you in the morning."

Rising Wolf looked at his friend and knew what he was feeling. "It's not all her fault," he softly pointed out.

Hazard sighed. "I know."

"Don't be too hard on her. Our ways are new. She didn't understand."

Hazard deferentially listened to his best friend's advice and smiled a little. "I've never struck a woman in my life," he quietly answered. "Take that worried look off your face."

"In that case," Rising Wolf said, smiling that light-hearted smile that reminded Hazard of a thousand boyhood memories, "pleasant dreams." But Rising Wolf had never seen Hazard run for any woman. Never. And he doubted whether Hazard's woman would go unscathed after the smoldering kiss he'd seen her give Spirit Eagle.

Upright and hostile, she was standing waiting for him when he walked in.

Regardless of what Hazard had said to Rising Wolf he was, by then, extremely short-tempered, for the image of Blaze kissing Spirit Eagle fed a fierce jealousy that burnt away his habitual self-control. He felt like shaking her until she promised never to kiss any man again. Ever. Territorial rights were crowding his rationality and pressing his sense of possession past the point of moderation.

"Did you think of Raven Wing when you kissed her little sister?" Blaze vindictively asked, ever on the offensive.

The words detonated on impact, explosive as the enraged woman, poised like a lethal weapon in the center of the lodge. Hazard stopped as if someone had slapped him, the name—rarely spoken since her death—charged with a life of its own. Hazard looked at Blaze, his back stiff with displeasure, he opened his mouth to speak, then closed it again in a grim line. He walked past her to the far side of the lodge and pulled his fringed shirt over his head, his muscles flexing across his back.

"What do you want, damn you?" she cried, outraged at his behavior. And his present silence. "I'd like to know! Why me, Hazard? When any woman out there would gladly change places. I understand you need a hostage, but why all the rest? Why bother with the endearments and the love words? They don't mean anything to you, that's obvious. That young girl out there tonight. She could take my place in a minute. If it's a servant you want, to cook and clean, you know I can't do that. And if it's an unpaid courtesan you want, surely the line must be long for that position!"

He turned and stared at her in disbelief. Only two days ago, he'd told her that in his eyes and that of his clan, she was his wife. Although unplanned, it wasn't a casual decision, lightly made. And now he'd found her in another man's arms. "Courtesans at least know—" he testily began, but Blaze wasn't listening, only pouring out her fury, only intent on exorcising the frustration of the past hour, a frustration based on unparalleled forfeiture of her independence, going back to Hazard's first kiss weeks ago. Tonight was only the ultimate effecting balance that toppled, not the underlying cause.

"Or maybe . . ." she sarcastically went on, disregarding his utterance. She was pacing wildly in the small space between the doorway and the fire, her eyes flashing like storm signals. ". . . Maybe *I* should be paying *you*. After all, *you're* the one with the notorious reputation and expertise. She stopped in midturn, spun around, and archly declared, "How much do I owe you by now? Do you charge by the hour or by the week?"

He walked away rather than hit her and dropped down on the fur robes piled into a bed. Her angry words continued rolling over him in an undisguised litany of rage while he shakily counted to fifty—ten wasn't enough. He would have been on his feet after ten, letting her feel the extent of his reaction to her bitter sarcasm.

The episode with Spirit Eagle was still in the forefront of his mind: Blaze in his arms; the ungovernable urge to kill overwhelming him; the necessity to curb the impulse. But the situation was only defused, not resolved; still infinitely complex, aggravated by Blaze's continuing presence, potentially dangerous, and at base—he grimly thought—unsolvable. Damn the noise levels. Why did the yellow eyes always feel they had to shout to be heard? Would she ever stop? He reached down to untie his moccasins, slipped them off, and lay back on the bed.

Blaze was standing over him in two short seconds. "What the hell do you think you're doing?" she tersely demanded.

"Going," said Hazard with simple truth, "to sleep." He didn't trust himself at the moment to do anything else.

"Aren't you going to answer my question?" she furiously asked.

There was a moment's complete silence. "No," said Hazard, repressing his own fury with visible effort.

But Blaze wasn't, currently, sensitive to delicate nuance. "I want an answer!" she screamed, standing above him stridently, unfamiliar with not having her way, unfamiliar with not carving her own path through the universe—magnificent, flushed, intensely proud. But not as dangerous as Hazard.

He saw it coming—the stiff-armed lashing palm reaching down to feed the fury, and he caught her slender wrist a foot from his face. With a wrenching twist, he tumbled her to the bed and in primitive lust fueled by rage, jealously, and primordial need for possession, and in one smooth movement, flung his body over hers. His hands on her shoulders were cruelly rough, his temper unconcealed now in his narrowed eyes, his voice too soft. He said, "You want an answer? I'll give you an answer." Brutally he bore down, grinding his lean hips into hers. "No," he whispered, his face grim, answering her question at last. "I'm not looking for a servant. Or a courtesan. Although Spirit Eagle seemed interested. And no, I don't want you to pay me, sweet bitch," he smiled then, an unpleasant leer. "You don't have enough money." Forcing his knees between her thighs, he settled his body familiarly between her legs. "All you understand, spoiled child, is *I want.*" And with smiling violence, he snapped the shell belt clasp at her waist. "All you've ever understood is *I want.*" He tossed aside the shattered shells. "It's time, sweet puss," he quietly went on, roughly pushing her dress up past her waist, "to learn the world doesn't revolve around your wishes. It revolves around mine, and I don't choose to share you with any man who catches your eye."

Blaze pushed against his weight, against the hands forcing her body to accommodate his. "Don't touch me, you damned hypocrite," she stormed, gasping for breath with his dead weight on her. "And don't lecture me on . . . fidelity!"

"It's not a lecture. It's an order." His voice was awesome in its moderation. "I'm sorry, but in future you'll have to forgo extracurricular lovers. My contract doesn't allow it."

"I see. *Hazard's Law!*" she hissed. "Only playmates for you!"

"I didn't kiss that woman," his soft voice continued, but his brows met in a black scowl, belying the subdued tone, "because I wanted to. I kissed her because it was expected of me. Just like now, *bia,*" he growled, his hand tracing an ungentle pattern up her inner thigh, "I expect you to play the dutiful wife."

"Damn you, I won't! Not after—all those people watching you—I won't!" She struggled against the prowling hands and failed to stop their progress. She tried to arch away from contact with them but he lay atop her like a vise.

His fingers circled her wrist in a bone-threatening grip. "You will." His voice was like ice. "I'm sure of it. Look at me."

She turned away, deliberately, hot anger boiling inside her.

His hand forced her head back. "You shouldn't have gone off with Spirit Eagle." His eyes were pitiless.

"Were the little sister's lips to your taste?" she spat, her own eyes like hurricane seas.

"You're a long way from home, Boston, and what you don't know about our culture would fill a thousand volumes. Perhaps," he murmured, tight-lipped, "I've been derelict. Lesson one: I won't have you going off with other men."

"He forced me," she panted, the blood pulsing in her white throat, all her struggling useless against his strength.

"Like hell he did," Hazard snapped, his fingers biting into her wrist. "Not from where I was standing."

"I thought we were going to dance," she breathlessly insisted.

His teeth showed for a moment, white against his grim mouth. "Oh, you would have danced all right," he snarled. "The oldest dance in the world."

"That's not fair." She pushed against the relentless weight of him. "I had no intention—"

"Remember, Boston, I know how hot your sweet body can be. Don't tell me you had no intention. Not after the kind of kiss I saw."

"You don't own me, Hazard!" It was a heated, angry cry, at frustrated odds with her circumstances.

"Here I do. Here I very much do, sweet wife," said the passion of an Absarokee chief who had fought like his forebears had, to retain possession of his land and property. "At least as long as I want you," he rudely added, the thought of her mouth on Spirit Eagle's etched on his memory.

"I might leave you first," said Blaze, her voice thin. "Everything's egalitarian here, isn't it?"

"You might run into a little trouble leaving. Unfortunately, theory and practice aren't always synonymous in real life. You're very much mine, Boston. Predispose yourself."

Glowing with a furious incredulity, she stared at the man lying atop her. "And if I don't?" she hostilely countered.

His low, derisive laugh was exquisitely soft. "Then I'll have to adjust my schedule," he said, brutally courteous, "to allow time to persuade you. We'll discuss it again," he murmured drily, "one hour from now."

"You'll have to force me," she spat, flushed and glowering.

His mouth curved into a genuine smile. "Don't be stupid. You're usually"—his mouth widened—"how do I put this delicately . . . agreeably anxious?" he murmured.

"And you're usually," Blaze hotly returned, her magnificent eyes narrowed, her small body still fighting against Hazard's steely fingers and solid weight, "like a damn rutting bull."

"That's why we get along so well, I'd guess," Hazard said approvingly and laughed quickly. A warm, pleasant sound. "Some like it tame, Boston. And some like it wild. And some say they like it tame but eat you alive when all is said and done. So don't accuse me of obtuseness; you get exactly what you ask for. But we will in future," he growled, "see that the asking is confined to me."

"Maybe and maybe not," Blaze pugnaciously answered.

"Positively and unequivocally," Hazard commanded, his grip near to snapping the bones in her arms.

"You can't tell me what to do," she stubbornly cried.

"You need tutoring in holding your tongue. You're a shade too noisy for my taste."

"And you're too insufferably under control for mine," she retorted, stony-faced and obstinate.

Thoughtfully, his gaze scanned Blaze's stormy face. "You're willful," he murmured, "exasperating as hell, and dangerous to my peace of mind." Then he sighed, a deep and baffling sigh. "*What* am I going to do with you?"

"Let go of my wrist," she whispered pleadingly, a tiny wan smile toughing the corners of her face. "Peace of mind," she tentatively continued, "is much overrated."

Hazard groaned mockingly, released his grip, and dropped his head into the curve of her neck.

"Speaking of peace of mind, though," Blaze ventured, "*since* you brought it up . . . not that I subscribe to it as a virtue, but tell me something," she abruptly finished in a quick rush of words.

Hazard had felt her body tense beneath him and when he looked up was relieved to see her attempt a small smile.

"Honestly now," she added, her face grave once again.

"Of course." He eased his weight lightly on his elbows.

"Does she mean anything to you?"

"The girl at the dance?"

Blaze nodded, chastened and subdued and so unlike herself, Hazard worried for a moment he may have hurt her in their struggle. "No," he said very gently. "It was only duty, ritual, ceremony . . . whatever you want to call it."

"No memories, no twinges of regret?" she asked, warily peering at him.

"I don't even know her. She was eight when I left for Harvard the first time."

"Then," Blaze said in an altogether different voice, the familiar one with a touch of wanton cheerfulness, ". . . I didn't have to try to make you jealous by kissing Spirit Eagle."

"You're telling me," he said, harboring his own suspicions, *"that* was deliberate?"

Blaze's mouth curved sweetly. "I saw you coming. Before that I'd been fighting to protect my virtue."

"Really?" His tone was vaguely dubious.

"Don't you believe me?"

"Well, pet . . ." Hazard's experience with Blaze had been rather the opposite; he'd been the one protecting his nonexistent virtue, so one must allow him his doubts.

"Hazard!"

"Of course I believe you," he quickly acceded, warmed suddenly by memories of his darling, if vexacious lover, warmed by her astonishing diversity and plurality and fighting instincts. But being a realist, he made a mental note to see that Blaze was safeguarded when out of his protection.

"You really don't care about that girl?" she repeated, her anger gone but some niggling anxieties persisting.

"I don't care about Blue Flower or Little Moon or Lucy Attenborough or even—" He stopped before pronouncing the name and gently smiled at Blaze. "Even my memories are gone," he softly went on. "You've taken every iota of space in my consciousness. "I love you," he said, very, very quietly. "Stay with me." Then suddenly he rolled off her and collapsed on his back, his fingers raking brusquely through his sleek black hair. "Damn it to hell," he muttered. "How we'll ever manage—" He left the unanswerable question unfinished. "I shouldn't be saying any of this," he went on, his arms thrown restlessly above his head, his eyes trained on the distant sky visible through the opening in the roof.

All he could see was streams of yellow eyes overrunning his country, the prophecy of his long-ago medicine-dream disastrously true. The Indian tribes in dealing with the yellow eyes had never had any political advantage. They lacked the guile the white man cultivated like a precious virtue. Expediency, they called it, not ruthlessness. Progress, they said, instead of extermination. Was it possible to win? He didn't know.

In every generation there were men with outstanding powers; his father possessed the sacred gifts to see the future. And he did as well. But the success as a visionary chief rested on an individual's consciousness of the ascribed powers, on self-sacrifice and compassion. The supreme test for both himself and his clan was near at hand. Winning might be possible; there was a remote chance with the gold. Or at least the contingency of not losing too disastrously. But he should nurture his sacred powers, focus on the seriousness of his clan's future. Not let personal feelings interfere with the substance of his life as a chief and leader.

Then suddenly all the conflict in his heart was submerged by the flow of love he felt for Blaze and duty faltered. Tonight he was willing to drown in the welcoming forgetfulness, settle only for his tremulous feelings. "Tell me," he said, turning his head quickly back to her, "tell me you care. Tell me," he pleaded, wanting her, at that instant, more than honor itself.

Blaze threw herself across his body, loving beyond doubt, beyond differences, with all her heart and soul. "I love you," she joyfully breathed. "I love you, I love you, I love you, I love you." Butterfly kisses punctuated each blissful declaration. Blaze was suffused with the magic of her love, feeling a wondrous unity with the world, as if everything had fallen into place with the simplicity of a child's dream. And she wanted to shout it from a mountaintop into a cloudless sky.

Hazard's arms were close around her, and looking

into her sparkling eyes he asked, "How can you be so sure?"

She nodded an emphatic, unequivocal affirmation. "I know," she said.

"Why is it so easy for you to say?" he wistfully murmured.

"If you feel it, you say it," Blaze explained. "No restrictions, spontaneous; I live, I feel, I am," she went on in her impulsive rush of words. "Very simple. Don't you ever feel that way?"

"No," he replied without hesitation. He wished his feelings were as uncomplicated. His love for her was hindered, enclosed, obstructed by a multitude of impediments, all mutually destructive.

"Kiss me," she urged, drawing him from his morbid musing. "And love me."

"Little dictator," he muttered. "You never change." But he was smiling when he said it.

She kissed him first, as it turned out, lushly and heatedly, a flaming prelude to passion, and in a few brief seconds he forgot the bittersweet sadness as the floodgates of pleasure opened in a rushing torrent.

Chapter 28

THE following days were perfection; mostly play, all precious. A time to be treasured forever. Hazard kept Blaze near. He liked to be able to reach out and touch her, as if her tactile presence were talisman against the future he chose to ignore these few sweet weeks of summer.

They rode out with the other lovers and sweethearts, picking berries and hunting wild rhubarb in a delicious season of merrymaking, laughter, love, and their own special oneness. They spent long, lazy hours in the sun-tinged willow bower playing at love and ignoring anything but the present.

Sometimes at night they'd climb halfway up the mountain to some small hillside pasture and Blaze would lay curled against Hazard's shoulder while he rested in the sweet-smelling grass. Under the glittering night sky, he'd point out the constellations, giving their Indian names, or he'd recount to her some of the Absarokee legends. Once he told her of his first vision on this mountain.

"My uncle had died, killed by a Lakota on Powder River. My family mourned. I cut my flesh and bled myself weak."

"These are mourning scars?" Blaze's fingers trailed over the ridged pattern of old scars on Hazard's chest.

He answered yes, quietly, but it was as if he had returned to that time, as if he remembered the grief anew. His eyes were lifted to the starry sky and the memory was so vivid for a moment, he thought he heard his mother's wailing cries. "My uncle was young and brave," he softly continued, "had counted coup many times already; he was an inspiration to me."

"How old were you when he died?"

"Twelve, and I loved him dearly." Hazard was silent for a moment. It seemed like yesterday when the crier had come back with the news. He sighed. "My heart fell to the ground and I knew I must dream if I ever hoped to avenge him. It was almost this time of year. The chokecherries were black and the plums red on the trees. I took extra moccasins and a good buffalo robe and walked to the mountains."

"What did your parents say? Twelve seems so young," Blaze murmured, her cheek warm on his shoulder.

"No one saw me leave the village. I slipped away. As soon as I reached the mountains I covered a sweat lodge with the robe and cleansed my body. Then I made a bed of sweet sage and ground cedar. The day was hot and, naked, I began walking on the mountaintop, crying for Helpers. But no answer came. I grew tired as the sun went down and lay down on my bed. For three days I fasted and walked and slept, and then I wakened the third night and heard someone calling my name. They had come for me. The People had come for me.

" 'Come,' they said, and I stood up, my head clear and light as air. I followed them, the wind cool on my skin, the trail smooth as the plains, although it was the mountaintop." Hazard was speaking now as if he were back on the mountain.

"I came to a burning fire. Six Little People were sitting around it in a half-circle."

Blaze was frightened suddenly; Hazard's presence had altered, his voice taking on a remoteness. "Jon," she murmured, placing her palm on his cheek, "I don't understand."

Her touch seemed to bring him back. He shook his head slightly and then hugged her close. "It's nothing, *bia*. It's like a dream. We see signs in our dreams sometimes, that's all." He didn't say, the medicine men had known when he came back from the mountain, had listened to his vision of the dwarf people, the spotted buffalo, and Four Winds, and had told him when was twelve that he already possessed the power to be great. Ah-badt-dabt-deah has given it to you, they told him, but the difference between men grows out of the use or nonuse of what is given them by Ah-badt-daht-deah. Learn to use what he has given you. You will become a great chief. From that day he had *known* himself.

"It's so different. I don't feel I know you when you talk that way."

"Think of it like a religion and it seems less strange. All the white man's religions are different, too. Scarcely any two white men can agree on which one is the right one. Some have two gods and a goddess, some many gods, some one, and the black robes talk of visions and miracles. Does that make it seem safer, *bia?* I didn't mean to alarm you." He gently stroked her hair.

"It's so much a part of your life, though," Blaze softly said.

"We simply meet our divinities face to face, without priestly go-betweens. And individual visions if successful are seen as a great source of power and a blessing to the tribe. We see mystic power in the wind and sky, in the rain, the rivers, in birds and mountains and prairies."

"The land's important, isn't it?" Blaze whispered, only half understanding the merging of self and religion, and oneness with nature.

"It's everything," Hazard pronounced with reverence. Ah-badt-daht-deah, The-one-who-made-all-things, has given us the most beautiful land on all the world. No other country compares with Absarokee country. And it's my dream to keep it for my people." Now, as so often when he spoke of the future, he trailed off into moody silence. But he held her tightly while he gazed into the great star-filled sky.

"You can do it, Jon," Blaze whispered.

"Maybe," he softly murmured. "Just . . . maybe."

"I want to help. If I can in any way." Her warm breath drifted across his chest.

"You're my second-by-second reminder that life is joy and happiness, *bia*. You're my staunchest help. Now give me a kiss."

She did, and tasted the tears on his cheeks.

Blaze came to understand on those quiet summer evenings Hazard's pride in his heritage and the ties that bound him to this land. They were ethereal as a faded memory from childhood, yet indelible as a fingerprint. This land nurtured his spirit and his body, and in turn he loved it with supernatural mysticism.

The summer encampment made their idle pursuits easy. Pleasure was everyone's avocation. They were gathered together in their annual renewing of friendships, sharing the events of the last year. Relatives met each other again, and the days and evenings were spent in rounds of dining, dancing, game playing, horse racing, and sport.

Overlooking acceptable social behavior, Hazard brought Blaze to council meetings. It was a gallant defiance done in the name of love. He warned her, though. "You're welcome to come," he'd said, "but expect some scowls. It's not that it's unheard of. We've had women warriors occasionally and treated them as equals in council. But not in the last decade, and people forget. Plus you're attending as my wife, not a warrior. Don't let anyone upset you."

Rising Wolf had said straight out and bluntly, "You can't bring her in," when Hazard told him he was bringing Blaze to council.

"She wants to, and I'll bring her," Hazard had replied.

"They'll crucify her," Rising Wolf said wildly, looking at Hazard as if he'd suddenly gone mad.

"No one will remark on her presence or they answer to me. You can pass that information along."

"Damnation, Hazard," he groaned in despair. "She's a woman!" Rising Wolf's glance was tender. He was an old friend whose favorite companion appeared to have lost his senses.

"She'll sit beside me tonight," Hazard responded, his gaze clear and untroubled. "Tell them."

"Are you sure it's all right?" Blaze asked one last time before they left their lodge that evening, aware of the etiquette involved.

"It's fine," Hazard cryptically replied, his smile disarming. There were sure to be objections, but he was willing to put up with them. "A chief is the consequence not only of the individual merit of his coups,[18] but also recognized for his medicine and his accomplishments for the clan. You prove your courage in battle and your fortitude in situations that try the heart of a man. And that capacity allows you to lead and govern.

"In theory, it's not a hereditary position, and the clans are democratically organized," Hazard reflected, "but family's important. In our variety of communal living," he continued, "a large and rich family ensures one's own prosperity.[19] In fact, the greatest insult you can direct at a person is to call him an *akirī' hawe,* a person without relatives. Although my mother and father died last year, I still have a network of relatives, all supportive. In addition, my medicine has allowed me much success on raids. And the gold from the mine, the more prescient of the council realize, will ensure our survival. I am considered a *kon-ning,* 'a man that knows and can,' so"—he smiled—"you see, *bia-cara,* in the aristocracy of *batsē' tse,* or chiefs, I'm able to do damn near anything I want."

"That, dear, is a source of both great joy and vexation to me—that predilection of yours." Blaze's smile was mockingly deprecating.

"Similar feelings have crossed my mind on occasion, too, puss." He tapped her lightly on the nose. "Your father indulged you much too much."

"And you find me unattractive?"

He grinned. "Not altogether."

"How reassuring."

"One small assurance for me, love, if you don't mind. In council, if you would refrain from outright ordering me about, my dignity would be preserved."

"You mean I can't drag you away when I feel an unaccountable urge to make love to you?"

"It might be embarrassing. We warriors are supposed to be above such frivolous emotions while in council."

"And are you?"

"Hell no," he said with a grin. "Another discredited theory, but we keep up the fiction for reasons of self-interest."

"I promise not to embarrass you in council," Blaze declared with mock solemnity.

"What a relief," Hazard teasingly responded, wiping imaginary sweat from his brow. "But you might consider winking at me discreetly when you take such a notion and I'll immediately recall some crisis that requires my attention."

"Resourceful."

"So I've been told." One look at Blaze's nettled expression and he hurriedly added, his smile broad, "By friends, love, only friends."

So Blaze sat through two council meetings in the following week, but she understood very little of the language and nothing of the nuance. Hazard was, despite his assurances, more formal at the public meetings; after the second lengthy session, Blaze chose to stay at the lodge during future councils.

Red Plume, Hazard's young nephew, was chosen to guard her. With Spirit Eagle present in council, Hazard wasn't alarmed about leaving Blaze alone, but it never hurt to be cautious, and Red Plume was good entertainment for Blaze. He was teaching her how to handle a bow and arrow.

The first meeting Blaze was absent from, Hazard asked the assembled chiefs whether any had been approached by Colonel Braddock. He explained the circumstances of the Colonel's pilgrimage into the mountains and through various replies was able to trace Billy Braddock's progress up to his meeting with the Sore Lip Clan near Dog Creek. After that, no one had seen him. "Where's his guide?" Hazard inquired, searching for more specific details after the Colonel's last sighting.

"Gone to see his Shoshone wife's relatives."

"When did he leave?"

"I'm not sure. Maybe ten days ago."

About the time, Hazard thought, when he'd first heard the rumors of a yellow eyes death north of the Clearwater Mountains. "Gone for the summer, then." Hazard knew the distance involved. The guide and his family could be absent a long time. "If anyone hears of Colonel Braddock, let me know," he advised them, but in his own mind, he was more than half certain Blaze had lost her father. He'd check with One Heart's brother-in-law—if he could find him. His description of the man killed might tell him something.

The discussion turned to a raid in the planning. A scout had brought in news of Blackfeet traveling north with a herd of ponies cut from the Lakota south of the Yellowstone. It was agreed they'd leave before first light the following day.

As they were dispersing, Bold Ax, Raven Wing's father, touched Hazard's arm. "Walk with me," he said. He and Hazard strolled toward the river, talking of the coming raid, exchanging gossip about mutual friends, recalling their years of friendship; following the preliminary protocol to a discussion Hazard wished he could avoid. But courtesy forbade his evasion. "You've known Blue Flower since she was a baby," Bold Ax said, broaching the subject prompting his invitation for a walk.

"Yes, she was always my wife's favorite sister."

"She's been a woman now for over a year and has refused two marriage offers." Hazard only waited, wondering how to offend the least. "You know our customs allow a man to marry his wife's sisters."

"She's young," Hazard quietly replied. "Perhaps at this encampment she might find—"

"She speaks only of you."

Hazard stopped, indicated a grassy plot on the bank of the river and suggested, "Sit with me." For a quiet moment, they both looked out over the placidly flowing river under the twilight sky capricious with magenta. When Hazard spoke, his voice was as calm as the water before them. "I'm honored, Bold Ax, with your daughter's regard. Her sister, whom I loved, brought much happiness to me. I've always felt the welcome of your family. It wouldn't be right now for me to accept the feelings Blue Flower offers me, that you offer me. The yellow eyes woman is *bua* to me and I care for her. Please try to tell Blue Flower the way of my heart. Perhaps at another time, it might have been possible."

"You can have more than one wife."

"In my heart, I can't."

"You're young, and even as a child, you were ungovernable." Bold Ax said it with affection. "A yellow eyes wife can bring many problems. The heart can change. I speak as your father would."

"Perhaps, but my spirit dictates over a sterner logic. Thank Blue Flower for the warmth of her affection."

"She's going to be disappointed."

Hazard smiled. "At her age, she'll forget in a few days."

Bold Ax placed his broad palm on Hazard's knee and smiled back. "You're probably right; I hope you're right. Good luck on the raid tomorrow," he said, rising.

"The Blackfeet should be tired. I don't expect problems."

After Bold Ax departed, Hazard sat watching the river flow by. It was comforting to realize that this river had been crossing Absarokee hunting ground since before they had horses. He knew, his eyes unfocused on the clear water passing before him, that six months ago he would have accepted Bold Ax's daughter in marriage. And he wondered, with the same nagging unease that prompted much of his musing, whether he'd taken a route in his life which would prove not only disastrous but deadly.

How great a fool was he to brazenly disregard convention by taking Blaze as his wife and standing up to a menacing conglomerate like Buhl Mining as well? A very large fool, he decided. A reckless, illogical fool, he thought. An enormously happy fool, he smilingly recognized, and in depth and breadth and intensity, the happiness diminished all else.

THAT night, before they fell asleep, Hazard told Blaze of the raid.

She didn't answer for so long, he thought she may have fallen asleep and not heard him. "Am I going to be a widow?" she inquired at last, sitting up and gazing down at him as directly and straightforwardly as she queried him. The summer moonlight streaming in through the opening at the peak bathed her in bright and shimmering silver, making her pale skin radiant. Though she trembled slightly in apprehension, she wanted to know; wanted to know how much danger and what kind, and how far he would be from her. She thought for a brief second of saying, "Don't go—please, for me," but refrained.

"Nope."

"I'm not a child, Hazard. I'd like the truth."

"It's only a raid for horses, love, not revenge." His hand touched her reassuringly, soothingly. "When we raid or 'cut' horses, it is a greater coup to accomplish it undetected, since that requires more finesse. We pride ourselves on finesse rather than brute force."

That simple statement explained to Blaze a great many pleasurable variables in Hazard's nature. "You're sure it's not dangerous."

"Positive."

"How far do you have to go?"

"Not far. The Blackfeet are slicing through the upper tangent of our territory on their way home. Maybe two hundred miles."

"That's close?"

"Damn close. If we strike out diagonally in the direction of their flight, we should overtake them in less than a day. We're the short side of the triangle and they have to wade the Bowstring at Ottertail Gap. It's the only way through the mountains there."

"Do women ever go on the raids?"

Hazard hesitated, wondering how much to tell her. If she came, it would present problems, since Spirit Eagle was in the party. Although women did go on some raids to cook for the men or help with the ponies, Hazard didn't think Blaze could keep up. If he told her that, however, she'd rise to the challenge immediately. He chose an answer that deviated marginally from the truth. "Not unless they're very safe."

"I thought you said this one was," she nervously replied.

He curled her small hand into his. "Basically it is," he calmly explained, "but the Blackfeet like to take scalps,[20] and I'd hate to see yours on a Blackfoot lodge pole."

"What about yours?" she significantly asked.

"I can take care of myself, but if I had to guard you as well, it would halve both our chances."

"Do you have to go?" By this time Blaze's apprehensions were anxiously raised. It wasn't the innocuous expedition he'd initially suggested.

His answer was softly worded, but plain. "I want to."

The bright moonlight illuminated Blaze's face, drawn and serious. Tugging her close, he nestled her in his arms. "It's only two days, *bia,*" he whispered into her soft hair. "Red Plume will keep you company." Touching her grave face with a gentle caress, he murmured, "I'll bring you a present."

"Don't try to bribe me with presents," Blaze protested, drawing herself up and resting on his chest, her chin perched on her crossed wrists, "when I have to spend two days wondering if I'll ever see you again."

"I'm not trying to bribe you. You probably own half of Montana by now with Buhl's larcenous instincts. I just mean I'll be thinking of you, that's all."

"Keep your mind on staying alive, Hazard, if you don't mind. That's all the gift I want."

"I can guarantee that. I've been practicing survival for twenty-six years. This is a lark compared to Vicksburg and the Wilderness Campaign."

"You really enjoy it, don't you?"

In the half-dark of the shadows where Hazard lay, she could only imagine his smile. "Horse raids are amusing sport. Now tell me you'll miss me."

"You know I will; I just hope," she murmured, her mouth pursing in a brief moue, "it won't be permanently."

Hazard laughed, then kissed the tip of her nose. "Would I risk my life when I've you to come back to?"

"No, I guess not," Blaze replied, a smugly mischievous smile lighting her face.

He laughed again, pleased her plaintiveness had disappeared. He much preferred her playful arrogance. "If you need anything while I'm gone . . . besides that," he amended viewing her half-raised brow. "And keep in mind," he facetiously went on, although dead-serious at base, "my ideas of territorial rights are decidedly primitive."

"Is Little Moon going along?"

"I don't know."

"Keep in mind, if she should," Blaze firmly stated, "I have notions of territorial rights as unequivocal as yours."

"You have my word of honor," Hazard solemnly pledged. And when his strong arms closed around her, she felt the love of the universe was hers.

AT THE last moment, though, she wasn't admirably brave when he left, throwing herself weeping into his arms. He kissed her tenderly and, far from thinking her tears foolish, felt like crying himself. It was their first separation.

"You *will* be careful?"

"I'm always careful," he lied.

"No heroics!"

He kissed her rosy cheek and smiled. "None."

"Are you sure you need more horses?"

"Need?" He gave her a startled look, as if sure she should have known. "It's a game, *bia*. Need doesn't signify."

"How about my need?"

"That," he said, his voice warm as an August sun, "is

another matter." Their eyes met, like two small children on a lark. She'd remember the magic all her life. "Red Plume will take care of you. Be good."

"And if I'm not?" Azure eyes were saucy.

"Why do you think I'm taking Spirit Eagle with me?"

"Don't you trust me?"

"Of course," he soothed.

"What if I'm bored?"

"I'll be back before the boredom is fatal. My word on it." He pulled an eagle feather from his headpiece and tucked it behind her ear. The Absarokee considered the eagle feather a sign of success. Hazard looked down into the face of his woman, looked long, for he might never see her again. Then he kissed her and he was gone.

HAZARD and twenty braves with their guns and their knives and war clubs and sticks, their saddlebags of meat, dressed in full war regalia, rode their ponies away toward the High Blue Mountains.

Hazard's heart sang as he rode along through the vast, lonely, still plain. There welled up within him a deep love for this land of his, the land his people had fought and died for. Miles of sagebrush and greasewood, miles of waving buffalo grass, rustling softly, buttes and hills and rivers and plains. Cottonwood trees and quaking aspen and willows and pines. Widespread, still distances under the blue skies hovering close. And the majesty of the mountains so much a part of his youth, so vital to his background, he couldn't imagine he'd lived in Boston without them.

Rising Wolf, keeping pace beside him, flashed a smile. "Two horses says we overtake them before the Mussleshell."

It was joy to be riding with his best friend at his side. Like the voice of the night wind which one could not understand, could scarcely hear, could only feel, Hazard was imbued with pleasure. "You're on." His own smile was cheerfully assured. "Not a mile closer than the North Slope. And that horse you're riding will do for one."

"Remember, I talked to the wolves this morning and

you didn't. You were too busy being all gooey-eyed with your woman."

"Gooey-eyed?" Hazard pronounced the word as if it were a new taste.

The new expression had struck Rising Wolf forcefully when he'd watched Hazard and Blaze say goodbye. His grin was ear to ear.

Hazard's own smile was untarnished benevolence, as only that of a man in love can be. "For someone who's spent the greater part of two days sweet-talking Breeze of the South Wind down by the river," Hazard retorted, cheerfully at peace with himself and the world, "I'd be careful about casting the first stone."

"I may have sweet-talked, but"—Rising Wolf's eyebrows rose—"I don't think anyone heard me mention marriage. That's for gooey-eyed smitten men," he teasingly mocked.

"I had my reasons for marrying her."

"Sure, and anyone looking at her knows them," Rising Wolf drily replied.

"They were cogent reasons."

"Delude yourself if it salves your rakish soul, but it's gooey-eyed to everyone with clear vision."

"Call it what you like," Hazard replied with serene imperturbability and a tranquil smile, "but it's as close to paradise as I've ever been." His brow lifted sardonically. "Might I recommend it to your libertine sensibilities; it's a unique sensation."

"If she has a twin sister, I might be persuaded," Rising Wolf waggishly retorted. "Otherwise the marriage trap's not for me. I like variety."

"Someday you're going to find someone to change that."

"Just so long," Rising Wolf said with a wicked grin, "as it's not too soon."

IN THE next two days Blaze alternated between blind faith in Hazard's ability to survive in any situation and mind-numbing fear. If she were to lose him after knowing so briefly such love and fulfillment, she didn't know how she would cope. For a woman who had always felt only supreme confidence in herself and her own sufficiency, Blaze now reckoned her life as only half of a whole—only complete with Hazard by her side.

And she had another fear as well, adding to her sense of insecurity, an anxiety still hovering on the fringes of certainty. An anxiety which became less avoidable with each passing day. If, as she thought, Hazard had put life in her body, would he, she hesitantly wondered, welcome fatherhood? Would he, after this raid, even be alive to ask? She sent up her own silent prayer for his safety.

"He *will* be back, won't he, Red Plume?" Blaze had asked within minutes of Hazard's leaving. "There's nothing to worry about, is there?" Blaze only wanted the right answer. And if the truth was different, she didn't want to know.

Red Plume understood the pleading in her voice. He'd seen the love and fear in her eyes when Hazard said goodbye. "Dit-chilajash will be back," he assured her. "He has the power with him." It was true. Hazard had always led successful raids, but Red Plume knew, with an inherent fatalism, that their enemies were numerous and the spirits unpredictable. He'd seen it happen when he rode against the Lakota with the great chief Long Horse, the day Long Horse's medicine lost its power; the day Long Horse died.

Red Plume was left ostensibly as Blaze's companion. In fact he was there for one purpose only: to guard Blaze's life with his own. Hazard was taking no chances on any possible abduction by rash young bucks. Red Plume was a matchless friend in Blaze's current state of unease. In his adolescent openness he responded to her seesaw moods, diverted her with a variety of activities, answered her curious questions about their way of life with patience and thoroughness. And in the process of becoming friend, guardian, companion, and helpmate to his uncle's beautiful wife, he fell a little in love with her himself.

They spent the mornings riding over the peaceful countryside. Red Plume taught Blaze the names of all the wildflowers and showed her the butte they called

Coyote's Ear and the point on the Arrow River they called The-place-where-the-cranes-rest. The sanctuary was beautifully serene, hundreds of magnificent cranes feeding in the lush green inlet. They rode along Arrow Creek where the sage thrashers whistled and called among the bushes and box elders. And they dismounted and sat down to watch the colorful birds the Absarokee call the-bird-that-makes-many-sounds. In the afternoons, when the sun was hot, they rested in the shade of the lodge. Together they practiced Blaze's Absarokee. Red Plume was a patient teacher, quick with his praise, an adolescent delighting in his role as tutor. But he seemed very grown-up when he demonstrated how to sew moccasins. Every warrior carried a sewing kit for moccasins, he explained. It was a basic necessity. And when Blaze, confounded at the image of Hazard sewing moccasins, inquired in astonishment, "Dit-chilajash too?" he said complacently, "Of course."

Young girls brought their meals to them; Hazard had arranged it. Rising Wolf's young nieces he'd asked for, intent on avoiding any confrontations between Blaze and women from his past.

It was a peaceful time, if Blaze's underlying fear for Hazard's safety could be discounted. And in the evenings Red Plume sat across the fire from Blaze and recited, in his beautifully careful English, some of the timeless legends of his people. Legends of courage and hope, love and honor, and some of the private depths of Hazard lineage were revealed to her in the haunting tales. She came to see the deep respect for tribal custom, the quest for the realization of individual dreams incomprehensible to a white man, the veneration paid to courage. The new understanding seemed to bring Hazard closer to her in his absence.

When it was time for sleep, Red Plume would always say good night politely and leave. Blaze was unaware he curled up in a robe under the stars and guarded her.

It was late at night when she felt the most terrible unease. Alone in a vast Indian village, certain she was carrying Hazard's child, she prayed, "Please, God, let him come back safely."

On the morning of the third day, Blaze was awakened by a soft whinny, unusual in its proximity. Rolling over half asleep in the predawn coolness, she dozed off again. Moments later, the sound again awoke her. It was distinctly a horse and very close. Lying awake now, she looked up and saw the pale morning sky just beginning to shade into color.

At the third clear nicker followed by an answering soft neigh, she slipped her fringed dress over her head, rose from the bed, and, walking across the silent lodge, lifted the entrance flap.

A magnificent golden palomino, its glossy coat glistening like new minted gold, its powerful neck looped with a braided rope, was tied to the lodge pole. And slipped under the rope circling its neck was a bouquet of summerflowers. Hazard was back! Her heart danced with joy. *He was back.* And it wasn't until the splendid palomino whinneyed again, only to be answered by several neighboring nickers, that Blaze glanced beyond the gilded beauty of the horse tied to the lodge. Her eyes widened in astonishment. Numerous other horses, each as beautiful, were tied beyond.

"Do you like them?" said a lazy voice, warm and familiar, over her shoulder.

She spun around. No more than a foot away, Hazard stood smiling. And she imprinted on her memory the image of him that morning: tall, collected, naked from the waist up, his hair still wet from his bath in the river, morning mist rising around him, a birdsong lifting on the breeze. He had a necklace of brown-eyed susans encircling his strong neck, spilling golden color down his sculpted chest. She ran toward him through the dew-wet grass, her face alive with happiness.

He crushed her to his cool chest, pungent flower scent invading their nostrils, and felt a glowing contentment seep into every tired pore of his body. "I missed you," he murmured, his chin resting in her hair. And they clung to each other, their love a tangible blessed presence. Feeling silent tears on his chest, he gently lifted her face and brushed away the wetness with his knuckles. "No need for tears, *bia*. It was a marvelous raid."

"I'm just happy," Blaze sniffled, attempting a small smile.

"It's hard to tell," Hazard teased, brushing away a smudge of pollen on her cheek. "Are you happy about your present, too?"

Blaze looked up at him, thinking no other man could give her such joy. "They're beautiful . . . and the flowers . . ."

"You're a woman of property now, in our clan."

"I am, you say." She blithely giggled.

"That many horses is considered an extravagant gesture," he banteringly quipped. Hazard didn't mention he'd risked his life to get the golden palomino.

"Does a herder come along with the extravagant gesture? Because I don't think I'm up to the job."

"Of course, princess. Chiefs' wives don't herd horses."

"I'm relieved to hear it," she murmured. They hadn't moved, content to stand holding each other, touching, talking under the rose-tipped rays of the rising sun, knowing that in each other's arms there was joy.

HAZARD slept for half the day and Blaze watched him, memorizing every line and plane, every muscle and silken hair, but restrained herself a dozen times from touching him; after all, he hadn't slept in two days. And while she sat at his side she realized, now that he was back, how dreadfully frightened she'd been. How beneath the busy activities during his absence had been not just loneliness but a flood of fear. When he finally woke, she curled into his arms and lay at peace. "Tell me about the raid," she said. And he did. Concisely, with a minimum of drama, editing the portions in which Spirit Eagle endangered his life.

The true story was left unsaid between the carefully selected words: The Blackfoot raiding party had entered a friendly village late at night just within Blackfoot territory. Feeling safe, they had begun celebrating and five drums were going at once when Hazard's band overtook them. The big flat was covered with horses.

Hazard and several of the Absarokee had stolen into the camp to spirit away some of the prized horses kept close to the lodges, while the rest of their party rounded up the ponies out on the plain.

Hazard saw the palomino tied to a tall lodge standing a little apart from the others. Immediately he set his heart on having it for Blaze. The palomino was eating grass before the Blackfoot lodge and a rope around its neck reached inside. Somebody loved it and slept with his hand on the rope. Hazard didn't blame him; the horse was a beauty.

Hazard was flat on the ground by the palomino, his knife lifted to cut the rope, when someone stirred inside the lodge. Even with the drums beating he knew he couldn't stay there too long. Even if the Blackfoot inside the lodge didn't see him, one of the other Absarokee might be discovered, and then he'd be caught and killed when the alarm was sounded. He was trying to decide how long to wait when a shot cracked, then another.

He cut the rope, sprang upon the palomino, and lashed it into a run. As he careened out of the village, the first Absarokee he saw was Rising Wolf. He was waiting for him, astride a bay. By this time the whole village was aroused; guns were cracking.

"What happened?" Hazard shouted.

"You were the last one in there and Spirit Eagle accidentally stampeded the loose horses." They were both racing for the place where they'd left their clothes with two men to guard them. Quirting their mounts, they dashed through the night.

The palomino was fast, and Hazard reached the place first. Springing from the horse, he began pulling on his leggings. He could hear the pounding hoofs even before he'd finished tying his braided belt. Rising Wolf was just ahead of the pointers—men in the lead to guide the running horses—and close behind them thundered the frightened ponies rounded up from the plain.

"Hell of an accident!" Hazard yelled above the

noise of the approaching horses, and tossed Rising Wolf his leggings.

"We should walk with Spirit Eagle down by the river if we get out of here alive!" Rising Wolf shouted back, reminding Hazard with that pertinent phrase of an event in their own impetuous youth.

Hazard's eyes gleamed in the moonlight and he laughed suddenly, recollecting a similar calamity many years ago, the jealous result of his and Rising Wolf's amorous inclinations. "Like Bell-rock!" he cried, his grin wide. "Come on. Let's see if we get out of this one as well. We'll try the steep cut bank."

Hazard and Rising Wolf sprang to their horses and fought through the band of horses to the lead. The enemy was after them, guns flashed in the moonlight. Riding like the wind, they made straight for the canyon wall. The crest where the ground dropped away was only yards away. Taking a deep breath, Hazard gave his war cry and lashed the palomino over the brink. Rising Wolf on the bay soared simultaneously over the escarpment, his own yell screaming in the wind. Horses, riders, like a swirl of dry leaves in a gale followed and came down twenty feet below—alive!

The Blackfeet stopped dumbstruck atop the precipice.

Hazard's raiding party sprinted for the timber and, out of sight of the enemy, leisurely headed home.

Blaze listened to Hazard's laconic narrative, but the casual words fell on a concentration attuned to other things, and she scarcely heard a word. His eyes were different from those in her memory—darker, under a strongly jutting brow. She had forgotten how they danced with amusement. He was smiling, asking her something. Without each other there was no calm center in their lives. "It was the longest two days of my life," he whispered, bending to kiss her. "Did you miss me?"

"It seemed like six months of an arctic winter without you." Then their lips met and the ice of their separation melted.

*   *   *

THAT evening everyone in camp celebrated the profitable raid. They'd captured two hundred horses without any loss of life. Visitors drifted from lodge to lodge, jubilant over the triumph, and Hazard as a chief had more than his share of well-wishers. Everyone, too, wanted to see the yellow eyes up close, wanted to see the woman to whom Hazard had given thirty horses.

They entertained all evening, Hazard holding Blaze's hand, smiling at her often, translating when he could. And when Blaze haltingly attempted some of the Absarokee words Red Plume had been teaching her, he beamed like a proud parent at her effort.

Bold Ax and his family arrived late in the festivities. He apologized sotto voce to Hazard, "She insisted on coming," he said, indicating his youngest daughter, Blue Flower. "She thinks the horses you sent are for her."

"They were for our old friendship."

"I know that," Bold Ax muttered, "but try and tell her."

"It doesn't matter," Hazard said mildly. "We'll be leaving in a few days to go back to the mine."

While Hazard and Bold Ax had been quietly conversing, Blue Flower had been staring at Blaze with undisguised curiosity. Blaze smiled at her politely, secure in Hazard's love, no longer suspiciously viewing Blue Flower as a rival.

"She doesn't even cook for him," Blue Flower said to her mother, who immediately cast a warning glance at her daughter. It wasn't a malicious remark, only a mild bafflement. Blue Flower's passion for Hazard was absolute and devoted, and it bewildered her that a wife who loved her husband wouldn't cook for him. She would have been more than happy to cook for him, if he would only have her as a second wife. The yellow eyes wife could be as lazy as she pleased. And even if he didn't love her now, in the course of time she knew she could make him love her. The stars had fallen from the sky the night he'd kissed her at the owl dance, and she saw that as a propitious omen for their future together. "Who will take care of him," she softly asked her mother, "when they go back to the mine, if she can't cook or sew?" Her glance strayed briefly to Hazard, her expression demurely anxious.

Before her mother could reply, an unruffled voice said, "I don't need taking care of, Blue Flower, but"—Hazard smiled—"thank you for your concern."

Blue Flower blushed, a young girl's shy response. Hazard didn't seem to notice the fresh glowing bloom of an adolescent on the verge of womanly splendor, nor the doe's eyes alive with adoration. Hazard was oblivious, but Blaze wasn't. It evoked a twinge of jealousy after all. There was no denying the apple-blossom innocence of her beauty.

Hazard diplomatically redirected the conversation into channels unlikely to cause anyone embarrassment. And after a decent interval the family left. Within the hour the last of the guests making calls was gone.

"Did you see those soulful eyes? *That* is adoration," Blaze couldn't help saying, her voice infused with an unwarranted testiness.

"I'm not interested in adoration, *bia-cara*," Hazard soothingly replied, making no pretense of misunderstanding. He leaned back against the elaborate willow backrest and exhaled a deep sigh. "I hope that's the last of the visitors tonight," he said, deliberately diverting the subject. "I haven't had you to myself for hours. And, princess, your Absarokee is charming; thank you for learning it." His smile was affectionate.

"You needn't try enchanting me with your compliments when you've just insinuated that I'm not adoring," Blaze hastily retorted. Blue Flower's fresh innocence was still maddeningly vivid in her mind.

Hazard laughed. "You're definitely not adoring, pet. Adorable, yes, but adoring? Definitely not. Why would you want to be, anyway?"

"Didn't you notice those puppy-dog eyes trained on you? You could have drowned in their idolizing reverence."

"I'd much prefer drowning in your enormous storm-tossed eyes, Boston. Relax, we won't be seeing them again anyway. We're going to have to think about going back to the mine."

Even though Blaze knew their summer idyll must end, she felt a lurching sense of disaster at Hazard's words. A visceral feeling, far removed from rational considerations. She knew he couldn't leave the mine for long. She also knew, eventually, they must face her father, Buhl Mining, the uncertain future. She knew it but her heart resisted. "Couldn't we stay a little longer?"

"We've already stayed longer than I planned." Hazard too had been ruled by his emotions. They should have started back a week ago. But the past days had been as close to paradise as he'd ever reached, and he resisted leaving their summer retreat.

"When?" Blaze quietly asked, having promised herself she'd tell Hazard about the baby before they returned.

"Day after tomorrow."

She had another day, then, to put off her disclosure.

IT WAS well past midnight of their last night in camp and all was quiet save the fireflies dancing thick among the bushes along Arrow Creek. Hazard had been sleeping while Blaze lay awake. She hadn't told him. She'd begun to a dozen times that day, but each time her courage had failed, uncertain how he'd take the news of impending fatherhood.

Their lives were so complicated by extraneous forces: Buhl Mining; duty to his clan; the depths and shades and differences of their lives; the hundreds of whites streaming into the territory each day. It was like standing on a small island whose shores were being eaten away, inches at a time, but inexorably. And when the water finally reached their feet, what would they do then? So she hadn't told him. But she knew she must.

When she touched him, he woke and reached for his knife in one reflex action. He slid it back in its sheath when he saw they were alone. "Is something wrong? A nightmare, *bia?*" In the diffused moonlight he could see the worry lines above her downy brows, and her hands were clenched together, the knuckles white.

"No, no nightmare," she softly replied.

Hazard was sitting up now, his dark glance searching

her face, his powerful, muscled body braced as if reading her unspoken thoughts. "Whatever's worrying you, *bia,* tell me. I'll take care of it." And he meant it. He'd move mountains for her. "Is it . . . the going back?"

She shook her head.

Lifting his hand, he touched her smooth cheek with the tip of one of his fingers. "Are you afraid?"

"Not of that," she whispered.

"Of what then, princess?" he gently asked. His slender fingers took hold of her clenched hands, smoothing the backs of them with his thumbs.

There was no subtle way to say it, although she'd considered a hundred possibilities in the last few days. "I'm pregnant," she said.

Hazard's thumbs stopped their movement, and his eyes met hers calmly. "I know."

Blaze's face was startled. "You know?"

His thumbs' soothing rhythm resumed. "I thought," he quietly said, "maybe *you* didn't know."

"How could you know?" she bluntly asked.

"I've been with you every day, from *maré à ape así E* to *batsu(w)ō' oce.* I would have known if your monthly cycle had come. It hasn't."

"Are you angry?" she inquired, a breathless apprehension undisguised.

"No."

"Are you happy?" And she waited for his answer, her heart filled with dread.

It terrified him, but he couldn't tell her so. He was vulnerable now for the first time in his life, vulnerable to the fear of death. His courage as a warrior, the courage which surrounded him with the sanction of invincibility, all the enviable successes hadn't been based on an absence of fear. His courage wasn't that. It was disregard of fear, a detachment from personal safety. And now his personal safety mattered for Blaze, for their child. Unlike his other children, who would be nurtured by his closest knit clan, even if he died, this new child would be alone in the world with only a mother if he should be killed.

He had always known it was his destiny to save his

beloved clan or die in the attempt. Either way, he'd be true to his vision. And he'd always been at ease with the truth of his mission. Now his neutrality in the face of danger was impossible, and he was terrified.

Pulling her close, lifting her into his lap, he buried his face in her scented hair. Raising his head a moment later, he whispered, "I'm happy, *bia-cara*, about the child." His mouth lightly caressed her cheek. "Our spirits are one now. When you breathe I feel it, when you smile the warmth touches my flesh, the pulse of our child's heart echoes in mine."

"Do we have to go back?" she implored, feeling safe and protected here in the mountains.

"My duty lies there. I must," Hazard said, feeling the same sadness at leaving Blaze felt. "A lodge in the mountains with you and our child . . . someday . . ." His voice trailed off, the future too troubling.

Tears filled Blaze's eyes. "Can the baby be born here, in the mountains?"

Hazard nodded, affected by the same impulse, wanting his child born in peace and in love. He and Blaze had found the very best the world can give here in the land of his people, and he dearly wanted the same bounty of love for his child.

"Promise me," she pleaded, needing to hear the words to counter the lurking apprehensions, willing to cling to the words against the trepidation filling her mind.

"I promise," Hazard said, because he loved this woman. It was a promise he wanted to believe, a promise he hoped he'd be able to keep.

Chapter 29

THEY started back at dawn escorted by Rising Wolf and a dozen warriors, for after the raid on the Blackfeet there was always the possibility of retaliation.

The cabin was untouched when they reached the mine site, except for some supplies Jimmy had brought up. The mine entrance was intact; no visitors there either. Rising Wolf and the escort searched the entire area before they proclaimed it safe. No signs anywhere of trespassers. It was shortly before sunset when Hazard and Blaze bade them goodbye.

"It feels like home," Blaze said, standing just inside the doorway, surveying the small, primitive cabin. Everywhere she looked triggered memories.

"Our first home," Hazard said, coming up behind her and putting his arms around her waist. "Are you tired?"

She leaned her head back against his strong chest. "No, the trip back was leisurely." Hazard had intended it that way. He wasn't taking any chances with Blaze's health.

"You have to be careful now. Don't do too much."

"I feel fine."

"Ummm," he agreed, hugging her close, bending his head to kiss her cheek. And he wondered, as he'd often done since she'd walked up the mountain so many weeks ago, how he'd existed before her. Which brought to mind a recurring thought much on his mind since Blaze's announcement of the baby. Turning her around in his arms, Hazard softly said, "Now with the baby coming. . . ."

Blaze's brow crinkled expectantly when he hesitated. "Yes?" And she worried momentarily at Hazard's serious look.

"We should locate your father. He should know about the baby, about our marriage." Or, Hazard thought, if he *is* dead, Blaze should be told so she doesn't keep waiting for him to appear.

"I'd like that. I know Daddy will be happy for me, for us. He'd always said 'when you find love you'll know,' but until I met you I wasn't sure he was right. Do you suppose we could send him a message somehow . . . with Jimmy, perhaps?"

"I'll check into it," Hazard replied, certain that if Jimmy didn't know where the Colonel was, Rose could find out. Now that he knew the Colonel was no longer using his guide, if he was alive, he would have returned to Diamond City or Virginia City.

On THE same evening Blaze and Hazard were settling in back at the mine, on the same evening they were discussing means of getting in touch with the Colonel, Yancy and Millicent Braddock were discussing their marriage plans.

"We *should* wait a year, Yancy darling. You know what protocol demands."

"Millicent," Yancy returned with a solicitous smile, "I can't wait a year. I've told you before. Please don't insist. Do you know how long I've searched for a woman like you?" His low voice was intimate, but hoarse now since Hazard's knife had pierced his throat. Yancy had hovered between life and death until the hired trackers had come back to Confederate Gulch shortly after Hazard's attack. Even drifting in and out of a coma, Yancy had heard the words: The Colonel was dead; victim, they had coarsely laughed, of renegade Indians. The news had revitalized Yancy's spirit and he'd fought to live.

A month later, he was recovered, and the Colonel's body was at the mortician's awaiting transportation east as soon as his grieving widow found her daughter.

Millicent preened, looking up at him from under modestly downcast lashes in the way she'd been taught as a young debutante so many years ago. "How very sweet of you."

"It's God's own truth, honey," Yancy drawled, and he meant every word. He'd been looking for a rich southern lady to marry all his adult life. "We could have been married after the funeral, if you'd let him be buried out here. No one outside Montana would know exactly how many months one way or another."

"Buhl Mining, love," she prudently cautioned him. "They're all his friends. I'd be cut dead in Boston society if we rushed into this marriage."

"So? We'll be moving back to Virginia anyway."

"Be practical, darling. Probating the will"—she raised her pale, carefully groomed brows—"will take months. Months in Boston. Months in Boston dealing with William's friends. Plus, the mining property is held in common with all his Boston colleagues. A return to Virginia is in the future. Right now, all the money and property are tied up in Boston."

"Where *is* the will?" Yancy inquired. As long as the conversation was so frankly candid tonight, Yancy didn't feel obliged to feign needless tact.

"With William's attorney, Curtis Adams."

"Do you know how things are divided?" It was gently put, the new hoarseness in his voice more prominent now, in his anticipation.

"Between myself and Venetia, I presume."

It was expected, of course, although it would have been smooth as silk if the troublesome girl had been eliminated also. "We really will need her, then," he conceded. "If she's missing, it could hold up everything."

"I think under the circumstances of William's death"—Millicent looked pointedly at Yancy—"our case would appear more respectable if my daughter returned east with us. A mourning mother and daughter accompanied by my 'distant cousin,' rather than you and me alone returning with my husband's body, would attract less comment. Indians generally don't have access to new Winchesters, and suspicious minds might gossip. Venetia's presence would be reassuring to the doubters. Then after the will is probated and the property disposed of, I'm sure Venetia can be settled somewhere on a modest stipend—perhaps Europe. If she should prove disagreeable"—Millicent shrugged her small delicate shoulders, bare tonight above nonmourning red-colored silk in the privacy of her sitting room—"we can think of something else."

"Your plans seem quite complete," Yancy huskily murmured, his light eyes shrewdly approving.

"It's not as though I haven't dreamt of this before," Millicent silkily said. "But until you came along, Yancy darling, I'd no one to—ah—confide in." Millicent delighted in Yancy, but they both delighted in the prospect of becoming millionaires much more. Although their common backgrounds drew them close, their common lack of scruples was the true bond, and at base the marriage they were discussing was decidedly practical. It was a match of passionate, resentful natures, a match of genteelly poor southerners, intent, finally, on coming into a great deal of money; above all, it was a match of limitless greed, a marriage of *extreme* convenience.

"In that case, Millicent, love, I think we should immediately consider rescuing your daughter from her abductor. The longer we wait, the longer it will take to reach Boston and clear up the property matters."

Millicent brushed a particle of dust off the shimmering silk of her skirt and, looking up, casually inquired, "You have the necessary men assembled?"

"Have had since the Colonel's body was brought down."

"And they're both back?"

"Lights in the cabin windows tonight, my lookout informed me no more than a half-hour ago."

"At last." Millicent sighed. She and Yancy had been waiting in Diamond City for over a week and she was thoroughly disgusted with the primitive conditions. "I don't want her hurt. My reputation wouldn't survive my daughter's death as well as my husband's. You understand," she said evenly.

"Of course, Millicent. I understand." Until they were married, Yancy had no intention of countering her slightest whim.

"Will it take long?" She was already mentally arranging the necessary orders to her maid for an early departure.

"We should be ready to leave by midafternoon. Midmorning, if all goes well."

"I've everything arranged." Her mouth twisted into a faint smile.

"Good." Yancy's eyes flashed with an inner fire. At this time tomorrow night they'd be on their way to Salt Lake City on the Overland Stage. In less than two weeks, with good connections and no mishaps, they'd be in Boston. And he'd be on the brink of the riches that had eluded him all his life. He got up to leave, careful of appearances in this small mining town.

"Oh, and one thing, darling . . . I don't want to hear any details about the Indian." She'd had to warn Yancy off when he'd begun being uncomfortably explicit about William's death.

Yancy would have liked to tell her of his smoothly implemented plan. He was proud of how easily the Colonel's death had been accomplished. Of course, it helped that Billy Braddock had been in the wilds, where Indian attacks as well as robberies were common. Ned Gates had told him it was like taking candy from a baby: They'd seen the Colonel and his guide from their lookout on the last butte before Virginia City. Their high-powered rifles had picked off the two men effortlessly, attack that close to town being unexpected.

The Indian had gotten away, Ned had said, but was

trailing blood. No one had bothered going after him, but Yancy was unconcerned. The Colonel was dead and the Indian, even if he lived, wasn't going to come into town with any accusations.

Millicent had appreciated Yancy's polite concurrence to her wishes, relieved she didn't have to be involved in any way with the unsavory details of murder.

"Don't forget the note," she reminded him, gesturing toward the table near the window. If anyone investigates we want them to think Venetia left of her own free will."

Chapter 30

YANCY'S small army of scum and scoundrels came up the next morning after Hazard entered the mine. A hundred of them, armed to the teeth with the latest-model Winchesters and Colts. A Blackfoot Indian, like Yancy a mortal enemy to Hazard, was guide. Because the attack, brutally heedless of Blaze's presence, came full-scale in broad daylight, it caught him unaware. Even if the Colonel was dead, Hazard never anticipated such rash disregard for Blaze; surely some of the Colonel's partners, his wife at least, would never risk her life so blatantly. The surprise was total and complete. Never underestimate the rapacious greed of the white man.

The Blackfoot reached the cabin first and stifled Blaze's horrified cry. He was holding her cruelly tight, one large hand over her mouth, when she heard Hazard scream her name in a roaring crescendo of anguish and alarm.

And then a hundred rifles fired, an erratic, terrorizing series of crackling death, and she fainted.

Pressed against the cold rock face of the south drift, Hazard, bleeding, his left arm shattered below the elbow, his breath labored from pain that was tearing his head apart, looked down fifty yards of tunnel with horror. Then his vision blurred. Rubbing his eyes, he brought away fingers soaked in blood. He must think. There wasn't much time, but the pain was spreading up his arm into his shoulder, filling his consciousness. He heard the scrambling above him, saw the ricocheting splinters of rock flashing in the sunlight, the hundred rifles trained on the mine entrance keeping up a steady barrage like an unreal scene from hell.

He shook his head and his vision cleared. He was sure now, blood dripping from his fingertips to the black dampness of the tunnel floor, a doomed sense of frustration and rage assailing his mind, that the Colonel was dead. And clearly the man he thought he might have killed at Rose's hadn't died. The voice was harsh and grating now shouting orders, but the southern inflections were distinctive. Yancy Strahan was in control. The Colonel was dead. Blaze was in their hands. His child was in their hands. And if the black powder he smelled was being handled by anyone even rudimentarily versed in explosives, he was about to be buried alive.

He'd shot three of them before the heavy onslaught of rifle fire drove him back into the mine. And no one was brave enough to risk his life coming in after him.

Hazard forced himself to move although he felt giddy and nauseated and the splintered bones grated at every twitch, the pain forcing him to stop and rest after each advance. He needed his supplies before the explosion made the tunnel pitch black. Even as he moved toward the small wooden box containing candles, the impact of the first explosion drove him against the wall.

When the smoke cleared, half the entrance was sealed.

He tried to hurry after that, estimating that one, no more than two, explosions more and his light would be gone. He didn't think beyond that. He only considered the cache of candles as his goal. The pain was too intense to think clearly past that short-term essential. It was smothering his thought processes, almost shutting down his mind completely. It was one of the most appalling acts of will he'd ever performed, standing upright with the crushing agony tearing at his brain, and forcefully holding off the swirling darkness. Lurching down the tunnel, each step seemingly intolerable until, grim-faced, he took the next, he tried to focus on Blaze, knowing he had to help her. Only a hairbreadth from black oblivion, his numbed brain absorbed the frantic sense of panic her name evoked. But it was beyond forming the messages coherently, beyond deductive reasoning. Her name floated around the hazy interior landscapes at the basest level of dread, and simply echoed like a living scream down the pain-racked corridors of his mind.

Stopping, he leaned, panting, against the tunnel wall, drawing in great labored gasps of air, absently watching the blood drip from his fingertips. Stunned, he didn't know how long he'd been propped against the wall, his own time running out along with his blood. He shook his head twice to clear his eyes and reactivate his sluggish brain. Distantly he heard the multitude of voices, the commands, affirmations, hurried suggestions, snapped orders. And when he shook his head a third time, he realized where he was. The box of candles. The box of candles. He repeated the litany, his survival instinct badgering his half-conscious brain. *Hurry,* it frantically commanded.

He compelled himself to move. The pain swamped him like a tidal wave. He grunted deep in his throat and took another step, leaning on the wall for support. Agony hit him in a fresh wave and he clenched his teeth against the shock.

The second blast knocked him down, and it was a full five minutes before he found the energy to pull himself to his knees. He tried crawling, but his limp shattered arm accidentally dragged on the rough floor, spiraling an excruciating spasm along his battered nerve endings so dreadful and excessive that he lay shuddering uncontrollably for long moments. He tried to think of other things, tried to draw his mind aside from the monstrous hurt if only for a moment so he could rise. He was sweating profusely, his body nearly in shock, only his strength of will holding off the darkness. Inch by agonizing inch he pushed himself up the wall until he was upright. He could see the box then, a dim shape thirty yards away. The next explosion would seal him in. Don't think, just walk, he commanded his limbs. Walk or you're going to die.

He was sunk in an exhausted sprawl next to the box of candles when the third explosion detonated. After that he could smell the dust settling but he couldn't see it anymore. He was in total darkness. As if on cue, his brain released its feeble grip on its own interior light and Hazard slipped into unconsciousness.

WHEN Blaze awoke, she saw her mother first. It was a face lit with an inner triumph, a face that gloated. A face that she recognized as her mortal enemy. *"You,"* she accused quietly and bitterly.

Millicent touched the pearls at her neck. It wasn't a nervous gesture. It was languid and indifferent. "You'll thank me someday when you're older and wiser. Only foolish young girls make the mistake of falling in love with undesirables." Blaze had been calling out in her sleep, calling for Hazard, crying for him. And Yancy had described Blaze's struggle to break free before the explosion when she'd heard Hazard scream.

"He's a thousand times better than you," Blaze sharply replied, her eyes cutting like daggers. Hazard possessed qualities that people like Yancy and Millicent would never possess, that their greed couldn't buy.

Millicent laughed lightly. "Petulant child. You'll change your mind once you grow up."

"I don't intend to argue with you. Where's Daddy? I want to see Daddy."

Millicent didn't move, her fingers arrested on the gleaming pearls at her neck, the light of rejoicing burning brightly in her pale grey eyes. "He's dead," she said.

It struck Blaze like a physical blow, so violent and brutal she had to forcibly draw her breath upward from deep down in her lungs. When she spoke it was a pained whisper. "You lie."

Millicent smiled then, a malignant, delighted smile. "His body's in Virginia City. You can see for yourself."

"You killed him," Blaze accused.

"Really, how distasteful a child you are. Of course I didn't kill him. He never came back alive from his frantic journey into the mountains to save *you.* Some of those renegade savages you cohabit with no doubt killed him. If you want to blame someone," she went on, malice and resentment behind the suave tone, "you're as likely a candidate as any. Yancy told me *you* insisted on going up to talk to that savage. *I'd* say, *missy,* you are as much to blame for your father's death as anyone."

"You bitch."

"I'm quite immune to your insults," she tranquilly said, neatly straightening the lace cuff on her silk gown. "Money does that."

"That's all you ever cared about, isn't it? Not Daddy. Just the money."

"Well, of course, what else was there? Your father was a peasant. And it appears his blood runs true in you. Did you enjoy sleeping with your ill-bred Indian?" she silkily inquired.

"His breeding is more pure than any Hatton from Virginia."

"Was, dear. He's quite dead."

White-faced, Blaze was struck with stark reality. She'd been thinking of Hazard as alive despite her knowledge of Yancy, despite the swarming cutthroats that had besieged the mine. In the back of her mind, she'd been planning on leaving this bed, this room, this hateful woman, and going back up mountain to the cabin. Dear God, let her be wrong! "It's not true!" Hysteria was a thin thread through the calm cadence of her voice.

"He's dead." There was no attempt to hide the enmity now. Venom infused the pale grey eyes.

"No. He's alive. He *must* be." The hysteria was rising into a sharp, piercing wail.

"Very dead."

"No, no, he isn't!" Blaze's heart was thumping against her chest wall, her palms ice-cold.

"Dead and buried in that filthy mine," Millicent softly declared.

"No!" It was a thin, high cry of pain, primitive and ageless. "No, no, no, *no!*"

"He's dead and under tons of rubble. Tons and tons."

Blaze pulled a pillow over her head, trying to shut out the coolly detached voice. But it didn't help; each word was still heartbreakingly audible. Each word stabbed at her very being. Each word was crushing her will to live. Hazard dead. Sobs shook her slender form. Hazard, who'd become life itself to her—dead. Tears streamed down her face. And suddenly she gave up. Numb with grief, she sorrowfully thought, *I'm dead.*

TWO days passed and she'd hardly moved. Huddled under the covers, she mourned her loss. The tears were over. She couldn't cry anymore, but the pain had worsened. Hazard filled her mind, every moment, every breath, and the poignant memories turned the melancholy into agonizing torment.

On the afternoon of the second day, a weakness pervading her mind and body, she was easily convinced she should accompany her father's body back to Boston. She wouldn't talk to her mother or Yancy, but Hannah reminded her of her duty to her father and his memory. She'd whitened out her mind to avoid the pain of Hazard's death and foreshortened her thoughts deliberately. "I'm coming back then, Hannah," she said, her voice hardly sounding like her own. "As soon as Daddy's properly buried, I'm coming back." She wanted their child born where Hazard had been born. She wanted to raise their child in the country Hazard had called home. She didn't tell Hannah that, but her old nurse understood her grief for the man she'd loved.

"It's a fine and fair country to come back to. And you will. But for now, you should go home."

"This is my home." Pale and lethargic, Blaze looked very small in the large carved bed, but her eyes were burning fiercely, and Hannah was reminded of the small girl in a large bed in a cavernous room on Beacon Street. Even then, she'd known what she wanted.

"I know, child, and you will be back," Hannah soothed, just as she'd soothed so many childhood tears in the past. She wished, though, with all her heart, this sadness could have been as trivial. She'd known Millicent Braddock for too many years to blandly accept the story about an accidental explosion. And Yancy had struck her from the first as a ruthless hoodlum, however grand his family lineage.

She couldn't change what had happened. She couldn't bring back Blaze's love. But she would give to Blaze what she always had: love and comfort.

ON THE day Blaze left Diamond City, Hazard started hacking at the greenstone in the ceiling of the east drift, no small achievement considering the periods of dizziness which still plagued him.

He'd made a makeshift splint for his left arm, wrapping two boards from an old powder box with rawhide strips from his leggings. The procedure had taken half a day because he'd fainted repeatedly from the pain. His arm, swollen to monstrous size, made every jarring movement torment. He watched the color of his arm change from pink to red to angry magenta that day, and he knew from experience that if his fingertips turned blue, he'd lose his arm. That first day after he'd managed to get the splint in place, he lay in a half-faint, his body's message that it required rest to recoup its strength after the ravaging it had suffered. He'd only light a candle for a few moments when he awoke, check the mounting color in his arm, and then blow the candle out.

He had a vague plan that was incubating even as he slept. In his lucid moments he'd review it, cast and recast it, allocate his time against his candles, against his lack of food and water. He had to rest; his body demanded it be easing him into unconsciousness whenever he overexerted himself. But he'd have to move soon. With no food and only the moisture collecting on the rocks for drinking, he didn't have a lot of time to hack his way out. Each day his reserves of strength would diminish. But if there was a way out, if there was a way to rejoin Blaze and their unborn child, he would find it. Or die trying. It was inherent in his spirit, in his code as a warrior. It would be his ultimate test and he knew it. Jon Hazard Black versus Death.

BY THE time a subdued and shaken Blaze was helped into the hired carriage early in the morning of the third day after the blast, Hazard had been working already for five hours. In his best estimate, the east drift at its high point was eight feet underground. He'd chipped away two feet the day before and then had to rig up some scaffolding. He planned on proceeding with as little rest as possible from now on, for he knew he'd become weaker with every day. And at the rate he was progressing, it was moot which would give out first: the greenstone or his strength.

It kept him going through the pain and the agonizing doubts, bolstering the despondency when he didn't think he could raise his arm above his head one more time. It gave him the strength each time he pushed "one more time." It mitigated the pain and breathed fresh life in him when he fell exhausted to the rough scaffold floor. Thoughts of Blaze and their unborn child kept him alive.

BLAZE wasn't dragged away crying and screaming; she left Diamond City an unsubstantial shadow of herself.

But on the stage to the railhead, she refused to speak to her mother or Yancy, a latent anger dwelling deep below the vivid grief of her loss. And once she was settled in her bed on her father's rail car, she told Hannah very quietly, in a voice that wouldn't have carried two feet on a still night, "They're not going to win."

"That's my girl talking," Hannah said, unconsciously putting out a weathered hand to stroke Blaze's hair. "That's my baby girl." And tears shone in her eyes at the first spark of life she'd seen since Diamond City. "Your dad would'na want that trash holding court in your mother's drawing room to have his money."

"I know," Blaze quietly said. "And he won't. It's all mine, you know." And then Blaze's eyes went lifeless for a brief moment; it could have helped Hazard so. But it was too late now . . . for him . . . for them. Tears started welling up.

"She'll be surprised," Hannah quickly declared, attempting to deflect the direction of Blaze's thoughts.

"It doesn't matter, though, does it?" Blaze was morose, defeated, back in the dim, shadowy purgatory of her torment.

Hannah's heart bled to see the life and energy slip away from the young woman she'd known always volatile and gay. She hadn't intended mentioning it, and she hesitated a brief second even now, not wishing to intrude on Blaze's privacy. But when the tears spilled over the pale cheeks and slid down the small face, its expression indicative of retreat from everything but pain, Hannah spoke, "It matters for the wee one, now, don't it?"

Blaze's gaze shot upward.

"You don't want them two in there"—a jerk of her greying head indicated Millicent's drawing room—"taking away your baby's birthright. And they will, child, as sure as I breathe, if you just lay there like you been doing."

"How do you know?" Blaze whispered.

"That's a silly question, child. I've been dressing and undressing you for nineteen years."

"Do you think they know?" Blaze struggled up to a seated position, and a touch of color rose on her cheekbones, too prominent now after ten days of scant appetite.

"Not yet they don't, but nature will tell them soon enough. Now you can lay there and cry your eyes out, or you can get up and make sure your babe has the silver spoon it's entitled to when it's born."

"They'd try, wouldn't they . . ."

"Sure as the sun rises each day."

Blaze fingered the Irish lace bordering the linen sheet. "I suppose they'd say I wasn't married."

"That for starters and anything else they could think of."

"But I can name anyone I wish my heir." Her back had straightened and a healthy pink suffused her cheeks. "It's my money, after all."

"You're going to have to have your wits about you, child, to see that it stays that way."

Blaze looked point-blank at Hannah and there was fire again in her sapphire glance. "In that case," she said, throwing the covers aside, "I'd better get dressed. And then," she went on, striding toward the small rosewood desk as her old energy returned, "I think I'll rewrite my will. Is there still paper here? There is." And she turned to smile at Hannah. The first smile in ten days. "Find me a dress, a pen, and another witness, Hannah. Bring Cookie. He can be trusted."

The Blaze who stepped off the train in Boston was starkly different from the one who'd boarded it in Nebraska. Millicent and Yancy should have noticed, but they were too deep in their own plans, plans to spend Colonel Braddock's inheritance. They failed to notice the light, determined step of the young woman proceeding them down the platform.

It was their first mistake in the battle about to erupt.

Chapter 31

WHEN Hazard's last candle went out for the last time, he leaned against the wall of the narrow shaft he was chipping out of the greenstone and allowed the first wave of fear to subside. Then he opened and shut his eyes twice. No difference. Pitch damp blackness either way. It took him another length of time to beat back the second wave of panic. He forced himself to breathe calmly; he ran through the calculated assessment of the days he'd been entombed; he tallied the number of feet he'd raised the shaft through the ceiling of the east drift and then, pressing down the fiends of alarm, he reckoned the equation again.

There should be fresh air and light and green grass and freedom no more than a foot or two above his head. He was being conservative in his estimate to cushion the possible disappointment. But his gut feeling said more like ten inches.

His grip on the pickaxe began slipping as his palm

sweated from fear and apprehension—the dreaded possibility of being wrong in his calculations. He hadn't eaten in five days, and he needed more rest between work spells now. He'd hallucinated the last time he'd dozed off and thought he was on the Blue Mountains until he woke to the dank underground smell and the brief touch of fear. He counted now when he chipped away, forcing himself to swing thirty times before resting. He made it to thirty each time though a clenching of teeth accompanied the last few strokes. And once, when he'd missed the rock and his ax had slipped onto his broken arm, the scream had echoed for endless moments down the underground tunnels.

He'd had to rest then, and the arm throbbed in a steady, undiminished agony after that. He was only able to swing ten times now before the pain forced him to stop. He almost sobbed in frustration. It would take even longer with his slowed pace; time he didn't have. Time was his enemy as much as Yancy Strahan had been. And where Yancy had failed, sheer attrition might not.

He didn't dare breathe when he felt the faint, thin waver of sweet air. If he was hallucinating again, he thought . . . and held his breath waiting, hoping that if it was a hallucination, it would quickly pass before hope became too vivid. So he was holding his breath when he felt the second whisper of air. Exhaling slowly, he murmured, "Blaze," very, very softly.

The pickax swung up a second later and he didn't count this time, didn't count and didn't stop, his body and mind energized by the breath of freedom, the breath of life a few scant inches away. The dense greenstone gave way reluctantly, but once he broke through it, the layer of sand and topsoil poured in.

He'd been working above his head, so there was still the problem of pulling himself up four feet of shaft, but it was a problem he was more than pleased to confront. His left arm was useless, his left shoulder too painful to put any weight on, so he cautiously inched his way upward in a pressure climb, his right shoulder taking the entire antipodal force of his legs buckled almost double in the narrow shaft. He ascended by millimeters rather than inches, keeping even pressure on his feet and good right shoulder. He rose laboriously, ever conscious of the damp rock walls. He didn't move one foot until the other was securely placed. If he fell, he might tumble on his broken arm and it could be hours again until he was able to move. He couldn't afford the fall, not only in terms of time lost, but also because he was running on sheer adrenaline, and if he had to reclimb the shaft, he might not have the strength. To die within sight of freedom would be a torture too painful to bear. Go slowly, his mind cautioned. Don't slide, his inner voice directed. Two more feet, his brain deliberately noted. *Do not rush.*

When his shoulders broke the surface, his heart was beating so thunderously he could taste the drumming in his mouth. But he forced his feet to continue their slow climb up the shaft sides until his right arm was free. And then he hauled himself up and out of the shaft in one superhuman surge of power and lay panting on the buffalo grass, a faint breeze cooling the perspiration covering his body. Placing the palm of his good right hand on the cool ground, he talked to the earth spirits, could feel their presence, thanked them for his release. Then softly he sang his spirit song, his deep rich voice drifting like the silvery night air over the mountain. When his song was finished, he rose, slowly, painfully, turned toward the cabin, and began the long descent.

HE STOOD in the open doorway, silhouetted against the moonlight. The door had been wrenched from its hinges and lay half in and half out of the cabin. Everything had been vandalized. Hired thugs operated that way; they had an urgent need to break and crush and maim and kill—a hostility Hazard had never understood. He'd been hoping his Navy Colts or Henry repeater would still be there. They weren't. Nothing remained in one piece. What was too large to cart away had been broken. The table was smashed along with the chairs. Even the heavy stove had been tipped over and the chimney pipe hung like a weary stalactite from the ceiling into nothingness.

A melancholy sadness overwhelmed him. He and

Blaze had lived the first days of their love in this room, now open to the weather and animals and moonlight streaming undisturbed through the broken window openings. Stepping over food and broken glass strewn across the floor, he searched the rubble for some clue that might tell him of Blaze.

He walked by it twice before a beam of moonlight caught a corner of the envelope, lying flat on the mantlepiece.

He took it down, with a gunpowder- and dirt-blackened hand, leaving dark smudges on the paper, and brought it over to the open doorway. It wasn't sealed. He pulled out the single sheet of paper with his teeth and dropped the envelope. Unfolding the note he read:

Hazard,
I don't make a good hostage. I told you that. I'm going back to Boston.

Blaze

From his moon-gilded hair to the bloodied wound at his throat, Hazard went pale. Stupefied, he read it again. And again. He read each word individually as though somehow the message would alter with a change of rhythm. But the pitiless words were callously fixed on the page, mocking him, revealing all as counterfeit between himself and the beautiful society lady from Boston. He felt cold, chilled to the marrow by an icy rage and then a great boiling tide of anger, surging slowly at first, built in momentum to uncurbed violence at the thought of his entombment. So the millionaire's daughter had gotten tired of playing the noble savage in the wilderness. He'd somehow always thought she would—the bitch. She'd gotten tired and decided to go back to Boston. Not very decent of her to try to kill him in the bargain.

But come to think of it, his death would neatly tie the bow on Buhl Mining Company's package of Montana wealth. It would be easy enough to settle his claims on his child. No messy transfers of title, no complicated litigation over scraps of paper like the one Yancy had tried to make him sign. Just a neatly inherited parcel of gold-rich land. He'd never imagined, of course, how premeditated the child's conception was. It was staggering even to contemplate. Was it possible Blaze would go to such lengths to secure the land? He didn't like to contemplate such base deception. But he'd seen such corruption over gold—usually other people's gold—so he knew the possibility existed, however inconceivable.

It was too bad, he malevolently thought, dropping the note on the floor and grinding it into the rubble with his heel, their program wouldn't be so easily implemented. As soon as his arm healed, he intended reopening the mine. And this time, no one would catch him unaware.

The forty-minute trip into Diamond City took him four hours, his body remaining erect through sheer force of will. No guards were posted around Rose's anymore, he noted. With all the loose ends neatly tied, Yancy had called off the dogs.

How convenient.

When he walked into Rose's parlor a few minutes later, he had only enough strength to cover the distance to the nearest chair. Falling into it, he fainted, and Rose found him that way a moment later. Bloody, dirty, his arm in a makeshift sling, thinner than she'd ever seen him, his head lolling back so awkwardly that for a terrifying moment she thought him dead. But she saw him breathe at last and her frightened heart slowed its racing.

So Yancy Strahan had been wrong. Even a hundred armed ruffians hadn't been able to kill Hazard. And then her heart sank.

What was he going to do when he regained consciousness and discovered Blaze Braddock had gone back to Boston?

But when he did wake late the next morning, bathed, bandaged, and lying between crisp clean sheets, Rose told him; he only said, his voice cooled to its usual irony, "I know. I only wish the pampered princess had left with less fanfare."

Chapter 32

BUT in the early days of Hazard's recuperation, when he still slept a lot and started putting back the weight he'd lost during the days without food, Rose would come upon him unaware at times and always glimpse the same brooding look.

When he saw her, his expression would instantly alter and he'd become the same Jon Hazard she'd always known. But Rose felt he wasn't indifferent to Blaze—hadn't been, at least—and the dark, brooding look was persistent in his solitude.

She finally said, the day he stood outside on the balcony for the first time, "Do you want to talk about it?" He'd been looking toward the mountains, his profile stony. He turned to her when she spoke, his eyes startled, as if he'd forgotten she was there, and after a short silence replied, "It's going to take a lot of work to open up the mine again."

"I didn't mean that."

The harshness in his features eased. "I owe you a lot, Rose: You've taken me in twice now."

"You don't owe me anything, Hazard. If I didn't want to, I wouldn't. Are you going after her?"

There was a short silence again as his brain assessed possible answers; then one dark brow rose. "Are you going to give in," he asked pleasantly, "to that young clerk who's had moon eyes for you so long?"

"Don't change the subject, Hazard."

He shrugged and ignored her with a mocking, tantalizing smile. "He's been giving me threatening looks for days now. I expect to be called out any time by the pup."

"The pup, as you call him, is only four years younger than you."

Hazard's eyes opened a fraction, and while his voice was light, his dark eyes held the fragments of melancholy. He was simply smiling and talking to forestall her questions. "He seems young."

"He is young, but so are you."

At that he snorted, with a delicacy that reminded her nostalgically of all the other sensual delicacies in his nature. With half-ironic tenderness he said, "So you've taken pity on him?"

"Not that way."

"What other way is there? In my experience—"

"He's led a sheltered life, Hazard."

"And you and I haven't." It was both mocking query and pressing statement.

"No."

Hazard smiled—an ironic, leisurely smile—when he thought of all the living and all the dying he'd seen in his own short life: careless, coarse, brutal. Next to that even Rose's experience paled. "You're very sweet, Rose," he said like a gentle uncle, although they were of an equal age. "You should be nice to that young clerk."

"Like you should be to your woman. Why don't you go and bring her back?"

Hazard's eyes met her violet scrutiny and held it for a considered moment. When he answered, his voice was controlled and mild. "She was a pawn in the game. Only a pawn in a game they lost, for I'm still alive. That makes the pawn forfeit now—to me, to them, to everyone. No, I won't be needing her."

"I'm not talking about the mine or a game, Hazard."

His mouth lifted in what should have been a smile, but his eyes were fatalistically cold. "You're too romantic, Rose. That's all it ever was . . . only the mine and the game—Buhl versus Jon Hazard Black. Why would I be interested in going after her anymore? I have my mine and Buhl's got her back."

"You're sure?"

"Well, if I'm lucky," he said, smiling, "they won't give my address to the next female hired to deliver their sales pitch. The last one was more trouble than she was worth."

"Forget the mine, Hazard. Are you sure about Blaze Braddock?" Rose wanted to believe more than she didn't that Hazard had no interest in going after Blaze, for selfish reasons of her own. But she'd been dealing in human emotions too long to accept Hazard's answer at face value.

"I'm sure," he affirmed grimly, reflecting on how his love for Blaze had jeopardized not only his life but his clan's very existence. "I'll admit it was interesting." He shrugged faintly. "She had the moral instincts of a jungle cat and that has its moments. Unfortunately, she also had the cat's cunning deceit. It almost cost me my life. It reinforces a lesson about the yellow eyes: Never mind the words; watch their trigger finger. Present company excepted, of course." The tall, lean man flashed her a smile. "I wonder, though . . ." he stopped, hesitating.

"What?" said Rose, levelly.

"Do you suppose," he said drily, "my child will have flame-red hair?" The brooding look was back in his eyes, and in a restless motion he squinted up at the sun. "Is it too early for a drink? This arm's the devil today."

A moment later Hazard was lounging in Rose's parlor in a black mood, his back curved low against the embroidered sofa, his long legs sprawled out casually; his arms rested on his chest but his slender fingers cradled the brandy glass so rigidly Rose expected it to shatter any second. Nursing his brandy, he wondered what he would have done if Blaze hadn't left the way she did, and he someday had to choose between his clan and her. The clan must come first, of course. Of course. He drained the glass.

"Would you like another?" Rose asked, coming in from the adjoining room where she'd left instructions with the maid for lunch.

Slowly Hazard straightened, the tense fingers holding the snifter out forcibly relaxed, and he apologized for his dull company with a rueful smile and a quiet "Sorry."

"Everyone has bad days," Rose sympathized, pouring a generous measure of her Napoleon brandy into Hazard's glass.

He laughed. "Bad days? I like your eternal optimism, Rose." Such a mild phrase, he thought, lifting the refilled glass to his lips, for a wayward chieftain who knew in his heart he wouldn't have chosen against Blaze whatever the situation. Who knew also that with all their differences, it couldn't have ended any other way. Who knew that because he had loved her, he had forgotten his duty. He drank most of the bottle that morning, but it didn't wash away the images, the memories, the old unanswered questions, the closely averted calamity.

Or the fury.

Chapter 33

ON THE third week of Hazard's recuperation at Rose's, on the same day he was first able to move the fingers on his damaged arm without breaking into a cold sweat, in Boston Millicent Braddock, outraged, came explosively to her feet in the office of Curtis Adams, where her husband's will had just been read, and viciously snarled, "There must be a mistake!"

Curtis Adams had been a friend to Billy Braddock as well as his attorney; he knew there was no mistake. And the circumstances of Billy's death, together with Millicent's new "cousin," affirmed in spades, he thought, Billy's own estimation of his wife.

It wasn't as though she'd been left destitute; as his widow she could live in the house as long as she wished and would receive an adequate monthly allowance. Personally, Curtis wouldn't have been so generous. He'd known Millicent too long. But Billy had a kinder heart than he.

"I want that will broken," Millicent curtly ordered, a pinched look of fury on her face.

Curtis neatly folded his hands on his polished desktop. "It's legal, Millicent."

"I'll contest it."

"It's airtight."

"I'm sure I can find a judge who might disagree."

"Suit yourself," he politely declared. He turned to Blaze. "Will you be staying on at Beacon Street?"

"Not for long. I'm going back to Montana." Although friends had called and offered their condolences on her father's death, and the men friends sent enough flowers daily to perfume the entire city of Boston, Blaze longed for the mountain landscapes of Hazard's native country, wanted to be close to him in spirit, wanted their child to grow up in the land where Hazard had spent his youth. "Very soon," she added, the sadness in her eyes as deep as the ocean. She was dressed in black silk, her skin pale, faint blue shadows beneath her strained eyes, yet she was splendid still, capable of drawing every man in Boston with her beauty.

Strangely, mourning seemed to enhance her fairness. Unadorned, delicate now in her paleness, her heavy hair simply styled, her eyes dominating her face, a new fullness to her figure. Innocence and melancholy existed paradoxically with an underlying sensuality no longer flirtatious but real. She was a woman now, not the girl she'd been the spring before and there wasn't a man alive who wouldn't feel the overwhelming urge to console her in her grief. But Hazard had spoiled her for other men. Next to his memory, other men seemed tame. Hazard, wild and reckless, had filled her universe. No other man could compare.

"That's ridiculous," Millicent brusquely objected. "You'll stay in Boston where you belong."

"I'll go where I please, Mother." And Blaze stared at her mother in the special way she'd learned in childhood: features composed, her thoughts of other things behind the cool facade. It was a way of winning against a mother who expressed only hatred and contempt.

"We'll see about that," Millicent malevolently repudiated, giving her daughter a look of such pure hatred Blaze was shocked at the naked emotion. Millicent was infuriated. At her deceased husband, at Curtis Adams, at Blaze, at anyone or anything standing in her way to the fortune she'd married—as mercenarily as a Gypsy horse trader—twenty years before. Only taking time to draw breath for a harangue, she hissed, "You conniving little—"

"Don't be hasty," Yancy warned, his voice mild but his eyes like chips of stone. "You're distrait." He took Millicent's hand in his. "She's distrait," he explained to Curtis, careful to keep his own boiling anger under control. He'd been so close this time . . . twenty-two million dollars. And Blaze got it all. Smug little bitch. She'd probably known all along; she didn't seem surprised.

Then a brilliant idea came to him like a lifeline thrown to a drowning man. Graciously excusing himself and Millicent with every nuance of southern manners called into play, he ushered her out of the office without further damage.

Blaze stayed behind to sign the required documents, meticulously signing each and every paper. For the first time she became genuinely concerned for her child. She had never seen such hatred before. Such loathing and fury were uncommon. Uncommon enough to murder.

WHEN Blaze returned from Curtis Adams' office, Yancy surreptitiously followed her to her room and locked her in while Millicent waylaid Hannah in the drawing room. They had given the upstairs servants the afternoon off in deference to the Colonel's memory. Together, they told Hannah that Blaze had left for Montana directly after the reading of the will and offered her a lavish advance on the annuity Billy Braddock had left her in his will.

Hannah protested at first. "Blaze wouldn't leave without telling me," she insisted.

"She's been so depressed lately. *You* know that. I think all she had on her mind was going back. I told her it was impolite to leave without saying goodbye to you, but you know Venetia. Rash as ever, even in her grief.

Her father left her everything, and she's more independent-minded than usual. You can ask Curtis Adams if you like. He helped her into the hired carriage. I'll take you down there to talk to him if you like." Millicent dabbed delicately at her eyes with an embroidered handkerchief. "She's been so unhappy lately," she murmured. "Would you care to talk to Curtis?" It was a calculated bluff.

"Poor child," Hannah pensively declared, less wary once Curtis' name was mentioned. He'd been a friend of the Colonel's for years. And all Blaze had talked about since leaving Montana was going back. "She wanted to have her babe born in that wild country," she recalled, half to herself.

The only sound in the enormous drawing room was the ticking of the Meissen clock. Restored to the present after her brief musing lapse, Hannah noted the electrified silence. "She hadn't told you yet, had she?"

Millicent recovered first. "No, but it makes it even more understandable . . . her precipitous departure. Under the circumstances, poor darling," she solicitously maintained, "she'd want to return at once." Millicent smiled an understanding motherly smile. "We both know how headstrong Venetia is. But you needn't worry, Hannah. With her father's millions, she can afford the finest care wherever she lives."

"I hope the babe brings her peace." Hannah had blinders on when it came to Blaze's happiness. If she needed to go back right away, she understood. Blaze still cried every night over the babe's father.

"I'm sure it will, Hannah. Now, would you like a draft on the bank or cash?"

"When you get her address, would you let me have it? I'll be with my sister in Lancaster; I'll give you the address." And Hannah carefully wrote the street number on a sheet of paper Millicent pulled from the rolltop desk.

"There," Millicent observed, folding the sheet of paper. "I'll keep it right here on top." And she placed an Italian crystal weight over it. "We should have Venetia's whereabouts in three to four weeks. Thank you, Hannah, for all your devoted years of service. If the Colonel were alive, I know he would add his gratitude as well. Now, Yancy, dear, if you'd see to Hannah's packing, I'll write a draft for the first six months of her annuity . . . and I think perhaps six months' cash payment as well to begin with. Will that do, Hannah?"

"It'll do fine, ma'am, but I'll do my own packing," Hannah pointedly replied.

A short time later, all amiability and charm, Yancy escorted Hannah to the carriage drawn up to the side door, saw that her baggage was stowed, gave the driver directions, and waved her off.

Now, Hannah wasn't taken in by all the artificial, overdone politeness. She knew it didn't make any difference to either one of them whether she lived or died. But if Blaze and her babe were gone, there was no reason for her to stay.

YANCY came back into the drawing room, carefully closed the double doors, leaned back against them, and smiled gloatingly. "One old bitch closer to twenty-two million, my love."

"It went rather well, didn't it?" Millicent agreed, looking up from the small desk.

"Perfectly, and thanks to old Hannah, it should be much easier now to convince darling Venetia to see things our way. No young mother as determined to pine over her lover as she seems to be would relinquish her child once it's born, would she? The last link, as it were, to her true love." His voice was malicious with mockery.

"The child as leverage . . ." Millicent murmured thoughtfully, tearing up Hannah's address.

"But how"—Millicent paused for a moment to toss the scraps of paper into a wastebasket—"do we get the money? The will is quite explicit."

"Simple. We'll have her sign power of attorney over to us. Then the money's ours." Yancy contentedly examined the polished toe of his boot.

"What happens after that? We can't keep her locked up forever. People will talk."

His eyes met hers calmly. "Once the child's born,"

he said in low, even tones, as one might tick off items on a list, "if she leaves, say, for the south of France, or a quiet home in the Cotswolds, she'll be sent an allowance and the baby won't be harmed."

"All very neat," Millicent said with interest.

"For now, we simply have to say she returned to Montana, leaving us with power of attorney in her absence. After the baby's born, we'll see that she leaves for Europe. And then you and I will have our twenty-two million dollars to spend."

"I find your imagination delightful."

"Yours, no doubt, will do adequate justice to ways of disposing of that large amount of money."

And Millicent laughed.

THAT evening they carried Blaze's dinner tray upstairs, after explaining to the servants that the reading of her father's will had caused an emotional collapse, which they hoped would respond to bed rest and solitude. After carefully locking the door behind them, they appraised Blaze of their plans.

She listened quietly, although her mind was racing to find a way free.

"So, if you cooperate," Yancy finished, "everything will work out well."

"For you," she replied briefly. "Not so well for me."

"You'll have your child."

"And you'll have my money."

"A fair trade."

In truth, Blaze didn't care much about the money. She had her trust fund, which even they couldn't touch, and it was more than enough to live on. It annoyed her, though, the extent of their greed. And frightened her a little too. How far would they go to ensure their claim to the twenty-two million? Wasn't Hazard's death answer enough?

If she turned over her inheritance to them, her child —Hazard's child—would lose. She wished he were here to talk to. Maybe he'd say none of the money mattered. Then again, maybe he wouldn't. Look how hard he'd been working to give a measure of security to his people.

Just that afternoon, she'd legalized the will she'd written on the train. Curtis had it in his files now. If she gave them power of attorney, her child would never gain its birthright. On the other hand, if she didn't, it might not live. A small child would be much easier to kill than Hazard. And if he hadn't been able to stop them, how could she? "I want to think about it," Blaze said evenly.

"Don't take too long," Yancy ordered.

"I've six months until you can implement your threat."

"In the meantime, we can make your life uncomfortable."

"Thanks for the warning."

"I'll give you three weeks," he said.

"I expect she'll be sensible, won't you dear?" Millicent murmured, languidly waving her feather fan.

"Three weeks," Yancy reminded her, moving toward the door to unlock it. Millicent followed him, and Blaze was left alone, as the door clicked shut locked.

Hannah was gone. That had been her first question. Hazard was dead. Curtis and her friends who came to call would be told she'd returned to Montana. And the servants thought she had a nervous breakdown and was being shielded from society's prying eyes. She and her child were alone . . . between Yancy, Millicent, and the twenty-two million they coveted. She hadn't liked the look in Yancy's eyes when he'd said "uncomfortable." She'd seen that look before in men's eyes who hadn't even been coveting her money.

She wished that night very hard, as a small child might, wished that Hazard wasn't dead, wished that he and she and their child could live together in the cloud-covered mountains, wished she'd met him without gold and greed coming between them.

And then, as if wishes came true, Yancy came in the following morning with her breakfast tray and with what he referred to as an interesting bit of gossip. "You might want to change your fantasy about returning to Montana," he said, lounging against the doorjamb, dressed to go riding.

"I'm supposed to ask why to that leading question,

aren't I? All right, Yancy, I can be accommodating. Why?" And she closed the book she was reading, folded her hands atop it and gazed at him calmly.

"Because your lover found another bed."

"Is this some metaphorical allusion? If it is, I don't find it amusing." But her heart began pounding because Yancy wasn't subtle enough for that. When he said bed, he meant bed. She consciously willed her hands to unclench before Yancy noticed.

"The bastard lived somehow," Yancy churlishly said, "under a hundred pounds of black powder."

Joy, lately arrested by hopelessness, flooded back in one intake of breath. Blaze's spirits were singing wild songs of happiness while she casually said, "In that case, you'd best unlock that door permanently and slink off to Virginia. I don't think it'll be safe for you here."

"You didn't hear me, did you?" he silkily drawled, his raspy voice incongruously harsh. "He's not coming. He's in Confederate Gulch. He's in Rose's bed in Confederate Gulch. And he has been for almost a month."

The words turned her to ice. There had to be some mistake. She was his wife. He'd said so. They were going to have a child. He wouldn't have gone to Rose. He'd come after her.

"My offer stands, little rich girl. Three weeks. Sign over power of attorney then, or I'll have to resort to some ungentle persuasion."

Blaze rose from the loveseat and walked to the window before he saw how distressed she was, and he left when she refused to reply to his questions, but his parting words echoed gloomily in her mind: "Don't wait for him, little rich girl. All those Injuns love 'em and leave 'em, and Hazard, hell, they say he sets records."

But she did wait. Despite it all. Despite Yancy's vulgar assertions, despite the enormous distance separating them, despite the lingering uncertainty in her mind when she tried to think as Hazard might.

At the end of the third week, Yancy came to her room as promised. She hadn't signed in the interval. She'd held out. But when she saw him walk in that night, in his jacquard silk dressing gown, hand-braided ropes looped loosely over his arm, a hungry look in his color-less eyes, she'd half turned away and stared through the window overlooking the Charles River for a brief second. As she turned back, her small shoulders slumped a little. "That won't be necessary," she whispered. "I'll sign."

Yancy left with her fortune in his pocket.

And Blaze cried herself to sleep. Not tears for the loss of her inheritance, but tears for the loss of her love. He hadn't come for her. He didn't even care about his child. But then Jon Hazard Black had children already and lovers too. He'd probably even forgotten her name by now.

YANCY and Millicent were up most of the night toasting their newly acquired wealth with the late Colo-nel Braddock's rare, fine champagne.

"He may have been a peasant, my dear, but he knew his wines," Yancy remarked, uncorking another well-pre-served bottle from the Colonel's perfectly stocked cellar.

"One positive quality in an otherwise flawed charac-ter is hardly enough to endear him," Millicent replied, loath, even though indebted to her husband's perspicac-ity in amassing a fortune she could now enjoy, to give him his due. "Peasant blood is peasant blood," she em-phatically declared.

"Which brings to mind," Yancy pointedly said, "a proposal to terminate said peasant blood."

Millicent laughed a trill little ripple. "You're too late, Yancy. He's been cold-dead these many weeks."

"I had in mind," he paused, "his grandchild. Insur-ance," he said, "against some future claim."

Millicent sat up from her lounging ease, perplexed. She set her champagne flute down. "How do you pro-pose to do that?"

"There's a specialist in New York who takes care of girls in trouble."

"She'll never agree to an abortion."

"She doesn't have to *agree*. We have the power of attorney, now; we can *tell* her what to do, not *ask*."

"Where and when?" Millicent asked, immediately recognizing the future security in such an action.

"The one everyone here goes to—Madame Restell's[21] in New York. There's even a possibility," Yancy added, "Venetia may not survive the abortion." His brows rose suggestively.

"That's enough, Yancy. I don't want to hear any more."

"As long as you don't hear it, then?"

"I refuse," she replied, not at all flustered, only cautious, "to listen to any more."

"I know, love, you hate the details. Well, never mind, I'll handle those."

"Better, I hope, than you did in the case of the Indian."

Yancy shrugged, nonchalant after three bottles of champagne. "Impossible to kill like a normal man . . . but two small claims don't matter now, do they? . . . not with the millions we have."

It was easy to shrug off Hazard since he was two thousand miles away, but Millicent disliked loose ends, loose ends so close to home, so she inquired with a significant emphasis on each word, "When will you take care of our present detail?"

"Tomorrow," Yancy said with a smile. "First thing tomorrow."

Chapter 34

HAZARD stayed with Rose for slightly less than a month, and in that time summer slipped into autumn. Yancy had been right about Hazard sharing Rose's bed, but implication and circumstance weren't the same. Hazard could have made love to Rose, and once his arm began to heal, she'd said as much in an offhand, casual way, "No strings, Hazard, same as always. If you want. If you don't, I understand too." Years ago she'd given up the luxury of illusion.

They'd been lying in bed when she brought it up. It was a warm, sunny late-summer morning and Hazard was fighting down memories of Blaze under the sun-dappled willows. "You're too damned good to me, Rose," he ruefully acknowledged. "The guilt is mounting." He hadn't touched her and his broken arm wasn't an excuse anymore.

She rolled over on her elbow, at the courteous declining, and looked him straight in the eye. "Why don't you go after her, dammit?"

"She doesn't want me to," he replied as plainly as she, "that's why."

"How do you know?"

"A note I found made it pretty clear."

"You think she knew of Yancy's plans?"

"Apparently." The date on the note was etched on his liver. It preceded the invasion by a day. "She must have known about it somehow. Don't ask me how."

"She didn't really think you'd survive to read it. What was the point?"

"I don't know. Best I can figure, it would absolve her of any implication in my death. A gratuitous gesture out here where people die unnoticed every day. But they were probably operating under eastern rules of judicial procedure. It never hurts to be safe, especially if she was interested in having our child inherit the claim."

"Does it bother you? Having your child raised out there?"

He allowed the anger to show for the first time, and Rose unconsciously sat up, retreating from the cold fury. "It outrages me if I allow it to," he said tersely. "She told me she wanted to stay here, have the baby born in the mountains. I've never viewed myself as gullible, but damned if I wasn't, Rose. Like a wet-behind-the-ears adolescent."

Rose touched him gently on the shoulder, her fingers warm and soothing. "You couldn't have known."

"But I should have, Rose, dammit. I lived in that phony Boston society. I should have known better."

WHEN Hazard returned to his people, the comfort he sought never came. He saw Blaze in his memory wherever he turned: wearing her elkskin dress, trying to learn the Absarokee words, touching him when he sat in council, warm against him in the coolness of the night.

He was alone, preferred it that way, so people talked. But never to his face. He didn't sleep with any women. He didn't go on the raids. When he hunted, he hunted alone. They worried, his clan and relatives and friends. It was as if the living spirit had left him. But he didn't want help and he didn't want advice. Then his evening visit to Bold Ax soothed the alarm. He was coming out of his black spell. Those sorts of negotiations were a good sign.

It had been protection, rather than emotion, prompting his marriage proposal to Blue Flower. He needed a solid barrier, an unassailable fortification against the insidious, powerful yearning. Blue Flower was his fortification, marriage the final defense against his wanting Blaze. Blue Flower had said yes with joy that evening, and Hazard kissed her cheek lightly like a monk.

The first frost colored the cottonwood trees and quaking aspen all along the creek, the fragile leaves ablaze with emerald and crimson and gold. Wild rosebushes and kinnikinnick were like splashes of fire against the mountainsides. Hazard, looking bronzed and rested, was lounging under a shimmering mass of saffron-tinged cottonwood, half leaning against the tree trunk, seeking some peace of mind. The warm autumn afternoon was glorious, the tinted leaves above him shimmering in a light breeze.

Two small children were playing near their mothers, who were preparing food for the evening meal. The children were two, probably less, because they toddled still on pudgy, unsteady legs. They were playing with soft toys made by their doting parents, vocalizing in their abbreviated version of Absarokee, giggling at their mother's occasional nonsense chants. They were healthy, happy, loved, and playing under a sun shining on tribal lands fought for and defended under sixteen chieftainships.

And suddenly Hazard wanted his child raised here with his people, with him. Not in Boston, where he deplored the grey, soot-coated snow in winter, the houses jammed one against the other, where you could never see a sunset slip below the horizon like liquid fire. He didn't want his child reared in a Beacon Hill pile of stone filled with servants and no love, by a mother whose words were only coldly calculating business devices. The thought suddenly of his child raised in the teeming grey city made his skin crawl.

So against all sensible argument, against the logic that had kept him firmly in Montana for weeks, against the rationale developed as a result of the three curt sentences in Blaze's note, he walked back to his lodge and started packing.

"In a hurry somewhere?" Rising Wolf asked from the sun-drenched doorway.

"Boston."

"Need help?"

Hazard tied his saddlebag shut with two quick jerks, snapping them forcefully. "No thanks," he said. "I know how to handle her." Then, straightening, he reached for his Colts and transferred them to the holsters belted on his hips.

"Are you sure you know what you're doing? Remember your—"

The icy rage wasn't meant for him, but it stopped Rising Wolf midsentence. Hazard had the rancor under control by the next heartbeat and smiled an apology for his lapse. "I think it's about time," he explained coolly, a lazy arrogance nicely prominent, "Miss Venetia Braddock finds out that even millionaires' daughters can feel the cut of the bit. She's had her head long enough. I want my child."

"What if Blue Flower—"

"She'll do as she's told." His voice was curt. "One impertinent bitch a year is about my limit. See you in a month or so."

"With your child?"

The smile cutting Hazard's lean face was wolfish. "In a manner of speaking."

HE TOOK the stage from Diamond City two days later, the fastest mode of transportation; they traveled around the clock. If he'd ridden himself, he would have had to stop and rest. As it was, he slept most of the way, slouched in the corner of the stage to protect his still tender arm, his hat pulled down over his face. He wasn't in the mood for conversation and simply didn't reply when addressed. Passengers didn't press a second sentence on the dark-skinned man dressed in black. He only moved noticeably once on the long miles to the rail line. Road agents held up the stage the third day east of Salt Lake City, and Hazard, his automatic response to violence swift and sure, shot them—all three—in less time than the human eye could follow. The five other passengers only saw him slip his smoking revolvers into their holster as easily as if he were putting away his change, pull his hat a little lower on his brow, and shut his eyes again. When the driver shouted his thanks down, Hazard grunted something inaudible. After that display of marksmanship, the passengers afforded him an even wider berth, but he heard the whispers: "Hired gun."

He reached Boston in record time—ten days, six hours, and thirty-two minutes.

YANCY only told Blaze his plans an hour before he escorted her down the stairway to the waiting carriage.

"I won't," she said, sharply combative. "You can't make me."

"You don't realize how many reluctant young women pass through Madame Restell's," Yancy smoothly drawled. "Parental pressure is quite common. You'll be just another in a long line of young women who've unwisely chosen to love below their station in life. You'll do it," he bluntly said, all pretense of politeness gone, "if I have to tie you down to the table myself. And Madame Restell won't ask any questions when I offer to double her fee."

"I'll tell her about you."

"She won't believe you. All you young darlings get hysterical when you can't marry your dancing instructor or groom or gamekeeper. And even if your story's a bit different, she's not in the counseling business. She hasn't built the grandest mansion on Fifth Avenue by turning lucrative business away. We leave in an hour, so don't waste your breath."

Realizing argument was useless, Blaze acquiesced.

She at least would be out of her locked room, and escape was more probable than in her current circumstances.

She dressed carefully. Since she was in mourning, her string of black pearls wouldn't attract notice. She would have liked to empty her jewel case into her reticule, but didn't dare. Yancy was very likely to search its contents, and if she was carrying a fortune in jewelry out of the house, he'd dash her chrysalis plans. Today was the first time in three weeks she'd been allowed out of her room, the first time there was even a remote possibility of escaping.

The black pearls drew no undue notice against the black silk of her gown; she had simply chosen the most appropriate jewelry for her mourning. She had also chosen the most costly of her jewels, for in their rarity black pearls exceeded any other gem. And their value, appropriately dear, was about to buy her freedom. If Madame Restell was the businesswoman Yancy said she was, Blaze was certain she could be persuaded to let Blaze escape Yancy.

Not only Yancy, Blaze discovered on approaching the carriage, but two hired thugs as well. Two burly, beefy men towered over her, one on either side of the carriage door, as she stepped into the curtained brougham. Her expression remained suitably contrite on the trip to the station and on the train ride into New York, but her mind was busily contemplating the myriad details of her flight. The time required for an abortion should allow her at least a modest head start before Yancy discovered the deception. If she could reach her father's bank in New York, she could draw out funds for her trip west from her trust. Best avoid the train stations, she decided. She'd hire a carriage and driver for the first two or three days and board at Baltimore or Washington. No one would be expecting her to head south.

Chapter 35 ⟫

MILLICENT Braddock looked every inch the upper-class lady. She wore a plum silk mourning dress with only two strands of small matched pearls. Her light hair was immaculate in a ribboned chignon, her posture upright, her hands gracefully clasped in front of her. She had just set aside her first cup of tea and was standing at the window admiring the late roses in the small garden adjacent to her writing room.

The door swung open sharply and she turned irritably to chastise the servant imprudent enough to enter without first knocking.

"Where is she?" It was an order in a tone that disregarded entirely her position and the ambiance of a stately thirty-room mansion on Beacon Street.

For long enough to appear rude, she didn't answer. "I beg your pardon," she finally said. "Who do you think you are barging in here?" He only looked at her with a withering glance. "She doesn't want to see you," Millicent acidly declared.

"Get her down here."

"She doesn't want to see you." The repeated phrase was haughty and dismissive.

"I'm going up."

"She isn't there," she blandly said.

He stopped halfway to the door and spun around. "Then where is she?"

"Away," said the mistress of 12 Beacon Street, sweet contempt in her voice.

"Obviously. Where?"

"It's hardly your business."

"Don't push your luck, Millicent. Where is she?"

"I'll have you thrown out. I will not tolerate this flagrant violation of my home. If you do not leave instantly—"

"Cut the affronted southern belle. Do you think I give a damn what you want?" He shook his head almost imperceptibly. "Besides, you and I both know there's no one here that can throw me out. Now. You have exactly ten seconds to tell me where Blaze is or I'm going to strangle you right where you stand."

"Haven't you done enough to her already?" Total iciness. The prospect of being strangled in broad daylight in one's home could be discredited as mere rhetoric.

He looked up from the heavy gold watch he'd pulled from his vest pocket. "She told you that?"

"She did."

"Then we differ on the particulars of who did what to whom," said Hazard levelly. "Five seconds."

"You can't intimidate me, you rude savage!" Her grey eyes were icy pits of cold outrage.

"Three." A cabochon gem of some price on the hand holding the watch caught the sunlight and flashed a subtle green prism.

"You won't get another word out of me."

"Pity. Two."

Malevolent and assured, Millicent said, "Yancy will kill you when he returns."

A quick glance up to assimilate that interesting fact.

Yancy was gone. He hadn't been sure. His eyes returned to the watch held in his large, steady palm. "One. That's it. Say your prayers." Snapping the case shut, Hazard pocketed the engraved gold watch and moved across the room with astonishing speed. She tried to run, but he was firmly blocking her path.

"New York!" Millicent squealed, raw reality shockingly apparent when Hazard reached out toward her.

"Big city," he casually said, slipping his slender fingers around her neck and dragging her toward him. Their faces were so close she could feel the heat from his skin.

"Madame Restell's," she whispered, his grip leaving marks on her pale neck, stark fear crumbling her patina of arrogance.

The name made Hazard sick with despair and he was overcome by nausea. "When did they leave?" he asked, very low.

"An hour ago," she managed to croak, with the vise-like fingers unconsciously tightening.

A cold sweat covered Hazard's body. He might be too late. Desolation swept over him and for a long, terrible moment he relived the horrors of the past. It was the odd choking sound that brought him back. He dropped his hands and ran. He ran faster than he'd ever run before.

Chapter 36

WHEN they reached Madame Restell's four-story brownstone on Fifth Avenue, Blaze was whisked through the side entrance on Fifty-second Street and shown to a richly decorated bedroom by an attendant while Yancy met with Madame Restell in her ground floor office. The two hired guns guarded the marble foyer like prison wardens.

Let Yancy talk all he wanted, Blaze thought, looking around the room draped with a baby-blue brocade that she thought put a strain on good taste. I'll have the final bid. And no one, she knew, could afford to turn down $100,000 for *not* performing an abortion. She heard the door open and prepared to meet the most notorious woman in New York City.

"You're looking well, Miss Braddock," a deep, familiar voice she hadn't heard in seven weeks said. It was

Hazard's rich and drowsy tone. Hazard's accent. Hazard's beauty of cadence. Impossible.

Blaze whirled, clutching the heavy black pearls. He stood half in shadow, impeccably dressed in dark wool, the velvet collar on his topcoat lush in the dim light, his hair ordered and gleaming. His eyes accusing.

Her immeasurable joy wilted under the cold dark eyes and guilt overwhelmed her. How had he found her? What must he think? Her heart was thudding. "How did you know I was here?" she whispered. It was the worst possible choice of first words to him.

Hazard fractionally lifted his brows at the unexpected candor and then remembered it was typical of her type—selfishly self-centered. In Boston that afternoon, Millicent had information Hazard badly wanted, and her well-honed sense of preservation and the deadly look in Hazard's eyes warned her she'd best not withhold it. His reply omitted the less subtle details of garroting. "Millicent is easily persuaded," he smoothly said, in a voice as sharp as a knife blade. He was leaning against the door favoring one shoulder. A relaxed, casual pose, an odd contrast to his sudden ghostlike appearance.

"How did you find it?" Blaze's hands fell from the pearls and tightened on the heavy black silk of her skirt as if the stiff fabric would hold her upright. Astonishment, wonder, colored her breathy voice. He misread it from his jaundiced point of view. Ruffled resentment, he thought, and misjudged her clenched fists as well.

"The woman boasts of a six-figure income, pet, and lives openly in grand style on Fifth Avenue. Not exactly a difficult person to find." The cool, familiar voice brushed through her nerves. "And besides," he softly added, "I've been here before." When he saw the demonstrable disbelief, he finished with silky contempt, "Madame Restell is well patronized by Boston society. You can't think you're the only soiled brahmin daughter to spend a few hours here." He allowed an unflattering stare to include both Blaze's prickly new stance and the floridly furnished room.

"I might have known," Blaze said, a sudden sharpness cutting through her quiet voice, images of Rose and Hazard strong. "With your track record."

"No, you don't know," he replied, equally sharply. "Unlike you, I value my progeny. I came down here one time with Cornelia Jennings and a friend of hers. A friend whose husband was unwilling to accept a pregnancy as his responsibility after returning from an extended trip to Europe."

At the curt explanation, embarrassed color rose revealingly in her pale face. "I . . ." She swallowed. "Forgive me . . ." Her grip loosened on the silk crumpled in her hands, and her heart suddenly ached at the sight of him. He'd come after all . . . all the way from Montana. But so remote, she thought, gazing at him resting casually against the door. Remote . . . and affronted. There wasn't time to decipher the nuances in the polished stranger before her. Not with Yancy likely to appear any minute. "It's dangerous," she warned, almost in a whisper, moving a step nearer, and as if in choreographed response, he slowly pushed away from the door and strolled out from the shadows with his deceptively lazy stride. He stepped full into the lamplight by the window. He looked like any rich man of leisure in his exquisite tailor-made clothes. But different from most in one stunning way. He was as beautiful as sin, she thought. As always. And as if all her dreams had come true, he was really here.

"Yancy's here with his watch-dogs. How did you escape their notice? They're guarding the door."

"I know." Her breathlessness he saw as fear of betrayal, not concern. "I came in through Madame's terrace door. I told her I was your heartbroken beau." He enunciated each word in clipped syllables. ". . . And paid her twenty thousand dollars in gold to let me see you."

"Why?"

"Why? Because ten thousand didn't get an eyelash to move and fifteen only brought a knowing smile. Paternity is expensive." He would have gone much higher if necessary. He was carrying a sum of gold which could outfit an army.

"No, why did you come? After so long . . ." Underlying her joy was a thin frost of resentment.

"Call it nostalgia for fatherhood," Hazard silkily replied. "With near-perfect timing, fortunately, since you
decided not to become a mama after all, it appears." His
eyes traveled insultingly over Blaze's curvaceous figure.
"I expect it cut into your playtime more than you anticipated."

On the defensive again, shame coloring her cheeks,
Blaze quickly replied, "It's not what you think, Jon."

"How would you know what I think?" he retorted so
brusquely that she moved back a half-step. He followed
her the half-step, his kidskin boots silent on the carpet,
and towered above her, menace in every line of his tall,
lean body. "What I *do* think, Miss Braddock, if you're
really interested," he went on in a deliberately emotion-
less voice, "is that it's my child, too, and," he said with
simplicity, *"I won't allow this."*

"Jon, I'm sorry," Blaze whispered, tears suddenly
welling into her eyes, her tender, full underlip trembling.
He remained brutally silent, steeling himself against the
fleeting impulse to drown in those huge pleading eyes.
"You're wrong . . . I wouldn't . . . you don't understand . . ." she faltered, deathly pale.

And if the memories of the mine had been less lucid, he would have pitied her. "How could you?" he savagely said, instead, angry she could still affect him so, his
forced reticence gone, his eyes like granite.

"I wasn't going to—I mean—they—" Blue eyes
breathtakingly huge with appeal. An enchantress still capable of casting her spell over him. Almost. The hate was
stronger.

"Don't tell me they made you do it, Blaze," he brutally pressed, inner rage resisting the spell. "Not *you.* Not
the woman who's willing to take on the world single-
handedly. Not the woman who thrives on independence.
Admit it, you bitch," he finished crisply, his eyes on
Blaze's pale face, contemptuous. "You didn't want my
child."

"No, no, that's not true. It isn't! I'd never—" and
then her feelings overwhelmed her; the weeks thinking

him dead, the dismay over Yancy's story about him and Rose, the tearing apart of her dream of happiness, and now he was here like a miracle, only a few feet away from her. "You're really alive," she quietly sobbed, her emotions tumbling wildly, disbelief and fear uneasily assailing her mind. "Alive," she softly cried, so distrait she didn't feel the tears or realize she was trembling.

He was determined to resist the drama this time with the ruthless implacability of a man once burned. "No thanks to you, pet," he smoothly drawled. "It was a good try, though, I'll give you that." The memory of those terrible days underground, not knowing if he was entombed forever, further strengthened Hazard's resolve against the poignant scene of Blaze's distress, the tears streaming down her face.

The distant sound of the front door bell abruptly recalled to him the time element. Madame Restell had promised they wouldn't be interrupted, but he didn't trust her overlong, once she had her money. "Put on your cloak," he flatly ordered. "We're leaving. Or," he added when she didn't move, "shall I put it on you?" The steely warning was clear despite its softly perfumed politeness.

"Where?" Blaze murmured, numb, stunned, fearful of Yancy, the guards, fearful for Hazard's life.

"Montana, where else? And hurry."

"Why didn't you write?" she asked as though he hadn't spoken. "You never wrote" she moaned, her voice ragged, perplexed. Wiping away a trail of drying tears with the back of her hand, she looked directly at him and quietly accused, "In all those weeks you never wrote."

"I was under the impression," Hazard flatly replied, intently watching her face, "after reading your fascinating note, that you weren't interested in corresponding with me."

"What note?" A printing of shock and wide-eyed surprise played across the pale exquisite face.

Slender, long-shafted hands languidly lifted and Hazard applauded softly, his mouth quirked in faint derision. "Marvelous, dear. I admire your talent for duplicity. That was exactly the right degree of dismay. But then you

were always a very competent actress, weren't you . . .
bia." He whispered the last word, and it drifted across
the plush, lamp-lit room, evoking sweet memories of a
one-room cabin in a no-man's-land of claims and gold
and contention. His eyes, unfathomable, held hers for a
long moment, recognizing the power of those memories
now in her presence. It took effort to stop remembering.
Steeling himself, impatient with his sensations, he moved
decisively, lifting the braid-trimmed wrap from the chair.
"Surely you remember the note, love," he said drily,
holding out the elegant jacket. "The note you wrote a
day prior to Yancy's attack."

"How could I . . . I never wrote any note. I don't
know about a note! I swear! Show it to me!"

"I wasn't in the mood to save it."

"I'll prove I didn't write it. Look! I'll write—"

"Forget it, Boston. It doesn't matter anymore," he
interrupted, waiting, impatience etched undeniably in every taut muscle and line of face and form. "Here . . .
put this on." The soft light underscored the dark shadows under his eyes.

"Jon, I'm sure I can explain—"

"Save your breath, Blaze," he dismissively remarked, draping the jacket over her shoulders. "I'm not
in the mood for any clever stories. It's been a long trip
from Montana and it's going to be an even harder trip
back with the dogs at our heels." His scowl forgave her
nothing.

"We're going back," Blaze murmured, her eyes shining with happiness. They had told her he was dead—and
he really wasn't. Nothing mattered but he was alive; all
else could be resolved. His anger, the misunderstandings,
Rose. She moved toward him.

His hand came out to stop her, touching her lightly
on the shoulder, his posture rigidly inflexible. "I came for
my child. I want it born with my people. I didn't come
back for you. Unfortunately, I can't have one without the
other." His eyes were cool and expressionless, without
depth or shade. His tone equally untouched. "After the
birth, you'll be free of me. But until then, I mean to keep
a close eye on you. Very close."

Blaze drew in a sharp breath, her mood volatilely altering. "Just like that?" She demanded, hurt and resentful.

"Just like that." It was the voice of a Absarokee chief, absolute, uncompromising.

"Don't I have anything to say about it?" It was inconceivable, Blaze thought, her temper responding to Hazard's laconic absolutism. Here they were again, all these months later, right back where they started.

"I think your wishes have been indulged enough in the last few months. The mine will take weeks to reopen, weeks of unpleasant hard work. Not to mention the little attempt to shorten my life. I may have been a fool, but I draw the line at being a martyr. And draw the line at this." His arm gently swept the room. "You may not want my child, but I do."

Blaze opened her mouth to vigorously deny his misconceptions, but Hazard continued speaking. "I won't keep you any longer than necessary. After the child is born, you're free to leave. I can find a wet nurse in the village."

The assured arrogance, the familiar command piqued, as it always had. "A brood mare, then. Is that it?" Blaze's soft voice was acid.

Hazard looked down at her. His voice was unhurried, his bronze face calm. "I didn't want it this way. You did. Your note was quite explicit."

"Damn you! I never left a note!"

"Well, someone else named Blaze did, then." The sarcasm cut through her sharply.

"And if I won't leave . . . won't be brushed aside when the child is born?" she hotly inquired. She expected an angry rejoinder. She was wrong.

"I'm sure you'll prefer leaving," he retorted in his most detached voice. "You won't be a first wife, *bia*. And"—A cold impersonal gaze was trained on her—"to be frank, the lot of a second wife isn't always pleasant."

"Second wife?" Blaze breathed so quietly if the room hadn't been absolutely still, the sound would have been inaudible.

Jon Hazard Black inclined his head.

Take a deep breath and the world will start up again. "Need I ask who?" A small whispered exhalation, for she was fighting off the tidal wave.

"Probably not. Blue Flower will raise my child. The betrothal was three weeks ago."

The words hung between them like death.

"I see," Blaze said.

"I thought you would."

They were no more than a foot apart, but Hazard could have been standing on the other side of the planet, so final was his utterance, his eyes distant as the open prairies of his homeland.

"And if I don't choose to agree with your interpretation?" Blaze's eyes were bruised pools in a bloodless face.

"You'll change your mind—given a few months in the village. Think, Blaze," he drawled sarcastically, his suddenly disconcertingly sharp glance sweeping the room, "none of this . . . no blue brocade, no down mattresses on gold and ebony beds, no servants." His nose curled distastefully at the room's cloying scent. "We don't have hothouse flowers in Montana either. How will you survive?" He had no stomach anymore for what passed for upper-class deprivation.

"I survived well enough at the summer hunt." Her heart was quivering sickeningly.

"It was temporary and you're a good actress. Don't expect me to succumb to the same performance twice."

"It wasn't a performance, damn you." Some of her old spirit shone through, but her voice was only a whisper.

Hazard's by contrast was perfectly modulated, as though they were disagreeing on nothing more untoward than the color of a hair ribbon. "You say it wasn't. I say it was. Stalemate. Now let's get the hell out of here. Our thousand and one differences can be debated later. How many months will you have in Montana?"

"Fuck you, Jon Hazard!" Shiny wetness filled her eyes, frustration like suffocating cotton wool stuck in her throat.

"Thank you, ma'am, but I'll pass." His mouth was a

thin, straight line, his voice low and brooding suddenly. Like I should have right at the beginning, he thought bitterly.

"You're afraid of me," Blaze asserted in a voice of discovery. There was a chink, after all, in his icy armor.

"No," Hazard replied, moving toward the window, provocation more real than truth at the moment. "I'm not afraid of anyone . . . least of all you, pet." Dousing the lamp, he pulled aside the curtains and threw up the window. "Now get your sweet bottom over here and perch it on this windowsill. I'll lower you to the ground." Turning sharply, he snapped his fingers. "Now, *bia*, now."

Blaze moved. "I'm not finished with you," she said, approaching him, a renewed confidence growing in her heart, and placed her palm lightly on his.

Already intent on their departure, Hazard only absently replied, his fingers curling over hers. "I'm not finished with you, either, *bia*. Not for five more months." And pulling her close, he lifted her, one arm around her waist, and swung her out the window.

Chapter 37

HAZARD'S gold bought them a carriage, a driver, and the best team of horses in New York. Within the hour they were headed west.

"They took all my money," Blaze told him when they were finally settled in the beautifully upholstered interior.

Hazard was sprawled on the seat opposite her, his eyes shut. "Doesn't matter. I've plenty."

"I don't mean that. I had to sign a power of attorney over to them for Daddy's inheritance. They threatened our child."

Hazard's eyelids levered half open over bruised, heavy black eyes and he looked at Blaze sardonically. "Forgive me if I find the story unlikely, after finding you at an abortionist's." His eyelids lowered wearily and he adjusted his head comfortably against the velvet squabs. "I'm not up to the melodrama," he murmured, already half dozing. "I've been on the road eleven days and without sleep for the better part of it."

And while Blaze stiffened at the unfair reproach, contemplating a suitably scathing retort to the rank injustice, she heard the rhythm of his breathing slow as he fell asleep where he sat. Even in her anger, her heart went out to him. How tired he looked. She ached to touch him, hold him, and comfort him, but he'd put up barriers that daunted even her. He felt she'd betrayed him, blamed her for the attack on the mine, viewed her as an enemy, as he had when she'd first gone up to his mine that summer morning months ago.

But she'd managed to change his mind then. Might it be possible once again? She loved him; that had never changed. And seeing him once again only strengthened that love. How could he talk about marrying Blue Flower? He was hers! Ten days, she thought, two weeks at the outside before they rejoined his clan, before he was reunited with Blue Flower. Certainly she mused, warming to the challenge, certainly it should be possible to reestablish her claim on his affection in that time.

Her anger was forgotten, borne away by a wave of tenderness, a restless intoxication only the man sleeping opposite her could evoke. We'll see, she thought, green-eyed possessiveness gripping her senses, who's first wife and who's second. We'll see if a second wife materializes at all. In her present frame of mind, her old assurance buoyed by Hazard's presence and her overpowering love, she wouldn't recommend anyone bet on it.

At the next stop, Hazard woke with a startled, quick alertness until he recalled where he was. He held his head in his hands briefly, hunched over his legs. Then he got up and left to see to fresh horses. When he came back and dropped into the same tired sprawl, Blaze quietly said, her blue eyes extraordinarily large in her pale face, "Could we please start over again? I love you. I always have. I'd never intentionally hurt you. Please believe me."

Hazard's gaze drifted over wearily. He looked at her, then looked right through her, his face expressionless. "The last time I believed you," he murmured, his soft voice grating suddenly with aversion, "I almost died. It was a sobering lesson, pet." He lifted a side curtain and glanced outside. "How far have we come?" His tone was conversational now, bland, Blaze's attempt at reconciliation dismissed.

"I want to talk about it, Jon. Tell me how you survived the mine explosion—how you got out. Were you hurt? You must have been. Tell me. I don't care how far we've come."

"No, I don't suppose you do." He took a last look before dropping the curtain back into place. "I think we can outrun them, though," he added as though her pleading questions had never been uttered. "Sorry to disappoint you, Boston," he finished, flashing her a brief glance, "but we're going to gain fifty miles on this route."

"Damn, Hazard," Blaze exploded, "there's no reason for me to side with Yancy. If you weren't so stubborn you'd understand. Yancy and Mother would as soon see me dead now, too. Can't you see that? Then all the money would be theirs without any legal maneuvering. And I want the baby, Jon. I do. Ask Curtis Adams. I willed everything to the baby!"

"So you say," replied Hazard, a shade of exasperation entering his deep voice. But the phrase "Willed everything to the baby" jarred momentarily against the solid wall of his defensive armor.

"Damn you, it's true."

He had had two hours' rest. Because of necessity and the bringing together of the ragged components of his self-command not entirely drugged by fatigue, he was awake, but shadowed by a hovering temper. He shot her an irritated scowl, all her arguments overridden by his temper. "It's also true that I'm only here because I was able to chip my way through eight feet of greenstone before I starved to death." A muscle clenched along his jaw. "It's also true," he said very softly, "your note greeted me on my escape. I can't begin to describe the indelible feelings it etched on my liver."

"How can I convince you I didn't leave that note!" She was looking at him with a kind of hurt anger, aligned with a bravura challenge. "Why would I leave a note, anyway, if I'd had a hand in with Yancy?"

"Protect yourself, I suppose. Hell, don't ask me to figure you out. I gave up on that quite a few weeks ago."

"Talk to Hannah. She'll tell you. She'll tell you about mother and Yancy and how I wanted to die when I thought you were killed."

Hazard looked at her wearily. "Hannah? Who's she? Another one of your cohorts?" He shook his head. "Give up, Blaze. None of it means a thing to me."

The carriage lurched momentarily as the horses settled into a gallop, but even that didn't move the lounging indifference of Hazard's posture. "I'm your wife," Blaze insisted, impatient with his obstinate disinterest. "Doesn't *that* mean anything?"

"You won't be for long . . . if I choose," came the expressionless reply.

"Meaning . . . ?"

"All I have to do is put your things outside the lodge and the marriage is dissolved."

"Damned convenient for you men!"

"Oh, no, you misunderstand," he mildly corrected. "A wife can do the same to a husband."

Blaze sniffed, mettlesome and moody as her husband when the spirit moved her, becoming increasingly piqued at Hazard's detached attitude. "Maybe I'll choose to exercise my option."

"As you like," he said in clipped accents. "All I want is the child."

"And if I want it too?"

"Don't make me laugh," Hazard scoffed. "Remember, I found you at Madame Restell's."

"It was the only time in three weeks I'd been allowed out of my room. I went because it was my only chance for freedom, but I took my black pearls with me," she insistently went on, "to barter that freedom from Madame Restell. These pearls are worth twenty times what an abortion would have brought her. Madame Restell would have accepted, I *know,* Jon. As God is my witness, I *want* our baby. How many times do I have to tell you I wasn't planning on going through with the abortion?"

"You haven't enough breath to convince me," said Hazard, his patience slipping. "Put on all the airs of affronted motherhood you choose. Cast those soulful Madonna eyes on the world at large. Weep tears of modesty and shame. Take up with the carriage driver once we hit St. Joe. . . . But kindly, *spare me the theatrics!*"

"You're impossible!"

He frowned. *"We're* impossible." Then he shrugged negligibly, as he might have in the early days of her captivity. "I said it the first day at the mine. I was right then and right now."

"And in between?" Blaze significantly reminded him.

The shrug this time was tossed off, one shoulder only rising slightly. And dismissive. "An unfortunate lapse in judgment." But his thoughts dwelled on the memories.

"How can you call our love an unfortunate lapse in judgment?"

"I had time to reassess it, dear wife, those five days underground, chipping my way out. Do you know what a calculated guess is?" He didn't wait for her to answer. "That's what my shaft to freedom was. I could have just as well been off five or ten feet and died in there. That sort of experience tends to temper one's love. Like an asp bite, it's deadly."

"Say what you will," Blaze replied, bold and assertive, "I'm not leaving after the baby's born. I never left you by choice and I never will. I might as well warn you now, so there's no misunderstanding. With the pattern of error and misinterpretation in our relationship, I'd just as soon avoid any more."

His eyes met hers and held them for a long time, but she didn't flinch or look away. He was reminded of the young virgin he'd told to leave so many months ago. She'd given him the same solid look and said she was staying.

That flat, blue-eyed gaze was Blaze Braddock and determination and Jon Hazard Black's wife. Its undeniable familiarity provoked the first fissure in Hazard's armor of resentments, invisible yet to a consciousness nursing a moody bitterness, but a fracture nonetheless. "Fair enough," he said. "I'm warned." And perhaps in self-defense against an inexplicable pulsing sensation of warmth stirring his nerve endings, he added, "Remind me to warn Blue Flower as well. I hope you two get along." The words were cynically said.

"Bastard."

"That's a yellow eyes epithet," he said, a thin smile curving his fine mouth. "Try again."

"I'll scratch her eyes out. She won't stay long," Blaze tightly declared.

"I'll have to protect her, then."

"I suggest you protect yourself as well."

Hazard's dark brows rose fractionally, his mouth twitching into a wider smile. "Is that a threat, sweetheart?"

"Read it any way you like, dear, *dear* husband," Blaze sweetly replied, more determined than ever to see that Hazard never married Blue Flower. If he thought she intended to share him with another woman, he was seriously deluding himself. She had no intention of placidly handing him over to another woman. And if Hazard had examined his own feelings more closely, he would have recognized the same possessive sentiment. Blaze belonged to him; no other man could touch her. And while the conscious impetus for his racing journey east had been his child, submerged beneath the intricacy of his rancor was the selfsame territorial imperative.

THEY boarded the Michigan Central and Great Western Railway at Niagara Falls. Hazard reserved one of the new Pullman hotel drawing room cars, splendidly luxurious and well appointed, but insisted on locking Blaze in whenever he left her alone.

"I'm not trying to get away from you," she protested, one time when he returned from his regular round of reconnoitering.

"And you won't," was all he said, pocketing the key,

his voice as guarded as his expression. "We agree on something at last."

"We'd agree on a lot more if you weren't so perversely intolerant."

"Not intolerant, just practical. I remember all your sweet talking from before." There was a bitter set to his mouth and his dark, thick-lashed eyes were forbidding. "And I had five extremely long and painful days underground to remind me about your style of sweet talk. Lunch?" he said coldly, and handed her a sandwich with such indifference that nothing more was said in the compartment for some time.

While Hazard kept Blaze confined, he maintained a low profile as well. Yancy was bound to be on their trail. Sooner or later. And he never worked alone. Bullies never did.

The second day, Blaze had one of her rare bouts of morning sickness, and when Hazard brought in her breakfast on a tray, she took one look at it and bolted for the tiny bathroom.

He opened the door she'd slammed shut and took in her green-faced misery for a silent moment before he reached down to help hold her steady while she vomited. After, he carried her to her seat and settled her comfortably with two pillows behind her head. "Are you sick often?" he anxiously asked.

"No," Blaze weakly replied. "Hardly ever. I think it's the movement of the train. Junior's objecting," she added with a wan smile.

"I'm sorry," Hazard quietly said.

"About Junior?"

"No, it's too late for that. I'm sorry about your sickness. If there's anything I can do . . ." His concern was sincere.

Blaze wanted to say, Forgive me for everything . . . for the mining company, for mother, for Yancy . . . but even in his tender attention, she felt the constraint and she didn't dare. "Don't bring breakfast in before ten," she said instead with a light smile.

"Never again, *bia,*" he replied with his own casual

smile, but instantly shuttered his gaze when he realized what he'd called her. Rising abruptly, he moved over to his seat opposite and lapsed into the moody silence prevalent since New York.

When Blaze complained of the boredom several hours later, he bought some books for her at their layover in Chicago. When she complained of his silence, he only looked up and said, "I'm thinking."

On the following afternoon, Blaze opened the window, dropped the books out, and demanded, "Talk to me."

Hazard opened his eyes and uncurled from the green and crimson upholstered seat which turned at night into a fine linen-covered berth. In extremely slow motion, he eased himself partially upright from his dozing sprawl. He'd been up at each stop during the night checking on passengers boarding. The closer they came to St. Joseph, Missouri, the more apt they were to run into Yancy. St. Joe was the jumping-off point for trails west. Yancy knew that, and although alternate routes existed overland, they were either too far south or passed through Lakota territory. Hazard might chance the Lakota on his own, but would never attempt it with a pregnant woman.

So the logical choice was stage west from St. Joe; not only a logical one but the only option. Yancy would be aware of the limitations, he knew, and that was why Hazard slept very little last night.

"Talk to me," Blaze repeated. "We've been on this train two days and you've barely said a dozen words." He had been either uncommunicative or abrupt to the point of discourtesy.

"We don't have much to talk about." He didn't seem inclined to change his pattern.

Blaze wasn't about to be ignored for a third day. "Are we going by stage from Council Bluffs?" she persisted.

"Most likely." He was lounging on one elbow, his voice as lazy as his pose.

"I heard you leave last night, more often than usual.

Why?" And when his eyes seemed on the verge of closing again, she firmly added, "I want an answer."

Slowly dropping his feet onto the deluxe compartment carpet, Hazard finally sat up. Apparently Blaze
wasn't going to be denied today. "Checked who came on
board."

"Yancy?"

"Not yet."

"Do you really think he'll follow us? Wouldn't it be
more sensible for him to stay in Boston and spend my
money?"

"Yancy never struck me as a moderate man. More
greedy than most and more vengeful. I'm sure he'll come
after you. And me. And our child."

"Can we get to Montana?"

He shrugged. "We'll make a damn good try."

"I could ride."

"Not now."

"I'm only about four months pregnant."

"This wouldn't be a leisurely cross-country jaunt.
You can't hold up to eighteen, twenty hours in the saddle. It's too dangerous for the child."

"Only the child?"

"You, too, obviously."

"Thanks for the concern."

"For someone found at the most expensive abortionist in the country, don't question *my* concern." His
answer was spiny-tempered and curt.

"I wouldn't have gone through with it."

"And then again you might have changed your
mind; women have been known to change their minds. I
couldn't take that chance . . . again." His eyes were
suddenly internally focused. And pained.

"Again?" Blaze breathed, the word conjuring up un-
revealed mysteries.

Recalled to himself, to the green and crimson decorated railway compartment, to the wide-eyed woman opposite him, Hazard simply said, "There're other ways
besides the Madame Restells of the world. All cultures
have their methods."

"Your wife," Blaze whispered, understanding suddenly about the dresses carefully packed away as reliquaries.

He didn't move, hardly breathed. When he spoke at last, his voice was disembodied, speaking from the distance of time. "She mortally damaged herself and our child . . . my child," he said very softly. He paused, all the old memories and pain vivid as bloodstains on snow. After a long while he looked up. "She was sixteen, and strong." He went on quietly, "It took her a week to die. I held her hand and watched her slowly leave me." And he saw her features again as though it were yesterday, saw her dying slowly in agony. He swallowed and exhaled gently. "We were young. I loved her very much. We were inseparable after our marriage. She'd come with me on the raids. When she discovered she was pregnant she didn't tell me. I wouldn't have allowed her to come along anymore. So she tried to abort herself—very crudely, it turned out." His eyes drifted up and caught Blaze's horrified gaze. "So don't," he said gently, a lifetime of regret in his voice, "do anything foolish. And don't talk to me about riding the way we'd have to, to stay ahead of Yancy. I won't let you."

"I'm sorry. I didn't know; I'd never have mentioned it had I known. Please, Hazard, don't hate me." Blaze murmured in a small, pained whisper. Don't hate me, she thought, because of another's mistake.

Hazard sighed and watched the landscape slide by.

"Can we be friends, at least . . . for now?" she coaxed, wishing it were possible to hold him and give him the comfort he needed.

"I'll try," he slowly answered.

It wasn't much, Blaze thought, but a concession of sorts, the first harsh anger mitigated, a step in the right direction. And Hazard always kept his word, so he would try.

It was better for the remainder of the day; they were able to talk a little, and when he locked her in, he apologized. He even smiled faintly—the first hint of a smile since he'd found her.

He'd been careful, during their days on the train, to

leave when Blaze readied herself for bed and when she rose and dressed in the morning. He'd learned his lesson well—learned it the hard way. Almost died from the education. And he didn't intend to be lured or enchanted again by Blaze's beauty or sensuality.

Chapter 38

ALL hell broke loose in Boston when Yancy returned with the news that Blaze had disappeared.

Millicent had hoped Hazard wouldn't get to Madame Restell's in time, had even vaguely hoped he couldn't find the place. But she had never considered he'd get past all of them to Blaze and manage to elude them as well. Millicent went so far as to feelingly declare, several decibels louder than those considered genteel, "You are a goddamned fool, Yancy Strahan. And if you don't find her, I can't imagine supporting you on my dower portion."

"He's back," Yancy brusquely replied. "It's not going to be easy," accepting her negation of their marriage plans with blunt agreement. He'd do the same to her under the circumstance.

"How much!" Millicent snapped, well aware, with Hazard's finger marks on her neck, that he was back. "Tell me how much it's going to cost."

They were partners in a venture that could have realized millions. It still might. Neither was willing to give up yet. She needed him and he needed her: his brawn, her money, and between them a plain, bare-faced predisposition to let nothing stand in the way of the fortune they coveted. Like duelists they had politely parried those early weeks in Montana, dropping a word or tentative hint here and there, waiting to hear the other's response, then moving to the next position, like calculating professionals until they were engaged fully, both understanding the other's strengths, both sure after the initial moves, that they would make better partners than adversaries.

And beneath their callous exteriors, they held each other in a strange respect, tempered at times with a curiously erotic attraction. Wickedness attracted to vice.

"I need trackers, horses, supplies. He's ahead of me, but if I can hire Hyde in St. Joe, he won't get away. *Neither* will get away. Hyde can track anything."

"Give me a figure and get packed. I'll have the bank draft ready when you come down. They are *not* to escape this time. Understand?"

Yancy nodded briefly. He understood perfectly.

"How far ahead of you are they?" Millicent briskly inquired, already moving toward her desk.

"A day or so by the time I'm organized, but Hazard's not going to be able to travel fast with her."

Millicent's silk skirt brushed the carpet as she half turned back. "What makes you so sure they're heading west?" she pointedly questioned.

"He's an Injun," Yancy matter-of-factly replied.

Chapter 39

BLAZE was the one who insisted they stay overnight in St. Joseph. She pleaded fatigue, the pregnancy, and a half-dozen other symptoms to make him agree. "I want to sleep in a real bed, not a poorly padded shelf attached to the wall."

He didn't want to stay. Speed was their only hope of staying ahead of Yancy, and he told her so.

"I'm so tired, Jon. Would one night really matter?" They'd transferred twice in the last leg of their rail journey—the Chicago, Burlington, and Quincy Railroad first, and then the ferry to the Hannibal and St. Joseph Railroad—and the travel was beginning to exhaust Blaze.

They were standing in a sheltered alcove near the carriage stand, and the sight, sounds, and smells of St. Joe in the afternoon bustled around them. Hazard would only feel safe hiring a stage and leaving in the next five minutes. But he cast an appraising glance at Blaze and noted the smudged half-circles under her eyes, stark with fatigue, and the lack of color in her cheeks; swiftly calculating the possible danger against her frail health, he nodded his agreement.

He wasn't expecting the sudden hug she gave him. If he had, he would have avoided it, as he'd deliberately avoided any physical contact with Blaze since New York. She felt warm and soft and very familiar against his body, and he only hesitated briefly before his arms closed around her back. He looked down at her in his arms and instantly felt desire burn his heart.

Blaze lifted her face, their eyes met, and she smiled. "Thank you," she said.

"You're welcome," he answered, crushing the smoldering longing, offering only a constrained reply. Here he was in St. Joe, on the run, in broad daylight, on the busiest corner in town, his entire life in the balance, and all he could think about was wanting her. It was madness. He couldn't afford it. "We should go," he said.

Blaze shook her head, leaning into him, his arms around her giving her new strength and joy. Make it last.

The crowds of passengers pushed past them, church bells began chiming somewhere in the heart of the city. "It's not safe here." And she felt his grip slacken. "This is the first place they'll look," Hazard said in a tone calculated to persuade her of the danger. He extricated himself gently from her arms. "We have to go."

NEITHER spoke in the carriage. Hazard's rejection, while gentle, was obvious and Blaze, hurt at the rebuff, turned her head away while tears silently splashed on her cheeks. Hazard was being his most calculating self and in that mood was virtually unapproachable. For the first time since her happiness at seeing him in New York, she began to doubt her ability to move him. All the old arguments were still cogent, and now the additional one of her alleged complicity with Yancy was seeming insurmountable.

It was a subdued wife Hazard introduced to Lydia Bailey at her small farmhouse north of town. Subdued, paler than usual and looking fragilely small next to Hazard's large form.

"Shame on you, Hazard," Lydia said the second she met Blaze. "This poor child is practically falling over. I don't know why you men never understand you can't drive a woman like an Indian pony."

Hazard looked sheepish for a moment. "I guess I need you to remind me occasionally," he confessed with a penitent tip of his head.

"Darn right you do." And Lydia Bailey, who even at sixty stood straight-backed almost eye to eye with Hazard, cast him a stern, scolding look. "Now you go unload that carriage and have something to eat," she ordered, "and I'll put this poor mite to bed." And Lydia shooed Blaze down the hall. "Now you eat," she said to Hazard before following after Blaze. "You look a bit peaked yourself."

"I'll wait," Hazard said. "Is she going to be all right?" The taut nerves were explicit in his voice, and he was mentally cursing himself for being so obtuse.

"Nothin' a little food and rest won't cure." Lydia placed a gentle hand on Hazard's arm and she felt tense, iron-hard muscle. "Relax, Hazard, she's going to be fine. Food over on the stove. You know where the plates are." And she bustled off to see to Blaze.

She was in and out of the kitchen during the next twenty minutes, fixing a tray, fetching warm water; once she asked through the screen door to where Hazard sat immobile on the porch steps, "Does she have luggage?"

"No," he said, turning, half rising. "I have some light baggage. Is there something—"

"Never mind. Eat now, Hazard, and that's an order."

"Thanks, Lydia, I will." But he didn't move. And it seemed a long time later that Lydia held open the screen door and said, "You can see her now."

Blaze was propped up in a large feather bed clothed in one of Lydia's plain cotton nightgowns and dutifully sipping the warm milk Lydia had instructed she drink before sleeping. "Now you can talk to her, Hazard, for five minutes; then she's going to nap. Five minutes. Understand?" She waited for his nod before brushing past him and returning to the kitchen, with the same energetic stride Hazard had first seen ten years ago when he'd met her at a trading camp her husband, Joel, had set up near the Powder River.

Hazard stood in the doorway, his head only inches from the lintel, the width of his shoulders dwarfing the opening. "I'm sorry," he apologized. "I didn't realize how tired you were."

"It's all right," Blaze politely replied, holding the warm cup of milk between her hands and wishing they could stop acting like strangers. Into a deepening silence, she nervously stammered, "I . . . it came on suddenly . . . actually."

Feeling the awkwardness as well, Hazard made an effort at conversation. "How do you feel"—he paused, searching for an appropriate word—"otherwise?" he finished lamely. "The baby . . . I mean."

"Good, I think." Blaze blushed. "I don't know what to expect."

She looked touchingly young, all in white, her flamed-red hair falling loosely on her shoulders, the nightgown, many sizes too large, rolled up at the cuffs. It struck Hazard for the first time since New York that she was Blaze, his wife. He walked the few steps to the window overlooking the orchard and stared at the even rows of apple trees, at the glossy green leaves and shiny fruit turning a deep autumn red. Had it been a mistake going back for her? He wasn't immune as he'd thought. He couldn't carelessly discard her simply as the woman bearing his child—a notion conceptually viable back in Montana when he'd made the decision to go east—it was all eminently more complex here in her presence.

"You must be tired, too."

He turned, hearing the sound but not the words, and Blaze was reminded of the first time at the cabin when he'd been silhouetted against the noonday sun. Dressed in black, affecting the white man's world, Hazard looked as tall and straight and powerful against the sunny window as he had that first day on the mountainside. But his eyes were shadowed with the strain of travel now. And when he didn't respond, she repeated, "You must be tired too."

"No," he said, "I'm fine." It was an automatic reflex, schooled into him many years before, schooled by arduous migrations, and fortnight-long raids and a man's code of endurance. "But you should sleep now. Lydia says you must."

"So I must?"

"Absolutely." He smiled a little. "I've never dared argue with her."

"Are you afraid of her?" Blaze playfully asked, running her fingertip around the rim of the plain pottery mug.

"I'm afraid of lots of things."

"But not of me."

"Oh, of you, too, *bia,*" Hazard said very very softly. Perhaps most of all, he reflected. "Now sleep. . . . I'll see to the horses."

Blaze finished the milk after he left, contemplating his softly worded reply. No sarcasm this time or anger as in New York. It was Hazard, honest and plain-speaking, and the words warmed her more than anything he'd said on the journey. She slept peacefully for the first time in weeks, buoyed by his soft disclosure, and dreamed glorious, luminous dreams of them as a family: she, Hazard, and their baby, somewhere in the mountains, somewhere safe with sun-dappled willows and clear running water.

AFTER Blaze fell asleep, Hazard ate.

"You can't take her overland at the same pace you're used to, Hazard," Lydia was saying. She and Hazard were seated on the back porch. It overlooked the road and while Hazard didn't anticipate anyone finding them here, it never hurt to be wary.

"I know. But it can't be too leisurely either."

"Why? Trouble after you?"

For a moment Hazard didn't answer. He looked down at his hands, then out to the vista of ripening cornfields. "There's always that," he said into the warm evening air.

"Some dead husband's relatives?" Lydia asked. She'd seen the mourning clothes and the first signs of pregnancy, and they both conjured up questions.

He shook his head. "The mourning's for her father."

"Is there a husband?"

"Not *after* us."

"What sort of trouble, then?"

"A greedy mother with less than maternal feelings and her boyfriend, who'd kill his own mother or anyone else for a nickel."

"Nice combination."

"It encourages speed on one's journey," said Hazard drily.

"Where you taking her?"

"Back to my people."

"Is she your wife?"

He nodded, then looked away.

"Problems?" Lydia said, the evasion too noticeable to miss. There was a short silence, and then she asked the question in the forefront of her mind. "Is the child yours?"

"Yes." An emphatic answer, and this time he looked her straight in the eye.

"If you're willing to take advice from an old lady who's been married forty years to an irascible fur trader with an itch to travel, I'd say you can work out about anything . . . if you want to."

"Thanks for the advice. I'll think about it." He was contemplating the dusty toes of his boots.

"She loves you, you know."

His eyes came up slowly, questioningly.

"No, she didn't tell me in so many words, but all you have to do is watch her eyes on you. That's love, Hazard, and I hope you're not too big a fool to know it. What with your child and all, she needs you. Now, more than ever. I should know. Had eight."

It was an opening for Hazard to turn the conversation. Everything was too confused now for easy answers to anything. He knew Lydia's favorite topic of conversation was her children and grandchildren. "How are your children?" he asked.

Lydia told him. In detail. Hazard knew all the children, although most were older than he. And when Lydia slowed occasionally in her recital of their latest experiences, he coaxed her with another question. Lydia's family was all nearby, although the boys often accompanied their father on the trading journeys. So he posed the polite inquiries and Lydia talked. It pushed aside the issues and problems confronting him—if only for a time. They were still on the porch when Blaze woke from her nap, exchanging reminiscences with each other.

Hazard was incredibly handsome, lounging back in his chair, all dark elegance against the bucolic green countryside. Blaze was reminded afresh how much of a stranger he was to her, how little she knew of his past. It added another small sadness to the chasm between them. Squaring her fragile shoulders, she shook off the melancholy, her chin came up, unconsciously stabilizing her uncertainties.

She padded out the door and across smooth wooden porch flooring worn shiny by forty years of children's feet, and the chatter abruptly ceased. The oversized nightgown trailed behind her, and Hazard, his eyes drawn to her fresh young beauty, had a glimpse of the girl she must have been long before he knew her.

"A swing," she said, her voice liltingly light, as though dark thoughts were strangers to her soul. "I love porch swings." She moved toward it, past Lydia and Hazard seated at a small table in the shade of a fruit-ladened grape vine. "Do you remember, Jon, the night of the Territorial Ball? There was a swing on the porch." Sitting down, she pulled up the excess skirt and set the swing in motion with her bare feet. Small, high-arched feet. With soft, warm soles, Hazard recalled. Soft, warm soles that had teased him; soft, warm soles he'd kissed.

She looked up when he didn't answer and smiled, a winsome, small-girl smile that tugged at Hazard's rapidly beating heart. He remembered the night—and every day since first seeing her—vividly. "I remember," he quietly said.

Lydia had never heard anyone call Hazard "Jon." She'd also never seen him with his heart in his eyes. "Why don't I let you two reminisce and I'll start something for supper," she said, and neither seemed to notice when she left.

"You look like a small child in Lydia's gown." He should have said something more neutral, mentioned the weather or the grapes or Lydia's hospitality, but the words were on his mind and came more naturally than meaningless chatter.

"I don't feel like one," Blaze replied. "This gown makes me feel very pregnant. I hope you like a fat wife." She smiled. "And you look like a misplaced hired gun dressed all in black on this sun-drenched porch. A *thin* hired gun . . . we'll make a fine pair." She spoke as she always did—spirited, frank—and memories of the mountain cabin poured over Hazard.

"That always came easy." His dark brow rose. "The pairing."

"And it doesn't now?"

"It can't."

"What if I want it to?"

He smiled that lovely smile she would have walked through fire for. "You always want it to. That's no reason."

"It's a start, Jon. It was before and it can be again." There was quiet hope in her voice.

The smile had disappeared and he had slipped back behind the confines of his mistrust. "I don't want it to start again. I had plenty of time in the weeks since the blast to think, and I couldn't come up with one logical reason for being together."

"How about an illogical reason like . . . love?"

"Grow up, Blaze. You're using the wrong word. You and I are nothing but problems."

"I don't agree with you."

"You never did, Boston." He smiled halfheartedly. "That's another problem." Pushing his chair back, he rose. "I'm going to take a walk before supper." Vaulting lightly over the spindled railing, he strode away.

Chapter 40

"WOULD you like some help?" Blaze asked, entering the kitchen. Then, more frankly, "I need advice."

Lydia turned from the sink window where she'd seen Hazard disappear down toward the creek. "Lovers' quarrel?"

"I wish it were that simple," and Blaze outlined the last few months in succinct phrases.

"He came back for you, though."

"Not me. He came for his child."

Lydia knew love when she saw it, and Hazard's feelings weren't strictly paternal. "That's what he's telling himself," she said.

"He won't even come near me."

"Skittish, like a wolf that got hurt in a trap."

"Do you think so? I can't even tell if he cares anymore. I practically had to make a scene before he'd talk to me on the train."

"Oh, he cares."

Blaze smiled and pressed her palms to her cheeks; she could feel the warm glow rising. "If he still cares . . ." she whispered.

"No doubt there, child. He looks at you like . . . well, like I've never seen Hazard look at any woman."

"Have you known him long?"

"Since he was about fifteen. He came with his pa and a party of bucks trading on the Powder River. The Crows usually don't trade that area, but they'd heard Joel had some good repeaters. Hazard stood out even then in that bunch of young braves. The Crows are the best-looking nation on the Plains. But even then Hazard was just a little bit taller and a shade more handsome and dressed fit to kill. No other tribe can ever outshine a Crow warrior when it comes to dressing. That boy dazzled the eyes." Lydia smiled even ten years later at the memory. "Well, we traded him his first repeater, and he smiled then just as nice as he smiles now. Gentle too— 'course I expect you know that. Lost track of him then for a few years. Heard he married, then his wife died, and next thing you know he showed up at the Powder again . . . three, four years later, hair cropped, white man's clothes on and wanted Joel to help him get east from St. Louis. Me and Joel had become sort of parents to him. The paperwork had all been done by some adopted uncle of his who married one of his kin, and his pa was sending him off to white man's school. The kid was real unhappy, but he went. For his pa, I guess. Anyway after that, he'd visit with us coming and going to that eastern school each year. Liked us, he said, in that quiet way of his, because he could trust us. He didn't say the opposite—but he didn't trust most other whites."

Blaze nodded, trying to visualize Hazard at fifteen or eighteen.

"And I told him already," Lydia went on, snapping the green beans she was preparing for supper, "whatever problems you two have can be worked out. I should know. Over the years Joel and me have had a heap of problems. But once they're over"—she shrugged— "they're over and forgotten. Best thing in a marriage, if you ask me, is to have a poor memory for the bad times."

"It isn't just us, though," Blaze explained, gripping the back of a simple handmade chair. "It never has been. There's been all the obligations of his duties as chief to his clan, and then, the mining company. And Yancy, who's really the most dangerous. The combination has made everything impossible."

"Well, you can forget about those people and problems at my place. At least for one night," Lydia said with a wink.

Blaze smiled at her allusion and softly repeated, *"At least for one night.* That would be nice."

"Hard for a man and wife to hold a grudge when they're sleeping in the same bed."

"But he won't."

"He will tonight," Lydia forcefully declared, scooped up the beans in her large, capable hands, and tossed them into a pot. "Now, the biscuits. Do you want to do them? Most men get used to their wives' biscuits."

Blaze blushed. "I can't cook."

"Land sakes, girl," Lydia exclaimed, "how do you ever expect to keep him if you can't cook? Men can say all they want about lust and love, but good food brings them to their knees faster than a silk nightie any day. Pay attention now, child, and I'll show you how to make the best biscuits west of the Mississippi."

Blaze watched and listened and talked of her life some and then tried her hand at rolling and cutting until eventually Lydia was satisfied. "Good, you'll do just fine in no time. Just need a little practice. Now go wash up and get yourself looking pretty. Throw away that black dress. My Abby's about your size. She's small . . . takes after her pa. There's a dress or two of hers left in the cupboard in your room. Nothin' fancy, mind, but prettier than black. And your pa won't mind. He'd want you to be happy most of all, from what you said."

Soon after Blaze left to change, Hazard returned. He had talked himself back into physical control by the time he walked into the kitchen, his hair slicked back and still damp. "Nice creek for swimming," he said. "As always."

"The rope swing's still up there where you put it, Hazard. Grandkids love it."

"Nothing like a rope swing on a hot day."

"Amen to that. Sit down and have some lemonade. I'm almost ready."

Hazard's eyes widened momentarily when Blaze walked into the kitchen a few minutes later. Then he smiled and remembered, "The little flowers I was looking for in Diamond City. It's pretty on you."

"Thank you," Blaze replied, dropping him a small curtsy and smiling back. The compliment cheered and heartened her as much as Hazard's earlier remark. He seemed more relaxed, smiled more, spoke to her easily, as he used to.

"We should get some dresses like that for you. What's that called again?"

"Calico." Blaze swayed the skirt across her bare feet.

"Right. Calico. Could we get some, Lydia?"

"Take Abby's dresses."

"Blaze?" Hazard asked. While it was tempting to read a future and caring and a hundred other implications into Hazard's concern, Blaze warned herself to respond as casually as she'd been queried.

"If you're sure you don't mine," Blaze said to Lydia.

"Don't mind a scrap. Suits you, child."

And it did, Hazard thought, as sunshine suited summer. Barefoot, her hair falling in silky tendrils on her shoulders, dressed in yellow-sprigged calico, Blaze looked the very opposite of the woman he'd seen at Madame Restell's four days ago.

"Why doesn't Lydia keep my black pearls, Jon, for her hospitality. I can't possibly use them anymore."

"Heavens no, child," Lydia protested. She'd seen the two-strand necklace of perfectly matched pearls on Blaze when she'd walked in with Hazard. Even her unpracticed eye knew they were worth a small fortune. "Just take the dresses with my blessing. Now sit down and eat. Hazard looks as though he could stand a meal."

Hazard ate like a man who had lived on snatched meals for two weeks. And after supper, the three of them sat on the porch and watched the twilight turn to dusk. Lydia talked; Hazard, on his best behavior with his old friend, answered an occasional question, contributed an anecdote or two on his friendship over the years with the Baileys, and exercised his practiced ability to charm. Blaze listened, and learned more about Hazard's past in those two twilight hours than she had the entire time she'd lived with him. She saw him here on Lydia's porch devoid of the mantle of chief so prominent in Montana. It was almost as though a weight had been lifted from his shoulders. He was only a man, relaxing in the Missouri countryside, enjoying the dwindling twilight.

When it was time for bed, Lydia bluntly said, "While you're under my roof, Hazard, you can forget whatever troubles you and Blaze have. You'll be sleeping in that guest room with your wife tonight, and if you give me any guff, I'll lock you in, damned if I won't."

Hazard had risen and was about to make some excuse about checking the horses; he was planning on sleeping in the carriage or in the hayloft, but at Lydia's peremptory words, he quickly brought his glance around and searchingly scrutinized her face. She was dead serious, and suddenly he felt like a teenager again. She had power over him—always had. While he silently contemplated his options in face of what sounded like an order, Lydia added, rising to her full height, only three inches shy of Hazard's, "And don't think I can't make you do it, Hazard. I've got thirty pounds on you, and years of experience."

At such determination, Hazard's considerations abruptly terminated and he smiled. "And you've still got a left hook I envy."

"Damn right. And I'm not afraid to use it on you."

"You've managed to scare the hell out of me, Lydia." His smile was genial when he turned toward Blaze and bowed in a parody of courtly politeness. "Would you care to retire for the night, dear wife?"

"I'd love to," Blaze replied, her own smile tentative and she put out her hand toward Hazard's proffered one. His fingers closed around hers as they'd done a hundred times before, and she felt a small measure of comfort.

"Any further instructions, Lydia?" Hazard jestingly queried. "I wouldn't want to disappoint you."

"Humpf," Lydia snorted, plunking down in her chair and setting the rockers into a vigorous rhythm. "You ain't needed no instructions about that since long before I ever set eyes on you, Hazard. Now get yourself off."

"Yes ma'am," Hazard softly murmured and gave her a casual salute with his free hand. Then he pulled Blaze behind him through the door and down the hall.

After they entered the bedroom, he dropped her hand, turned to shut the door, and then leaned back against it, his fingers still lightly curled around the porcelain knob. "My apologies if Lydia's bluntness embarrassed you," he said cautiously, as one might explain away an idiosyncratic relative to a new acquaintance.

"Not in the least," Blaze replied, resting her hands on the carved footboard of the bed and facing Hazard across the hand-braided carpet. "In fact, I think she's very sweet."

Suddenly Hazard's glance was suspicious and his voice held a daunting mildness. "Was this your idea?"

Blaze's tone was one of vicious respectability. "I'd never presume to bludgeon you into sleeping with me. There're subtler ways of dealing with men."

"And you should know." It came out before he could stop it.

"Jealous?" Her glance of tolerant appraisal was calm.

"No."

"Hardly a remark, then, for a man who knows all the intricate subtleties of dealing with women. Something like the pot calling the kettle black. And if you recall, all my dealings with men were quite innocent. I was a virgin, after all . . . until I met you," Blaze coolly replied.

His answer was sharp and immediate. "You asked for it—a dozen different ways, if I recall," said Hazard rudely.

Blaze stared at Hazard, scowling. "I'm not quibbling over that. But you didn't refuse either."

"I tried to," said Hazard drily.

"But you didn't."

There was a brief silence. "Are we assigning blame?"

"Not in the least," Blaze crisply answered, well aware of her own initiative. "Just don't assume an unnatural posture of piety, that's all."

His dark eyes fixed on her for his own moment of recollection; then, fighting for equanimity, he quietly said, "Fair enough. I'm sorry if I offended you." And he turned on her the fluid smile and excessive charm that recalled a splendid man in evening dress in Virginia City. He obviously was determined to maintain a polite charade, and she rose to the occasion.

"And I, if I offended you," she neatly returned, her smile as blasé, contradicting the distress in her eyes. "Now, do you think we could sleep together in some polite amiability? Obviously, you'd rather not, but there's no sense in hurting Lydia's feelings. She's been very good to both of us. I wish," Blaze said with the smallest of pensive sighs, "I'd had a mother like her." And then Blaze pushed away from the bed and walked to the window to hide the stupid wetness in her eyes. How different life might have been, she thought, tugging restlessly on the ruffled curtain tie. Instead she had a mother determined to have her father's money at any price. Until now, she had never questioned her privileged life, had always accepted the numerous and lavish accoutrements of wealth as her personal right. She hadn't realized all she'd been deprived of. Lydia's warmth and genuine affection brought with it a poignant sense of loss.

"Speaking of mothers," Hazard noted with a sudden sharp irritability, "I'm going to check the road once more. We leave before sunrise."

When he returned, Blaze was in bed wearing Lydia's oversized nightgown. The room was dusky with the new risen moon diffused through the drawn curtains. "Everything looks fine," he said, unbuckling his gun belt, unaware of Blaze's fretting sense of loss. "The carriage is in the barn. Lydia owns enough land so the neighbors aren't close." He sat down on the edge of the bed and pulled off his boots.

Blaze watched the muscles in his strong back flex under the light fabric, saw a pulse beating very fast above the dark collar of his shirt, and wished longingly that she could touch him and calm his hurried heartbeat. He stood to unbutton his shirt, then stripped it off in an agitated jerk and tossed it over a bedpost. With restless, abrupt movements he unbuttoned his trousers, stepped out of them, and added them to the drapery on the bedpost. Retrieving his gun belt from the chair near the door, he walked back to the bed and without a word looped it over the headboard with a quick twisting motion.

Blaze studied him and wondered—had he changed? Her gaze took in the nakedness, the nervous, taut muscle and lean power, the pulsing strength, the unsmiling face. He was thinner, his hair a shade longer, his frame more spare and hard. And his strides had been almost pacing tonight. Fascinated by his restlessness, she was reminded of his predator namesake and experienced an unsettling sensation. She didn't know him. Didn't know this silent fierce man who was called her husband.

Hazard looked over after he'd secured his gun above his pillow and saw her eyes on him, dark and luminous in the dim light. "Good night," he said, his voice empty of emotion, and slid under the hand-quilted coverlet.

They both lay silent, the furthest extent of the large feather bed separating them, but each intensely aware of the other. The silence was unquiet, as if invisible fingers were drumming nervously. Hazard's hands were locked behind his head, his eyes surveying the papered ceiling, while the pulse in his neck signaled his consciousness of Blaze's nearness. How the hell was he going to sleep tonight?

A great despair came over Blaze like creeping fog smothering her last shred of hope, and she could no longer stop the tears swimming to her eyes. Silently, they slid down her cheeks and nose, dripping onto the pillow as she lay on her side, only inches from the only man she'd ever loved. She had never felt so miserably alone, and the tears were admission at last that all the wishing in the world was never going to bring Hazard back. He really didn't care. "Good night," he'd simply said; "Good night." Nothing more. As if they were chance acquaintances somehow thrown together by fate.

It was impossible to be strong any longer. It hurt too much. She'd been maintaining the fiction against tremendous stresses, and her resources were depleted. She'd been fighting Millicent and Yancy for weeks over the inheritance, the baby, her own life. And suddenly she was tired of fighting, tired of being torn apart emotionally, unable to face the world with her old determination. She had no one to turn to now. Even Hazard would never care.

So the tears came, but she bit back the sobs. She might not have much strength left, but she had a fragment of pride.

He lay there after he heard it and wondered how long she'd been crying. She was curled away from him on the far side of the bed and he hadn't realized, hadn't heard until the small sound escaped. The windows were open to the autumn night and a breeze stirred the plain muslin curtains. Maybe the night sounds had masked the quiet crying; more likely, knowing Blaze, she'd stifled it. She wasn't the kind of woman who welcomed pity.

He hesitated only a moment, then reached out and lifted her into his arms, sliding partway up the headboard so he was holding her, all muffled in yards of nightgown, like a young child. He felt the warm tears on his bare chest, the intimacy of her soft cheek smudging the wetness against his skin, and his heart went out to her. She was unhappy, and suddenly it mattered fiercely to him.

Having Hazard hold her, his strong arms cradling her close for the first time in weeks, only forced the welling tears into a gushing flood. The revelation pervaded her mind and body and senses with awesome simplicity as she lay protected within his embrace, the sudden truth so astonishing and undeniable and frightening that she felt a transient moment of fear. For she understood at last how much she needed him, how much his caring mattered to her, how little everything in the world meant without him. How *alone* she'd been without him.

"What's wrong, *bia?* Tell me," said the soft, roughened voice. His long-boned fingers smoothed her fall-gold hair, brushed it back from her forehead with infinite care. Bending, he caressed the delicate curve of her temple. "Tell me."

She couldn't answer, overwrought, gulping for air like a child who's cried too long. He waited, holding her tightly, but carefully—infinitely less tightly than he'd like —for fear of hurting her. After so many weeks of being deprived of her warmth and softness and tangible presence, he wanted to crush her into his bones.

Her weeping quieted at last, her head resting on his shoulder, her fragile frame encircled by Hazard's strong body. "I'm tired," she said at last, bleakly, in a very tiny voice.

"I know, princess. The last days have been hell." He tugged the sheet up and wiped away her tears. Their faces were very close and Blaze's wet eyes were unbearably naked.

"I don't want to be strong," she whispered. "I can't anymore." And fresh tears flowed.

He comprehended: too many burdens too fast; more responsibility and uncertainty than a young woman should have to assume alone. "You don't have to be strong all the time, princess. Everyone gives up or falls occasionally. You were doing fine, only it was all too much, taking care of yourself and the baby, plus warding off Yancy's threats. I should have been there to fight him for you. But you're not alone anymore. I'm here now, to do the fighting. So rest; lean on me. I'll take care of you and the baby." He said it without thinking . . . and meant it, everything swept away except his need for her.

"Truly?" Blaze whispered, afraid to believe, afraid the words were only words. But hoping desperately that Jon Hazard Black was true to his character now—plain spoken, honest.

"Truly," he quietly replied. "There've been too many misunderstandings in the past. But it's over." He shook away the dark spirits. "I don't even want to think about them anymore." His hand came up and lightly brushed her cheek. "You say you don't want to be strong all the time. I, *bia-cara,* don't want to be dutiful all the time. I can't help it, I love you," he whispered. "And if I lose my protecting vision, my clan and my soul, I must have you."

"I'm yours . . . until the pines turn yellow," she softly assured him in the old Absarokee formula for infinity. "Don't ever leave me," she breathed from the safety of his arms. "Don't ever leave me. . . ."

"Never . . . starting from this minute." He lifted her face tenderly from the curve of his shoulder and touched her lips with his. "Our first night together" he murmured, and swallowed hard to keep back his own tears, "on our long and enchanted trail." His dark eyes held a potent magic as they gazed into hers. "I can fight them all, princess . . . if you're beside me."

"I am—I will—oh, Jon, I love you so." Her voice was sweet with hope. "We *can* do it, you know," she added, the old vivacious gleam in her eyes.

Always charmed by her innocent and determined optimism, Hazard generously replied, his own gaze tender, "Of course we can, Boston. With you and me against the world, how can we lose?" His answer was like that of a war-worn, worldly veteran to a fresh young recruit, unblooded yet to the small viciousnesses in man. And while he dearly hoped she was right, privately, a cautious skepticism questioned both their sanities. "Tonight, though," he quietly murmured, "we've no dragons to slay. Tonight there's only us."

"That's what Lydia said. How did she know?"

Hazard adjusted her in his arms and squeezed her lightly. "We owe the bully a lot."

"Would you have stayed with me otherwise . . . tonight, I mean?" It was a woman's question, measuring love. It was a Blaze question, straight to the mark.

He was silent for a moment, then shook his head. But his grip tightened and she knew that while the chief answered no, the man said yes.

"I never wrote that note, Jon. I didn't."

His anger flared briefly; he could set aside the demons, but not forget. That time was never really gone, even though he wanted to believe her. "It's over," he said tightly, withholding all the convoluted fragments of doubt. "I don't want to talk about it."

"I could punch you," Blaze retorted, her own sense of injustice equally thin-skinned, "when you get so damned masculine and condescending." And she suited her actions to her words.

Hazard caught her small fist easily, lightly, just short of its mark, and enveloped it in his large hand. Smiling into her heated eyes, he pleasantly declared, "I've a better idea right now. But I promise," he murmured, his mouth descending to brush hers tenderly, "you can assault my condescension afterward, if"—his tongue slid over the upper curve of her lips—"you still have the strength."

"Have you considered," Blaze whispered back teasingly, her lips wet from Hazard's leisurely roving tongue, "you might be consorting with a wicked evil woman who may have tried to kill you?"

Hazard's breath was warm on her throat as he nibbled her tender flesh. "Wicked sounds *interesting,*" he exhaled softly, sending shivers up her spine, "and evil." His dark head came up, his long lashes brushing her chin, and he looked assessingly at her exquisite blue-eyed face, fair and fresh as a spring morning. His seductive glance turned beguilingly merry and he laughed softly at her teasingly and at his own ludicrous doubts. "With you and evil, fairy princess of the May, I'll take my chances," he sportively assured her. "And the only way you can kill me tonight, sweet-scented woman," he whispered, his dark fingers unbuttoning the collar of her nightgown, "is a sweet death I welcome." Unfastening the last of the buttons, he slid the loose gown over Blaze's shoulders, his fingers splayed and drifting like silken caresses down her arms. "I've missed you like hell," he murmured. "Do you know how long it's been?" His breathing had altered, and Blaze felt his arousal come to life, felt the heat and pulsing splendor.

Her hands were being slipped free from the sleeves and she thought, as she did each time Hazard touched her, that such gentleness was like liquid pleasure. How could a man trained to warfare have hands that moved on her body like velvet? "Too long," she softly sighed, reaching up to bring his face to hers. "Way too long," she informed him in a low voice lush with promise, and holding his face with her small hands lying fragrant on his cheeks, she kissed him as if the world were going to end in the next minute. When her tongue invaded his mouth, softly demanding, his arms locked around her, one curving around her neck and shoulders strongly, pulling her closer, smothering her hair, crushing her to him with a desire unrequited for so many weeks.

What happened tonight, he thought, was past judgment or analysis, whatever the cruelties or failures. It was inevitable. And that it might be hopeless too no longer mattered. With joy he held her. With joy and disquiet and aching tenderness.

She was his wife. There was no turning back.

It was the jubilant spring of his soul's hardest winter.

It was walking on air.

It was madness.

He entered her hesitantly as if he were a young boy, uncertain. And glided into her melting moistness so slowly she protested.

"Jon," she softly cried, arching up to draw him in, demanding more, pulling him closer. He resisted briefly; she could feel the strong muscles of his back beneath her hands contract. "Please . . ."

"I don't want to hurt you," he murmured, withholding himself.

"Oh, Jon, please, *please*. You won't hurt me. It doesn't hurt. I'm going to die, Jon, if you don't let me feel you. Jon, please!"

But the "please" ended on an explosive sigh as Jon Hazard Black did what he'd been wanting to do since he first set eyes on his wayward wife in New York. He buried himself in her silky sweetness. "*Di awátsiciky* [I love you]," he breathed against her ear. He was home.

Blaze wouldn't let him go, wouldn't let him leave her. He was her lover, her friend, her husband. She wanted all his attention, and she got it. Much later that night, when Hazard rolled off her, he teasingly noted, "Only a rest, *bia* . . . don't get alarmed."

The bed was a shambles. They were both damp with sweat.

"I'd forgotten how demanding you were, puss," he mocked, stretching his arms high and flexing his back.

"Complaining?" Blaze purred, smoothing his hair slickly behind one ear.

He turned his head and looked at her. She was flushed, tousled, adorable . . . and his. "Do I," he said with a slow smile, "look like a fool?"

Chapter 41

VERY early in the morning while Blaze still slept, Hazard bathed in the creek and then ate breakfast with Lydia.

"You look as though you were able to mend your differences," she observed. Hazard's smile was contagious.

"Thanks to you."

"No thanks needed. You would have figured it out sooner or later yourself. She sleepin'?"

Hazard nodded, his mouth full of bacon and eggs.

"Don't be too hard on her, Hazard." Even under Hazard's deeply bronzed skin, the faint blush was visible. Noticing his discomfort, Lydia hastily amended, "Didn't mean that . . . meant the long trip ahead. She's not strong like a farm woman or one of your tribeswomen. She's game, mind, but those hands ain't seen no hard work—ever."

Hazard set down his fork and quietly said, "I know

that more than you do. It was one of the reasons I tried to tell myself to stay away."

"I ain't sayin' it can't work, Hazard. Just take it a mite easy at first, that's all."

"I'll try, but"—he shrugged—"they're bound to pick up the scent soon."

"Stay here if you've a mind to."

"That would only postpone it. Once we reach my people, Blaze will be safe . . . and the child."

"You're not thinking about doin' anything foolish, are you, Hazard?" She'd noticed the significant absence of his own safety factor.

"He's got to be killed eventually. Yancy Strahan's the kind who doesn't stop taking until he's dead."

"Take an old crone's advice, Hazard. Killing doesn't always tie up all the loose ends like you think."

Hazard looked up from the corn muffin he had begun buttering. "It depends," he said softly, "on who it is you kill."

"Better think of your wife and the coming babe before you get all heroic. I know you damn Crows and your sense of justice."

Hazard set down the knife and studied the butter melting on his muffin. "Right now," he said, looking up with the same grave look Lydia first saw in his dark eyes on the Powder River years ago, "I'm only interested in reaching the village safely. There's plenty of time to take on Yancy later." His mouth curved in a sudden grin. "He has to catch us first, and right now I'm hoping like hell he doesn't. And if I knew how to pray to your carpenter spirit, I'd add that prayer to mine."

"Prayer don't hurt, I suppose, but if I was a betting woman, I'd put my money on your Colts."

"Let's hope we need neither," Hazard diplomatically said, and took a bite of his muffin.

Several minutes later, after harnessing up the team, Hazard carried a sleeping Blaze out to the carriage.

"Safe journey," Lydia called to Hazard as he climbed aboard the driver's seat.

Hazard waved and blew her a kiss. Then the whip snapped over the horses' heads and the closed carriage rolled out of the farmyard. Following Lydia's instructions, Hazard traveled off the main roads. At noon when Blaze woke they stopped at a stream to refresh themselves and the horses. After eating the lunch Lydia had prepared, Blaze put on traveling clothes and climbed up top with Hazard. They traveled the remainder of the day on sparsely populated byways, but by nightfall the settlements had fallen away and only the main routes west were left.

Leaving Blaze inside the carriage with the curtains drawn, Hazard drove into the next stage station, a small village with no more than a dozen families, and bargained for a stage, a team and two drivers. From here on, there was only one road west, and Yancy would know it if he trailed them to this point. They'd have to run like hell to the borders of Absarokee territory.

No one questioned the Indian dressed like a white man. Gold was the universal voice of commerce on the prairie, and the fabulous strikes in Montana the last three years had made idiosyncratic behavior common. Gold spoke volumes. And Hazard had plenty of gold in his saddlebags. Some might covetously eye the heavy saddlebags and the single man holding them, but he carried a dangerous aura about him and wore his guns down low like the gunfighters did who lived long lives. With such palpable strengths no one dared lay a hand on him, so Hazard, authoritative and roughly dressed for riding, got his stage and team and two drivers.

And no one remarked on the request for two pillows any more than they did the quietly spoken order for grapes. They managed to find some at Widow Brown's, and the tall Indian said thank you softly and paid Widow Brown twice what she was asking.

It was almost dusk when they started out again, the dying light of the setting sun a dim glow on the horizon. Hazard rode inside that night, having left instructions to drive straight through. With two drivers, they could spell each other, and Hazard descended at each stage station to bargain for the fresh horses. He always carefully selected them with an eye to stamina and speed.

Traveling by stage on a well-traveled road was his

idea of the worst possible way to avoid Yancy and his trackers, but with Blaze he didn't have much choice. He always bought the best food he could at the stops and only dozed occasionally once Blaze went to sleep. They could make it to Absarokee land in six hard-driving days from here if they were lucky, and he figured he could sleep after that.

It was midafternoon of the second day on the stage road when he sighted the faint cloud of dust on the horizon behind them. He climbed on top of the stage and watched the landscape behind them for perhaps twenty minutes. They were so far behind that if he hadn't been trained as a scout, taught to read the most minute changes on the horizon, they wouldn't have been visible at all.

From the dimension of the dust cloud being raised, Hazard guessed maybe eight or ten men. And they were riding hard; maybe an hour, he estimated, before they were distinct enough to count.

Climbing forward on the stage roof, he explained what he was going to do to the two drivers and reviewed what he expected of them—for a generous bonus, of course.

Swinging down through the window, Hazard proceeded to apprise Blaze of their situation. He was calm, explaining that the trackers were a good hour behind. He was also pulling off his boots.

"How many?" Blaze asked.

"Eight, maybe ten. But don't worry," he quickly said when he saw the panic rising in her eyes. "They're going to have to split up to come after us." He slid his moccasins on and retied his small sack. "They're not going to know whether we left the stage or the drivers did. And if we run into a real streak of luck, they may not notice our tracks at all. There's a creek coming up, and if I can get the horses cut out fast enough, we'll head out that way. Now give me a kiss, *bia*, and be ready to go out that door when I ride up."

The kiss was sweet and warm. "We can do it," Hazard reassured her, throwing the strap of his leather satchel over one shoulder and heaving the saddlebags over the other. He smiled a quick encouragement and then pulled himself up and out the window. He hung for a moment or two, his moccasins visible, their red-beaded fringe swinging, before he secured his grip and swung atop the stage.

"Just remember to go full speed to the next station," Hazard reminded the drivers before he launched himself with a light leap onto the back of the nearest offside horse. Balancing for a brief moment, with what was incredible poise, Hazard jumped over to the middle offside bay and without hesitation, as though he were walking on solid land, leaped aboard the leader. His knife was in his hand before he was fully astride, hacking away at the harness connecting the leader with the middle team. Six economical slashing strokes later, he pulled the lead team free of the swiftly racing stage with Herculean strength and a miraculous finesse.

The two horses ran alongside their stablemates for the time it took Hazard to cut away the excess tack, but the sudden lightening of the controlling leathers bewildered them and they fell behind. With the lead reins still in place, Hazard guided the leader he was mounted on, pulling the second horse in their wake with its reins twisted twice around his wrist. As he kicked his mount into more speed, they soon caught up to the stage; but he had to manhandle the frightened animal over to the stagecoach door against the wheel noise and flapping door that was spooking it.

Hazard glanced ahead once, briefly, gauging the distance to the creek just this side of the approaching rise.

Clutching both sides of the door frame on the wildly careening stage being whipped along at the full-out gallop Hazard had ordered, Blaze had watched Hazard cut the horses loose, her heart in her throat. It was impossible, she thought the whole time he was dancing atop the horses' backs like an acrobat; he was going to fall and kill himself; he was going to be crushed by the back teams before he could pull the confused horses free; then, dear God, he was free. He slowly drew near over the lost ground and, yanking at the terrified horse, forced it to within a foot of the swaying coach. Then he moved it up parallel with Blaze and the door.

He had only one free hand, since unlike Indian ponies, which could be guided by the rider's knees, Hazard's horse needed a firm hand on the reins. But he steadied the frightened horse for ten galloping yards alongside the stage and then, leaning over, gripped Blaze securely around the waist and shouted "Jump" through the noise and dust.

He had her. Five seconds later the stage had whipped past and, slowing the horses slightly, he swung Blaze across his lap. He was smiling. "Said we could, didn't I?"

"You're a maniac," she remonstrated. But she was smiling too.

"*Your* maniac, until we cross the slippery log, darling," he reminded her with a teasing lift of his eyebrows and a nervy smile.

"My Lord, I'm going to have my hands full."

"Lucky girl," he mockingly teased, then, setting his gaze on the rough wash ahead, whipped the horse, forcing it into the creek. "Can you ride for an hour or so?" he asked once his mount was safely splashing through the shallow stream.

"More if necessary."

"I've orders from Lydia . . . so we'll start slow." The next hour would be the critical one anyway, Hazard thought, but he didn't tell Blaze that. If they were followed, they'd know in an hour. And if they were followed, they'd know by how many of the men. And if they were followed, they'd have to stand and fight because Blaze didn't have the stamina to ride day and night to stay ahead of professional trackers.

Making sure Blaze was comfortably seated on his mount, Hazard pulled the second horse up and swung across to it. He kicked his horse into the lead, and Blaze followed him down the shallow, sparkling creek.

Chapter 42 ⌘

IN THE country north of the Platte and south of the Powder[22] River, the prairie gave way to rolling hills and patches of badlands. Hazard had his eye on an outcropping of rock used for generations of Indians as a lookout, and after almost an hour of riding, they eased their horses out of the creek onto coarse river-washed gravel that left few traces or tracks. The rugged needle of sandstone towered over them, casting long shadows of shade over the cottonwood and willow scrub beneath it.

Settling Blaze in the cool shade, Hazard scrambled up the rough pinnacle of pale yellow stone. Looking back the way they'd come, it didn't take him long to spot them. Four. He counted them twice before carefully surveying the surrounding country to see if any more were riding flank positions. No more, he noted with reflexive exhalation of relief.

They were coming up the creek slowly, checking for signs, and although he had tried to be careful, any tracker with experience could follow them. The danger set his adrenaline pumping, and he forced himself to stay calm. If they'd only had a day's start, he thought, even a half a day's, they might have made it into Lakota territory. And while it would have been dangerous for them to traverse the Absarokee's enemy's land, it would have been infinitely more dangerous for the four heavily armed trackers. Weapons, new weapons, were always at a premium in the Indian tribes, and such rich spoil would have been sighted within five miles. Either the Lakota would have taken care of Hazard's problem for him or the trackers would have turned back. His eyes searched the surrounding countryside . . . he needed a special place to ambush four well-armed men.

After several minutes of scrutiny, he was forced to conclude that the outcropping offered the only opportunity, something he must have realized an hour ago. Not a first choice, by anyone with options, but for them an only choice.

Sliding down the steep incline in a swift descent of tumbling gravel, he helped Blaze climb the rocky treacherous trail and concealed her safely behind a natural redoubt. "Stay down," he instructed. "Don't make any noise. I'll be back in a few minutes."

"Do we have a chance? The truth, please," she said, her expression a curious combination of fear and challenge.

He sighed and looked away, contemplating the lie. But he changed his mind. His dark gaze returned to her face and he said simply, "A slight chance. Can you shoot?"

Blaze took a deep steadying breath, her eyes on the man she wanted to live a long and happy life with, and reaching deep for a courage she'd never had to call on before, said, "Moderately. Target practice, that sort of thing."

"If you have to, can you do it?"

She knew what he was asking. It was their lives at stake. "Yes," she said, "if I have to."

He smiled, a quick flash, gone almost before she saw it. "Good. Take the rifle, then. I'll be back in a few min-

utes. I'm going to try to split them up so we can get two
of them before they have time to reach cover. Then the
odds will be even and I'll feel a helluva lot better."

"There're four?"

He was checking the ammunition in his Colts and
only nodded. "Don't move from here," he said, looking
up, "until I get back."

"If you get back," she very softly replied, a sadness
clear as bell sound in her voice.

"When," he emphatically repeated. "My word on it.
Now get down and watch the creek at the spot we came
ashore. I'm going to leave one of our horses down there
and another at the base of the outcropping. The trackers
may separate to approach them. At least I'm hoping like
hell they're cautious enough to."

STANDING in the middle of the stream, Hazard
wedged one rein between two large rocks, nudged the
horse over a few feet so the rein was taut, and left the
second rein trailing in the water. He was hoping to create
the impression the horse had snagged itself to a standstill
accidentally. It was not very subtle but sometimes, when
one was being extra wary as he hoped the trackers were,
even the obvious was suspect. The other horse he left
loose in a small clearing near the outcropping. The grass
was thick and lush; the horse wouldn't wander.

Climbing back up, he relieved Blaze of the rifle, settled them safely behind the redoubt, and sighted in on
the horse standing in the middle of the stream. He had to
take out at least two of them right away. Motioning Blaze
to silence, he sat waiting.

He recognized the lead tracker when they came into
sight—a half-blooded Cheyenne named Hyde who'd
fought with Price's Army in the war. He hired out as
scout or tracker now. The Mexican, known as Montero,
"The Huntsman" rode with him, two paces back. Behind
were two white men, large, dressed in eastern riding
wear, obviously Yancy's men. Hazard knew the two in the
lead could track a sandpiper over solid granite washed
clean in a rainstorm. It at least obliterated any doubts

about their options. With those two, they couldn't have run. They might as well make their stand here.

He knew whom he had to kill first. Hyde's reputation as a butcher with a knife made him most dangerous. The Mexican had handled a killing or two in his past as well; he'd have to be next. They were approaching the horse in the stream as if it were booby-trapped.

About ten more yards and he'd have an unobstructed shot. Hazard could hear Blaze breathing, his own respiration momentarily arrested. He counted the paces in his head as the men moved upstream. *Come on, come on,* he was silently urging. *Five more steps . . . four . . . three . . . keep going, Hyde . . . keep going—* And then his trigger finger squeezed hard once, twice. Pandemonium erupted in the stream, two bodies fell, horses squealed, reared, the white men jerked their mounts around and raced for cover. Hazard pressed off two more shots but they were just a gesture—there wasn't enough time to sight. He was lucky to have gotten the two. "Now," he said, turning to Blaze, "the fun begins."

"Yancy's men?"

"Exactly, how moderate is your shooting?"

"I only said moderate in contrast to the dazzling displays your Absarokee so effortlessly perform on galloping war ponies." She smiled, the old assurance replacing the previous fear.

He was pleasantly surprised. "I didn't realize you had any modesty." He grinned. Home seemed more certain every second.

"Only practical, love. I was answering your question with your standards in mind. From a steady vantage point, very much *not* a galloping pony, Daddy taught me to shoot out the bull's-eye ninety times out of a hundred."

Hazard looked at the mother of his child dressed in calico and decided he was a very lucky man. "You never cease to amaze me."

She shot him a telling glance. "In the interest of continuing that pleasure, tell me how we're going to get out of here."

He exhaled softly and began ticking them off on his

fingers, casting a glance occasionally at the wooded area where Yancy's two men were hidden. "No food, no water, we can't stay up here long; they can wait us out; they have time; we don't. When Yancy discovers we're not on the stage, he'll be back tracking at top speed. I'm going down and get them. You take the rifle and cover me." He waited and she nodded. "We're short of time. Yancy could be backtracking already. It's about four hours into the Lakota hunting grounds. From there I'll get us home. Shoot straight," he softly said and slipped over the side so quickly and quietly he seemed to disappear right before her eyes.

Her rifle poised on a large boulder, Blaze crouched down so only her eyes scanned the country below. For ten minutes she didn't hear a sound or see any movement other than those normal to the woodland, although she knew Hazard was down there somewhere.

Then suddenly Hazard catapulted into the clearing between the outcropping and the creek. His reckless maneuver drew both men to their feet from their concealed positions. Frantically Blaze searched for her front sight. At last, after what seemed a lifetime, she managed to catch it and sighted in on the man behind and to the left of Hazard. There was no time left to think, only react. She pulled the trigger as Hazard rolled to his right with both his Colts blazing at the man in front of him.

Ravens and finches squawked and fluttered their disapproval at the hail of gunfire tearing up the underbrush, their scolding falling into a deathly silence. When the smoke cleared, Hazard cautiously uncurled from behind a windfall and, rising, walked slowly over to the two white men, his pistols drawn, to make certain they were dead. He did the same for the two trackers face down in the creek.

Then he turned to Blaze standing high against the blue sky and blew her a kiss.

Within ten minutes they were heading north-northwest, four additional horses tied behind with food, weapons, supplies, enough to last them home. Blaze had changed into the leather trousers Hazard had purchased for her at their last stage station, and she looked comfortable astride the Indian pony once belonging to the half-blooded Hyde. "I'll take you for backup any day, Miss Venetia," Hazard drawled, a warm, encompassing smile taking in her new apparel and exotic beauty. They were cantering knee to knee through waving buffalo grass, with a light wind in their faces. "If I'd known Boston society misses were so damnably accomplished I'd have considered some of the other debs more seriously."

"For your information, the rest aren't similarly accomplished, so you can dismiss all those old memories. I, Mr. Black," she replied in a primly mocking affectation of a Boston deb, "am singular in my accomplishments."

"No quarrel there, *bia.*" And Hazard reached over to give her an affectionate brush on the cheek. "Singular in every way." She was fire and ice, steel and gossamer. He adored her. He smiled. She smiled. They were at peace with the world, with themselves, even though they were about to enter enemy territory.

They spoke quietly, haphazardly, in the next hour about their immediate plans—the next three days' plans when they'd cut through Lakota country. By unspoken but mutual consent, neither marred the serenity with any long-range plans.

Yancy was still alive, Blue Flower was in the mountain village waiting for her bridegroom to return, Blaze had forfeited her inheritance, and Hazard's mine would require weeks of unbearably hard work to reopen. It was in the way of love that, at that moment, even such shattering obstacles couldn't impinge on their happiness.

Once they reached the Powder River country, they only traveled by day; Hazard knew of shelters in badland caves and harsh ravines where they were safe from any normal scrutiny. It was against his principles to dally on dangerous journeys such as theirs—against his principles, better judgment, and training—but Blaze wanted to be held while she slept and he'd never been able to refuse her. So he indulged her, with one eye on the approaches to their shelter, and after she was sated and sleeping, when he sat watch, he'd think about how she'd come into his life and changed so much, the changes both had brought to each other's lives. And he thought about his child. His child's imperiled future terrified him beyond the limitless joy the child itself evoked. In the previous three years more whites had settled in Montana than in the last three million years. And the settlers never left once they came. The miners left when the gold was gone but not the farmers.

While The Seven Stars—the Big Dipper—turned around The Star That Does Not Move—the North Star —and the night moved westward, Hazard, sitting awake, staring into the darkness and listening to the even breathing of the woman he loved, wondered how long there would still be choices for his people before a gener ation would come, born into captivity. And then a weariness would assail him, a seasoned warrior born too late. Too late to live his life out in the old ways. Too late to stop the inexorable tides of civilization. Too late to know the peace of his father in a land dark with buffalo and plenty.

And then, when the universal issues were left unexplained, uncertain, and undealt with, the less universal remained—imminent and spectacular—how to handle his wife-to-be, Blue Flower.

Chapter 43

IN FOUR more days that issue faced him squarely as he and Blaze rode into the village, weary but alive. Hazard was almost to the point of exhaustion. It had been nearly a month since he'd slept more than snatched hours here and there. And in the last few days, he'd carried Blaze when she tired, watched over her while she slept, gave her the bulk of their food.

In his weariness, more short-tempered than usual, he was hoping they could reach the security of his lodge and sleep for a few hours before he confronted Blue Flower. When they reached his lodge, however, Blue Flower was waiting at the doorway, beautifully dressed like a young bride, smiling her welcome. Calling on what few reserves of restraint he still possessed, Hazard very deliberately, in a subdued voice, said to Blaze, pleadingly, "You're tired. I'm tired. This is a very large favor I'm asking, but if you'd do it for me without argument, I'd be eternally grateful."

Blaze turned her head, saw the fatigue on his face, heard it in his husky voice, looked into his dark eyes trained expectantly on her.

"Please," was all he said, low, gently, poignant in its need.

She mutely nodded her consent and Hazard smiled his thanks. A frugal smile, symptomatic of his exhaustion.

"Will I have to sleep in the same lodge as—" Blaze's glance took in the young girl standing possessively by Hazard's lodge.

"No," he quickly interposed. "But I might have to be gone for a few hours. I was hoping this would wait until"—he paused and exhaled—"later." His explanation to Blue Flower and her family would tax the most adroit diplomat, and Hazard knew he was too tired to be at his best. But, he thought, squaring his shoulders, it had to be done.

"I wish I could say I'm sorry, but I'm not," Blaze said. "I would have fought for you. I still will if I have to." Her lush cerulean eyes glimmered hotly.

Among all the other things he loved about her, Hazard loved her intrinsic strength. Here was a woman as strong and determined as he. In all places in the world, through fate's most convoluted machinations, he'd met his match. And in the mystic core of his being, he gave thanks to the spirits. He smiled a little when he answered. "That won't be necessary, *bia*. But thank you. I would fight for you as well." Something, he reflected, he was just about to do.

Before he greeted Blue Flower, he lifted Blaze down from her pony, a quiet opening statement of his intent. It was also the first move in the complex procedures to follow, and he wanted his intentions clearly visible to the village.

When he greeted Blue Flower a moment later, the adoration in her eyes was momentarily disconcerting. He had forgotten, with his own private disinterest, that polygamy was an accepted fact in a female's education. Some liked it less than others, while many who were sisters lived happily and harmoniously with the same husband. A woman's own nature determined her acceptance. He had also forgotten, he recalled with dismay, how passive, how *young* Blue Flower was.

She opened the lodge door for Hazard and Blaze and followed them in. His home was immaculate, food was cooking on the fire, his clothes were all neatly arranged near his bed. Even his favorite medicine bundle was hanging in the place of honor. He briefly—and uneasily—wondered how she knew so much about him.

"Lie down, eat, rest. I'll be back," he murmured to Blaze, and turning to Blue Flower he spoke rapidly to her in Absarokee. Formally, he apologized for his appearance, thanked her for keeping his lodge in his absence, and then asked her if she would walk with him.

She accepted, pleased to be seen with her betrothed before the village, acquiescent by nature and agreeable to any request he might have made. He walked with her to her father's lodge and, after a lengthy welcome which Hazard was obligated to endure in the name of courtesy and which further depleted his resources of energy and diplomacy, he put forward his proposal. Somewhat more bluntly than he'd planned. Somewhat more precipitately than he'd intended. Sweetened with an enormous gift, much more lavish than necessary.

But he was driven by fatigue and urgency, beyond sensible calculations of propriety. And he felt more guilt than anticipated. Blue Flower's expression was artless in its worship. He gave them his entire herd of horses, keeping only Peta and the palomino he'd given Blaze. He apologized for his rough manners; it was impolite to offer a gift directly. He should have gone through a relative, but he'd been on the trail for twenty-eight days, he said, and hoped they'd forgive the rudeness.

Bold Ax remembered Hazard's first refusal and understood his heart now. He knew Hazard's honor and integrity, knew his daughter was too young and beautiful to be seriously affected. He accepted Hazard's proposal with good grace. Blue Flower was crying, though, when Hazard left, and he felt a sharp twinge of unease at her tears.

*   *   *

"IT'S over," Hazard said when he walked back into his lodge.

"Thank God," Blaze softly breathed.

"Thank Bold Ax for his understanding," Hazard replied, hauling his shirt over his head. "It could have caused hard feelings for years." He kicked off his moccasins and fell down on the bed. "I'm too tired to bathe." He shut his eyes and breathed deeply twice, then opened his eyes and said, "Sorry."

"You're forgiven." Blaze was sitting cross-legged beside him, having spent the last hour waiting, unmoving, trying to anticipate what was going on, frantic to know, terrified to know.

"Have you eaten?"

Blaze nodded.

"I'm too tired to eat."

"You shouldn't go without—"

His dark, slim hand went up and his midnight glance silently stopped her. "Just because you're my only wife now," Hazard said, a boyish smile gracing his classic features, attenuated by the fatigue of his cross-country journey, "does not entitle you to nag."

"How about friendly persuasion?" Blaze countered with the faintest of grins, never in the least intimidated by Hazard.

"That's allowable," he replied, his arms opening wide, his smile crinkling his eyes half-shut.

"*How* friendly?" Blaze teased, falling into his embrace.

"Your usual friendly will do nicely. And an extra-friendly friendly wouldn't be out of line on this single occasion in our life when I've diminished my wealth by three hundred horses to maintain your position of only wife." It was an unheard-of gesture of apology, costing him all his horses.

"Three hundred horses?" Blaze repeated, astonished.

"Every one I owned, save Peta and your palomino."

"That's rather sweet." She kissed him lightly. "Just think, I'm worth three hundred horses."

"The first solid night of sleep in twenty-eight days was worth three hundred horses," he mockingly retorted.

"Are you really going to sleep *all* night?" Blaze quickly asked in a touchingly doleful way.

He looked at her. At the woman he'd traveled four thousand miles for, had fought and killed for, the woman he'd paid three hundred horses for, who'd almost cost him his life. He looked at the woman who made life worth living and smiled. "An hour?" he indulgently inquired.

Chapter 44

IT WAS only the time when wild geese fly south to the winter sun, but the first snow came early in November that year and postponed Hazard's plans to reopen the mine. With the arriving snows, the clan broke up into smaller units, migrating to sheltered locations in the Wind River Valley where hunting and grazing for the horses was made easier. Hazard and Blaze chose to go into winter camp alone.

He didn't mind that his plans had been altered by the early blizzards. The mines everywhere were shut down for the winter; mining needed water to operate, and once the rivers and streams were frozen, operations ceased. He and Blaze welcomed the peace and solitude. They had stayed a month in camp but were now snug in a small mountain valley with enough buffalo grass to last their two horses the winter, and a stream he chopped open daily for their water and his bathing. Hazard had improvised a buffalo-skin tub for Blaze supported on a

folding wooden framework and rubbed with tallow until
the hide was waterproof. In the evenings he'd watch her
bathe or help her bathe by the light of the fire and watch
his child growing. They had food in good supply, enough
firewood on the mountainside to last several lifetimes,
fur-lined moccasins, and warm buffalo robes. The lodge,
heated by a fire, was snug and warm against snow, wind
and cold. So when snows covered the mountainsides and
every twig and tree and bush snapped with cold and even
the rushing waters of the Echeta Casha were frozen over,
their short winter days by the Yellowstone were theirs
alone.

They had books to read; he taught her some Absarokee gambling games, and she taught him bridge with
a set of cards she made. She was learning Absarokee and
improving as a cook, although Hazard still did a healthy
share of the meal-making. Hazard made them a sled
from a hollow log, and on warm afternoons they went
skimming down the powdery snow on the mountainside.

Their winter alone was one long honeymoon—perfect, joyous, distant from the outside world, with love and
their child growing strong and healthy amid the mountain splendor of Hazard's homeland.

At Christmas the mercury was stagnant at twenty
below and the sky had been clear with Northern Lights
for a week. Hazard brought in a small pine tree for
Blaze, and she trimmed it with ribbon bows and strings
of berries. On Christmas Eve, Blaze insisted he unwrap
his present first and, like a young child, eyes alight with
the pleasure of giving, she watched him carefully undo
the small fur-wrapped package. She had unstrung her
black pearls and sewn them in a flower pattern on Hazard's ceremonial tobacco pouch. The stitches were irregular and knotted in places—she had never acquired the
necessary skill as a child, much preferring less sedentary
pursuits—and all the imperfections of her rudimentary
sewing technique were candidly exposed on the fine light
leather. Hazard touched the asymmetrical flower, the
petals tilted slightly lower on one side than the other, ran
his slim fingers lightly over the precious black pearls, and
looked up at his beloved wife, her expression expectant

with anticipation, and softly said, "It's the most beautiful tobacco pouch I've ever seen. When I wear it at the ceremony in the spring, everyone will be green with envy." She was radiant with happiness, and he had never loved her so much. "Open mine," he gently prompted her, nodding at the large deerskin-wrapped bundle he'd placed beside her. It hadn't been intended as a Christmas gift, but when Blaze started very early talking about Christmas, he'd saved it to give her then.

In her excitement, she struggled with the leather ties until Hazard calmly helped undo the knots. Seconds later the deerskin was tossed aside and even the millionaire's daughter was momentarily at a loss for words. Silently she unfurled the lush ermine until it was spread in a large opulent drapery across her lap. "It's magnificent," she whispered at last. "Absolutely magnificent." Hundreds of skins had been sewn, with stitches so fine they were invisible, into a flowing hooded cape, lined in black velvet embroidered in traditional Absarokee geometric patterns.

"Put it on. I hope it fits." Standing, he scooped it up and held it out for her.

It fell gently around her shoulders. Grasping it under her chin, she swung in a slow circle before Hazard, the supple fur gleaming in the firelight.

"It fits," he drily commented, "my Boston princess."

"How did you ever think of it?" Blaze asked, burying her chin in the plush softness.

"Couldn't have my princess cold this winter. There's something in the pocket, too," he added.

Blaze slid her hand into the deep inner pocket and pulled out a small birch-bark box. Lifting the cover, she found a tiny pearl on a gold chain lying on soft green moss. "It's very lovely," she said, lifting the locket out.

"Do you recognize it?" Hazard asked.

She looked at him, faintly perplexed. Although she had pearls in her jewelry collection, she'd never had a single pearl. "Should I?" she asked.

"It's from your dress. . . ."

"The Territorial Ball!"

"I found it after you fled from the summer kitchen. I

don't know—didn't know why I saved it then. The spirits must have known even that night how our lives would turn out. It was the first time I kissed you. Do you remember?"

She nodded. "No one had ever kissed me like that before."

"I'd never kissed anyone like that before," said Hazard, the man who had been a favorite of all the women in his life.

"Show me again," she impishly said, moving a step nearer.

"With pleasure," he murmured, taking her in his arms. "Merry Christmas, *bia-cara.* And may we have a thousand more."

"Next year we'll have another person to buy presents for," she reminded him."

"How nice," he said simply, but his heart was overflowing with his love of her. "Now kiss me and I'll see if you've improved," he teased, "since that June night in Virginia City."

"You know I'm the best you've ever had," she retorted with sweet arrogance.

"I know," he said very, very softly, and kissed her.

IT WAS a night early in March with a blizzard blowing in over the mountains when Blaze woke Hazard and said, "I feel funny."

He was fully awake before she'd finished speaking. I shouldn't have given in to her, was his first panic-stricken reaction. We shouldn't be up here alone, with the midwife at Beaver Dam. "What feels funny?" he calmly asked even though his pulse was racing.

"I don't know. I can't sleep. My back aches."

"Let me rub it. Turn on your other side . . . here? Does that feel better?"

"Ummmm, better."

Hazard remembered Yellow Shield's words. "Her back will ache, down low. You'll know then, it's started." They'd both talked to the midwife, the medicine woman in their village, last fall. She had explained what to expect, had given instructions on the birthing. Blaze had been the one who wanted to be alone, who wanted Hazard to deliver the baby, who didn't want some stranger alone with her when she gave birth. Hazard had tried to talk her out of it, had seriously argued with her about it, didn't feel competent to handle the procedure. But he'd given in eventually when he saw how important it was to her. After the time Yellow Shield had come to the lodge and described what would happen so he and Blaze would know what to do, Hazard had walked the old woman back to her own lodge. "Now tell me about the problems," he had said. "If we're up there alone, I have to know." So she had, Hazard had written everything down and memorized it. Since then he'd gone over Yellow Shield's advice a hundred times in his mind. He'd made all the preparations weeks ago, digging away the snow and gathering the sweet sage and ground cedar they'd need, making sure they had plenty of containers for warm water, checking and rechecking the soft furs the baby would need.

Soon they were both sure Blaze's contractions had started, and Hazard lifted her to her feet. "You have to walk now."

"I don't much feel like it. Tell me everything's going to be fine."

"Everything will. Walk now, *bia*. Please. Lean on me." So they walked, stopping occasionally for Hazard to rub Blaze's back and legs, and when the pains came too fast and hard and Blaze couldn't walk anymore, he carried her over to the buffalo robes stacked between the two stakes driven into the ground. Lowering her to a kneeling position, he leaned her against the robes piled up before her. "Hold on to the stakes. Put your elbows on these robes here. I love you." Oh, damn, he thought, terrified, how in the world were they going to manage?

Now, Yellow Shield had said, you can feed her the medicine. Hazard had asked for something to relieve the pain. "She's healthy," he had explained to the old medicine woman, "but not used to hardship, not raised like us to withstand pain and discomfort. I want something to help her." So he spooned the juice of the *batsé kice* weed into Blaze's mouth a spoonful at a time to mitigate the pain.

After that, Blaze existed in a pleasant, misty haze, neither celestial nirvana nor the harsh aching hurt of moments before, but something midway between and manageable. The medicine tasted of licorice and took away all sense of fear. Hazard was with her, she was healthy and strong, and whenever she opened her eyes from the internal world in which she was floating, Hazard was there to smile or kiss her or murmur words of love. It was his spirit in her, their child she was bringing into the world and, like its father, there was a gentleness now, even in its journey into life. She had heard much about the pain, the horror, the danger, had felt the first licking daggers of agony. But little of it continued for her now.

"Another spoonful, *bia,*" Hazard would whisper, his breath warm on her cheek, his fingers smoothing the curls away from her face. And when she'd open her mouth, he'd spoon in another portion of the sweet syrup. "I love you, angel. You're doing just fine."

He'd been warned about the dosage, so he watched her eyes and pulse and timed the contractions. But he didn't want Blaze in misery, didn't want to be the cause of any hurt, so he carefully balanced on the fine line between too much and too little. Occasionally, he'd say, "Open your eyes, love," so he could check her pupils, and Blaze would languidly obey, her lashes sweeping slowly upward, revealing deep blue, velvety eyes.

"I can feel the baby," she'd say. "We're going to have a baby." And she would smile and ask to be kissed.

If Hazard could have given her the world and the sun and the stars then, he would have. She was in his heart, inhabiting his soul, more important to him than his own life. He'd kiss her with a quiet intensity that sang through both their senses.

"I can feel your love, too, and the baby's. Aren't we lucky, Jon?" Her heavy lashes rose, and blue eyes warm as sunlight gazed out at him.

Hazard blinked back the wetness stinging his eyes. Lucky—it was such an American word, effortless, genial. Less than what he felt, puny and small against the fullness of his senses, but he smiled back into the radiant eyes and obligingly agreed. "Lucky . . . the luckiest people on earth," he whispered.

And at the end, when even the sweet syrup couldn't smother the stabbing torment that gained over mind and tissue and nerve like an avalanche, Blaze was suddenly afraid and screamed for him.

Hazard, gripped by his own panic, forced the words to be soothing. "I'm here, love. Open your eyes. I'm here." But for all his calmness, he was frightened for the first time in his life. He could lose her. Terrifying memories whispered through his mind, "I'll never leave you, *bia-cara*. I'm here." And when his fingers gently touched her brow, her taut, frenzied body relaxed.

When the baby's head appeared, Hazard's heart was pumping so furiously he could feel the blood coursing through his veins. Blaze was panting, her pale hands grasping the stakes tightly, her mind focused on the corroding, clawing contraction. And then a small shoulder slid free and, moments later, Hazard measured off three fingers on the wet umbilical cord, cut through it, and held his son. He was small, perfect, lazily sucking his thumb, his eyes tightly shut, immune to the world he had just entered, content and placid. Hazard smiled at the wet scrap of humanity, small enough to sleep comfortably in his two large hands, smiled his own smile of contentment, and whispered, "Welcome, *barā' kbatsë*, to your world."

Wrapping him temporarily in a small lambskin, Hazard settled Blaze comfortably on the bed of robes and waited for her to open her eyes. "We have a son," he said, grinning from ear to ear.

He presented the boy to Blaze, who instantly said, "He's the handsomest baby in creation, and the strongest and the best, the most wonderful. Don't you think?" Her eyes were soft with love.

"Absolutely the best, *bia-cara*. A miracle that's entered my life, like you."

"Don't ever leave me," Blaze whispered, suddenly frightened by so much happiness.

"Never, kitten."

She gazed up at him and felt as though her heart would burst. "Tell me things will work out . . . for our son." She needed the reassurance. Alone with Hazard, away from the fractious world, she knew unadulterated bliss, and she wanted as much for her son.

"It will. I'll make it work." His voice was low and determined. Then he smiled faintly. "Remember, Boston, with you at my side, we can take on the world."

They laughed together, feeling, in the afterglow of their son's birth, warm and blessed and invincible.

Blaze gazed down at the baby at her side and said half in astonishment and half seriously, "He's awfully small."

Hazard's lips twitched. "Something you should be grateful for, child. Your labor was as long as I would ever care to endure."

Blaze looked up. "Were you frightened?"

"I'd rather face a thousand Lakota. Does that answer your question?" His voice was without its familiar mocking irony. "You're very courageous, darling," he said softly, reaching out a hand to touch her cheek. "Thank you . . . for our son."

"You're very welcome, now that it's all over," Blaze replied. She was holding a tiny hand in hers and tugged it gently. "Do you think he might open his eyes soon?"

Hazard laughed at the artless naiveté. "You can be certain of that, love."

"I'm going to sit and watch him. Will it take long?"

"Why don't you sleep while you can? When he does wake, he's going to want to be fed."

"Oh," Blaze said, then smiled and added, "I knew that."

Hazard's grin was enchanting. "Good, because I can't do that for you. Cooking and cleaning I can manage, but you're on your own there."

"Will you help?"

"Yes, lazy child," he gently replied, his glance warm. "In any way I can." Then he bathed Blaze and put her to sleep near the fire.

While Blaze dozed, he carefully bathed his son, greased him and dusted him from his hips to his knees with a fine powder Yellow Shield had given him. Conscientiously following the instructions he'd memorized in the preceding weeks, he next put a layer of buffalo hair all around the child's body and wrapped him in soft buckskin before laying him on a strip of stiff buffalo rawhide to keep his little head from falling backward. After that, he wrapped his son in tanned calfskin and held him in his arms, talking to him, firelight illuminating one dark head bent over another, very much smaller one.

It was nonsense and baby words, part low crooning spirit song and some quiet spoken promise. "There will be no Trail of Tears for you, *barā' kbatsë*, my son. The land of your ancestors will be yours. The rights and privileges of a chief's son will be yours." Hazard's face was filled with pain and resoluteness and a desire, strongwilled as his heart. "I will not fail you." The hunger of his ambition for his child was fused with a restless yearning that his country and people could spring free from the exploitation and struggles he knew they faced.

And he allowed himself to dream for a moment— his cherished dream, a dream of unity in which all races could live in peace. It comforted him at the moment of his son's birth even though he knew it was an unlikely vision of the future. Peace would come at a heavy price, he suspected, to be paid yearly and daily until the spirits called.

But he dreamed his dream anyway, in the glowing happiness that inundated his senses. And all the time he'd been speaking to his son, telling him of his love and wishes and hopes, he was unaware his face was being bathed by unheeded tears. "Beloved son," he whispered, and bending his head kissed his small son softly. They were a family.

THEIR child's name came as gently as his birth. He was the treasure of their hearts, the sum and differences of their spirits melded into one being and unconditionally loved. He became Baula-shela, Golden Treasure —abbreviated very quickly with everyday usage into Trey. His eyes when he opened them several hours after his birth were neither dark like his father's nor sapphire blue like his mother's. They were, when they steadied themselves into a constant color several weeks later, a pale silver warmed with scintillating flashes of hazel. His hair, although dark, was downy silk now, not yet the heavy black satin of his father's. His small nose was straight and pure refinement, and he favored his father in bone structure and size. But the silver eyes were like restless tides as he grew, and the silken brows and thick lashes framing them held the bold sensuousness of his mother's.

"He's yours, all right," Blaze remarked the first time he demanded his supper.

Hazard was sprawled out near the fire. "I never once considered denying paternity, love. And haven't I been a perfect father?" he teased.

"Personally, I find perfection revolting, so don't expect any compliments," Blaze cheerfully retorted.

"What can I say? You yellow eyes just don't come up to our high standards," he mildly challenged with a gleam in his eyes. While a facetious comment, it was true that Hazard's personal standards had always acknowledged only the exceptional.

"Maybe not, but some of us yellow eyes make beautiful babies, you must agree," Blaze brightly returned.

Hazard eased himself out of his lazy sprawl and sat straight-backed across the fire from Blaze, holding Trey to her breast. "No argument there," he quietly said, adoration in his eyes. "Absolutely none."

EACH night all Trey's dressing was removed, he was washed, greased again, and left to kick up his heels while his mother and father played with him and talked to him and he talked back in irresistible gurgles. They marveled at his eyes, bright and alert in the firelight, exclaimed over the perfection of his tiny fingernails or toes or lashes, and decided, unanimously, that he really was a treasure.

"Are all babies so adorable?" Blaze wondered aloud.

"I think it helps if they're related to you," Hazard replied with a smile. But they both agreed he was the most perfect baby in the world.

Chapter 45

SPRING came very late that year, but it seemed to them all too soon. Warm suns melted ice and snow, buds came out on the bushes, in the low places grass showed green, and every run was babbling with water leaping down to the plains.

The mountain passes were open last, and then their first visitor reached them.

Rising Wolf became unofficial godfather to Trey and, in the way of Hazard's clan, a substitute father. He was suitably impressed with his new godchild, to please the two most doting parents he'd ever set eyes on. "May his moccasins," he said to Hazard, "make many tracks in the snow." Blaze smiled at Rising Wolf's wish of long life for Trey.

Hazard gripped his hand and softly said, "Your heart and mine have always spoken as brothers and always will while snows continue to fall upon my head. Thank you from my son."

Rising Wolf brought other news as well, in addition to his congratulations on their new son. He told Hazard of it the afternoon of his first day, when they strolled away from the lodge to check the melting ice in the creek.

Yancy Strahan was back in Diamond City. The winter had driven him back to Boston, but he had returned in mid-April and set out a week earlier with a Cheyenne scout for Lakota territory. "Should we go after him?"

"No," Hazard answered, his breath spiraling in the chill air. "I want him."

"He may get away."

"He'll be back, greedy soul that he is. I'm sure he'll give another try for the mine . . . and try to ensure his inheritance once again."

"It's possible he's given up. There's talk of gold in Lakota land. Maybe he goes for that."

"Yancy Strahan has failures in his past that require more and more money to pacify," Hazard replied. "He never has enough. A character flaw I look forward to correcting," Hazard mildly said, "when I kill him."

"And if he kills you first?"

"He can't touch me here," Hazard lazily replied, "and down the mountain, I move with a bodyguard this time."

"We're going to the mine?"

Hazard nodded. "It has to be reopened, because the sooner we buy land and have it registered, the better. I want to buy it all at once and register it in Blaze's name. If it's done swiftly, there's no time for the legislature to push through a law making it illegal. There's not going to be any reservation for my clan. I saw the Indian Territory north of Texas; it's pure hell. I'd sooner kill myself."

"Blaze won't be at the mine this time, will she?"

"No."

"How did she respond?"

"I haven't told her yet. It's going to be one hell of an argument. But it's too dangerous. I want scouts around the clock this time, and if we're lucky and the vein holds, in two or three months, combined with the reserves we have already, we'll have enough for all the land and homes and horses we'll ever need. After that, if Yancy hasn't come looking, I'll go looking for him. He was going to kill my child, you know. I wish I had the stomach for torture; he'd be a perfect candidate. As it is, I'll console myself with sending him off to his eternal hell with a well-placed bullet. He doesn't deserve it, but we Absarokee are just too damn refined."

BLAZE protested, but logically knew Hazard was right. Until Yancy was dead, she and Trey would be safer in the village.

"It won't take long. Rising Wolf and I are taking twenty warriors, and I'll come back whenever I can to spend a few days. By midsummer"—he shrugged—"I'll probably be back for good."

When Hazard readied to leave the village, it was the final week in May. Blaze's eyes were liquid with feeling, and with a little sob she leaned into his chest. "It won't be long, will it?"

"No."

"How long?"

Hazard hesitated. "Weeks."

"Tell me."

"Maybe two weeks."

"You'll be back then?"

"For a visit."

"And then?"

He sighed. "I'll be back whenever I can." In his arms Blaze seemed small and vulnerable; her face was ashen.

"I know you have to go. I know it, but—"

"It won't be forever, *bia*. Take care—I need you. And take care of our son. He needs you."

"Can't I come with?" It was a forlorn desperate hope, anxiety in her voice and face.

"Not yet," he said gently. Not until Yancy's dead, he thought. "When the baby's bigger, then you both can come."

"Don't keep me waiting too long."

His hands tightened on her. She seemed delicate and fragile. He loved her more than he should. "Two weeks, no more," he promised.

*   *   *

WITH the machine gun manned twenty-four hours a day this time, Hazard worked shifts around the clock. He wanted to get enough gold out for the land, and after that a more leisurely pace would prevail. If he was lucky —and with gold veins, luck was a predominant factor— the mine would keep them all comfortable for life.

Chapter 46

A WEEK later, a full moon shone on both the mine and the Absarokee village on Ash River.

Hazard was sleeping before going on the third shift at midnight.

Blaze had left Trey with Red Plume and was practicing some new Absarokee words in the lodge of Rising Wolf's mother. She intended to surprise Hazard and speak his language well when he returned.

The dogs barked once that evening, a loud, clamoring sound that drifted across the river but abruptly stopped almost as suddenly as it began, unnoticed.

When Blaze walked home under the silver moon two hours later, a cool spring wind was blowing down from the mountains, bringing with it the smell of rain.

A tingle of unease, dim and obscure, fluttered through her mind when Hazard's wolfhound didn't rise to greet her at the lodge door. He'd been raised by Hazard from a pup and was the most loyal of guard dogs. She brushed away the irrational premonition, silently listing a dozen reasons he wasn't there to greet her. She opened the lodge flap and stepped inside.

And screamed.

Red Plume lay in a pool of blood only inches from her feet. The wolfhound, his rough coat matted with blood, lay dead with his fangs bared in attack. Trey's cradle was ripped from its frame. *Her baby was gone.*

Her second scream pierced the clear, moon-drenched night like a cry from hell.

Hazard received the news thirteen hours later. A relay of horses had ridden at a murderous pace through the night and early morning.

Yancy. No one else would single out his son to kidnap. He knew what Yancy was capable of, knew brutalization meant nothing but a means to an end for him. And closing his eyes, he steadied himself against the messenger's final words. When the last awful sentence was through, he walked to Peta and leaned his face against the smooth warmth of her neck until the nausea passed and the blackness cleared from his brain. Then he mounted his favorite horse and rode through the rough, wild country, far in advance of the troop sent to fetch him.

BLAZE was trembling when he pulled her into his arms. She was close to collapse. A note had been found, she sobbed, left on a war lance driven into the ground near the river ford.

Hazard had already been apprised of its contents.

"He'll kill him! He'll kill our baby!" she wept, clinging to Hazard with the wild strength of hysteria.

"No, he won't. He won't," Hazard soothed, not really believing it, but saying the words. "He wants the mine. Trey's ransom for the mine. We'll give him the mine, that's all. And we'll have Trey back." His large hands were stroking Blaze's hair, her back, gentle, calming, although his own brain was wrought with terror.

"Can you find him? Where did they take my baby?" Blaze whispered, lifting her face to Hazard. "Where is he? He has to be fed. Jon, what if no one's fed him?"

"They'll feed him, *bia*. Yancy needs him alive for the mine. Don't cry, angel. I'll find him." He started to disengage her clinging arms. "I have to go now. They're waiting for me. Pearl Light will take care of you. Please, love." Her hands had tightened on him. "Every minute counts."

"I'm coming too!"

He looked down at her and softly said, "No." Even if she was strong enough, which she probably wasn't so soon after Trey's birth, Blaze presented added dangers. Yancy would as soon see her dead as alive. Hazard had never underestimated Yancy's callous greed.

Blaze whirled away from him, then turned back in the same sweeping motion, her eyes feverishly aglow. "He's my baby!" she cried.

Hazard put his hands over his eyes and inhaled deeply. Dropping them a second later, he exhaled quietly and spoke, his voice harsh and raw. "If you fall behind, I can't wait for you," he said. "I just want you to understand." He was tautly adamant. Yancy had his son and every minute wasted was danger to him.

"You won't have to," Blaze replied in an unearthly calm voice. "I'll keep up." She stood splendid in her determination—slender, pale, but no longer trembling.

Their eyes met and he reached out to her. They clung to each other for a brief moment, then Hazard swept her up in his arms and strode out of the lodge. "Six more horses," he ordered, carrying her toward the waiting mounted men. "And bring up the palomino."

They rode at a frightening pace, without stopping, swinging over to a fresh mount when the pony they were riding flagged. Blaze maintained her place at Hazard's side. He gave her marks for courage. If she'd faltered, he would have had to leave her with an escort home. They both understood. Their son's life was at stake.

The party of Yancy's hired Lakota they were trailing was large and riding hard for their own territory. When they crossed out of Absarokee land midafternoon of the next day, they paused briefly to check their weapons, water the horses, set up two flanks riding protection, and throw a scouting party forward several miles in advance.

Hazard quietly passed the word along that ranks were to close around Blaze if they were attacked.

He wasn't anticipating trouble, but it never hurt to be prepared for the possibility. Yancy's note had been succinct enough, and at least until the mine was signed over an attack was not very likely. Provided Yancy could control the Lakota braves he'd hired.

The Lakota tribes were many times more numerous than the Absarokee, and Hazard had only ninety warriors with him from his small clan. But none of these possibilities mattered; his son's life was at stake. They rode without rest or concealment straight to the Lakota camp.

When they sighted the village, Hazard gave instructions to Rising Wolf, terse, succinct instructions regarding Blaze, then readied himself. He rode down alone on his war pony.

He was visible from a long distance, coming down the grassy rolling rise east of the village. And he was watched. He was painted ocher from his hair to just below his eyes, the rest of his face was black with green stripes, while his chest and arms and legs were streaked with bright vermilion. Stripped as he was for battle to breechcloth and moccasins, the colors on his lean body were like an angry message vividly explicit in the golden rays of the setting sun.

All the specters that had haunted him on the swift ride east were gone. He was a warrior at war, on the attack and with the imminence of action, his mind settled as a resolute determination took over. He was riding in for his son.

They watched him as he slowly rode down. Armed, painted for war, displaying the courage of a spirit-god, his war pony was as splendid as he, the single war bridle feathered and tasseled with silver. Hazard was entering the first circle of lodges when a rising murmur from the crowd made him turn.

A golden palomino glittering in the hot orange sunset was being whipped down the grassy knoll. Flaming hair, vivid as liquid copper, flowed out in the wind behind the reckless rider. Hazard stopped Peta with a faint pressure of one knee and waited for his wife.

It was rash, foolhardy, a blind, headstrong bargain with the devil. But it was the Blaze he understood far more than the trembling, clinging version he'd seen a day ago. She was his wife and he calmly waited for her, surrounded on all sides by his lifelong enemies.

When she neared him the crowd parted, and when she pulled to a stop a foot shy of Peta, he smiled his welcome. They rode into the inner circle side by side, one dark and warlike, the other a flash and gleam of saffron beauty. Neither was surprised to see Yancy beside the Lakota chiefs. They dismounted.

Hazard addressed the chiefs, ignoring Yancy. His strong arms, braceleted at wrist and biceps with painted black bands signifying his grief, moved in an easy sweep of salutation. And then his slender hands rapidly spoke in the sign language common to all the Plains tribes. He told them he'd come for his son. He told them Yancy Strahan was a thief and a murderer. He told them he didn't intend to leave camp without his son.

And in a dramatic gesture, bringing gasps from the assembled crowd, he whipped Peta off.

The war pony didn't move at first, but turned to look at Hazard. Hazard had spent much time alone with his war horse. Peta had fought with him and fasted with him and knew his heart. The white men didn't believe a horse had a soul, but the Absarokee knew it to be true. Many times Hazard had seen Peta's soul in his eyes. And this day in the midst of the Lakota, Hazard knew Peta understood. "Go," he said softly to him. "You must."

Peta hesitated a second more, then whirled and galloped away.

Everyone knew Hazard intended to stand and die if necessary. It was rarely used—this act of courage taking precedence over all others and seen on rare occasions in a lifetime. It earned him unqualified respect and admiration. Enemies they may be, but courage, remarkable courage, was highly esteemed by all warrior codes.

Yancy indignantly spoke through his interpreter. He

wanted no luster ascribed to Hazard, wanted his signature on the mine sale and then wanted him dead.

Hazard understood the English, of course, and caught much of the Lakota interpretation as well. Although Yancy was vigorously insisting, the Lakota chiefs were talking among themselves, weighing Yancy's payment of rifles against Hazard's valor. They understood abduction, the use of hostages, they dismissed Yancy's greed for the mine as white man's foolishness, but felt obligated to uphold the contract for the rifles.

As they argued, Hazard's optimism was bolstered. He'd known only an extraordinary audacity would weigh in his favor, and he'd played all his cards on the first round. And the longer they argued, the better chance he had of accomplishing his mission. He considered outbidding Yancy for his son's life but decided not only couldn't Yancy be trusted to uphold a bargain, but that approach would have served him ill in the eyes of his enemies.

"If things go wrong," Hazard murmured to Blaze standing beside him, "jump on your pony and try to whip your way out of here. Rising Wolf is watching you with the field glass. He and the others will fight through to your aid."

"If. Don't say that."

"I have to. Look for Rising Wolf. *Remember!*"

She didn't answer, reluctant to consider leaving without Hazard. Instead she asked, "What are they going to do? Yancy seems furious."

"Things might not go his way. They're arguing about it now. I'm going to offer a challenge," he said, his eyes on the chiefs' conversation. "If they accept, I'll try to have Trey brought out to you. The Lakota don't care about the mine; only Yancy does. So Trey as a hostage has become superfluous now that I'm here. If"—he looked down at her, a world of love and regret in his glance,—"if I shout for you to go, do it. Take Trey and whip the hell out of that pony."

"Jon, no—"

"Don't hesitate. Not for anything." Horror drained the color from her face. "I won't say it unless I have to." And he knew if he had to say it, for him it would be over.

"Now promise me," he insisted. "I have to know you and Trey have a chance. That you'll take that chance. No false heroics on your part; it won't save me. If I tell you to go, go. Now say yes, they're about done with the wrangling." He touched her hand, cupping her fingertips lightly for a moment.

"You're asking me to—"

"Good God, *bia*, do you think I'd ask if there was a choice? Please, think of Trey. He's the future. You can give me that." Sober, he watched her with bleak gravity.

Blaze nodded, curling her fingers around his and holding him fiercely. "Damn, it's not fair. Just shoot Yancy. He's the cause of every misery in our lives."

"The rules don't work that way here."

"I want you and I want Trey—both."

"I know, princess," Hazard said softly, "but if fortune turns, I don't want you and Trey dying without trying to get out. Just try—that's all I ask."

She couldn't speak, suffocating with an impotent sadness that silently questioned why people like Yancy existed.

"Now, say a prayer for my diplomacy," Hazard said, squeezing her hand. "Here goes." And he gently disengaged his fingers.

Hazard offered to challenge any man in their tribe for the life of his son—with any weapons, and with an added codicil. If he won, he wanted Yancy. Not handed over to him, not unfairly. He'd fight him as well, one on one.

He heard Yancy reject the offer when the interpreter explained. Hazard saw the papers Yancy drew out, the ones he wanted Hazard to sign. But papers were worthless as arguments with a direct challenge in the air tossed like a gauntlet waiting to be picked up. It was a matter of honor. And if Yancy didn't accept the challenge, his credibility would be wiped away.

So it was agreed.

Then Hazard began the delicate negotiations to have his son brought out. Thirty nerveracking, cautious, sensitive, cool, and tactful minutes later, Trey was placed in his mother's arms. He took a moment to greet his son and silently say his goodbye should the spirits choose this day to desert him. Laying his large palm gently on the baby's downy head, he spoke in a soft whisper to his child. Silver eyes looked up at the familiar touch and recognized his father through the ocher paint and green stripes slashing the symmetry of his face. Feather lashes fluttered and his tiny mouth curved into a lingering smile. His father smiled back at him and whispered one last word, then his muscled arm, streaked with vermilion and braceleted with black, fell. He murmured to the flame-haired woman as tears sprang to her eyes, and then he walked out into the center of the space cleared for combat.

Hazard knew, as he stood there, that before him lay the ultimate test of all his accomplishments as a warrior: his skill and courage and cultivated knowledge of killing. But first, the Lakota champion. Holding no personal grudge like Yancy, the chiefs had decided on a wrestling match between Hazard and their favorite. It was enough to test him, and who won or lost mattered less to them than the prospect of entertainment. They had no vested interest in the child or the enmity between the white man and the Absarokee chief. Their concern was the wagonload of rifles, and with casual disinterest in the outcome, they had honorably respected the limits of their contract with Yancy Strahan.

Opposite Hazard waited the Lakota warrior chosen to represent the tribe. He stood, loosely bent, a man bigger and more solid than Hazard, his braided hair tied back, his muscular body oiled.

The circling began slowly, both men narrow-eyed, crouching, advancing in progressively smaller arcs. Then, like a snake striking, the Lakota lunged and caught Hazard in a death vise. The steel embrace locked and then pressed, and Hazard was lifted into the air like a trapped animal. Blaze looked away, her face gone white.

Hazard was fresh yet and before his breath was choked from his lungs launched his knee upward with all his strength. You could hear the impact of the blow. A smaller man would have fallen, but the Lakota grunted and stumbled, easing his grasp enough for Hazard to break free. Or half-free, for as he twisted away the Lakota's splayed right hand dug into Hazard's shoulder and managed to slow him enough to gain a hold. As he slammed into him, they both fell flat on the ground, Hazard underneath. The crowd murmured its approval; a hubbub of talk circled the area.

Hazard's legs were free and, drawing in a breath, he heaved his weight up, taking all the force of the drive on his thrusting legs. The dead weight atop him barely moved, but twisting under the slight lift, Hazard's hand flung out and wrenched hard on the coiled braids. The Lakota emitted a thick roar, and Hazard flung himself free. One fall. No pin.

In utter silence they faced each other again and this time the Lakota came at him with great speed, an outthrust thumb aiming straight for Hazard's eye. Hazard's head jerked aside to protect himself, and this time the Lakota filled his hand with Hazard's hair and pulled him to the ground. Hazard landed on his knees, his outstretched hands catching his face only a hairbreadth from the dirt, and the Lakota was on top of him, trapping him in a classic hold. Hazard knelt on the packed dirt, breathing in fast, gasping breaths, setting his muscles in an attempt to hold off the grinding effort to press him into the ground. The pressure mounted breath by breath, the heavy body atop him crushing him downward, the Lakota's sweat dripping past his face. As the leverage increased, Hazard began slowly inching his hand toward the moccasined foot planted like a post near his knee.

He touched it, wrenched his body toward it with his last ounce of strength, and with a grunt, grasped, twisted, and heaved so the Lakota rose, turning in the air, and fell crashing to the ground. His head bounced once hard and a second time lightly, and then he was still.

With well-bred passivity, the crowd absorbed the shock.

Blaze turned her eyes around at the stifled silence and saw Hazard swaying slightly, coming to his feet . . . but alive . . . and, her spirits quaking, she managed a tentative breath of relief. His eyes searched the crowd for her and, finding her, he favored her with a flickering smile.

Now for Yancy. More intent on murder, he had chosen knives as their weapon. Silently, Hazard welcomed the choice.

Hazard's body was glistening with sweat, and now he held a knife in his hands. It felt slippery in his grasp, but solid and comforting on this, his day of reckoning. He glanced at Blaze, a hurried half-glance to see that she and Trey were still safe. Flexing his knees on a deep inhalation of breath, he relaxed for a moment and thought: Now he'd test Yancy's spine, if he had one. Balancing the knife, a reassuringly familiar gesture, he swept the sweat from his eyes with his free hand and moved into the offensive.

It was as though he'd waited for this moment all his life, as if the time had come to claim some small share of satisfaction from those who would take his land, his wife, his child and future. As if Yancy represented all the greed and stupidity that was forever altering his and his people's world.

But Yancy hadn't survived so long in the aggressive world without developing some properties of self-defense; he was fit, hardy, and a shade more ruthless than most. His massive sandy head sat squarely on broad shoulders, and he was braced on legs sturdy as tree trunks. "I'll take her home with me after you're dead," he snarled, "to share a bed with her mother and me." His eyes were filled with hate, but they met only a chill, dark glance and open contempt.

"Somehow," Hazard said, looking every painted inch the vision of his black cougar spirit, "I don't think you'd survive the experience. She knows how to kill now. Since," he said gently, "the Powder River."

Incensed at the gentle disdain, furious that a savage would dare bait him, Yancy hurtled forward like a charging bull, slashing upward with his knife. Hazard hurled himself sideways in time, almost in time. Yancy's blade drew first blood, leaving a trail of crimson down Hazard's side.

The crowd gasped with delight, Blaze smothered a

cry of alarm, and Hazard swore softly. Lunging at Yancy before he had time to fully complete his turn back, Hazard's knife ripped up the fabric covering Yancy's arm, slicing deep into the muscle. Yancy grunted hoarsely like a wounded boar, and blood wet his white shirt, but feinting to the left, his own thrusting arm raked down Hazard's side as he passed. Hazard stumbled but recovered and stood braced, a man's length from Yancy.

"Someone's going to have to teach you a lesson, boy," Yancy growled, his injured arm inciting his fury.

"But not," Hazard levelly replied, "you." He spoke clearly although he was breathing hard; the wrestling match had taken its toll, and blood was pouring from his newest wound. He waited watchfully, his knife hand steady, and took Yancy's next rush with a swirling turn, spinning away with extended arm and blade. Yancy's big sweating frame bore another red slash.

He heard the scream of warning, Blaze's voice, a second too late. Then a tooled leather boot spurred with a large Mexican rowel thudded into his groin, offside and diagonally. But at least the warning had started him moving in time. Had the kick been straight on, he'd never have gotten up again. A stabbing spasm tightened his stomach, and then the agonizing pain came rushing in, doubling him over, settling him to his knees. With a blinding crash the spurred boot swung into his ribs. He rolled away, but the pain, ricocheting through his skull like a hot branding iron, followed and he struck the ground on his fresh wound, knocking the breath out of him. He dropped his knife.

Kicking it aside, Yancy towered triumphantly above him.

He was barely conscious, and it seemed, in his pain, that he was looking up through a tunnel of light surrounded by a bordering darkness, a shapeless monster with red-rimmed eyes looming over him.

"Take a last look at them," Yancy gloated. "I think I'll leave the bastard to the Sioux."

Hazard's head cleared and Yancy came back into focus.

"The hot little piece I'll take back with me."

Hazard only had one chance. The next time he went down, he knew he wouldn't get up.

"I wonder what it's like with a stepdaughter." Yancy chuckled.

Hazard's blood began to pound, adrenaline blasting heat and pulsing blood through his veins. It warmed him. He could feel the surge clear down to his toes. For a moment there was only the sound of Hazard's labored breathing, and then, his eyes half blind with pain, he came up from the blood-soaked ground so fast Yancy didn't have a chance to move away. Hazard caught him in the groin with a crashing fist, doubling Yancy over. The sequence that followed, fists and feet and a chopping blow to the back of the neck, finished the fight in four seconds more. Yancy's neck was broken just above the spine. His mouth dribbled foamy blood across the crushed grass, his body slowly settling into an openmouthed sprawl, the head loose, like a broken toy. Hazard stared briefly at the face turning blue, then gradually sank to his knees, short of breath, his hair streaked with dust and sweat, blood coursing steadily from his wounds. "You . . . can't . . . have . . . them . . ." he said at last, with cold, exhausted finality.

Yancy was dead and with him the swagger, the rapacious greed, the most overt threat to Hazard's property. Yancy had been the epitome of all that was most base in human nature, of the worst of free enterprise and the pioneer spirit. Would that it were possible to deal so finally with all the enemies confronting his people and his life.

A sudden weakness came over him, dulling his gaze until the ranks of Lakota merged in one dim, formless mass of staring eyes. He shook his head to clear it, exhaling a deep, shivering rush of breath that sprayed sprinkles of blood. Then the weakness passed and his head cleared. Hazard moved from his knees, back on his heels, slowly, testing his body's responses, then laboriously pulled himself to his feet. As his legs took his full weight, he swayed, then forced himself to stand perfectly still. He must walk to Blaze, put her and the baby up on the pony.

Somehow mount himself. It seemed a daunting prospect. He hurt; he stifled the moan deep in his throat.

The Lakota warriors watched the Absarokee chief hold himself upright with obvious effort and tentatively take a step. The second limping step was accompanied by a sharp gasp of pain, and he dully hoped he wasn't over-estimating his strength. He was still panting, his arms hanging limp. Looking up, he saw Blaze, then his eyes closed and he wished he had something to lean on. Blaze, his tired brain repeated down the lacerated corridors of his mind. And Trey. It wasn't over yet. He had to move. Not just stand. He had to walk. He opened his eyes.

Summoning the will from reserves he'd never plumbed before, Hazard took a step toward Blaze standing on the rim of the crowd clutching Trey. She hadn't moved. No one had moved. No one but Hazard, as if this was the last test of his courage. They waited silently to see if he would fail.

He was bleeding from a dozen wounds, sweat and blood in glistening rivulets mingling with the vivid war paint on his chest and arms and face, every muscle in his fine-tuned body taut with the simple effort of standing. And when he took his next step, collective breaths were held. Would he manage another?

He did finally, and then several more—painful, un-nerving to watch, slowly traversing the twenty yards that separated him from Blaze. She wanted to run to him and help him, but she was afraid to move. "Jon," she breathed when he was close enough to her, the single word full of hope and fear and courage.

His eyes caught hers briefly and his lips formed her name, but he made no sound; he was using all his breath to walk.

As he drew near, his hand reached out to grasp the palomino's mane, and he hung there panting, his bloody fingers laced through the gilded mane. "Leave now," he murmured at last, and loosening his grip, he bent to give Blaze a leg up. He swayed unsteadily, then, marshaling his strength, stabilized himself. "Up," he said. With the baby in one arm, Blaze placed her foot in Hazard's cupped hands, gripped a handful of mane, and felt him lift her. The effort nearly felled him.

Straightening, he leaned against the pony until his ears stopped ringing. Feeling powerless and distraught, Blaze reached toward him. "I'll get down," she said, "and help you."

He nodded his head side to side in a slow movement, his forehead resting against the palomino's neck. It was a full minute before his head lifted. "Don't fall," he said very low and very slowly. "I'm coming up." And he hauled himself up shakily behind her.

They rode out, the palomino restive with the smell of Hazard's blood in its nostrils. Hazard held the reins lightly in one hand, the other high around Blaze's waist, steely-tight, holding her close. And on the way out it was she, as anchor to his viselike grip, that kept him upright. Leaning against him, she could feel the rapid beating of his heart, his warmth. Trey's small form was cradled in her arms, a light evening breeze ruffling his soft dark hair.

"Don't look to the left or right. Keep your head up. We're going out slowly." Hazard's instructions were quiet, low, the strain of the past hour harsh in his breathing.

She felt rather than saw the blood trickling over her arm, the rhythm of the drops sliding down her skin. Hazard was savaged with oozing knife slashes, dirty with blood and sweat and earth. He shook his head once, his long hair swinging across his shoulders, to clear his vision from the wound bleeding over his right eye.

Miraculously, as if his future were indeed secured by his father's bloody and devoted courage, Trey slept peacefully in his mother's arms.

They were halfway through the village now, Hazard's grip tightening reflexively each time the palomino sidled and pranced restlessly, hauling her back in line, forcing her through the staring crowd, holding her in with the pressure of his hand and legs. She wanted to bolt, her eyes rolling, her ears pressed flat to her skull.

Blaze sat rigidly erect, Hazard's efforts to control the pony forcing his wounds to bleed more freely. "Are you all right?" she asked, fearful of the extent of his injuries, uncertain whether he had the strength to see them through the camp.

"Damn pony's not trained for war—the blood's panicking him."

"Are *you* all right?" She reached back and touched his arm.

"I'll make it." And he swore softly, wrenching back the palomino's wildly tossing head.

"Will they truly let us go?"

"A step at a time, *bia-cara* . . . that's all I know."

It was a slow, ticklish gauntlet, a lifetime in the balance. But at its end, the prairie stretched green and wide, the twilight sky met the rolling hills in the lilac kiss of evening, and freedom beckoned. At the furthest lodge, a dozen yards past the last group of Lakota, Hazard nudged the palomino with his heels and set him into a canter.

He held the pony to an easy rhythm, displaying a fearless confidence to the end.

They talked about him for many snows around the Lakota fires. And about his flame-haired woman who'd come down with him to save their child; they told of his boldness, how he had ridden in alone, whipped off his pony; they painted the story of his combat on their lodges as a commemorative chronicle. Hazard the Black Cougar was always painted larger, like a spirit-god, and in the course of time the tale grew into folklore.

Chapter 47

AFTER they reached Rising Wolf and the rest of the party, they didn't dally, uncertain how long the Lakota feelings of cordiality and respect would last. Hazard transferred to Peta and Rising Wolf took Trey; once the initial congratulations were offered they rode fast and hard and silently until they reached Absarokee land.

Hazard helped Blaze down, carried Trey to her and then cradled his family in his arms and kissed them. At last they were safe. Moments later, after he had seen them comfortably settled, he collapsed. He had lost too much blood, had pressed on too long beyond the last pulsing beat of his straining heart, and the last thin light of his considerable will wasn't enough.

Hazard lay, eyes open and sightless, bloody from head to foot, and there was no comforting Blaze's terror-stricken cry until Rising Wolf looked up from where he knelt opposite her and said across Hazard's body, "He's alive."

They sewed and stitched and washed and bathed and did all the gruesome patching while he was unconscious, and then they waited. Blaze anxiously watched his shallow breathing, uncertain whether he was asleep, in a coma, or worse . . . and Rising Wolf couldn't be trusted to tell her the truth. But Hazard's respiration was stronger by afternoon; the wounds eventually stopped bleeding and when she touched him tentatively once, afraid of hurting him, his dark, smudged eyes opened and far down in the tired eyes a smile shone. "Love you . . . home," he whispered, then fell back to sleep. After that they all slept, except the warriors on guard.

When he woke several hours later, he insisted on washing himself in the icy mountain stream nearby. It was a ritual of their medicine, but he returned very pale. His two worst wounds were bleeding again; one high on his left arm was open and oozing, the other—tracing an arc over his ribcage—was ghastly-looking, like an angry red painted line. They remained there two more days until Hazard was strong enough to ride home. Scouts had gone out ahead, so the entire village was out to greet their triumphant arrival, and the victory celebration lasted through the night. Red Plume, too, was on the mend after anxious days when he had hovered near death, and Hazard's first act on arriving home was to present his young nephew officially with his first coup stick in recognition of his defense of Trey.

Hazard excused himself and Blaze from the festivities when the morning star first came up pale in the east. They walked back through the camp of reveling merrymakers and returned to their lodge. Blaze placed Trey snugly asleep in his cradle suspended on swinging rawhide ropes. Hazard, coming up behind her, drew Blaze into his arms, and they both stood silent and proud and thankful above their sleeping son. Trey's fluffy lashes rested on silky plump cheeks, and he smiled faintly in his sleep as they watched him.

"I didn't think I could love anyone as much as I love you, *bia-cara,* but in a different way I do. He's you and me and also specially himself, and I want to give him everything. Unrealistic . . . but a father's dream."

Bending his head, he slowly rubbed his chin against her hair, fraught suddenly with a rush of random doubts.

"And a mother's dream," Blaze whispered back, twisting around in his arms so she was facing him. "We can give him a life in these mountains. A life of freedom and worth. We *can.*"

Hazard smiled a little. "My determined angel." He kissed her lightly on the forehead. "But we'll try." And he vowed to himself to protect them always.

"When do we go back to the mine?" Blaze asked.

"You say a very assured 'we.' "

"Why not? Yancy's gone, so we're safe again."

"As safe as we'll ever be," he ambiguously answered.

"So don't even think of going back there alone. We're coming with." And she glowered at him as only she could, until, knowing that she'd won, her wonderful smile took over.

Hazard's arms tightened around her and they both felt the peace. He returned her smile slowly and leisurely. "Are you telling me you're going to be in my pocket the rest of my life?"

"The rest of your life, Jon Hazard Black, so what do you think of that?" Love welled up between them, incomprehensible, uncontrollable, but like a quiet victory in a world tarnished with madness . . . theirs alone.

His smile warmed his eyes. "I think," he said, very, very gently, "I'm a remarkably"—and he tenderly emphasized the word, giving just the proper inflection to the American slang—"a remarkably *lucky* man."

Out there, beyond the lodge wall, beyond the village boundaries, lay the future.

Epilogue

By 1872, ONLY nine years after the first major gold strike in Montana Territory, the Absarokee, who had roamed their land in freedom for a millennium, were on reservations. With one exception.

Jon Hazard Black's gold purchased security for his small clan in the form of thousands of acres of mountain land. Blaze's inheritance, restored by a brief and uncontested judgment of the Boston courts, bought additional acreage, both parcels carefully deeded in her name. Furthermore, sufficient wealth came from the mine so that Hazard's clan prospered. The Absarokee always had been the best horse breeders, dealers, racers: avocations acceptable in the state which grew up around them. The process of assimilation had begun with Hazard's father, Hazard and Blaze made it happen, and Trey inherited a frontier world of rapid change and altered circumstances with a privileged ease and panache.

"Do you think, *bia*," Hazard would protest occasionally as the boy grew to manhood, "he's being given too much?"

"Nonsense," his doting mother would reply. "No more than you and I had."

But born of such parents, both more audacious and bold than average, Trey Braddock-Black was truly their child—spoiled and reckless and, some said, handled with too light a rein. But he was also warm and gentle and imbued with a charm that dazzled like meteor fire. And when he came of age in the raw, turbulent early days of Montana statehood, he cut a swath a mile wide, supported by his parents' wealth and a semiprivate army at his back, an army of Absarokee warriors he referred to as "family."

Montana politics at the time was a confusion of interminable squabbling, focusing power for varying lengths of time in the hands of men who didn't know how to use it, misused it, or abused it. Hazard's private army assured his clan a modicum of influence in his corner of the state and protected his son against interests unsympathetic to the notion of a live male heir to Hazard's vast holdings.

With Trey's reentry into local society after the years away at school, gossip flew and tongues clucked in disbelief at his rash and reckless ways. Fathers fingered their guns in nervous readiness when Trey showed their daughters too much of his careless, indiscreet attention, while deb mothers prayed Jon Hazard Black's starkly handsome and wealthy son would settle down at last.

NOTES

p. 2 1.   For simplicity's sake the name Montana is used, although in 1861 there was no "Montana." The northern reaches of Unorganized Indian Country had been made a part of Nebraska Territory in 1854; then the area was placed in Dakota Territory, carved out of Nebraska in 1861. After the mining frontier moved into the northern Rockies, Idaho Territory was formed in early 1863 from parts of Washington Territory and Dakota Territory, encompassing present Idaho, Wyoming, and Montana. Montana Territory came into existence May 1, 1864, with Bannack as temporary capital.

p. 2 2.   The Absarokee were a secessionist group from the Hidatsa and moved farther westward anywhere, depending on the source, from five hundred years ago to as recently as 1776. After the move, they came to call themselves Absarokee or Children of the Large-Beaked Bird, a species no longer seen in their country.

In Hidatsa, "Absa" refers to a large, crafty bird. From this came the French translation, *gens de corbeaux,* hence Crow. They never called themselves Crow even though this was the name used by all their neighbors. And in sign language, the sign for Crow Indian is made by extending the arms forward at shoulder height and imitating the flapping of a bird's wings.

p. 61 3.   Granville Stuart, one of the earliest pioneers in Montana, who later became one of the influential settlers and state historians, prosaically relates a story about the hanging of some horse thieves. After the men were captured, notice of their arrest was sent to Fort Maginnis and Samuel Fischel, deputy U.S. Marshal, started at once to get the prisoners and take them to White Sulphur Springs. At the mouth of the Musselshell a posse met Fischel and took the prisoners from him. They hanged them from a log placed between two log cabins, burned the cabins, and cremated the bodies. He calmly mentions that several of the men hanged belonged to wealthy and influential families, and there arose a great "hue and cry in certain localities" over what was termed the arrogance of the cattle kings. The cattlemen were accused of hiring gunmen to murder these men. He then goes on to declare, "There was not a grain of truth in this talk." And that took care of that as far as he was concerned.

p. 61 4.   If a claimant fixed his surface boundaries on a claim in such a way as to embrace the apex (that is, the top) of the vein, he might follow the vein through the limits of his claim. In practice this meant that millions of dollars could depend on the geological whimsy of whether the apex of a vein was within a claim. In other words, Hazard could follow a rich vein that began on his claim across to other claims. Much court litigation involved the mutually contradictory testimony of what constituted a single deposit, a lode, and a replacement deposit.

p. 66 5. François Larocque, a fur trader with the Northwest Company, traveled with the Absarokee in 1805 and left an account of their life. In trying to discover whether the term *leggings* was meant literally, as in leggings and breechcloth, or used as "trousers," Larocque solved the mystery. He left a description of how they dressed before the white men came. He noted that the men usually wore tight leggings rather than a breechcloth, and that the tops of these were tucked under a belt or girdle.

p. 93 6. In the spring of 1851, Congress appropriated $100,000 for the holding of a great council of "the wild tribes of the prairie." Assisted by agent Tom Fitzpatrick and the celebrated missionary-explorer Father Pierre de Smet, Supt. D. D. Mitchell managed to gather, on September 1, eight to twelve thousand souls. The Cheyennes, Arapahoes, Snakes, and several Sioux branches arrived en masse, while the Crows, Arikaras, Gros Ventres, and Assiniboines were represented by delegations. The Comanches declined for fear of losing horses to the Crow and Sioux. During the eighteen-day encampment, Mitchell wrote: "The different tribes, though hereditary enemies, interchanged daily visits, both in their sectional and individual capacities; smoked and feasted together, exchanged presents; adopted each other's children."

   The document signed there established federal right to build roads and military posts in Indian country, fixed tribal boundaries, and provided for the annual payment of $50,000 in goods for a fifty-year period. Then the Senate chopped this to ten years and only the Crows refused to sign; thus, the treaty was never ratified.

p. 94 7. There's no need to go over the government's treachery in its history of treating with the Indians, nor to detail the thousands of corrupt and malevolent men sent out as Indian agents. The following passage perhaps says it all. Keep in mind that this statement was made in 1864, before the territory had an Indian policy or even a legislature. The newly arrived agent for the Blackfeet, who lived just north of the Absarokee in what is now northern Montana and southern Canada, in 1864 called his charges "the most impudent and insulting Indians" he had ever met, and remarked that were it not that their treaty expired the next year, he would recommend that their next annuity be paid "in powder and ball from the mouth of a six-pounder."

p. 148 8. The Absarokee were unusually indulgent to their children. Fur traders detested their undisciplined children. One clerk at Fort Union noted that "young Crows are as wild and unrestrained as wolves," and another trader observed that "the greatest nuisance in Creation is Crow children, boys from the ages of 9 to 14." On occasion, crying babies were even allowed to disrupt the solemn proceedings of treaty commissions. And one particularly tender story describes an Absarokee father with his young son at an early Fourth of July celebration in Helena. The young child already had an ice-cream cone in each hand and saw some candy he must have. His father bought it for him without comment, and kindly held one cone while his son tried the new candy.

p. 238 9. Present-day Pryor Gap received its Absarokee name of Hits with the Arrow from the legend about a boy who had been befriended by dwarfs dwelling there. Absarokee passing through these mountains were instructed to make offerings to these dwarfs by shooting arrows into a certain crevice. Hence the gap was called Hits with the Arrow, Pryor Creek was named Arrow Creek, and the Pryor Mountains were known as the Arrowhead Mountains.

p. 251 10. About two days after a child's birth, its mother pierced its ears with a heated awl and then stuck a greased stick through the perforations. When the sores cured, earrings were put in. The ceremonial piercing of ears was not an Absarokee custom.

p. 251 11. Crow warriors risked their lives to perform defined deeds on a raid. Most praiseworthy was the striking of an enemy with a gun, bow, or riding quirt; then came the cutting of an enemy's horse from a tepee door; next, the recovery of an enemy's weapon in battle; and finally, the riding-down of an enemy. The winner of all four could decorate his deerskin war shirt with four beaded or porcupine-quill strips, one running from shoulder to wrist on each sleeve and one over each shoulder from front to back.

p. 256 12. The native word for *clan* is *ac-ambaré axi à,* "lodge where there is driftwood," the idea apparently being that clansfolk cling together like driftwood lodged at a particular spot.

p. 256 13. Denig, the trader in charge of Fort Union, the principal trading post on the Missouri, estimates the Crow nation at 460 lodges in 1855–56, separated into several bands, each governed by a chief.

p. 257 14. Denig notes: about one half of the Crow nation have a plurality of wives, the rest only one each. The property of husband and wife is separate. Each has a share of horses, merchandise, and ornaments. Not being accustomed to depend much on each other's fidelity (Denig found their love lives scandalous), they wisely prepare for immediate separation in the event of any great domestic quarrel. When from certain causes they decide on parting, the husband takes charge of all male children unless they are too small to leave the mother; the female part go with the wife. Guns, bows, ammunition, and all implements of war and the chase belong to the man, while kettles, pans, hides, and other baggage fall to the woman's share. The lodge is hers, and the horses and other property having been divided years before in an anticipation of this event, each has no difficulty in selecting his or her own. Denig's entire account is the disapproving white man's point of view of a culture different from his own. However, when one ignores the disapprobation, details are gleaned from his journal. As a trader, the Absarokee failed to find favor with him, for he wrote: "The trade with the Crows was never very profitable. They buy only the very finest and highest priced goods." (In fact, they traded the least of any of the tribes with the white man.) Another prominent trader further noted that they were wise enough to refuse to be debauched and swindled by the use of alcohol—the most profitable item in a trader's stock. They called whiskey "white man's fool water" and left it alone until after they settled on the reservations.

p. 258 15.   When a man wished to visit another man in his lodge, he stopped by the door and called out, "Are you there?" If the friend wanted company, he asked the visitor to come in and set fat meat before him and they smoked and talked together. A woman wishing to visit always lifted up the lodge door and peeped inside. But unless asked to come in, all visitors went about their business, without getting mad over not being invited into lodges.

p. 305 16.   A legitimate form of "mutual wife-stealing" (*batsú Erā u*) was practiced by rival warrior societies for a brief period in the beginning of spring.

p. 305 17.   Not all women and men took kindly to some of the woman-stealing tactics of certain societies. When one group tried to take the wife of His-Medicine-Is-Bear, she called to her husband for help. He picked up his gun and warned, "There is no one of you who are man enough to take her." Such action was practically unheard of and started a controversy, since accepted behavior restricted a husband from showing any concern. However, this anecdote clearly indicates there were exceptions, as in any society, to custom and mores.

p. 319 18. There are four types of deeds that were generally recognized as meritorious and counted for the title of "chief": the carrying of the pipe, that is, the leadership of a successful war party; the striking of a coup; the taking of an enemy's gun or bow; and the cutting of a horse picketed in the enemy's camp. The principal aim of a leader was to successfully complete a mission, whether horse raiding or war, and bring his own party safely to camp. If some of his people were killed, no credit would follow the feat.

p. 319 19. Individually, a warrior could gain fame, standing, honor, riches, and as much influence over the band as anyone, except two or three leading chiefs. To these offices one could not expect to succeed without having strong family connections, extensive kindredship, and a popularity of a different description from that allotted to outsiders.

p. 324 20. Scalping, though extensively practiced by many of the Plains tribes, was not regarded as a specially creditable deed by the Absarokee and did not count for the chieftaincy. An informant said to Lowie, "You will never hear an Absarokee boast of his scalps when he recites his deeds." And this statement was confirmed by Lowie's experience.

p. 373 21. Madame Restell practiced her operation for three decades in New York and her business flourished so that she could afford to build one of the largest mansions on Fifth Avenue. People called her Madame Killer behind her back and gawked at her when she rode up Fifth Avenue behind a pair of matched greys for a pleasant drive in Central Park. Two men attired in black livery with plum-colored facing

on the coat lapels rode on the seat ahead of
her. Her dressmaker was the best in town, and
she affected a small muff of mink in the cold
weather, much as the famous pianists or vio-
linists used to protect their hands from harm.
The police knew of her existence but didn't
disturb her, for she had threatened again and
again to expose some of the fanciest skeletons
in New York society if anyone had the temer-
ity to bother her. As a matter of cold truth,
Madame Restell could not have existed a
month if people hadn't wanted her there.

p. 433 22. Two Leggings says the Powder River was
named because along its arid banks buffalo
and riders churned up great clouds of dust,
like ash or powder, while Larocque's memoirs
state ". . . that is the reason they call it Powder River, from the quantity of drifting fine
sand set in motion by the coast wind which
blinds people and dirtys the water."

ABOUT THE AUTHOR

SUSAN JOHNSON, award-winning author of nationally bestselling novels, lives in the country near North Branch, Minnesota. A former art historian, she considers the life of a writer the best of all possible worlds.

Researching her novels takes her to past and distant places, and bringing characters to life allows her imagination full rein, while the creative process offers occasional fascinating glimpses into complicated machinery of the mind.

But perhaps most important . . . writing stories is fun.

Look for Susan Johnson's thrilling
historical romance

SEDUCTION IN MIND

Turn the page for a sneak preview.

AN IMPOSING BUTLER ushered them into Frederic Leighton's studio, despite the inconvenient hour and the artist's custom of receiving by appointment only, and despite the fact that the artist was working frantically because he was fast losing the sun. Although perhaps a man like Leighton was never actually frantic, his sensibilities opposed to such plebeian feelings. Ever conscious of his wealth and position, particularly now that he'd been knighted, he cultivated friendships in the aristocracy, as his butler well knew.

The room was enormous, with rich cornices, piers, friezes of gold, marble, enamel, and mosaics, all color and movement, opulence and luxury. Elaborate bookshelves lined one wall, two huge Moorish arches soared overhead, stained-glass windows of an oriental design were set into the eastern wall, but the north windows under which the artist worked were tall, iron-framed, utilitarian.

Leighton turned from his easel as they entered and greeted them with a smooth urbanity, casting aside his frenzied air with ease, recognizing George Howard with a personal comment and his two male companions with a cultivated grace.

Lord Ranelagh hardly took notice of their host, for his

gaze was fixed on Leighton's current work—a female nude in a provocative pose, her diaphanous robe lifted over her head. "Very nice, Sir Frederick," he said with a faint nod in the direction of the easel. "The lady's coloring is particularly fine."

"As is the lady. I'm fortunate she dabbles in the arts."

"She lives in London?"

"Some of the time. I could introduce you if you like."

"No, you may not, Frederick. I'm here incognito for this scandalous painting." A lady's amused voice came from the right, and a moment later Alexandra Ionides emerged from behind a tapestry screen. She was dressed in dark blue silk that set off her pale skin to perfection; the front of the gown was partially open, but her silken flesh quickly disappeared from sight as she closed three sparkling gemstone clasps.

"It's you," Ranelagh softly exclaimed.

Her eyes were huge, the deepest purple, and her surprise was genuine. "I beg your pardon?"

"Alex, allow me to introduce Viscount Ranelagh," Leighton said. "My lord, Alexandra Ionides, the Dowager Countess of St. Albans and Mrs. Coutts."

"*Mrs.* Coutts?"

"I'm a widow. Both my husbands died." She always enjoyed saying that—for the reaction it caused, for the pleasure it gave her to watch people's faces.

"May I ask how they died?" the viscount inquired, speaking to her with a quiet intensity, as though they were alone in the cavernous room.

"Not in their beds, if that's what you're thinking." She knew of Ranelagh, of his reputation, and thought his question either flippant or cheeky.

"I meant . . . how difficult it must have been, how distressing. I'm a widower."

"I know." But she doubted he was distressed. The flighty,

promiscuous Lady Ranelagh had died in a riding accident—and very opportunely, it was said; her husband was about to either kill her or divorce her.

"Would you men like to stay for drinks? Alex and I were just about to sit down for a champagne." Leighton gestured toward an alcove decorated with various colorful divans. "I reward myself at the end of a workday," he added with a small deprecating smile.

A bottle of champagne was already on ice atop a Moroccan-style table, and if Alexandra might have wished to refuse, Leighton had made it impossible. Ranelagh was more than willing, Eddie had never turned down a drink in his adult life, and George Howard, like so many men of his class, had considerable leisure time.

Ranelagh seated himself beside Alex, a fact she took note of with mild disdain. She disliked men of his stamp, who only amused themselves in ladies' beds. It seemed a gross self-indulgence when life offered so much outside the conventional world of aristocratic vice.

He said, "Meeting you this afternoon almost makes me believe in fate. I came here to discover the identity of the exquisite model in Leighton's Academy painting, and here you are."

"While I don't believe in fate at all, Lord Ranelagh, for I came here today with privacy in mind, and here you all are."

He smiled. "And you'd rather us all to Hades."

"How astute, my lord."

He'd never been offered his congé by a woman before and rather than take offense, he was intrigued. Willing females he knew by the score. But one such as this . . . "Maybe if you came to know us better. Or me better," he added in a low murmur.

Their conversation was apart from the others, their divan offset slightly from the other bright-hued sofas, and the three men opposite them were deep in a heated discussion of the best routes through the Atlas Mountains.

"Let me make this clear, Lord Ranelagh, and I hope tactful as well. I've been married twice; I'm not a novice in the ways of the world. I take my independence very seriously and I'm averse, to put it in the most temperate terms, to men like you, my lord, who find amusement their raison d'être. So I won't be getting to know you better. But thank you for the offer."

Her hair was the most glorious deep auburn, piled atop her head in heavy, silken waves, and he wished nothing more at the moment than to free the ruby pins holding it in place and watch it tumble onto her shoulders. "Perhaps some other time." He thought he'd never seen such luscious peaches-and-cream skin, nor eyes, like hers.

"There won't be another time, my lord."

"If I were a betting man—"

"But you are." Equal to his reputation as a libertine was his penchant for high-stakes betting. It was the talk of London at the moment, for he'd won fifty thousand on the first race at Ascot yesterday.

He smiled. "It was merely an expression. Do I call you Mrs. Coutts or the Dowager Countess?"

"I prefer my maiden name."

"Then, Miss Ionides, what I was about to say was that if I were a betting man, I'd lay odds we are about to become good friends."

"You're too arrogant, Ranelagh. I'm not eighteen and easily infatuated by a handsome man, even one of your remarkable good looks."

"While I'm not only fascinated by a woman of your dazzling beauty but intrigued with your unconventional attitude toward female nudity."

"Because I pose nude, you think me available?"

"So blunt, Miss Ionides."

"You weren't interested in taking me to tea, I presume."

"We'll do whatever you like," he replied, the suggestion in his voice so subtle, his virtuosity couldn't be faulted. And that, of course, was the problem.

"You've more than enough ladies in your train, Ranelagh. You won't miss me."

"You're sure?"

"Absolutely sure."

"A shame."

"Speak for yourself. I have a full and gratifying life. If you'll excuse me, Frederick," she said, addressing her host as she rose to her feet. "I have an appointment elsewhere."

The viscount had risen to his feet. "May I offer you a ride to your appointment?"

She slowly surveyed him from head to toe, her gaze coming to rest after due deliberation on his amused countenance. "No, you may not."

"I'm crushed," he said, grinning.

"But not for long, I'm sure," she crisply replied, and waving at Leighton and the other men, she walked away.

Everyone followed her progress across the large room and only when she'd disappeared through the high Moorish arch did conversation resume.

"She's astonishingly beautiful," George Howard said. "I can see why you have her pose for you."

"She *deigns* to pose for me," Leighton corrected. "I'm only grateful."

"I'm surprised a woman of her magnificence hasn't married again."

"She prefers her freedom," Leighton offered. "Or so she says."

"From that tone of voice, I'm surmising you've propositioned her," Eddie observed. "And been refused."

Leighton dipped his handsome leonine head in acknowledgment. "At least I'm in good company, rumor has it. She's turned down most everyone."

"Most?" Ranelagh regarded the artist from beneath his long lashes, his lazy sprawl the picture of indolence.

"She has an occasional affair, I'm told."

"By whom?" Ranelagh's voice was very soft. "With whom?"

"My butler seems to know. I believe Kemp's acquainted with Alex's lady's maid."

"With whom is she currently entertaining herself then, pray tell?" The viscount moved from his lounging pose, his gaze suddenly intent.

"No one I know. A young art student for a time." He shrugged. "A banker she knew through her husband. A priest, someone said." He shook his head. "Only gossip, you understand. Alex keeps her private life private."

"And yet she's willing to pose nude—a blatantly public act."

"She's an artist in her own right. She accepts the nude form as separate from societal attitudes."

"Toward women," the viscount proposed.

Leighton shrugged again. "I wouldn't venture a guess on Alex's cultural politics."

"You're wasting your time, Sammy, my boy," Eddie told Ranelagh, waving his champagne glass toward the door through which Alex had exited. "She's not going to give you a tumble."

The viscount's dark brows rose faintly. "We'll see."

"That tone of voice always makes me nervous. The last time you said *We'll see*, I ended up in a Turkish jail, from which we were freed only because the ambassador was a personal friend of the sultan's minister. And why you thought you could get through the phalanx of guards surrounding that harem, I'll never know."

"We almost made it."

"Nearly cost us our lives."

"You worry too much."

"While you don't worry at all."

"Of course I do. I was worried Lady Duffin's husband was going to break down the door before we were finished last week."

"So that's why Charles won't speak to you anymore."

The viscount shrugged. "He never did anyway."

Alexandra didn't have another appointment, but feeling the need to talk to someone, she had her driver take her to Lady Ormand's. This time of day, she'd have to sit through the tedium of tea, but not for long, since Rosalind's guests would have to leave soon to dress for dinner.

She felt strangely agitated and annoyed that she was agitated and further annoyed that the reason for her troublesome feelings was Viscount Ranelagh.

He was just another man, she firmly told herself, intent on repressing her astonishing reaction to him. She was no longer a missah young girl whose head could be turned by seductive dark eyes and a handsome face. Nor was she some tart who could be bluntly propositioned, as though he had but to nod his perfect head and she would fall into bed with him.

But something remarkable *had* happened when they met, and try as she might to deny his startling sexual magnetism, she was impossibly drawn to him.

Unfortunately, that seductive power was his hallmark; he was known for the carnal eagerness he inspired in females. And she refused to succumb.

Having spent most of her adult life struggling against conformity, trying to find a role outside the societal norms for women of her class, *needing* the independence denied so many females, surely she was strong enough to resist a libertine, no matter how sinfully handsome or celebrated his sexual expertise. Regardless, she'd not slept with anyone since her disastrous affair with Leon.

Reason, perhaps, for her injudicious impulses now.

But after Leon, she'd vowed to be more prudent in her choices.

And Ranelagh would be not only imprudent but—if his conduct at Leighton's was any evidence—impudent as well.

Inexhaustible in bed, however, if rumor was true, a devilish voice in her head reminded her.

She clasped her hands tightly in her lap, as though she might restrain her carnal urges with so slight a gesture. Impossible of course, so she considered spending a few hours with young Harry, who was always so grateful for her company. But gratitude didn't have much appeal when images of Ranelagh's heated gaze filled her brain. Nor did young Harry's sweetness prevail over the shamelessly bold look in Ranelagh's eyes.

"No!" she exclaimed, the sound of her voice shocking in the confined space, as was the flagrant extent of her desire.

She desperately needed to speak with Rosalind.

Her friend was always the voice of reason . . . or at least one of caution to her rash impulses.

But when the last teatime guest had finally departed and the tale of her introduction to Ranelagh was complete, Rosalind said, "You have to admit, he's the most heavenly man in London." She shrugged her dainty shoulders. "Or England or the world, for that matter."

Alex offered her friend a sardonic glance. "Thank you for the discouragement."

"Forgive me, dear, but he *is* lovely."

"And he knows it and I don't wish to become an afternoon of amusement for him."

"Would you like it better if it were more than an afternoon?"

"No. I would prefer not thinking of him at all. He's arrogant and brazenly self-assured and no doubt has never been turned down by a woman in his life."

"So you're the first."

"I meant it facetiously."

"And you've come here to have me bolster your good judgment and caution you to reason."

"Exactly."

"And will that wise counsel suffice?"

Alex softly exhaled. "Maybe if you're with me day and night."

Rosalind's pale brows rose. "He's said to have that effect on women."

"And it annoys me immeasurably that I'm as beguiled as all the mindless women he amuses himself with."

"You wish your intellect to be in control of your desires."

"I insist on it."

"Is it working?"

Alex shoved her teaspoon around on the embroidered linen cloth for a lengthy time before she looked up. "No."

"So the question becomes—what are you going to do?"

"I absolutely refuse to fall into his arms." She glared at her friend. "Do you understand? I won't."

"Fine. Are there matters of degree then?"

"About what?"

"About falling into his arms. Would you, say, after a certain duration, or never in a million years?"

Alex shifted uncomfortably in her chair, tapped her fingers

on the gilded chair arm, inhaled, exhaled, and was silent for several moments more. "I'm not sure about the million years," she finally said.

"You're boring the hell out of me," Eddie grumbled, reaching for the brandy bottle at his elbow.

Sam looked up from his putt. "Go to the Marlborough Club yourself."

"I might." Refilling his glass, Eddie lifted it in salute. "As soon as I finish this bottle."

"After you finish that bottle, you'll be passed out on my couch," Sam murmured, watching the ball roll into the cup on the putting green he'd had installed in his conservatory.

"You don't miss a night out as a rule," Eddie remonstrated. "Did the merry widow's refusal incapacitate you?"

"Au contraire," Sam murmured, positioning another ball with his golf club. "I'm feeling first-rate. And I expect she's in high mettle as well."

"She turned you down, Sam."

"But she didn't want to." He softly swung his club, striking the ball with exquisite restraint.

"And you can tell."

The viscount half smiled. "I could feel it."

"So sure . . ."

"Yes."

"And you're saving yourself for her now?"

"Jesus, Eddie, if you want to go, go. I don't feel like fucking anyone right now and I drank enough last night to last me a week."

"Since when haven't you felt like fucking someone?" his friend asked, his gaze measured.

"What the hell are you insinuating?"

"That you fancy the voluptuous Miss Ionides with more than your usual casual disregard."

"After meeting her for ten minutes?" Sam snorted. "You're drunk."

"And you're putting golf balls at eight o'clock when you're never even home at eight."

Sam tossed his club aside. "Let's go."

"Are you going out like that?"

The viscount offered his friend a narrowed glance. "None of the girls at Hattie's will care."

"True," Eddie muttered, heaving himself up from the leather-covered couch. "But don't do that to me again. It scares the hell out of me."

Sam was shrugging into his jacket. "Do what?"

"Change the pattern of our dissolute lives. If you can be touched by Cupid's arrow, then no man's safe. And that's bloody frightening."

"Rest assured that after Penelope, I'm forever immune to Cupid's arrow," Sam drawled. "Marriage don't suit me. As for love, I haven't a clue."

"I'll drink to that," Eddie murmured, snatching up the brandy bottle as Sam moved toward the door.

But much later, as the first light of day fringed the horizon, Lord Ranelagh walked away from Hattie Martin's luxurious brothel pervaded by a deep sense of dissatisfaction. What had previously passed for pleasure seemed wearisome now; a jaded sense of sameness enervated his soul, and sullen and moody, he found no pleasure even in the glorious sunrise.

Walking home through the quiet city streets, he was plagued by thoughts of the bewitching Miss Ionides, wondering where she'd slept or, like him, not slept. The rankling thought further lowered his spirits. By the time he reached his town house, he'd run through a mental list of any number of men who might be her lovers, the image of her voluptuous body in the arms of another man inexplicably disagreeable.

It shouldn't be. He should be immune to the nature of her liaisons. He had met the damned woman only a day ago and there was no earthly reason why he should care who the hell she slept with.

He snapped at the hall porter when he entered his house, immediately apologized, and after making some banal excuse, pressed ten guineas into the servant's hand. When he walked into his bedroom a few moments later, he waved a restraining hand at his valet, who came awake with a start and jumped to his feet. "Go back to sleep, Rory. I can undress myself. In fact, take the day off. I won't be needing you."

His young manservant immediately evinced concern. The viscount was accustomed to being waited on, his family's fortune having insulated him from the mundane details of living.

Recognizing his valet's hesitation, Sam said, "I'll be fine."

"You're sure?"

"Why not take Molly for a walk in the park," the viscount suggested, knowing Rory's affection for the downstairs maid. "She may have the day off as well."

"Thank you, sir!"

"Go, now." Sam waved him off. "All I want to do is sleep."

In a more perfect world, he might have slept, considering he'd been up for twenty-four hours; but Miss Ionides was putting an end to the perfection of his world *and* to his peace of mind. He tossed and turned for more than an hour before throwing aside the blanket and stalking over to a small table holding two decanters of liquor. Pouring himself a considerable amount of cognac, he dropped into an upholstered chair, and sliding into a sprawl, contemplated the injustice of Miss Ionides's being so damned desirable.

Half a bottle of cognac later, he decided he'd simply have to have her and put an end to his lust and her damnable allure. He further decided his powerful craving was just the result of his not having what he wanted—her. And once he'd made love to the delectable Miss Ionides, that craving would be assuaged. Familiarity breeding contempt, as they say, had been the common pattern of his sexual amusements. In his experience, one woman was very much like another once the game was over.

But this particular game of seduction was just beginning, and glancing out the window, he took note of the position of the sun in the sky. The races would be starting soon at Ascot, the entire week scheduled with prestigious races, the Season bringing all of society to the track.

Including Miss Ionides, if he didn't miss his guess.

Rising from his chair, he walked to the bellpull and rang for a servant. He needed a bath.